'*Black Drop* is a joy from start to finish. I particularly liked the glimpses of the grubby machinery of government from the inside, giving a real sense of the intrigues behind closed doors. Jago is a very sympathetic hero, with all his flaws, virtues and secrets, and Philpott made me want to smile and cheer'

Andrew Taylor, author of *The Ashes of London*

'A gripping, intricate story of Georgian high politics and low life. Leonora Nattrass's historical spy novel is top notch'

W.C. Ryan, author of *A House of Ghosts*

'A riveting political thriller, set at a fulcrum point in global history. The setting is viscerally immersive and the characters spring to life from the page. This masterful narrative of deception, intrigue and heroism unfolds with compelling pace, wry humour and acute psychological observation. Gripping, moving and utterly engaging'

Philippa East, author of *Little White Lies*

'A thrilling slice of pitch-dark historical fiction, led by a superbly engaging narrator. Entertaining and deftly written, this gripping tale of murder and treachery on the smouldering streets of eighteenth-century London deserves to be huge'

Emma Stonex, author of *The Lamplighters*

'Lovers of historical thrillers have a treat in store. A splendid twisting tale of murder and espionage at the political heart of Georgian Britain'

Kate Griffin, author of *Kitty Peck and the Music Hall Murders*

'In *Black Drop* Leonora Nattrass has done that most dangerous thing: allowed fictional characters to mingle with real ones. I'm far too cowardly to do that in my writing, but she has pulled it off. Well written and well constructed, and Jago is a character readers will certainly want to follow'

Alix Nathan, author of *The Warlow Experiment*

'A sparkling evocation of a distant time, which is remarkably similar to the current one. I loved it. The sights, smells and eccentricities of eighteenth-century Britain are so perfectly captured. Other fictional worlds are going to seem a lot greyer in comparison'

Trevor Wood, author of *The Man on the Street*

'Leonora Nattrass brings Georgian London vividly to life in a delectable dose of secrets, lies and sinister skulduggery. Take care not to swallow this tincture of intrigue in a single sitting!'

D.V. Bishop, author of *City of Vengeance*

'This opium-fuelled gem is a murderous romp through the tangled roots of British democracy'

Janice Hallett, author of *The Appeal*

'Nattrass writes so beautifully. Absolutely compelling, and so atmospheric I felt I was there, following Jago around the mean streets of eighteenth-century London'

Frances Quinn, author of *The Smallest Man*

'A darkly atmospheric and utterly immersive tale. *Black Drop* is a thrilling, revolutionary ride through the coffee houses and committee rooms of a corrupt and fearful city. Grab your hat and pipe and keep your pistols at the ready!'

Miranda Malins, author of *The Puritan Princess*

'Superb. Nattrass convincingly recreates eighteenth-century London as a backdrop for spies, murders and a skilful blend of historic and imagined characters. Vivid and fast paced, it's an impressive achievement, and hugely enjoyable'

Guy Morpuss, author of *Five Minds*

'An astounding debut novel, written with style and confidence'

A.J. West, author of *The Spirit Engineer*

BLACK DROP

LEONORA NATTRASS

First published in Great Britain in 2021 by
VIPER, part of Serpent's Tail,
an imprint of Profile Books Ltd
29 Cloth Fair
London
ECIA 7JQ
www.serpentstail.com

1 3 5 7 9 10 8 6 4 2

Printed and bound in Great Britain by
Clays Ltd, Elcograf S.p.A.

The moral right of the author has been asserted.

A CIP catalogue record for this book is available from the British Library.

ISBN 978 1 78816 5914
Export ISBN 978 1 78816 5921
eISBN 978 1 78283 7404

FSC
www.fsc.org
MIX
Paper from
responsible sources
FSC® C018072

BLACK DROP

CAST OF CHARACTERS

IN DOWNING STREET

William Pitt (1759–1806): Tory Prime Minister

Lord Grenville (1759–1834): Whig Foreign Secretary

George Aust (1740–1829): civil servant, Permanent Under-Secretary to the British Foreign Office

Sarah Murray Aust (1744–1811): author, his wife

Anne Bellingham: her widowed daughter

Sir James Burges MP (1752–1824): Whig Under-Secretary of State to the British Foreign Office

George Canning MP (1770–1827): Prime Minister Pitt's protégé in Number 10

Harry Ransome, timber merchant from the West Indies

Will Benson: clerk to Canning, Number 10

Laurence Jago: clerk to Grenville, Foreign Office

Mr Gibbs: his dog

Dora: his landlady

THE AMERICANS

John Jay (1745–1829): American lawyer, founding father, and Washington's envoy to the British Government

Theodore Jay: John Jay's son, his secretary

Peter Williams (dates unknown): slave, valet and secretary to John Jay

THE LAWYERS
Thomas Erskine MP, KC (1750–1823): Whig barrister
Vicary 'Vinegar' Gibbs (1751–1820): his colleague, and
Laurence's former employer

THE ACCUSED
Thomas Hardy (b.1752) shoemaker, secretary and founder
of the radical London Corresponding Society
Lydia Hardy (b.176?): his wife
Robert Watt (d.1794): turbulent Scottish radical,
arraigned for treason
Paul Lemaitre and George Higgins (dates unknown):
members of the Corresponding Society, accused of
participating in the Popgun Plot against George III
Thomas Upton (dates unknown): their accuser

THE FRENCH
Maximilian Robespierre (1758–94): architect of the Terror
Aglantine: a Jacobin spy

THE WRITERS
William Philpott: loyalist journalist, lately returned from the
United States of America, editor of the *Weekly Cannon*
Hannah More (1745–1833): evangelical moralist and writer,
author of *Village Politics*
Thomas Paine (1737–1809): notorious radical, author of
The Rights of Man, 1790, and *The Age of Reason*, 1793–4

PROLOGUE

5 November 1794

S T D U N S TA N ' S C L O C K strikes twelve, and in the following hush I hear Gog and Magog thud back to rest in the clock tower, empty-eyed, hammers in hand. Curious to think they do this mechanical duty even in the depths of the night, when the lamps have died, a fine sleet falls, and the watchman is the only one to observe them. Even thus will I perform this last task, with no witness in the quiet darkness except God and Mr Gibbs, my old dog, who looks likely to outlive me after all.

I betrayed myself tonight at five and twenty minutes to ten, left immediately, vomited in the gutter, and fled home on foot. It was a poor sort of flight – near two hours' trek from Kensington through mud and icy rain – and by the time I reached Fleet Street I was limping. I felt dazed, as if I'd drunk a bottle of brandy. I wished I had that gentlemanly recourse at hand – knocked up Jeb Turner at the Cock Tavern – but he was abed, and only cursed me out of the window. So, I have resorted to more Black Drop, which has a similar effect at a fraction of the price.

There was no pursuit, not then, and in my right mind I would not expect it yet – the hammering at the door, the rush of officious feet on the steep staircase. It was past dawn when they roused the shoemaker, Hardy, threw him in the covered cart, and bore him off to prison.

I am unclear as to the true conditions to be found in the Tower. I imagine a medieval dungeon, with poor devils hanging from chains, pulled out of shape by the rack and the screw. I do not think this a likely picture, in these enlightened times, but you can tell by Hardy's sallow, bony face that he has suffered. In court he is clean and decently dressed, but if he is found guilty of treason, the Ministry is determined he shall endure a medieval punishment. He will swing, see his guts burned before his face, and be chopped in four quarters for the edification of the crowd. There is no need for torture when he must live that walk to the scaffold, each night, in tormenting dreams. In France, even Robespierre broke at the prospect of the tumbril, the jeering crowd, the waiting blade. For a man so expert in killing others, he made a sad fist of suicide. Only blew off his own jaw, and went to the guillotine alive, but in agony and degradation.

But it is not arrest, or the block, I most fear tonight, as I flinch at the settling of an old floorboard on the landing outside my chamber. I wish I still had the pistol, but it is gone to the bottom of the Thames by Blackfriars Bridge, and only my own dulled wits can save me from the soft footstep I listen for, the swift blow meant to silence me for ever.

If I am taken tonight – whether by law, murder or the devil himself – these papers must speak for me. Being in my right mind, despite the Black Drop and the terror, I will give you, reader, 'The Confession of Laurence Jago, clerk to the Foreign Office', the truth and the whole truth, as best I recollect it.

Though time is pressing, I will write down everything I remember, for it is only in such details that you will understand my story.

I light a new candle from the stump of the last, warm wax clotting on my fingers, and gaze for a moment into the yellow flame which spits in the damp draught from the window. Where and when to begin? The first cause for my involvement in the following tale lies in my birth, but I have no time for that tonight. Instead, I will begin with the coming of John Jay from America, in the hot days of June. It was that event which drew me down from my stool in the Foreign Office garret, and made me, at last, a person of interest.

I

THE CRUSH OF BODIES crowding into Newgate Street slammed me about like an angry flood. *Meet me by the scaffold*, Aglantine's note had said, and I could see her there by the steps, as I swept towards her, propelled by the mob. The sun shone down out of a cloudless blue sky, the heat was stifling, and the smell from the close-packed bodies foul. I let the current take me along the street, faces looking into mine unseeing, hands on my shoulders, pulling at my coat, inside my pockets. I held on grimly to my new green-lensed eyeglasses, determined not to lose them in the fray. Costermongers perched up on walls, out of the chaos, shouting out their goods in a singsong babble. Children were screaming on their fathers' shoulders, half in fear, half excitement. If anyone fell under the onward sweep of the crowd, they would be another unexpected casualty of the day.

Aglantine had managed to get in pride of place, like an old crone at the guillotine, with her tight black costume and wrinkled, scowling face. I washed up beside her and put my spectacles back on my nose. I had to shout to be heard over the din.

'Good God, Aglantine, it's hell on earth.'

It seemed a ridiculous place for a secret meeting, except that everyone else was bellowing, and no one was listening, not even the guards, only an arm's length away, lining the platform to keep some kind of order. Aglantine looked at me reprovingly, but the procession was already coming out of the press yard on its short walk to the scaffold, and we both turned to watch. The hangman first, followed by an uncomfortable official from the Home Office, then a couple of constables armed with clubs, and finally a pale stringy fellow who looked like a surgeon, probably come in hope of a corpse. There was something of a pause and then the condemned men appeared behind them, stumbling over their feet as they climbed the steps, white caps on their heads.

'Three at a time!' Aglantine looked from the three men to the three nooses dangling from the crossbeam. 'Is it to be three at a time?'

'There are only three. The rest have been reprieved for transportation.'

'Only three!' Such disgust. Her cold, amphibian eyes disappeared entirely within their folds of flesh. I had forgotten how hideous she was. 'Only three! For all this circus?'

She was right, in one way. They were a poor selection of villains. An old man accused of forgery, a postman convicted of stealing his letters, and a frail young highway robber, who had killed his first victim in sheer panic. The robber tripped on the stairs and the crowd roared, then clapped.

I realised Aglantine had turned her eyes on me, with a look rather like an undertaker measuring me for a coffin. 'I hear you are promoted. Senior clerk to the American talks. I had almost forgotten you, until I heard.'

'Then you've heard more than I have.' Had I really once admired her? Had I really thought her harmless? I had taken an odd dislike to marmalade in recent years, and I saw now that it was because she had always smelled inexplicably of oranges. When we first met, I had thought her a woman like my mother, adrift and alone in a strange land. In that, I had also thought her rather like myself.

The men on the scaffold were pushed into place beneath the nooses, ready for dispatch into eternity. Whatever last words they might have spoken were lost in the hubbub. Their women – wives, mothers, daughters – came up to bid them farewell, but the occasion seemed too much, and they stood there tongue tied. Only one was weeping. Then the caps were pulled down over the men's faces, the nooses affixed.

The drop was short, and they throttled slowly, jerking, legs kicking as their women watched. The young robber's mother threw herself at his feet, pulling with all her strength, but it wasn't enough to break his neck, and she stood up, defeated and bloody nosed from where he had kicked her in the face as he flailed. She shouted to men in the crowd to help her, but they only jeered.

'It *is* a spectacle.' Aglantine seemed to have recovered some-what from her disappointment. 'But so quickly over.'

Once they were dead, there would be an argument about the clothes and the disposal of the bodies, that was all. 'Shall we go?'

'Not until they stop kicking.' There was a hole in the post-man's boot, and his stockings were rags. The old forger was better dressed, but there was less fight in him. He was already still.

The fickle crowd was thinning as the thrashing above us lessened. An argument had begun between the hangman, the surgeon and the women as the old forger was cut down. He landed with a thud and the railing shivered.

Aglantine glanced at me, but she could not keep her eyes long from the stripping of the forger's corpse. The hangman seemed eager to assert his rights over the old man's clothes, but he probably wouldn't put up such a fight for the postman's rags and holed boots. I turned my eyes away, with equal measures of pity and disgust. Aglantine's small wizened face, like the capuchin monkey at Pidcock's Menagerie was, for once, a preferable sight. I didn't believe a word of this supposed promotion, but just now it was a welcome distraction from the close press of bodies about me, and the apprehension of contracting a sudden or lingering death from all their multifarious diseases.

'Where did you hear this preposterous tale about me?' I'd been in the garret of the Foreign Office decoding messages for ten years, and there had been no sign in Downing Street of any impending change.

'You are not my only set of eyes in Whitehall.'

'I didn't know.'

She looked at me pityingly. 'How would you?'

The surgeon had got his way as far as the young robber went, and was waving his cart to come through the thinning crowd. The boy's mother had fainted, and the hangman was gingerly reviving her, as if it went against all his training. Aglantine detached herself from the railing, smoothed down her dress, and steered me back along the emptying street. It was still blazing hot, and we kept to the shadow of the overhanging buildings.

'What manner of man is the American envoy?'

'Mr Jay?' I looked at her for a moment, trying to pick my words. In the end I only said what everybody knew. 'An enigma. The Government hopes for peace but fear his coming means war. He himself is entirely inscrutable. Pale, very cold, and appears calculating.' I'd heard rumours he'd tortured our spies in the Independence War, and from my first glimpse of his colourless face I could well believe it.

'They did not expect him?'

'No, he turned up without any warning. Claimed his previous letters had gone to the bottom of the ocean, but I don't know if they believe that. I saw him at St James's Palace, dressed so plainly the King was offended.'

The cart passed us, the young robber's body thrown in the back. One foot dangled dangerously near to the turning wheel, and I felt afraid for him, until I remembered he was already dead.

I only half heard Aglantine quizzing me about Jay's son, Theodore, who was come to England as his father's secretary. The boy had seemed altogether more animal than his father, his hair unruly under a bob wig. A shy smile. 'Yes, he was there too,' I said absently. 'An eager young lad.'

'Perhaps that might be an opening for you. You are both young; even if, as I see from your face, you are no longer eager.'

The cart was gone from sight, and I turned back to her with a sigh. 'Not so very young. I shall be thirty this year.'

'And I shall be ninety, one day, if I live. We need not speak in platitudes, Laurence. It is of the utmost importance to France that these talks between Jay and the Ministry fail. America is our natural ally and should come into the war on our side. It would make a very great difference to the war – and to Citizen Robespierre.'

Robespierre seemed bent on ruling his population by the expedient of exterminating them by the hundred, and even if the numbers reported executed by the newspapers were exaggerated by a factor of ten, they were still astonishing. They had always called him incorruptible, unswerving, and now he was single-mindedly pursuing his policy of Terror.

I stared at her. 'Aglantine, it's been over a year. Do you expect to come back into my life and find me unchanged? I won't do it. You say you have other eyes in Whitehall. Use them.'

She paused while I walked on a few paces. 'What do you hear about the army?'

'The British army?' I turned, cautious.

'Of course, the British. Are they in retreat?'

I searched for something to say that would tell her nothing she did not already know from the papers. 'They are in some trouble, I believe. The Austrians have made a deal with the French and are hastening home. Lord Moira has gone to the aid of the Duke of York and his army in Flanders.'

'And water is wet, and grass is green. Where are they heading? Inland, or to the coast?'

'I don't know.'

She frowned at me horribly.

'I don't know, and if I knew, I wouldn't tell you.'

'You are of no use to me, Laurence.'

'I am glad.'

'But I do not release you.'

It was absurd. I had released myself months ago, and she must be desperate to think of approaching me again. Behind her I could see the forger's naked body being bundled into a second cart, bound for a pauper's grave. I looked at the ignoble spectacle rather than meet her eye.

'Just wait till the traitor's trial comes on,' a voice said, approaching rapidly behind us from the direction of the scaffold.

'You mean Hardy? Damn me, I'll not come to that,' another

voice answered. 'There'll be trouble. Church and King on one side, and Jacobins on the other.'

'A right good mill,' the first agreed. 'I'll not miss it.' Aglantine turned her head to look at the fellow, but he only thrust out his tongue at her insolently before pushing past, just one of a faceless crowd.

They were speaking of Thomas Hardy, the latest man arrested among the radical reformers. In the quaint language of the indictment, he had been *moved and seduced by the instigation of the devil as a false traitor against our Lord the King*. He was a shoemaker, and the secretary of something called a 'Corresponding Society', which had a membership more vulgar than the Ministry liked, and a disturbing number of branches across the kingdom. They had threatened to call a mass meeting to demand the vote, and the Ministry, remembering Paris in 1789, had trembled, arrested the ringleaders, and thrown them in the Tower. It surprised me to see they had learned so little from the fall of the Bastille.

But at that time I knew nothing much about Hardy, God help me, save that he apparently intended to *break and disturb the peace and common tranquillity of this kingdom; stir, move and excite insurrection, rebellion and War against our Lord the King; subvert and alter the legislature, rule and government now duly and happily established in this kingdom; depose our said Lord the King from the royal state, title, power and government of this kingdom; and bring and put our said Lord the King to death*. It seemed an ambitious programme for an English cobbler.

Aglantine opened her mouth as if to say something on the subject, but then shook her head. 'Hanging is an unpleasant fate,' was all she said, reflectively. 'So English, so bungled, so undignified. When I die, it will be by the guillotine – or in my bed.'

I didn't answer, but as I walked back to work, I realised she could put the screws to me if she really wanted to. I wondered who her other spy in Whitehall might be, and why he couldn't tell her the army's plans. But then, for all I knew, he might only be a Chamber Keeper – *she* might only be a Necessary Woman with a mop and pail – with no access to real information at all.

2

I TRUDGED THE LONG way back to work. Over the Fleet, which runs close to my lodgings, and has become so vile it has been paved over, and slaps sullenly at its gratings before disgorging its swollen contents into the Thames under Blackfriars Bridge. Every other house a shop of some kind, with its goods set out haphazardly. A huddle of old women sitting in a doorway with a motley collection of useless objects: broken baskets, old walking sticks, a single left boot. But somewhere in the throng, a one-legged customer would be in search of it – a wounded soldier perhaps, discharged and left to fend for himself and make a living the best he could. Noise, mud, squalor, and a tide of small coin circulating up and down the street, without beginning or end.

I had walked under Temple Bar, and was passing the menagerie on the Strand, when Will Benson cropped up at my elbow. He worked in Number 10, in a position very like my own at the Foreign Office, and we sometimes ate a chop together in the Salutation and Cat, sometimes met at the revels in St James's Park. Though only a junior clerk like myself, and only five years in Downing Street, he was well known in Whitehall, having a sunny disposition that made him popular.

The mynah bird at the menagerie was greeting us from its cage at the bottom of the stairs, inviting us to ascend to view the animals, but Will hardly noticed, looking grey as he fell into step beside me with no more than a nod. He didn't ask me where I'd been, and after one look at his face I didn't ask him either. At the best of times he had a sallow indoor complexion and lank dark hair poking out from a grey scrub wig, but in the normal way of things you hardly noticed, his whole face redeemed by his ready smile. Now he was ashy grey, his usually cheerful eyes dark holes in his face. Hollow despair seemed to steam off him in the hot sunlight. Was he ill? Or had he received some dreadful news?

'Good God, what's wrong with you? You look—' But in truth I didn't really know how he looked. I couldn't exactly frame the words to describe the way he stared back at me, empty space behind the eyes that were usually so merry. 'Has something ...?'

'No!' He hastened his step away from me as we came up to the chaos of Charing Cross. 'No, nothing at all.' And dived across the road under the wheels of a builder's wagon, with reckless disregard for his own neck.

Ahead in the distance lay Westminster and its extraordinary muddle of crumbling medieval battlements, but here in Whitehall the pavements emptied, the pedestrians were more clerkly, and the buildings for a moment more genteel. I caught Will up as he turned into Downing Street, and we paused outside Number 10. I laid a hand on his arm. 'Will I see you in the park this evening? You look like a man sore in need of a drink.'

We should have been allies, for we were both country boys transplanted to the city, but the strange course my life had taken made intimacy too dangerous an indulgence and, though we moved in the same circles, I had rarely spoken to him alone. I knew where he lived, but I had never visited him, and I had certainly never invited him to my own shabby lodgings. There was no especial reason he should confide in me, and at length, when the pause grew awkward, I made my bow. 'Well, if you ever need anything …' But Will was only silent and I left him, crossing the road to the shadowy Foreign Office.

The lobby was cool, but the temperature rose inexorably as I climbed the three flights of stairs to my room. Up in the garret it was stifling from the sun hammering on the roof tiles and the windows close fastened against the pestilential air. I could feel the sweat gathering on my forehead as I pulled the stack of waiting papers towards me, come in overnight from Dover, and pushed my eyeglasses up on to my forehead. A symbol on the top right-hand corner of the first sheet was the key to the cypher and, dismissing Will Benson and his trouble from my mind, I reached the indicated volume down from the shelf, wiped the sweat out of my eyes, and opened the book at the relevant page.

L ATER IN THE AFTERNOON I was called down into Sir James Burges's comfortable old office, with its long, dusty mahogany bookshelves and the antiquated tapestry that led directly into the Foreign Secretary's mysterious domain. Lord Grenville has two under-secretaries, one political, one permanent. Sir James, the Political Under-Secretary, is the senior, and I expected to be sent on some menial errand, but instead he bade me sit. Then Mr Aust, the Permanent Under-Secretary, came in through the concealed door in the bookcase. He is a man of birth as lowly as my own, but with a long and meritorious history in the Department. He had taken off his shoes, as he often did late in the day, when they began to pinch. It was a habit we clerks much disliked, for it made it hard to hear him coming along the corridors.

Aust sat down among the cushions in the window seat, dust in the sunlight between us, and Sir James turned his moon face on me. 'This business with Mr Jay has caught us quite unawares,' he said. 'With Parliament about to adjourn for the summer there's hardly a soul left in town, and only eleven of us in the Department, if you can even count the young gentlemen upstairs in that number at all. How long have you been with us now?'

'It will be ten years at Christmas, sir.' Ten humdrum years in the garret, and another three before that, in Mr Gibbs' legal chambers in Lincoln's Inn.

'Is it really ten years? Well, well. Now, tell me, Mr Jago, what do you know of the American question?'

A very junior clerk, hardly more than a schoolboy, came in with a tea tray. It held three cups, and as the boy poured, I looked from Sir James's face, to Aust's. This unprecedented courtesy seemed to suggest that Aglantine's other eyes in Whitehall had been well informed after all. She now also provided me with an answer. 'I know that France seeks to bring them into the war on their side.'

The two under-secretaries exchanged looks, apparently impressed by my precocious knowledge of public affairs. 'Very good, Jago, very good. And if we are to prevent it, there will be a deal of advice to be sought, errands to be run, and the whole arsenal of diplomatic entertainments to be deployed.

If you're agreeable, you'll minute the meetings between Lord Grenville and Mr Jay, and act as Chief Secretary to a committee of interested gentlemen.'

I'd been forewarned, but this was a bigger step up than I had ever believed possible. So much has happened since then, that it's hard to remember exactly how I felt. Despite my unease at Aglantine's reappearance, on the whole I think I was pleased – mighty pleased – and with no presentiment of disaster.

'Mr Jay is no common-or-garden envoy, Jago. He would have signed their Declaration of Independence if he'd happened to be in Philadelphia at the time. He negotiated the peace treaty between us, in Paris in '84, and until recently he served as their Foreign Secretary. Yes, yes, a dignified gentleman indeed, and worthy of the greatest respect. You saw him at the palace, I suppose?'

'Yes, sir.' It was also at the palace that I first saw Philpott, I remember now. Hard to imagine a time before his large presence filled my life. Hard to imagine a future without him, but that day in the palace I had only laughed at him behind my hand. His warm Hampshire burr had made the courtiers shudder, as he shook his red face positively in the King's own, leaning closer than was at all proper to the royal person. 'Yes sire, my father was a farmer, and I often earned a penny scaring crows from his corn as a boy.' And then, to a whispered question, too low to catch, he replied cheerfully, 'Damned atheists and Jacobins, all of 'em. Don't you worry, sire, William Philpott will best them yet.' He was a journalist just returned from Philadelphia, someone said, and why he was there, at all, was a mystery.

But I wasn't thinking about Philpott just then, as I watched Sir James sip his tea.

'Have you met Lord Grenville much, since he came to the Department?'

'No, sir. Hardly at all.'

'You'll find him a very pleasant gentleman to serve, and you'll be at the hub of things, that's certain.'

A clerk poked his head around the hidden door in the bookcase. 'Lord Grenville wants you, when you have a moment, sir.'

'Very well.' Sir James stood up with weary resignation. Aust coughed discreetly.

'Your wig, Sir James.'

'Is it …?'

'I'm afraid so.'

Sir James tugged his headpiece to and fro until Aust nodded, and then pushed through the tapestry into Lord Grenville's office.

'So, if there are no practical matters arising?' Aust had got to his feet, ready to dismiss me.

'Well, sir …' I pushed my eyeglasses up my clammy nose for the twentieth time in an hour.

'You are wondering about the money? I imagine there'll be some increase to your stipend, if it would be helpful to you.'

I USED TO BELIEVE THAT in twenty years' time Downing Street would no longer exist, that my masters would be philosophers worth serving, and that I might even be one of them myself. But, as I cleared my desk in the garret, I was pleased enough with my more modest promotion. Though I had no more right to vote than the traitor Thomas Hardy, the devil that *moved and seduced* him had admitted defeat in my case, and these days I found myself quite willing to swear allegiance to Lord Grenville and his under-secretaries.

My new office was only a hat-box in the corner between the stairs and the chimney stack, with a view over the back alley that led into Fludyer Street, where a lively interview was now in progress between the clerks in the garret above and a purveyor of strawberries below. The boys were urging her to attach her basket to the strings they dangled; she was demurring, afraid for the safety of her stock. As they argued, I set out the few homely sticks of furniture I had found for myself in the lumber room. An antique wig stand, a worm-eaten bookcase and an old wine cooler that might serve as a footstool. It was almost the end of the day when I was finished. I took off my wig, set it carefully on the stand, and ran my hands through my damp hair. The new room was only a little less stifling than the garret, the window nailed shut, and I opened the door to let in a current of air from the lobby below.

'Ha – hm.'

Lord Grenville, the Foreign Secretary, was watching me from the doorway. I straightened, bowed, pushed my spectacles more firmly up my nose and reached for my wig all at the same time, but Grenville only waved his hand. He was good-looking in a way, with large eyes and a pronounced forehead. 'You're my new clerk. Mr Jago, I think?'

'Yes, sir – I mean, my Lord.' I had seen Grenville often, but never this close and certainly never to talk to. He had a pleasant, practical-sounding voice.

'I have a ticklish problem and can't find that damned Chamber Keeper anywhere. It's somewhat below both our dignities, but the Home Secretary is to come in shortly, and my room is in a state entirely unfit for visitors. Will you help me?'

Grenville was already crossing the landing, flinging open the door to his office. I followed, pausing in his doorway somewhat amazed. A large sash window gave out on to a vista of the park, and I blinked in the sudden brightness, before noticing the florist's display that filled the entire room.

'Look like a damned actress, don't I?' Grenville smiled with sudden good humour. 'The Home Secretary will never let me forget it, if he finds me in such a jumble.'

'What are they, my Lord?' I was still taking it all in – the air, the light, and the ocean of plants, all glossy green leaves and fat buds. Some had burst into blooms of extraordinary size, the innumerable petals ruffled in shades of white and pink. It was altogether a heaven I had never dreamed of.

'Peonies, Mr Jago, courtesy of an old friend, an intrepid collector of plants in the East Indies. I made the mistake of telling him my wife has a passion for the things, and an ambition to raise a blue variety – a thing never yet achieved.' Grenville was also eyeing it all, somewhat dazed. 'But I had not thought he would send so many. What the devil shall we do with them?'

'We could put some in my room. And some in the garret.'

'Make it so. And I dare say a few in the Cabinet Room would be cheerful.'

A clerk clattered down from the garret with a raft of trans-literations as I crossed the landing with an armful of foliage. When Grenville followed me into my room a moment or two later, he was holding a paper in his hand and seemed to have forgotten about the peonies.

'More bad news from Flanders, I'm afraid.' He put the paper into my hand and, remembering just in time that as a clerk I was supposed to understand no French, I resisted the urge to read it at once. 'Will you make a copy and take it across to Number 10? Make sure to put it straight into George Canning's hand. He is my channel to the Prime Minister on these military matters.'

'Very good, my Lord.'

I copied the note out with some difficulty amid the forest of plants. The message was written in the worst hand I had ever read. It was not the clerkish round hand that was ubiquitous throughout the Department. Almost too bad to be gentlemanly either, though I had seen some terrible specimens of that affliction in my time. But once I made sense of it, I scanned its French with a practised eye and perfect comprehension. It was bad news indeed. The Austrians were retreating towards the Rhine, while the English were in flight to the coast at Ostend. If the French only knew it, they could crush us at once, for our forces were split by the River Scheldt. The French had not yet learned of their opportunity, and God send they never would.

I sat back and looked at the words on the paper, remembering Aglantine's questions that morning about the army's flight. 'Inland or to the coast?' she'd asked. This must be a part of the same web of intelligence she navigated, and now I was brought down from the garret I would be a part of it, too. No wonder she had sought me out.

Once, God forgive me, I might have passed on what she wanted, just as I had occasionally let slip the name of an aristocrat fleeing France in the early days of the Revolution. Then I hardly thought my words of much consequence – nor Aglantine much of a danger, being only an old woman. But that was before the war. Now the newspapers screamed that there were scores of spies in London, everywhere from the docks to the House of Commons. French valets and maidservants could hardly be trusted, nor the tide of refugee émigrés, nor the general foreign element of the swarming humanity that filled the streets.

And I was certainly a foreign element lurking in a position of trust. The son of a Cornish farmer and a French widow, come together five years before my birth through an excise dodger out of Roscoff, I had omitted to mention at my Foreign Office interview in '84 that I spoke fluent French, for then it hardly seemed to matter. Later I drew a veil over the summer of '89, when Mother asked me to go home with her and we found ourselves in Roscoff in the middle of the Revolution.

Since Louis was guillotined and the war broke out in the February of '93, I had passed no more information, and the only incriminating item in my possession was the French pistol Aglantine had given me when we began our alliance. In '89 all of England was so delighted with the French Revolution that I might still have been forgiven, if I had spoken at the right moment to the right person. But I had spoken at the wrong moment to the wrong one. And now, with the war and the new Terror in Paris, any chance of confession seemed gone for ever.

3

WHEN I TOOK THE COPY across the road to Number 10, George Canning was in Pitt's outer office, ranting at poor Will Benson, who looked no better than he had done when I parted from him in the street. He had declined to confide in me then, but the trouble was now painfully clear. He kept his hollow gaze fixed on the ground, a tactic that only seemed to make Canning more histrionic.

'Have I not told you a hundred times? But still you go on in the same damned way. Such dumb insolence I have rarely seen, and I am as ready to throw you down as a hand of twos.'

I had come across Canning occasionally since he came up from Oxford but knew little about him. Only that he had come into politics an extreme Whig but had promptly turned extreme Tory when patronage by the Prime Minister seemed likely. No one seemed to much like him, and from current evidence he must be the very devil to work for. What Will could have done to incur such wrath was a mystery; as far as I knew, he was as well liked in the office as he was at the tavern.

Will was mumbling something, but Canning didn't ask him to repeat it. 'No, no, I have made myself clear, positively one hundred times, but there will be no more. Collect your things, sir, and get out. I never wish to see your snivelling features in Downing Street again.'

I think my jaw fell open at this public dismissal, made without any concession to my presence. If I'd been another kind of man, the humiliating news would have been round Whitehall within the hour. Will sidled past me, without a word, without meeting my eye, while Canning turned to take the note from me with fastidious fingers, quite as if nothing had happened. He looked at me – a cool grey gaze down his long nose – as if he was ten years my senior, not a callow youth of twenty-four, and I admitted grudgingly to myself that he had a manner likely to recommend him to women.

'From Grenville?' He read its French more laboriously than I had done, then looked at me again. He smiled, but not pleasantly. 'Thank you, Mercury. Are you Grenville's new clerk?'

'Yes, sir.'

'Who is your father? Do I know him?'

'My father is dead, sir.' I was purposefully obtuse, for I knew he took me for one of the young gentlemen who larked about the upper reaches of the Foreign Office building only pretending to work. I had no desire to be scorned like poor Benson.

'But still has a name?' He was studying me, green glasses and all. 'Good God! Don't tell me Grenville has promoted another Mr Aust?'

I didn't answer, and his eyes dropped back to the message. 'Well, supposing you merit your promotion by being less ignorant than the rest.' He was settling in for a little clerk-baiting. 'Know where—' He glanced at the paper again and affected a ludicrous accent, which he apparently supposed to be French. 'Know where *Oostende* might be?'

I was relieved to hear someone come in behind me, and see Canning raise his eyes over my shoulder.

'From Mr Jay, sir.' The voice had an unfamiliar inflection, and I turned to see a Negro in impeccable tailoring, proffering a note of his own. I nodded civilly, but he ignored me as completely as he might a beetle crawling past his foot, and watched Canning slide a knife under the seal and open the letter. Canning looked up at us both.

'Thank you, *gentlemen*.' His contempt was stinging. 'Back to your garret, Mr clerk-with-no-name, and back to your kennel, Mr ...?'

'Williams, sir.' Jay's man was imperturbable. 'Mr Peter Williams, at your service.'

I envied his unshakeable composure. Outside Canning's office he bowed and left me, striding easily away through the genteel crowd back towards Pall Mall. A few turned their heads to look at him, but only his gentlemanly suit distinguished him from the black footmen in their gaudy livery who were common enough among the well-to-do, and I dare say most thought him merely a novelty, a fashionable accessory to some rich gentleman or other. Which, as far as I knew, he probably was.

I ATE A MUTTON CHOP at the Cock on Haymarket, before walking home through the twilight. They were lighting the lamps and the streets were as full as noonday as I came to Charing Cross. Carriages clattered past, taking the quality over the river to Vauxhall Gardens, or up the Strand to the opera in Drury Lane, while market women were carrying empty baskets home on their heads. I remembered chasing Will Benson through the same crowds that morning and, on an impulse, I turned down Northumberland Street to his lodging. I suppose I thought I'd take him for a drink – exchange some caustic observations about George Canning – and satisfy my own curiosity, if he was willing to tell me the whole story.

But when I knocked at his door, there was a long interval before his landlady answered. When she did, she scarcely opened the door more than a crack. 'He ain't here, and pestering won't bring him any sooner.'

'Madam?'

Though I could not see her, she was evidently examining me. The door swung open a fraction wider. 'Beg pardon, sir, thought you was someone else in them clothes.'

'I was in search of your lodger, Mr Benson.'

'You too? Well, like I told the other gennelman, I ain't seen him all day.'

And I wasn't particularly sorry. It was getting late. Gog and Magog were chiming the hour with their upraised clubs, and a gang of feral children from Lincoln's Inn Fields were gathering around Temple Bar for the night, flocking to the lamps for safety like moths. One infant of indeterminate sex – perhaps five years old under its look of ancient apathy – glanced up warily as I passed through the old stone arch. A whore called out to me, but I only waved and walked on. I admired the fine chiaroscuro effect of the light from her doorway, which gave fleshly mass to her bare white breasts, but she was perilous goods and I had learned better than to buy.

God tells us it is a sin to spill the seed of life, but He hardly takes account of modern conditions, and I sometimes think He should issue a revised set of prohibitions, for like every other clerk in Whitehall I was preoccupied by the ever-present problem of abstinence. I had been in love with Mr Aust's stepdaughter, Anne, for almost as long as I'd been in Downing Street, but I knew the thing was impossible without a far better income than my clerk's pay. And yet I was still a young man with a young man's desires. Poverty put the clean Covent Garden ladies quite beyond my pocket, and the common whores were like belladonna, comely to look at, but likely bearing poison. So instead I'd learned to govern my desires with the tranquillising effects of a little laudanum. I now knew the number of drops of Godfrey's Cordial that, taken at bedtime, would produce a peaceful slumber free from arousing dreams and leave me passive through the following day.

As I came up to my lodging, there was a burly fellow I thought I recognised, kicking his heels outside the vacant shop next door and watching a herd of cows returning from their evening milking with a knowledgeable eye. He was dressed very like a farmer himself and was mopping perspiration from his forehead with a large handkerchief. As I caught his eye, I could see that he thought he knew me too, and by the time I had taken out my key, he had placed me in his own recollection. 'Clerk to Lord Grenville, I think?' Instead of a courtly bow, he thrust out his right hand. 'William Philpott at your service.'

'Laurence Jago at yours.' Of course, I knew him. He was the ridiculous fellow from the palace, who had spoken so familiarly to the King. His hand was hard and horny, a farmer's hand like my father's, and he was examining me with frank curiosity, china-blue eyes in a red face.

'Yes, yes, thought I knew 'ee. 'Twas those damned green specs. How do you see through 'em at all?'

I didn't take offence. I was willing to be quizzed a little for the sake of my health, for the apothecary had assured me that the glaring sun of this unusually hot summer would strike my weak eyes blind. I extracted my hand. 'Are you staying in England long?'

'Long enough to sort out this mess with Jay, I hope. Lord Grenville needs my advice but, God damn me, this city is a festering ulcer, and I'll quit it again as soon as I can.' He seemed to be waiting for somebody, for he had apparently lost interest in my spectacles and his active eye was scanning up and down the street. 'President Washington has a baying mob at his back, but he knows damn well they can't afford to fight us. He sends Jay for something to placate 'em, before Jefferson hurries them into war.' He turned his eyes back on me and seemed to swell even larger. 'I have exerted myself on England's behalf in Philadelphia these two years and landed many a blow on the damned Democrats.'

'I have heard your writing is …' I fumbled for a word that would adequately describe him. 'Pungent.'

'The Prime Minister called my efforts invaluable.' He looked fierce. 'Gather they wish to point the direction in which the *Cannon* will discharge its first load and are willing to pay handsomely.'

'The *Cannon*?'

'My new London paper, sir, quite ready to come hurrying to the gunwale of the national ship, to protect its country with a resounding blast.'

This explained his presence at the palace. 'A fine title. I wish you every joy of your gunpowder.'

'Gunpowder and balls, sir. Gunpowder and balls are all that is required.' He rubbed his hands and his fierce face blossomed into a disarming rosy smile. 'But come, do you not fancy a career as a journalist now? Can I not tempt 'ee? I fell into the profession quite by accident myself, driven to pen and ink by those damned Americans, but I find it answers exceeding well. The finest profession in the world, sir!'

For a moment I was tempted. He was so large, so full of life – everything the Foreign Office was emphatically not. But I only smiled, for I saw he meant it merely as a pleasantry, and I changed the subject. 'Do you really call this city a festering ulcer?'

'Oh.' He glanced about him at the filth and squalor of Fleet Street. 'Not here, I grant 'ee. This is quite to my satisfaction – puts me in mind of Basingstoke, where I was born. But those damned gilded streets and worthless tax-eaters in Whitehall! They, sir, are an affront to wholesome British values.'

It was clear that taking offence at anything the man said would be useless, and so I answered without resentment. 'You must know my stipend also comes from the public purse. Would it comfort you to know a half goes directly to my own mother's Cornish farmyard?' How seldom I mentioned home, and how impossible to imagine its soft light, its green dripping woods, amid this barren landscape of stone and dust.

'A farm, is it?' Philpott looked at me with some new regard. 'Then, if I may take the liberty, sir, I think I may hazard we are both men of the soil, transplanted to paper and ink.' He sounded tolerably satisfied by this state of affairs. 'Now, Laurence my boy, I am come to view this shop here. How do you find Fleet Street as a neighbourhood?'

But a small, vigorous figure was just then approaching, waving a set of keys, and after another handshake I left Philpott to his business and let myself in at my own door.

My old landlady, Dora, was dozing in the oppressive heat and darkness of the kitchen, where only the coals glowed in a dying grate. The washing was strung up above it as usual, the shifts hanging palely limp, like a row of corpses. As I came in, she roused herself from her slumber, and pulled herself to her feet heavily, patting her pockets and then putting a rough red hand up to check the washing was dry.

Mr Gibbs had been dozing too, but he now rose from his basket, stretched, and ambled over, making his curious ululation, halfway between a bark and a growl. Old Gibbs is a wolfish-looking animal with a nonchalant gait and a disconcerting gaze.

'Has the creature been good?'

'Middling. He do stare like old Nick. 'Tis a wonder the bread's riz.' Dora produced a letter from behind the flat iron on the mantelpiece. 'For 'ee. Come this morning.'

It was from my mother, and I held it close to my face to decipher the faint ink lines in the dull red gloom from the fire. The weather was too dry, she wrote, the crops wilting in the fields, and she would dance like a Red Indian if it would bring on rain. *This heat must make London mighty unhealthy, and I would have you come home if you are able – but, voilà, I say this in every letter.* There was a postscript scribbled on the back of the paper, so badly written it took me a moment to make out that my brother John had been beaten in Helston as a dirty Frenchman and told to 'go home'.

4

I T WAS, I SUPPOSE, the following Thursday, and I was sitting at the Cabinet table with a group of interested parties to the American question. A shaft of sunlight bisected Downing Street, throwing the pavements into shadow, and clerks were beginning to straggle out of their offices for the night. I felt peaceful, for Aglantine had not contacted me since the hanging, and although my mother's letter had troubled me, Cornwall and its problems seemed as remote as ever. Philpott had moved his family into the shop next door, with a good deal of cheerful commotion that I observed from a distance, with some amusement. Meanwhile, in Downing Street, there had been much gossip among the clerks about Will Benson's sacking. No one could understand it, and, accordingly, rumours had begun to swirl about, as full of filth as the Thames's incoming tide. I had called again, once or twice, at his lodging, but had never found him at home, and I half thought he might have left London.

'As Lord Grenville sees it, there are ways to placate Mr Jay.'

Sir James was sitting at the centre of the table, behind a formidable pile of papers, while from the lobby came the sound of crashing crockery and the rattle of cutlery. 'The dinner here tonight, of course, and Mr Pitt proposes another with the Cabinet next week. In the meantime, we are engaged in a preliminary discussion of the parameters—'

'God help us.' Harry Ransome was the committee's representative on trade, a timber plantation owner from the West Indies. He was a stout young man with a premature belly and an apparent belief that the world owed him its esteem. Sir James eyed him with the disdainful patience of a civil servant.

'Diplomacy is an exact science, Mr Ransome. Each stage must be observed, or disorder will ensue. And in any case, the longer the discussions drag on, the cooler tempers will become on all sides.'

'We'll *bore* him into surrender?' Canning asked, from his place next to Ransome. 'Well, I declare you quite capable of that, Sir James.'

A carriage had drawn up outside the window, and Aust's wife and stepdaughter climbed down, showing a good deal of ankle. I could see the embroidered seam of Anne's stocking, and with lightning thought followed the pattern up to the garter, the stocking top, and the bare thigh above it. There was nothing for it but a bigger dose of cordial. Mr Aust appeared, to lead his women inside, and their light voices echoed around the lobby like canaries.

As Sir James embarked on a lengthy explanation of diplomatic protocol, Ransome leaned over to Canning. 'What are those blue-stocking females doing here?'

'Come to inspect the preparations, I imagine. Aust's naught but a jumped-up footman, after all. He'll be angling for an invitation to Dropmore again, just you see. He longs to shoot on Lord Grenville's estate.'

'With his stepdaughter in tow, looking for a new husband?' They both chuckled.

'She had Grenville in her eye for a month or two, before he married. But it was too soon – she was still in black.'

'She could try her luck with Pitt.' This made them both laugh out loud, until quashed by Sir James's disapproving eye, and I mended my quill vigorously. Surely Anne was not fool enough to talk at large the way she talked to me. But somehow these men knew her ambitions.

As a matter of fact, she told me she intended to marry the Prime Minister the first time I met her. I was twenty, and newly appointed in the Foreign Office, she was just fourteen. Marriage had been much on her mind, for her mother had just fixed Mr Aust after some unsettled years and an unwomanly literary career. Anne had not seemed discouraged by Pitt's papery complexion with the veins running in his temples like rivers of ink, nor had she seemed a danger to my peace of mind.

But that was full ten years ago. Ten years in the garret, while she grew into something mesmerising – as formidable in her way as Aglantine – took a husband and lost him almost at once, at the bottom of the ocean. She would already know of my promotion, for she remained as captivated by politics as ever. Perhaps she had even recommended my promotion to her stepfather herself.

After the meeting dispersed, I followed Sir James into Grenville's room. We had thought him engaged at Pitt's Secret Committee, quizzing Thomas Hardy for the dozenth time, but he had requested our immediate attention, and we found him drooping in his chair, quite pale. 'Mr Philpott has been here.'

'I'm sorry, my Lord,' Sir James looked his concern. 'If I'd been at liberty, I should have been sure to deflect him.'

'I found myself hurried into inviting him and his wife to this evening's dinner.'

'My Lord!'

'Yes, yes, I know. But we need not speak to him, you know, any more than to that dreadful Miss More.' Miss Hannah More was a spinster lady of decided views and bracing writings for the poor, and the prospect of her company cast a gloom over Sir James's moon face, as he handed Grenville a glass of brandy.

'Philpott is a noisy fool,' Grenville went on, 'but I'd rather he wrote *for* us than against us, and I feel obliged to honour him with some token of our good will.' He knocked back the brandy gratefully and was holding out the glass for a refill when a clerk came in.

'Sorry to disturb you, my Lord, but Mr Aust wants Mr Jago.'

Mr Aust was looking particularly grey when I knocked on his office door. 'Come in, come in, and close that door behind you.'

I did as I was bid.

'There's some trouble across the road.' He meant Number 10 and, from his ashen look, probably the ire of Pitt himself, which might account for his reluctance to name that gentleman for fear of summoning him like a ghost at a banquet. 'One of Pandora's keys is missing.'

'Good God.' I considered this news. The Ministerial strong box reportedly contained many dreadful secrets that no one would want buzzing out into the ether with all their destructive consequences.

'They demanded a search of the Foreign Office, which I

have just now conducted to no avail. However, it seems there's a clerk lately dismissed from Mr Canning's service, who might have taken it.'

'You mean Will Benson? Nonsense!' But my mind was already busy. Was this why he'd been dismissed? If so, it was as preposterous a story as anything invented by the clerks. 'Surely not. He's a very agreeable fellow.'

Aust brightened. 'You know him? Well, well, that *is* fortuitous. Go and seek him out, Mr Jago, and whether he has it or not, we can at least tell Number 10 we have done our duty.'

As Will Benson's landlady opened the door to me, a faint but repellent odour came with her. Perhaps it had grown on her by degrees, so that she hardly noticed. At any rate, she was affronted by my look of revulsion as she leaned in the doorway suspiciously. 'What do you want now?'

'Is Mr Benson in?'

Either she didn't get enough to eat or she was suffering some wasting disease, for her clothes hung off her in folds. 'I told you all a dozen times, he don't want to see you. And besides, I ain't seen him for a day or two.'

It seemed I wasn't the first emissary from Whitehall in search of the missing key, but Aust was waiting for my report back in Downing Street. 'Can I look in his room?' She looked doubtful. 'I'm on Government business.'

'Well …'

'I'll only be a moment. It's Mr Pitt's particular orders.' If I was going to invoke the Ministry, I may as well go straight to the top.

She wasn't happy about it, but she could hardly argue with the Prime Minister, and stood aside to let me pass out of the sunlight into the dark hallway. For a moment I was blinded, but then bare wooden stairs materialised in the gloom ahead of me. Will's lodgings were as shabby as my own, but at least Dora's house didn't stink. I put my handkerchief to my nose, which didn't improve the woman's temper. 'Those damned Frenchies next door,' she said defensively, closing the front door behind us and immuring us in a deeper gloom.

There was certainly something badly wrong with the drains or with the cesspit. We went up one flight of stairs, and then another. Like me, it seemed, Will Benson lived high up in the tall thin house, the rent decreasing with every storey. All the doors were closed, and the only light filtered down the final set of stairs from a skylight in the attic.

The stink was worse up here. Even Will's landlady seemed to smell it now, for her breathing sounded a little ragged over the quiet creak of the floorboards behind me. 'That door. There.' She sounded queasy. 'It'll be locked, mind.'

It wasn't locked. The small brass doorknob turned easily under my fingers, and the latch slipped back at once. As I pushed the door inwards, the first thing that struck me was darkness. The next, a puzzling noise. The curtains were closed, and the smell was suddenly much worse, but I struck forward blindly into the darkness, my hands outstretched, aiming for the faint grey light seeping in around the curtains. The noise, which at first I had taken for a voice humming, resolved itself into an angry buzzing.

'You have a swarm of bees,' I said, over my shoulder to the woman in the doorway. 'They must have come in through the window. It's open a crack.'

The humming was growing into a discordant clamour, and I hunched my shoulders against the hovering of wings about me, my scalp prickling. Something landed on my neck, and

I slapped it away. At last my hand was on the curtain, and I pulled it back and threw up the sash as far as it would go.

I took a deep grateful breath of soot and horse dung, before turning back into the room. For a moment I was baffled. They were not bees but flies. Hundreds of flies. I felt a prick as one landed on my cheek, but I hardly noticed, for Will's landlady was prostrate on the threshold, in a dead faint, and Will himself was hanging by his neck from a knotted sheet, attached to an iron staple in the ceiling beam.

I should have gone to the woman's aid, but I was too dazed to think straight. The body was still recognisably Will, and for a moment I thought I saw his eyes shift, his tongue stir in his open mouth. But then I saw it was not his eyes, nor his tongue that moved, but flies, dozens of flies, crawling in and out of those glistening orifices.

The woman was groaning and rousing herself again. 'God love me,' she said hoarsely, and then began to sob loudly. I staggered towards her, pushing her out into the corridor and shutting the door.

'We must find a couple of strong men to lift him down. Send for the women to lay him out. And,' remembering reluctantly that suicide was a dreadful crime, 'I suppose we had better find a constable.'

5

WHEN I FINALLY GOT away from the gaggle of businesslike men and women taxed with handling the body, the rash of unimpressible officials, and Will's curious fellow tenants, I had to go home, wash off the stench of death, and change into my best suit for the Foreign Office dinner for Mr Jay, which, despite everything, I was obliged to attend that evening. Dora had excelled herself with the crispness of my linen and the polishing of my buttons. Smooth nankeen breeches, silk stockings and an embroidered waistcoat with a green lining. Embroidered lilies on my dress coat, too, the simple pattern running down from the lapels, to the pockets, to the tails. But I was pale as I examined my reflection in the silvered old glass, still shuddering at the memory of the fat satiated flies in that quiet room, and Will's evacuated corpse. I took a few drops of Godfrey's Cordial to fortify myself against the frivolity of the evening to come, wondering how I could bear it, after the horrors of the day.

Yet my mood rose strangely as Dora powdered my wig and

put a handkerchief in my pocket, before pushing me out of doors. As I found a hackney and bid it deposit me and my finery in Downing Street, the world seemed more than usually vivid. Perhaps it was the laudanum, or the prospect of seeing Anne – or the realisation that while death was very dreadful, I myself was still alive.

I had only just come into the Foreign Office lobby, where the guests had gathered for drinks before dinner, when Mr Aust appeared at my shoulder with the American envoy. 'Mr Jay, may I present Mr Jago? He will be Lord Grenville's clerk on this matter, and very happy to advise you on any practical matters during your stay.'

'Good evening, sir.' Jay's bow was stiff, his eye a little rheumy. 'Did I catch sight of you at the King's Levée, now? Your spectacles are familiar, I think.'

'Yes, sir, I was there.' I decided to say nothing about the spectacles, which seemed to speak for themselves. 'Though as a matter of fact, it was not a Levée, but a Drawing Room, as the Queen and other ladies were present for the King's birthday.'

'Drawing Room, was it? A curious kind of drawing room with no chairs.'

'There are never any chairs. It would be disrespectful to sit in the presence of royalty.'

'I see.' Jay seemed to be filing this information away in what might yet prove to be a capacious brain, but on first inspection he did not seem a brilliant man, though he was supposed to have a fine legal mind. His son arrived at his elbow. 'May I present Mr Theodore Jay? He accompanies me as my secretary.'

Theodore stayed at my side as his father was led away to meet Sir James, and I felt obliged to say the usual polite nothings. 'Have you been in England before, Mr Jay?'

'Never.' Theodore looked up at me with a shy smile. As before, at the palace, his curly hair was hardly tamed by his formal wig. 'I have never been much out of my father's estate in Westchester County.'

'Well, if you need a guide to the city then I'd be happy to oblige.' Hollow courtesy and, remembering too late that Aglantine had asked me to befriend him, probably unwise. But the boy looked surprisingly pleased.

'Would you really? I confess, all this is not particularly congenial to me. I am far more interested in finding out the ways of the real city.'

'You'll find that "all this" is a deal cleaner, safer and less troubling, I assure you. The city is excessively rough, and there are pimps and whores and thieves everywhere, with an unwholesome interest in your pockets.'

'So I have heard.' The boy sipped at his sherry with pursed rosy lips, and what almost looked like satisfaction. In ordinary circumstances this might have stirred my interest, but I was too tired for small talk. I made some murmured excuse and moved away.

After a moment, I wished I hadn't, for it soon became apparent that when the talk wasn't about the traitor Hardy, it was about Will Benson's disgraceful death. 'One does not mind the consumption, you know,' Sir James was confiding to a startled Mr Jay in a corner. 'And accidents occur all too frequently – I myself narrowly escaped death by market cart this very day in Charing Cross.' His voice lowered. 'But self-murder, sir! It does not reflect very well upon the Ministry at all.'

Anne had just come in and was being presented to Theodore. She looked cool. He was scarlet. *Women must frighten him, I* thought, turning my eyes away. Behind me, Lady Grenville was explaining the principles of cross-pollination to Sir James's wife, Lord Grenville was quizzing Mrs Aust about her latest book, and Sir James was reciting doggerel.

Philpott was suddenly at my shoulder. We had done no more than nod since we became neighbours, but he dispensed with any preliminary greeting, perhaps thinking me an old friend, merely on the strength of proximity. 'Did you know this poor clerk?' He was wearing a remarkable puce costume, which apparently constituted his idea of courtly dress. Mrs Philpott, a tall gaunt woman with a sensible face, stood beside him all in purple, so that taken together they rather resembled the inside of a fig.

'We all knew him a little, though only as a drinking companion.' Now, I realised, I was as intimate with Will Benson as any man alive, for he had shared the secrets of his putrefaction with me and I would never forget him.

'And you was the one discovered him hanging?' A slight gleam came into Philpott's rosy face.

'Yes.' I looked away again. 'It was horrible.'

'Dear me.' He sounded delighted. 'I suppose you'll give evidence at the inquest?'

'Yes, tomorrow afternoon at the Golden Cross inn.'

'Well, then, I shall certainly see you there.' Philpott took a glass of punch from a passing footman. 'A Government death is as good as a lord's and will sell me four score extra copies, I assure 'ee.'

'SOMEONE YOU KNOW?'
The lobby was empty except for Anne, standing on the stairs alone in a shaft of dying daylight, looking at a portrait.

She had her mother's shawl over her arm, but she'd evidently forgotten her errand. Her grey dress and pale face made her look rather spectral against the background of gathering evening shadows. She gave a cry as I trudged up the steps towards her. Voices murmured from the dining room, but here was only peace. 'Lord, Laurence, I did not see you there.'

I had escaped the gaiety of the dining room, having discovered that my appetite for the banquet was quite as dead as Will Benson. 'I beg pardon. You were rapt in contemplation of this ...' I pushed up my spectacles and bent to examine the portrait, which showed a middle-aged gentleman dressed rather improbably in full Scottish regalia, against a backdrop of mountains.

'My Uncle John! Would you believe it? I came upon him quite unawares.'

'What is he doing here?'

'Looking quite ridiculous, don't you think?' She looked up at me half composed, half impish. 'But you, too, are the great man, of a sudden. Mr Aust has been telling me all about it.'

'You mean my promotion?' I was admiring the slender neck she turned from me as she examined the picture, the dark hair powdered and dressed above it, and the contour of her spine as it disappeared under the neckline of her dress. For the first time that evening I forgot about death and decay.

'Mr Aust believes you will succeed him in a year or two.' She straightened to inspect me as closely as she had the picture. 'What glory for you, Laurence! No fear of losing office – it's a vastly better life than a politician's after all. They may blaze out for a year or two, but then fall quite into obscurity, along with all that belong to them.' She was looking at me in a way I didn't quite recognise, but even as I gaped at her like a landed mackerel, her smile was returning. 'Laurence, fie upon

45

you. What is that monstrosity upon your nose?'

I was still gawking, and she took matters into her own hands, plucking my spectacles from my face and putting them up to her eyes. They looked huge behind the thick green glass as she peered about myopically. 'How curious. Is it like this beneath the sea, I wonder?'

I knew exactly how the world looked to her behind my heavy lenses, for without them it now looked the same to me. We both blinked at a prospect suddenly blurry, like one glimpsed through rain on glass. I thought I could remember a time before the measles, when everything was clear, but I was very young. After that I moved in a fog that made reading more real to me than the fields and woods of the farm.

I took the eyeglasses from her hand. 'With myself the octopus?' I made to put them on again, but she stopped me with a hand on my own. There was unaccustomed colour in her cheeks, I could see that much even without my spectacles. She had always flirted with me – always known my preference and couldn't resist playing on it – but I hadn't ever seen that darting glance, the swiftly dropped eyes before. 'How you do hide your fine looks behind them, and that dreadful wig!'

She seemed to remember her mother's shawl and turned to go downstairs. I put my glasses back on my nose and offered her my arm in some confusion of spirit. She was still pink. 'But, after all, I shouldn't play the fool with a rising gentleman like yourself. You must not encourage me.'

I paused halfway down the steps. 'What strange new idea is this?'

She dropped her eyes. 'You are …'

'No longer an insignificant clerk in an attic?'

She was still blushing. 'Something like that.'

I can still feel the eager trembling of my heart as I followed her back to the dining room, such joy after the horrors of Will Benson's bedchamber. But trying to hold on to that feeling now is like glimpsing a sunlit scene through a moving window.

6

WE WAITED FOR THE carriages in the street, Mr Jay in earnest conversation with the dreadful Miss More. Mrs Philpott stood beside me, her clever face stolidly indifferent to my weary attempts to entertain her. In truth, I was no good companion, for the laudanum had long dissipated and I was suddenly dog tired. The world went on, seemingly, with one less man in it, quite as though he had never existed; but, in a way, it was soothing to let the political talk wash over me, running in its familiar channels. Mr Jay and Miss More were both staunch abolitionists, and their talk had turned naturally to Mr Wilberforce and his campaign in Parliament.

'Oh, he's an effective politician.' She was nodding her large head, the lace ruffle of her voluminous mob cap wagging. 'But he lived a very reprobate life before his conversion. He is useful to the cause of abolition, but I would not have him in my house.'

'Nor would I,' Philpott said from her other side, where he had been engaged in stilted conversation with Theodore, 'though for different reasons. Mr Wilberforce is a shade too *virtuous* for my taste. I never can like a fellow that sets himself up as holier than the next man. We are all sinners, ain't we? High and low.'

'That's true, in the strictest sense,' Miss More replied. 'But those who hear God's call must minister to those who do not.'

'And you set yourself up in that way, then? Are you so persuaded of your own virtue, ma'am?'

Pink spots appeared in Miss More's cheeks. 'I do not believe any man has ever questioned *that*.'

'Oh – I meant no disrespect to you personally, ma'am.' Philpott guffawed, and Miss More looked icier than ever. 'No man would fancy to assail your honour, I assure 'ee. But I am grieved by your disdain for the common people and their ways.'

'As I am grieved by sin, sir. I do not feel disdain for the wicked, only dreadful sorrow. How can the poor know any better, left as they are to wallow in ignorance, intoxication and vice?'

'What would you have 'em do?' Philpott was swelling, and Theodore Jay was blushing at his elbow. 'Drink tea instead of beer? Give up all their pleasures at the tavern? Spend their only day of rest destroying their knees in prayer, instead of taking the ease they deserve? I should like to see you, madam, labour in the fields from dawn till dusk, and then choose to spend your Sabbath mouthing pious nothings on a comfortless pew. Moreover, your agitation against the slave trade is right worthy, I'm sure, but your sympathies are misplaced. God damn me, I'd as soon be a slave in America with three square meals a day and a roof over my head, than a poor homeless orphan in a London alley.'

Mr Jay was stung into uncharacteristic energy. 'You don't

mean to say you support the institution of slavery? On grounds both spiritual and philosophical it is a scandal. Men and women treated as mere property, when they are possessed of immortal souls!'

Philpott stared at him, frankly perplexed. 'Mr Jay, I wish you the very best in these coming talks, but will you lecture me on such matters? God damn me, sir, *I* own no slaves, but I believe you do, and Mr Jefferson, too, for all his cant about *liberté, égalité, fraternité.* How many human creatures do you personally consign to such degradation?'

'Not above half a dozen.' Mr Jay looked whiter than ever. 'And I will be delighted to free them as soon as they are ready for liberty.'

'Ready for liberty! And when will that be? When they do as Miss More wishes, I suppose, and are as much in chains to your God-damned dismal morality.'

At this juncture Miss More's carriage appeared, and she was whisked away from Mr Philpott's brutal remarks, no doubt with a good deal of relief. As the rattle of the wheels faded, Mr Jay appeared to have been pondering Philpott's words.

'A slave is an expense,' he said stiffly. 'Food, suitable apparel – an education, if required – all these are burdens, quite beside the purchase price. But it is my plan. Buy them young, make such investments as are required and then, when the investment is returned by a reasonable length of service, I make it my business to free them.'

'Very rational, I'm sure, and vastly economic. Mr Adam Smith would approve.'

Mr Jay did not answer, and in the silence that followed we could hear faint strains of music wafting from the direction of the park. Theodore turned his head to listen. 'What's that?'

'A revel in the park,' Philpott answered, cocking his own head like a spaniel, and regaining his good humour directly. 'Now, now, Mr Jay, would 'ee care to see the English at recreation?'

It was a mischievous suggestion, for there seemed hardly anything less likely, but Theodore looked animated. 'Oh, Father, shall we?'

Mr Jay was predictably unmoved. 'I think not, Theodore. We have too much to occupy us, for such frivolous diversions.'

Philpott laughed, and nudged the envoy in the ribs. God knows how much of the Foreign Office claret he had drunk. 'You show your age, sir. Come, will you not take yourself off to the comforts of your rooms and let us introduce your boy to the pleasures of the town?'

Mr Jay looked speechless.

The discussion had now run into channels entirely novel, thanks to Mr Philpott, who was proving as good an antidote to horror as Anne had been, and I found myself suppressing a smile. 'I don't think Mr Philpott means anything improper. Merely a turn about the park, you know, to observe the people, hear the music and admire the scenery.'

Theodore sounded like a plaintive infant. 'Oh, mayn't I, Father?'

'Perhaps you could drop Mrs Philpott at her door on your way?' Philpott suggested. Mr Jay looked undecided, but just then his carriage appeared, and Mrs Philpott resolved the matter by climbing in directly. Jay's slave, Peter Williams, was sitting in the shadowy corner, a suit apparently inhabited only by deeper darkness until she poked him good-naturedly and his face moved into the lamplight. Mr Philpott looked after her with loving eyes. 'Now mind yourself, Nancy.'

'Get away with you.' She settled herself comfortably beside Mr Jay's investment, and beckoned Mr Jay to join her. 'I shall be as right as rain.'

Philpott was boisterously cheerful as we cut back down Fludyer Street and across Horse Guards Parade towards the canal. I had gone with them without reflection, but I realised now that I did not under any circumstances want to walk back home alone, past Will Benson's lodgings. I found myself afraid of sleep, and the dreams it might bring.

'Good God preserve us from strong-minded women,' Philpott was exulting. 'Unless, like my Nancy, they put their minds to their husbands' comfort.'

'Miss More is well respected.' Theodore was hurrying along beside us. 'And vastly pious. Folks in America hold her very high, I assure you.'

'America must be an uncomfortably solemn sort of a place,' I said.

'I wish it were, Mr Jago. Mr Philpott will tell you it is very, very dissolute indeed.'

'Scarcely more so than this city,' Philpott objected. 'But I begin to fear you and Miss More will change men's ways between you. By the time you're fifty and have made the world to your moral satisfaction, I'll be dead, thank God.'

The park has its dark parts, but near to Whitehall and the river, it was all light. A string quartet played by the canal, surrounded by a dignified audience of what London society remained in town. It was still warm, even this late in the evening, and as we walked through the female crowd it was an aviary of fluttering fans.

'Are these loose women?' Theodore asked with unexpected zest, and an offended old dowager bustled out from under our feet like a partridge.

'Apparently not.' I wondered how such an interest might sit with his earnest morality. 'I believe such females frequent another part of the park.'

'Steady, sir.' Philpott took Theodore by the elbow. 'I had thought you more tender of your immortal soul.' He called over a fellow selling shrub, and we took a cup, leaning on the balustrade that overlooked the canal. Theodore Jay gazed about him with pleasure, but every so often he glanced furtively over his shoulder, and I half-wondered who it was he feared to see behind him.

A pair of swans made elaborate figures in the water as I sipped at my drink of raspberries in brandy and watched the dancers take their places by the bandstand. Will Benson had frequently been among them, for we clerks often came here. While the rest of the lads banded together like a gaggle of geese, full of blustering banter, he had always slipped away to the music. I never saw him dance with the same woman twice but, being mere boys, the others used to tease him that he met some ageing paramour there – a woman of declining years but large fortune, far too eager, and splendidly accommodating in ways they enumerated amid raucous, callow laughter.

'Do you go home much, Mr Jago?' Philpott's voice roused me from this reverie, and I straightened, drinking off the last of the shrub.

'No, sir. I've not been home these four years.'

Philpott only nodded at this grave confession. 'And 'tis full ten since I saw my father down in Hampshire. Perhaps we neither of us dare to muddy ourselves again, for fear the stain will not come out. But I tell you, it's folks like our parents and their neighbours that are the true Britons, and we must not get ourselves too far above 'em. I shall tell Lord Grenville to look to the people for support. People like my father and your mother, whose feet are rooted in the English soil.'

'Country people are certainly more placid,' I said doubtfully, remembering my brother's beating.

'Your mother – my father – quiet country folks like them, see into things rightly, and understand what patriotism means, unlike that ruffian Hardy.'

I looked at him perplexed. 'I confess, I don't understand you. How can you praise up common people like our parents, but call Thomas Hardy a traitor for seeking the vote?'

Philpott was quite ready for another argument. 'How? Because it is merely a pretext for revolution, I assure 'ee, an infection caught from the damned French.' His face swelled. 'When neither you nor I have the vote, Laurence, what earthly use would it be to the poor? At home, in the countryside, the ancient constitution goes quietly on as it always has. If I took you back to Hampshire, you would see it. The poor with their cottage strips, a common to keep a pig and cow, independence, and pride in the things they own. And when they fall sick, the kindly attentions of my father and the squire himself. This city twists all social intercourse out of true. Those urchins that sleep at Temple Bar would be taken to the parish anywhere else in England, but here there's only the Foundling Hospital, and I'd not put a dog in there. The city destroys the ties of kindness between master and man, and the poor things will be beaten all their lives, worked like mules and not even shot when they lie dying. They are no better off than slaves, I assure 'ee. Hardy should spend his energy restoring the good old ways, not following the French towards murder and confusion.' But his own small blue eye was still fixed on the dancers and had begun to gleam. 'But come now, enough of politics, my lad. Will you be talking of nothing else? There is a rosy-cheeked creature over by the band, kicking her heels for a partner. She deserves to dance, and I will oblige. Mrs Philpott would quite approve, I assure 'ee, for there's no sin in a harmless flirtation. Yes, there are ladies for us all – even

Theodore. Eh, Mr Theodore Jay, what do you say?'

Mr Theodore Jay had absconded into the crowd and was not to be seen. We scouted about for a minute and then met up again with grave faces.

'You don't think …?'

'God damn me, I fear so.' Philpott looked aghast. 'What will his father say?'

Again, I repressed an urge to laugh. 'Lord, we'd better find him, or Mr Jay will never forgive us. Shall we meet again, here, in an hour?'

'An hour! God send we find him sooner than that.'

We parted, setting off in different directions into the shadowy realms, where vice of a kind that would have disappointed Miss Hannah More was in full swing. The music was faster, the voices louder and the dresses more shameless. I lost my sense of direction at once and wandered aimlessly from the orbit of one musical entertainment to the next. A woman caught hold of my sleeve and kissed me, before whirling away into the crowd with a drunken laugh.

I half-expected to meet the pack of Whitehall clerks, tearing through in search of amusement and flesh, but if they were here, I didn't see them. 'Fools,' I heard Will Benson say, equably, in my ear. But then he would grin. 'What would their mothers say?'

We were all mothers' sons, and all of us a disappointment if they only knew it. Had Will really stolen a key to the safe at Number 10? It was absurd even to imagine it. No, I was the only criminal in their midst, and if Will Benson had known my secrets, he would have turned his back on me. But he was gone, now, into a deeper blackness where I had no desire to follow.

It felt a good deal longer than an hour since I had parted

from Philpott, and I had begun to believe I should never find my way back to the canal even if I wanted to – should still be lost and drifting in the grey light of dawn – when I caught a citrus tang, and for the merest moment I thought I saw Aglantine coming towards me, her tight black clothing melting into the surrounding gloom, her face floating disembodied out of the torchlight.

It was at that moment I came upon Philpott, sitting on a stone bench asleep. The railings of Buckingham House were close by, and I knew where I was again. I looked around for Aglantine, but it seemed it had only been a trick of the light, for the vision was gone. Why I had thought of her I didn't know, but it was hellish enough in the darkness, and she had always put me in mind of bones and corpses.

The errant Theodore had turned up, apparently successful in his own hunt for loose women, for he sat across from Philpott surrounded by a bevy of low dresses and white-painted cheeks. It took me a moment to realise that they were all praying. I poked Philpott's shoulder, and he came to his senses reluctantly. 'What time is it?'

'I believe I heard a clock strike three.'

'God help me. It feels later.'

I sat down beside him, and we both looked at Theodore.

'Has he been doing this all along?' I asked.

'All along.'

'There has been no impropriety, I take it?'

'Him! Look at him. It makes my blood boil.'

'It appears he is his father's son after all.'

'It makes me tired, sir, that's what. Let us extract him and go home to our beds.'

Theodore would not be extracted until every woman had promised to attend church on Sunday and cook their old mothers a wholesome dinner instead of hanging about the town like common whores.

We dropped him at his lodging and tramped back through the deserted streets. As we came through Temple Bar into Fleet Street, Philpott grunted irritably. 'The boy is more agreeable than his father, I'll say that, but I wish he had some common sense.' He was off on one of his lectures again. 'You cannot possibly imagine the frenzy in Philadelphia when I left. The whole press of America is waiting for news, and Mr Theodore Jay will be a gift to 'em, if they find him out. It seemed to me the lad looked sheepish, as if he thought himself watched, but whoever it is that undertakes to guard him signally failed tonight. I think you had better look after him.'

I wondered if I had heard him right. 'Look after him?'

'Keep him in check. Protect him from himself. He'll likely listen to you, being of an age.'

'I'm nearer your age than his.'

'God damn me, sir, don't quibble, when the destiny of nations is at stake.' We had reached Philpott's door, where a single candle burned to welcome him home. 'Well, I shall see you again tomorrow at the inquest, Laurence. It seems we are fated to become regular companions, don't it?'

It was a relief to greet Mr Gibbs, strip off coat and waistcoat, and push my chamber window wide open, letting the night sounds of the city crowd in. There was a tremendous hooting of owls somewhere off by St Clement's Church, and foxes were fighting in some back alley, which made Mr Gibbs prick his ears, his forepaws on the sill. As I measured out my drops of Godfrey's Cordial, I caught sight of myself in the washstand mirror, a blurry figure in my shirt, with a long pale face, long pale hands, and eyes dark smudges in the candle-light. I looked as much a spectre as Will Benson, and for a moment I fancied the vision his ghost and shivered.

I turned back the covers and climbed into the bed, cocooned by its dusty hangings. I settled into the yielding mattress, with the dog pressed against my legs, snuffed out the candle, and let the laudanum propel me gently towards sleep, resolutely thinking about the events of the evening, to block out those of the afternoon. The dinner, the park – and Anne. Could she really want me now, despite my short sight, my rustic parents, and our long acquaintance? There was no novelty about me except my new standing. Perhaps money and position were all that had stopped her returning my affection all these years, in the same way that they had always prevented me from speaking.

7

THE INQUEST JURY, WHICH had assembled in the tap-room of the Golden Cross, seemed to have been plucked off the street quite at random. There was a weaver with crabbed hands, a cowman with a large hat, who informed the coroner he would certainly die if kept inside above a half-hour, and a collection of shopkeepers in aprons impatient to return to their usual business. I was there early, eager to get it over with, and watched as the coroner came in with Philpott on his heels, pushing through the small crowd of onlookers in the doorway. The coroner took his seat without delay and rattled through the preamble with a brisk solemnity that quietened the jury and made an unaccustomed hush fall on the cosy taproom.

'Gentlemen, we are gathered to take information on the death of William Benson, clerk, discovered this Thursday instant, in his rooms at Northumberland Street, in the Parish of St Martin-in-the-Fields. First, we have the deposition of the gentleman that found him, Laurence Jago of the Foreign

Office, I think. Are you here, Mr Jago?'

I stood forward, and the crowd looked impressed by this emanation of the Ministry in their midst. I was glad of the hat in my hands to cling to, for I had slept badly and was a little dazed and dizzy.

'You were sent to find Mr Benson, I believe?'

'Yes, sir. Mr Aust, Under-Secretary to Lord Grenville, sent me. I went to Mr Benson's lodging. His landlady took me up to his room, where we found him hanging by a bedsheet from the roof beam. The door was not locked, and the window was ajar.'

'I see.' The coroner looked at the jury. 'An unpremeditated act, then, I suppose we agree? The deceased had not gone to the trouble of providing himself with a rope.'

The makeshift jury nodded dutifully as Will's landlady was called to confirm my story and add her own colour to the proceedings. How she had fainted loomed as large in her recollection as the terrible image of Will's hanging corpse. Perhaps, like me, she did not want to remember it.

'And how would you describe Mr Benson's frame of mind, in the days preceding the death?'

'Not himself, sir, I shouldn't say. Not himself at all.'

'Distracted? Lunatic?'

'Well.' She paused to consider. 'I'd not have thought so, sir, but he must have been, mustn't he, to do such a wicked thing?'

'I'm afraid so, madam.' The coroner looked pleased as he turned to the jury, who nodded again. 'Very well then, having made thorough inquiry into this unfortunate business, I find as follows: *The Jurors aforesaid upon their Oath aforesaid do say that the said William Benson, not being of sound Mind Memory and Understanding but Lunatick and distracted in manner, and by the means aforesaid, did kill himself at his lodging at*

Northumberland Street in the Parish of St Martin-in-the-Fields some day in the last week of June 1794.'

THOROUGH! WELL, IT WAS as thorough as most trials at the Old Bailey, where the judges liked to dispatch dozens of cases in an afternoon. But in fact, the coroner was merciful in his brevity, as Philpott observed over his shoulder, as we set off briskly back towards Westminster. 'God help me, that fellow knew his business. He handled the jury damned well. The poor devil's family will not be fined, and he'll be quietly buried without drama.'

It might be expedient to call it lunacy and stop the whole panoply of a crossroads burial and the forfeiture of his possessions, but it still seemed wrong that I hadn't mentioned Canning's persecution, or Will's dismissal from Number 10. But then again, if these sudden misfortunes had really driven him to suicide, perhaps his wits had deserted him, just as the verdict said. The poor devil would go down into unconsecrated ground and be forgotten. But still I said, 'I wish I really knew what made him do it,' just as Philpott hastened his step in pursuit of Will's landlady, who was turning into Northumberland Street. By the time I came round the corner they were deep in conversation. She saw me following and nodded, climbing the steps to her door with Philpott on her heels.

I paused reluctantly at the bottom of the steps. 'What are you doing?'

'Visiting Benson's rooms.' Philpott seemed surprised to be asked. 'While everyone else is busy wringing their hands and drinking a skinful at the Golden Cross, his good landlady is perfectly content for us to have another look. She remembers you quite cordially, she assures me.'

'But in God's name, why?' I had no desire to follow him, but he was waving peremptorily.

'Investigation, my boy.' He stood aside to let me pass ahead of him into the gloomy hallway, which now smelled pleasantly of roasting capon instead of death. 'A journalist's stock in trade, I assure 'ee.'

I skulked at the bedroom door as Philpott bustled in, throwing up the sash as I had done. A nastier stench still lingered beneath what I saw now was a general squalor. The daylight revealed soiled shirts lying in a pile waiting for the washerwoman. The sheet still hung from the iron hook in the beam, but someone had taken away the soiled bedclothes, and only a handful of flies buzzed at the window glass and crawled over the mattress. I was very glad the body was gone. Death might be everywhere in the city, from cats flattened by cartwheels to men coughing up their last on street corners – and I had witnessed the felons hanged in Newgate Street a dozen times – but nothing could have prepared me for the dreadful stillness of that body brooding in the quiet room, or the dreadful seething of the creatures that gluttonised upon him. I felt a return of the superstitious dread I'd felt the night before, in front of my own mirror.

Desiccated snuff lay over the surfaces like dust, and as Philpott lifted up the lid of the bureau, I sneezed, coming to myself and venturing inside reluctantly. 'What are you looking for?'

He produced a letter, crossed and double crossed, that he took to the window. 'The answer to your question. Why he should find life so insupportable he'd choose a noose instead.'

'What are you reading?'

'A letter from his mother.' Philpott handed it to me and went back to the bureau. 'It can't be the only one.'

I read it while he rummaged through the bureau drawers. There was no sign of the famous key Aust had sent me in search of. Whatever Will had done to incur Canning's wrath, it had not been that, though he might have been arraigned for the theft of what looked suspiciously like the best Ministerial notepaper. Ink too, and good quills. But all blank. No written sheets at all, except the paper in my hand.

It was a workaday letter. Will's father was an attorney, it seemed, down in Kent, writing up wills and probate for the populace of Rochester. I folded the letter up again, feeling worse by the minute. He would not be forgotten after all, and it would kill his mother when she got the news.

Philpott closed the bureau, and went to the bed, rifling under the soiled mattress while I looked on with some fascinated disgust. 'Nothing,' he said, straightening. 'A Bible and a copy of *Robinson Crusoe* by the bedside, an engraving of Rochester Cathedral on the wall.' He peered at it. 'From St Paul's Churchyard, I see. It must have cost him a pretty penny.' He moved across to the wardrobe and flung it open. Two suits, grubby but neatly folded, a handful of linen. A pair of well-polished buckled shoes. I remembered Will's wiry grey wig, but it was nowhere to be seen.

Philpott was going through the pockets of Will's suits but came up empty handed. 'A poor legacy to leave to posterity.' He sat down by the window and looked about him. 'He had nothing to forfeit, and we're none the wiser.'

I picked up the copy of *Robinson Crusoe* and riffled gloomily through its pages. They were well worn and fell open at the page Crusoe met Friday for the first time. Will had been the merrymaker at the heart of every revel, but as I knew to my own cost, mere companions are not friends. Had Will been as lonely as Crusoe? As lonely as myself? If I had dared to hazard even a modicum of real friendship, I could have persuaded him that Canning's cruelty was no good reason to take his own life.

Philpott put his hands behind his head and put his feet up on the bed. 'What kinds of trouble can a young man get himself into? Looking about me, I might say debt. A towering sum owed to a moneylender in Cheapside, perhaps. A bill of hand about to fall due. Or a woman, of course. A love child in Whitechapel – a young lady compromised in Sloane Square. It could be either. And then I suppose there is sodomy. If someone found *that* out, he might prefer death to blackmail.'

There was certainly truth in that. If recognised in the molly walks of Holborn, or taken, perhaps, by a Bow Street Runner in disguise, the penalty was the pillory or even the rope. But more common by far was extortion. Someone with information could bleed a man dry, with no prospect of escape.

'All very true,' I said. 'But, in fact, it was none of those. I know why he did it.'

Philpott was all attention, though he feigned coolness. But as I told him about the scene with Canning in Number 10, his interest waned. By the end, he looked disappointed. 'Nonsense.' He stood up and closed the windows again. 'What man would kill himself for mere loss of place? There are a dozen other positions he might find in London with his qualifications.'

When I left home at seventeen, I was a marvel throughout the parish, the Reverend's prodigy, and the future entirely bright. They would think their confidence amply proved by my new position, and no doubt Will's home town felt the same. The only possession he still owned was that engraving of Rochester Cathedral. I thought I might hang myself too, before I went home in disgrace.

Philpott pulled the faded curtain across and the room fell back into a melancholy gloom. He was preoccupied as we walked back to Fleet Street, perhaps composing his newspaper article in his mind as he strode along. I was sombre again. When all alone, away from the mindless chatter of the clerks, was Will Benson often as grey and hollow as that last day in Downing Street? What worries had troubled him in the depths of the night? I had thought him an open book, as simple as all the other boys in Whitehall, but how much could any man really know of another? Every man had secrets, even if they were likely to be less damning than my own.

But then I saw that I did know him, after a fashion, and could answer these questions with a pretty accurate guess. His troubles might not be of his own making, or tantamount to treason as mine were, but we were the same. We were both young men dislocated from our homes and families, working with modest prospects in an alien city. How different, really, would my room appear, if anyone troubled to search it? I possessed my court suit with matching satin shoes, and a set of old clothes from the farm. A few more books than Will possessed, but nothing to tell the real story of my life. And whatever secrets Will might have had, mine were equally well hidden.

Well, I would not waste the prospects I now had. I seemed to remember that the wheezy gentleman in Dora's best front rooms was forever complaining about the laundry. If I could only inherit his apartments, I would fill them with belongings that might root me in the world and leave more than a feeble trace behind. A few gewgaws and a Turkey carpet might make them acceptable rooms for a young man on the rise, a young man with prospects, a man able to look about himself for a bride. And on Sunday, after church, I would go to Kensington and call on Anne.

When we got back to Fleet Street, Mrs Philpott was waiting in the doorway of the shop, spinning yarn on to a spindle she held in one hand, from a cloud of combed lambswool in the other. 'We are to take delivery of a half-grown pig tomorrow,' she announced as we came up. 'Mrs Beale from the jewellers is at her wits' end, for it will not endure its sty and is forever absconding to the greengrocer's apple store.'

'That is damned bad management.' Philpott came out of his reverie at once, the poor clerk apparently forgotten.

'I thought so, too, but did not like to look a gift pig in the mouth.' She laughed shortly and gave another smart twist to the spindle as it dropped. 'I have offered her a good price, and her boy is to bring it around in the morning. Your son is to take the charge of it, and Margaret is to have rabbits.'

I left them to their domestic confabulation and went home to find Dora in the kitchen, ruining her eyes over a badly printed broadside. The joint of mutton on the spit was scorched, and I went to turn it, while she wheezed and tutted behind me. 'Oh, my gawd! Oh, my laws!' There was something comforting in her clucking, like an old broody hen, and my despondency faded as she thrust the paper at me. A scantily clad female was wrestling with a French soldier, while a portly gentleman looked on, aghast. It wasn't exactly clear if the lady was being throttled or raped.

'What is this trash?'

'It's the war, ain't it? The Frenchies are coming.'

'Do you fear for your virtue?'

We looked at each other for a minute, then she cackled uproariously and took herself off to the mutton. 'My virtue,' I could hear her chuckling to herself, as I went upstairs to wash my hands and face. 'My *vurr-tew*.'

8

'CAN I HELP YOU TO a glass of brandy, sir?'
'I thank you, no, my Lord.' Jay folded the skirts of his coat carefully to either side as he sat down at the desk in Grenville's sunny office.

A week had passed since the inquest, but my mind still harped on Will's lonely death. I had heard Canning among the clerks in the back kitchen, asking where Will had lodged. No one admitted to knowing, though someone must, for I remembered his landlady's impatience at visitors. I would have thought better of the boys if they had been protecting Will's memory from Canning's spiteful enquiries, but in fact they were only distancing themselves from the squalor of his death. To my shame, I did not reproach them, but nor did I give Canning the information he wanted.

Instead, I remembered my resolution to make the most of my new position, for Will's sake as well as my own. That position unfortunately also entailed Mr Jay, who just now looked as cold and repellent as one of van Eyck's pallid Flemish merchants in oils. It was difficult to imagine how his son, Theodore, had ever come into being. The lad was sitting by the fireplace with a collection of papers and ink, wearing a dreamy expression, his brown eyes as soulful as a lapdog's and his curly hair rumpled under his wig.

Lord Grenville was examining the envoy through the stuffy fug and the shaft of sunlight that bathed the desk. 'We had no notice of your coming, you know. Rather expected a broadside than an envoy.'

Mr Jay wove his pale head. 'I am here to deliver a diplomatic broadside. Public feeling in America is quite against you, my Lord, and since your war with France began—'

'Their war with us, Mr Jay. They were the aggressors.'

'Nevertheless, the French expect us to honour our treaties with their former king and wish us to come to their aid against you.'

'And what does President Washington want?'

Jay lifted his head and spoke cautiously. 'He has asked me to state our grievances and keep the peace if it may be done with honour.'

'And if it can't?'

'Then regrettably ...' Jay waved a hand. 'I shall press on to Paris, for talks with Mr Robespierre.'

Grenville stood up and went over to the window, where a company of horse was exercising in the parade ground below. 'These matters may have quite a different complexion when viewed from our side of the Atlantic, you know. English sailors cowering under the decks of your ships, instead of coming to their country's aid in times of need. Your attacks on our Indian allies. You are not so well endowed with money and men, I think, to wage war against us, and might need to offer concessions of your own.'

Jay was unmoved. Theodore Jay seemed hardly to be listening.

Grenville turned back from the window. 'And if all these differences could be resolved, what then?'

'Peace,' Jay answered. 'And, therefore, a strengthened hand for you against the French, I imagine.'

'Well, that is a prospect I would be very happy to see, Mr Jay, if it could be brought about. We would not wish to murder our own children, you know, as a war between us would undoubtedly mean.'

'That,' Mr Jay replied with new coldness, 'is exactly the kind of language most calculated to offend.'

'I beg your pardon.' Grenville raised his eyebrows. 'Of course, murder is a strong word. Should I have said grapple with? Or thrash?'

'How you envisage defeating us, Lord Grenville, is not the point at issue, as you well know. Nor is it a pleasantry calculated to amuse me. What I mean to say is that we are not your children, and if Mr Jefferson heard you say so, he would reach directly for his pistols.'

I wondered what Jay would think of France now, so utterly changed from when he hammered out the peace with England in Paris in '84. Then France had been open to travellers, and even in '89 it had been easy to find a boat from Cornwall to Roscoff, when mother took me home. But the Revolution was coming, and the town was in a strange state of dislocation, which made my mother uneasy. Life went on, day to day, in the cool, high-ceilinged house on the Rue de Mat, but we were all eagerly awaiting the news from Paris, which came by word of mouth more often than by formal channels.

One hushed afternoon I went for a walk while the others took their *sieste*. The streets were empty, dogs and cats dozing in the shadows. I found myself at length in the church. Tall stone arches reminded me of home, while statues of the Virgin and the painted walls seemed like strange blooms on a familiar plant. The young, pale priest was going to his slumber, I suppose, but seemed constrained out of politeness to offer me confession. I shall never forget its musty peace. I had watched my mother work her rosary since I could understand what it meant, but she had never taught me the mystery of the Hail Mary. Perhaps, even when I was small, she had ambitions for me she knew could not be served by popery, and I found there was an illicit thrill in flouting my oath of office. Nascent treason that somehow Aglantine could see.

I met her for the first time in Dick's Coffee House, soon after I returned from France. She was sitting alone at a bench in the corner, sipping strong coffee and scanning the newspapers. She looked thin and worn, her black dress shiny with wear, and the men at the counter were discussing her, a solitary female in a bastion of masculinity, and a foreigner to boot. A damned Frenchie. Their faces weren't kind, and as I took my cup of chocolate I hesitated, and then strode over to where she sat.

'Forgive me, ma'am,' I said in her own language, 'but your presence attracts notice. May I offer my protection?'

She looked up at me with the scowl I have since grown to fear. Then, I thought her only uneasy. She hesitated, then nodded, and I sat across from her, a lamb gone willingly to its own slaughter. In fact, she was neither hungry nor poor. And she was only in Dick's Coffee House because she knew I frequented the place most nights after work. How she had learned of my existence I do not know, but at any rate, I have not set foot in the place now for near two years.

I was so eager to help Aglantine then, so proud when I

went home that first Christmas, that I bit my tongue to stop myself telling my mother all about it, as I watched her rake the curds from the whey in the dairy. Impossible to imagine my foolishness, now that ships fire on each other, and armies fight and flee. I was, in my way, as rash as Hardy locked up in the Tower, as bloodthirsty as the crowd at the hanging. Louis was soon a prisoner, and, God forgive me, I think I bayed for his blood with every passing day, gratified by every gloomy article in the English newspapers foretelling his death. Why we desire the worst, why we are secretly disappointed when amity and good sense prevail, I do not know, any more than I understand the pleasure in watching a tragedy unfold on the stage in Drury Lane. But when the blade fell, and the Queen, Marie Antoinette, followed her husband to the same fate, the spell was broken. It was no play, the blood was real, and even if war had not already come I hope I would have parted from Aglantine then.

WHEN I CAME DOWNSTAIRS from the meeting with Jay, Mr Aust and Sir James were huddled in the lobby in low-voiced conversation with a decent-looking couple. The man looked like a country attorney; the woman had been weeping. Aust and Sir James looked mighty uncomfortable, Aust patting the woman's sleeve.

'Distressing,' Sir James was saying. 'Most distressing, of course. We feel for you both, but I'm afraid the case seems quite clear.'

'My Will would never do such a thing.' The woman may have been weeping, but she was angry too. 'I know my son, Sir James. He is no suicide and deserves a decent burial.'

'Of course, of course.' Sir James was backing away, ready for flight from her embarrassing emotion, as I realised that these were Will Benson's parents, up from Rochester. I loitered on the pavement outside until Sir James was rid of them. They came down the steps and stood, hesitating and rather forlorn, amid the stream of active clerks on the pavement. They looked relieved when I accosted them.

'Mr and Mrs Benson, I think? I am Laurence Jago, clerk to Lord Grenville. Can I fetch you a hackney carriage?'

They took in my clothes, my age, perhaps my eccentric spectacles, and Mr Benson made a bow. 'You knew my son?'

'Yes, sir. I am so sorry—'

But Mrs Benson's face had lit up suddenly, and she grasped hold of my hand. 'Oh, thank God! We have been all over Downing Street, and no one seemed to know him. If I didn't think it all pretence, now they believe him a suicide, I should think he had no friends at all. But here you are and may tell us all about him!'

'Will you join us for a little refreshment?' Mr Benson was smiling too, through his sorrow. 'We are hungry for news of him, sir – have had scarcely a letter in a year.'

Their pain was dreadful, and I couldn't disappoint them. They took me to White's for coffee and a chop, where we settled ourselves in a window seat, amid a group of natural philosophers heatedly discussing comets. There were tearstains on Mrs Benson's cheeks, but she was a handsome woman for her age, not much unlike my own mother, and she watched me eat with maternal goodwill, though I had little appetite.

'Will was always hungry,' she said. 'He kept himself well fed, I hope?'

'Oh, yes. Ate like a horse.'

'And yet always so thin!' She shook her head, marvelling and, as I reflected with shame on how little I really knew her son, I thought it best to reverse the questioning.

'You come to contest the inquest?'

Mrs Benson's face trembled. 'We couldn't rest. Could not bear to think of him in …'

'In unconsecrated ground,' her husband finished for her, his face set. He waved his hand. 'Don't shake your head, sir, we know that is the fate of the suicide.'

Mrs Benson sobbed suddenly, and her husband took her hand. Tears were rolling down both their faces. All I could say was what I'd said before. 'I am so sorry.'

I WAS, INDEED, DREADFULLY sorry, but there was so little I could do for them, or for Will, except wonder again, for the dozenth time, what he had done to fall so far from grace in a matter of days. I was sure I had seen him laughing in the Salutation and Cat the week before he was dismissed from Downing Street. Something had happened in the interval to see him sacked, and apparently in such despair that death seemed preferable to continued existence. For myself, I thought only the discovery of my secrets and the fear of hanging would bring me to such a pass. And, in fact, my own affairs were about to take a turn that drove the Bensons' pain temporarily from my mind.

I made good my resolution to visit Anne at home, and on Sunday I walked out to Kensington in my best suit. The heat was still sweltering. A baker's shop was ablaze at Hyde Park Corner, and a crowd had gathered, calling out that the engine was on its way. Soon after, the streets thinned and gave way to market gardens, rows of stunted vegetables rising out of scrubby weeds, and a grim army of women trudging across the parched landscape with buckets of water. In Kensington, the palace gardens were in bloom, the Serpentine dark and quiet against the foil of lawns, and cows were grazing in the distance of Hyde Park. Aust's house stood back from the road with a bay tree beside the handsome front door, and upstairs in the drawing room, the Austs were sitting about in cool family comfort just returned from church. Mrs Aust nodded and smiled at me from her sewing, while her husband laid down his copy of yesterday's *Times*. 'Good afternoon, Jago.'

'Good afternoon, sir.' I feared my palm was clammy from my walk as I took Mrs Aust's hand, but Anne was just coming into the room with a dandelion in a jar. I had been here half a hundred times before, running errands for Mr Aust, who now retreated to his paper. It seemed he meant to make no special guest of me, despite – or perhaps because of – my new position. It was a compliment in a way, and I gravitated eagerly towards the table and Anne's shady grey presence.

She had laid aside a study of a rosemary sprig, the paint still wet, more in the manner of a botanical sketch than a lady's watercolour. 'You know my efforts aren't heroic.' Her hair smelled of soap as I bent my head over the paper, our faces no more than a foot apart. It would be easy to bend only a little more and kiss her mouth. She had been smiling freely, but now her expression changed, and she looked back to her paper and blushed. A fluttering feeling started up in my chest, and it was she who proved equal to the embarrassment, not I. She was a widow after all, no innocent maiden. 'Have you heard about the illuminations, Laurence? We are to have a dinner party and a bonfire in honour of the occasion, and I believe my stepfather should bid you come.'

Mr Aust only rattled the pages of his newspaper.

'Illuminations?' I was still preoccupied by her scent, by my own involuntary desire. 'For the Glorious First?' I dragged my mind back to the prosaic doings of Lord Howe. His naval engagement on the first of June had been the only real victory of the war, and a welcome distraction from the army's troubles in Flanders.

'And for the glorious sinking of the French supplies.' She raised her eyes piously, and at that Mr Aust was roused.

'Now, Anne, for God's sake don't say anything about the grain.'

'What's that, sir? Lord Howe's grain? Or Robespierre's?'

She was smiling, and Mr Aust shook his head. 'I should not have told you anything about it – Grenville would have my head if he knew I was gossiping at home.'

'We were not gossiping, sir.' She had her eyes on her step-father, but was speaking equally to me, eager to impress me with her political acumen. There was no need. She had always grasped the machinations of government better than I had. 'As far as I understood the matter, we were engaged in stimulating debate, in the course of which I made many observations you found most helpful. At least, you said so.'

'He would still call it gossip, my dear. I don't think his womenfolk are politically minded.'

'Well, I shall say nothing, if you wish it, and let the poor admiral have his victory.'

'He did sink a fair few ships, whatever else happened.'

'But "whatever else happened" was that the French got their grain anyway, and will eat to fight another day, while we rashly burn our best candles in all the windows.'

I realised I was smiling foolishly at her impertinent wit as Mr Aust finished his paper and motioned me to a chair by the cold fire grate. 'I've been telling Mrs Aust of your good work, Jago. She is very pleased to hear you deserve your promotion.'

'It's good of you to say so, sir.'

But Mr Aust was looking at his wife, as if the final judgement on my future lay entirely in her hands. 'Praise from Mr Aust means much indeed.' She was trying silks against her embroidery with a frown between her eyebrows. 'You are a good age for a promotion, Mr Jago.'

'Aye,' Aust said, before I could reply, for I was momentarily silenced by the possibility Anne's mother was also considering my eligibility as a suitor. 'I was about his age when I came to the Foreign Office – or the Southern Department, as it then was, under the Marquis of Bath. I arrived bang in the middle of the Falklands Crisis – what a beginning! The Marquis resigned over that farrago but came back in for the American troubles. Then came the Marquis of Downshire, he that died last year. They shook things up in '82 and turned us into the Foreign Office, whereupon I served Mr Fox, if you can believe it.'

I rather feared Aust was going to list every foreign secretary of the past quarter century, but instead the old man sighed. 'Aye, a lot of men, a lot of different views.'

'But you always there, throughout everything.' Anne raised her head from her painting and looked at her stepfather affectionately, before turning her gaze on me, her embarrassment and her mockery equally forgotten, almost as if I too was a rosemary sprig to be accurately sketched. 'A Permanent Under-Secretary becomes indispensable to the place and knows just as much as his masters.'

This new scrutiny made me uneasy, and I had taken off my glasses on the pretext of polishing them, the world becoming a comfortable blur, when the doorbell rang below. I did not know it then, but as the peal trembled into silence, my last peaceful hour was over.

A moment later Sir James came in, brandishing a copy

of the *Sunday Observer*, which Aust regarded as he might a snake – it was a mark of his Toryism that he would rather read day-old news in *The Times*. But Sir James was jabbing his finger at a passage in the paper under Aust's nose, his full cheeks quivering like a blancmange. 'Lord Grenville has gone down to Dropmore, to oversee the planting of his flowers. We cannot seek his counsel, but I fear something needs to be done.'

Mr Aust was looking entirely bewildered, still scanning the page for enlightenment, while the women had laid their occupations aside and were staring with as much attention as I was. Sir James took the paper back from Aust's pudgy hand and read aloud.

'A secret paper from Downing Street, received from hands unknown, makes grave reading. We learn that the army is separated, divided by the Scheldt, and the only plan our illustrious Duke can contrive is ignominious flight to Ostend. God send our forces speed, but God also send them better commanders.'

'Ostend!' Aust still looked blank. 'Where the devil—'

'The paper claims to have received a leaked internal memorandum from the Ministry, which contains this distressing news, and has published it this morning. True or not, I have sent a clerk down to the *Observer* with a rebuttal, and have demanded the return of the paper, whatever it is, so we may find the source.'

Aust nodded his approval, at which Sir James looked relieved. 'If it is a Government document, as they claim – and which I highly doubt – I think I am quite within my rights. To reveal the army's plans is tantamount to treason.' Sir James passed a hand across his face. 'God damn me, my own nephew is there. If a hair of his head is harmed from this disloyalty—'

I was remembering something Sir James apparently did not know, and that I should not know myself, if I was the monoglot clerk they took me for. George Canning was going to be in dreadful trouble.

9

THE FOLLOWING MORNING my guess proved right. The document recovered from the offices of the *Sunday Observer* wasn't just a copy of the message I'd given Canning, my first day in office, but the original itself, written in my own hand as Grenville had bid me, and which Canning had baited me about when I gave it to him. That morning I felt some honest satisfaction that he would now find his own fortunes on as much of a knife-edge as Will Benson's, as soon as Pitt and Grenville discovered it had gone directly from his desk to the *Observer*. How such a calamity had occurred I couldn't guess, despite the quizzing of the under-secretaries in Sir James's office.

'Tell us again, Jago, what you know of the business.'

'Lord Grenville gave me the message, just come in, and asked me to make a copy for Mr Pitt. I went to Number 10 and put it straight in Mr Canning's hand.'

'Did his Lordship say how the message had come in?'

'No, sir.' I tried to remember. 'I think he gave it to me just as a clerk brought down the day's messages. I thought it was one of those.'

'And the original?'

'I filed it with his Lordship's papers.'

'Very well.' Sir James looked at the message with a good deal of loathing. 'Mr Aust, I suppose we had better summon Mr Canning, and find out what happened to this after it reached his hand. I have also asked for an interview with the Minister for War. If the information is true, and Mr Canning has nothing convincing to say, he will find himself in worse trouble than he could possibly imagine.'

I was released to make fair copies of Mr Jay's first set of complaints, for the benefit of the Prime Minister. I settled to my task with little more thought for the leak than to wonder, caustically, what depth of misfortune could ever puncture Canning's self-love sufficient to drive *him* to self-murder. But then I heard the Minister for War cross the lobby below, with short, angry footsteps, and the reality of the business began to dawn on me. If the message proved true, and France took advantage of the information it contained, many more soldiers would die, or come home to join the ranks of the wounded and broken men in the streets. The war, so far away and unimaginable on a sunny afternoon in Downing Street, came suddenly closer.

WHEN LORD GRENVILLE FINALLY arrived from the consolation of his peonies, the Foreign Office cowered beneath his ill humour. All my new hopes for the future were driven effectually from my mind ahead of his scudding wrath, and if anyone's fortunes balanced on a knife-edge, it now seemed they were mine.

'This paper. You say you gave it into George Canning's hand?'

'Yes, sir.'

'I have just had a curious conversation with Canning. Says he has no recollection of the document at all. It's hardly so long ago that he should forget – or that you should.' Grenville looked at me coldly. 'You have no explanation for this discrepancy?'

'Well, my Lord.' The room had tilted, and I clutched for the chair back to steady myself. It had never occurred to me that Canning would deny his part in the business. 'Perhaps he has forgotten. In which case, I'm sure he'll remember our conversation if I remind him.'

'You made no other copy?'

'No, my Lord, I did as you bid me. I made this one copy for Canning and filed the original among your papers.'

'You and Canning are the only men beside myself to have had the opportunity to leak this paper.' Lord Grenville went to the window moodily, hands shoved in pockets. 'You understand that you are the most obvious source?'

I felt as if he had struck me. 'Not at all, my Lord. How could I wish to leak it, when I didn't understand a syllable? As far as I can see, it is only Mr Canning's word against mine.'

'You would call him a liar?'

'No, my Lord. That is – I do not see why his word should carry so much more weight on a mere matter of memory.'

A mere matter of memory – I didn't believe that for a moment. Canning was afraid, and like a coward sought to pass the blame.

'I could have you confined, and no one would question my judgement. However …' Grenville turned his eyes back to the damning note. 'As you observe, you are ignorant of the language. Mr Aust has also represented to me that you have served in this Department for ten unblemished years, and he has no reason, as yet, to doubt your loyalty.'

I had spoken in haste, alarmed by Lord Grenville's wrath, and now I realised with some dismay that I had talked myself into the very corner I had been wishing to escape these twelve months. Far from confessing my old misdemeanours with Aglantine, I had now positively denied any knowledge of French, and if I was found out it would look bad. Very bad. It seemed imperative I speak to Canning. I think, fool as I was, I resolved to appeal to his sense of honour.

Afterwards, I found Aust in the Cabinet Room, relieving his feelings by twitching the curtains violently and polishing the glasses with his handkerchief. 'Pitt is most displeased. They're saying Lord Grenville might have to resign.'

'God help us.'

'Sir James would be out with Grenville, of course. He is quite beside himself.'

'Mr Aust, sir … You know I would never—'

'No, no, Jago. Never fret yourself. Sir James and I quite agree on *that*.'

I wasn't entirely comforted to find they had been discussing me already.

'No, depend upon it, if we find that damned missing key we shall find our man. But I am at a loss, Laurence, to imagine what might possess him to do such a thing, unless he be an out-and-out Jacobin, a Frenchman in disguise. If he is found out, his head will be stuck on a spike on Temple Bar alongside Mr Hardy's.'

I went out to the privy and retched a little, but the sudden nausea did not pass. It seemed the knife-edge on which I balanced had death below it, and I was still sick to my stomach when I came through Temple Bar that evening. The gang of children had gone, probably off scavenging or picking pockets in Covent Garden, and Philpott was watching me from his door.

'Good evening to you, Mr Jago,' he bellowed, with a tremendous zeal that grated rather on my depressed spirits. 'Have 'ee heard the news of these illuminations we are to have? Damn me, I love an illumination above anything. Come inside and drink a toast with me to Lord Howe and the Glorious First.'

I had no great desire for my own company and despite his painful enthusiasm I submitted to his cheerfulness and the wholesomeness of his newly painted shop. There was new rush matting underfoot, and the place smelled remarkable. Cleanliness, I realised finally, as Philpott produced a jug of ale and set it on the desk between us.

'You like the place, my boy? I confess, I had my doubts, though the agent was so damned pleased with it. "Aye, aye," I said to him. "But what of the mice? There were decidedly mouse droppings in the pantry. Where is your cat, sir? Vermin must be routed out, Mr Shaw, they must indeed. I shall do my part, in print, but you must undertake to do your own." Upon which the fellow seemed quite bemused.' He poured us both a tankard and raised his own to me. 'But Nancy has been a-scrubbing, and I've routed out a prodigious number of rodents. We've acquired this fine old tabby to keep 'em in order in future, and Nancy declares herself quite satisfied.'

The fine old tabby had torn ears and a twisted paw, where she lay on a pile of closely written papers and as I put out a hand to stroke her she rumbled a warning and showed her claws. Philpott laughed.

'Yes, yes, how the creature do put me in mind of my wife! Quite as standoffish, when she has a mind to be. "The *spitting*

image of you, my dear," I says to her this very morning in bed.'
He gulped at his tankard. 'But now, my boy, have you heard
this astonishing news about that damned lawyer, Mr Erskine?'

Tidings that Mr Thomas Erskine KC was to defend the
shoemaker Hardy, for no pay, had reached the Ministry's ears
that afternoon, but it should hardly have surprised anyone.

'Hardly astonishing. Mr Erskine has represented every
political radical of the past fifteen years – even Tom Paine,
who I dare say you think the devil in human form.'

'Then he is a traitor himself.'

If I loved any man in London, it was Erskine. We had met
long before, through Mr Vicary 'Vinegar' Gibbs, a barrister of
acerbic temperament, from whose employ I had been eager
to escape. One day outside the Old Bailey we came upon a
poor young dog cast out on the street when his master was
taken up for debt. Erskine was there, and being fond of animals, asked me to take the creature home. It was a mere nothing, but Erskine was acquainted with Aust's wife from old
Edinburgh days, and recommended me when a vacancy in
Downing Street fell open. I named the dog for my former
master and might say I exchanged Vicary Gibbs's tyranny for
a canine one.

I told Aglantine this story once. She listened with a look
that told me she would drown puppies in a sack and lose no
sleep over it.

'Mr Erskine is no traitor,' I said with decision. 'He put me
into the Foreign Office, and I'll vouch for him against any
man.'

'Hey? Hey?' Philpott came down off his high horse and
seemed quite pleased to be contradicted.

'Besides, you'd find him a very interesting acquaintance and
full of information. He's a great defender of the constitution

– you'd have more in common with him than you imagine. He has a parrot and a very large Newfoundland dog, called Toss.'

Philpott looked entirely mollified by this eclectic list of recommendations. 'Well, well, we journalists are always glad to meet anyone, after all, friend or foe. Perhaps I'll seek him out.'

'I could introduce you, if you wished it.'

'Introduce me? Nonsense. If one man may not speak to another without an introduction, then a cat may not look at a king.'

10

BACK IN DOWNING STREET, Aust took to eyeing me anxiously, and Sir James gradually withdrew his favour. By positively denying I knew French, I had dug myself a grave if this new inquiry found me out in my old treason. In the end, Canning was the only man who could help me, and though in my heart of hearts I knew he would not do it, I resolved to endure his sardonic eye, and beard him on his own ground. He had rooms in Spring Garden Terrace, not far off Charing Cross.

The remains of the old gardens lay across the road from his lodging, half built over, with groundsel and dandelions seeding themselves into the gentle summer breeze, as if determined not to be vanquished by mere brick and mortar. Clouds of goldfinches lifted from the seed heads like butterflies as I turned the corner after work to see Canning himself coming out of his front door and running lightly down the steps to the pavement. I was still too far away to hail him but followed him along the street, until he turned into the art gallery, where the old French finance minister, Calonne, was staging an exhibition of paintings to be sold for the Bourbon cause.

It required a very genteel sum to gain entry, but I parted with my half-crown, straightened my wig, and wiped the sweat from the back of my neck with a handkerchief before pushing into the throng. It was the same old faces, those few of the gentry who had not left London for the summer, a clutch of lawyers from Lincoln's Inn, and the editors of the *Gentleman's Magazine* and the *Critical Review* arm in arm. The knots of spectators were mostly gathered about Canaletto's sunny Venetian squares, while a few others were inspecting M. de Calonne's extensive collection of paintings in the Flemish style.

I pushed on from room to room searching vainly for Canning's tall slim figure, but I couldn't find him. I had sat down on a sofa, defeated, when a voice hailed me. 'Jago, on my life.' It was Mr Erskine, my old mentor, and he sat down next to me, smiling. 'I did not take you for a lover of art.'

'Nor you.'

'I thought you would be buzzing about the hive in pursuit of this traitor.' He looked serious, and any impulse I might have felt to confide my troubles to him evaporated at once. His good opinion mattered to me more than anyone's. I looked into his melancholy brown eyes, which always reminded me of his dog, and changed the subject at random.

'What have you done with Toss?'

Erskine smiled, and the stern look vanished. 'Left him at my chambers. He ain't much for art either, you know.'

'Does he advise you on your clients? Sniff out their guilt or innocence?'

'He is not a *hound*, Laurence, but a very respectable dog of impeccable manners, and should not dream of sniffing anyone uninvited.' He sighed, leaned back in his chair, and pulled a box of snuff from his pocket. 'I hear you are making friends with that fellow Philpott. He called upon me this morning, with some cock and bull story of public duty. But I rather fear he was in pursuit of some scandal for his paper, some titbit about Mr Hardy.'

I was beginning to like Philpott almost as much as Erskine, but held my peace, for there seemed no denying he was a journalist before anything. 'How is the shoemaker?'

'Afraid, of course. But I tell him if we can get an honest jury and a fair trial, he has nothing to fear.' Erskine seemed to forget our surroundings and was ready to lecture me like the legal clerk I once was. I was happy enough to listen, watching the crowd for a glimpse of Canning. I could see the exit from where we sat and was pretty sure he was still somewhere in the gallery.

'You must understand, Laurence, Mr Hardy has been arrested for doing no more than Mr Pitt himself has done in his day. Parliamentary Reform is a noble cause, pursued by men of good conscience for years.'

'The papers say he fomented treason.'

'All my eye!' Erskine settled back in his chair more comfortably, opened the snuffbox and took a pinch. There was nothing he liked so well as a legal wrangle. 'They could not accuse him of sedition, for he's published nothing to be prosecuted. Instead, they must fall back on this nonsense about treason. But treason is a very old offence, Laurence, and quite specific in its terms. It must involve an overt attempt on the King's life. If weapons came to light, or they discovered a plot to kill the King, that would be entirely damning. Aiding and abetting the French in destroying our army, as this wretch in Downing Street has done, is also an indirect attack on the

King, and would merit the noose and the axe. But merely calling for reform is not an overt act. All Hardy desires is the right as a prosperous tradesman to have a voice in his country's government.'

He went on at some length about the iniquity of the franchise, the horrors of Old Sarum and the fact that my home town was in the pocket of a duke, but I had stopped listening after his mention of the noose and the axe. And now Canning had slipped out of a darkened alcove, full of neglected pictures unobserved by the crowd. As I turned to make my excuses to Erskine, a plainly dressed gentleman touched Canning on the shoulder and Canning turned to the fellow with a tight smile.

'Ah,' Erskine said, following my gaze and jumping to his feet. 'There's Mr Bourne of the *Observer*. I shall give him a piece of my mind about this leak. Thought theirs was the only paper in London with any sense, but it appears I was wrong. Good day to you, Laurence.' And so it was Erskine, not I, who hastened over to join them, the three heads in close conference.

But this spectacle changed the complexion of everything, and I would hardly wish to beard Canning now, in an apparent assignation with the very Mr Bourne of the *Observer* who had published the leaked memorandum. At first, I was astonished. Was *Canning* the leak after all? I had never even considered that, for what could possibly motivate him to betray government secrets to the press? Yet here they were, undoubtedly in secret conclave, and a tight triumph – a glow of sudden relief – gathered about my heart. Surely there were always reasons for misconduct. The lure of money. The mere pleasure of making mischief. If Canning was the culprit after all, he would be punished as he well deserved to be, on many other counts. Best of all, it would be at my own hands, for I now had ammunition to convince Lord Grenville of his guilt.

I abandoned all thought of confronting him, and slipped back towards the entrance, where I met Aglantine, and all these thoughts were temporarily driven from my mind. She must have been following me, and it disturbed me that I hadn't seen her. She led me out of the gallery at once, into the hot sunlight, and we paused at the foot of the steps. It was one thing to be summoned to meet her in a crowd, quite another to be accosted in a quiet street, and I glanced behind me, fearful that Canning or Erskine would see us together.

'What are you doing here, Laurence?' She looked as grotesque as ever.

I was cautious. 'Admiring the pictures. And you?'

She smiled her creased smile, but did not answer. Instead, she led the way around the corner towards Charing Cross where we loitered in the shadow of a wall. I had not confided in Erskine for fear of seeing disapproval in his eyes, but with Aglantine I found I had no such compunction. 'There's trouble in the Department. And I'm blamed.'

'A good reason to seek solace in art.'

'By George Canning—'

'*Hien?*'

'George Canning is blaming me for his own fault, and—' I broke off at the sight of her unsympathetic face. 'Oh, never mind.'

It seemed she had her own problems and didn't scruple to share them either. 'I am glad to have chanced on you, Laurence. You have heard that matters are disorganised in Paris at present?'

'*Disorganised?*' I was half perplexed, half bitterly amused. With every passing day, the world seemed to become more fantastic. 'That's one word for murder and tyranny.'

'Events have taken a turn these last weeks. First the attempt on Robespierre's life, then the new laws, which are too harsh and make men hate him. They say he has taken to his rooms and goes no more to the Committee. He fears for his life.'

'From more assassins?'

'From a Committee of them.'

She looked tired, I realised now, and perhaps even defeated. 'How bad is it?' For a moment she seemed human, even vulnerable, and it was a look I remembered – the look that had drawn me to her all those years ago in Dick's Coffee House. But then the brief look of defeat was gone, her expression unreadable again.

'I do not know. There are plots and rumours of plots. I may need you.' She pulled at her lace gloves and carefully arranged her cuffs. 'Be ready.'

'Need me? Aglantine, I've told you—' But she was already walking away.

If Robespierre fell, perhaps I would be rid of Aglantine for good, and hope put a spring in my heels as I turned for home. But then I remembered the flash of human emotion in her battered face, and I wondered who she really was, how she had come to England apparently alone with all this burden of espionage on her old shoulders. Why did she dress in black? Who was she mourning? She was a person just as I was, and so, though it was hard to credit the fact, was Citizen Robespierre. My mind glanced over the possibility that Canning might deserve the same charity, but that was a step too far, even for me.

LORD GRENVILLE'S FACE WAS in shadow as he looked at me from his seat behind the desk, late-afternoon sunlight pouring in through the tall windows behind him, straight into my eyes. They do the same to the poor defendant at the bar of the Old Bailey, I have since learned, reflecting daylight on to his face by way of a mirror so that the jury can study his expression. But I did not know that then. All I knew was that I felt at a considerable disadvantage.

Grenville looked tired. He had just come from the Secret Committee, and despite my fears I had compassion enough to see he disliked it. 'And you mean to imply?'

'Well, my Lord, it seemed to me—'

'I should think Mr Canning might very well talk to the editor of the *Observer*, in present circumstances, if only to express the Ministry's displeasure at such a breach of trust. The army is in considerable danger by their publishing. Damn me, I could have the fellow arraigned for treason too, whatever he might protest.'

I felt another clutch of anxiety and wished everyone would choose another word to describe the business, but I pressed on. 'In any case, my Lord, what I meant to say was that I feel it unjust that I am to be particularly suspected. Mr Aust has told you I have served—'

'Not so, not so.' Grenville jumped up and began to pace. 'Reflect, Mr Jago. You are a clerk, George Canning an MP. You are the son of a farmer, he of a gentleman. He has the ear of Mr Pitt, you of no one. However …'

I wasn't exactly sure, his face in shadow as he turned, but for a fleeting second I thought he pitied me. 'Let me propose this. We will conduct a search of your lodging for anything that might tend to incriminate you. If all is in order, I will consult with Sir James as to your future. Believe me, I have no desire to hang you, Mr Jago, but blame must fall somewhere for this business.'

'I understand, my Lord.'

I suddenly thought I understood too well. Lord Grenville knew I was innocent, but would damn me anyway, for George Canning was too secure in Pitt's favour to be questioned.

But it was worse than he thought, for there was a French pistol wrapped in a silk handkerchief in the top right-hand drawer of my dresser, and, next to it, a pile of incriminating letters from my mother. A sweat broke out between my shoulder blades. A Frenchman in disguise, Aust had said. If a search of my lodgings found either, there would be more to discuss than my future. I would find myself before the Secret Committee, Canning would be quite within his rights to smile his unpleasant, scornful smile – and I might wish I'd hanged myself, like poor Will, while I had the chance.

II

GRENVILLE HAD BEEN foolish to give me warning, but I took the advantage at once. Dora was entertaining Mrs Beale the jeweller's wife when I rushed home, barely a half-hour later, ahead of whatever party of King's Messengers I imagined might be assembled and sent in pursuit. I declined a drumstick from the pigeon she had dressed for their dinner and flew up the flight of narrow creaking stairs to my chamber, pursued by Mr Gibbs, in eternal hope of a walk.

'In a moment, sir.' The drawer of the dresser jammed, and I swore as I jerked it open and took out the gun. I'd forgotten how ornate it was, and how small. The butt fitted into my palm snugly, with an elegant curve. I wrapped it back in its handkerchief and thrust it quickly into the pocket of my fustian jacket from home. Mr Gibbs groaned loudly and flopped to the bare floorboards, eyeing me with disapproval as I pulled out the pile of letters from my mother. I lit a candle and watched them burn, holding the papers over the chamber pot with a shaking hand, for fear of setting a fire. Aglantine had told me never to keep a letter from Cornwall, but the danger had seemed long past. Names and places displayed themselves as the paper curled, and as I went back down to the kitchen with the dog on my heels I felt as solemn as if the old farm itself had burned to the ground.

The women were discussing the Philpotts as I hastened through. 'Lord save me, what a sad housewife she is! They have her measure down the market. Gets all their sweepings and dross, and don't seem to notice at all.'

Dora raised her eyes to me as I passed. 'I been working on your best coat,' she said darkly. 'Don't know what they put in that Downing Street gravy, but it's the very devil to get out.'

Mr Gibbs and I set out into the streets and, dressed in my old clothes, I was anonymous at once, just another working man on the crowded pavements. If I had met Lord Grenville in the lobby of the Foreign Office he would not have recognised me, still less turned out my pockets for the heavy pistol. The eyes of the wealthy slid over the troublesome poor unless obliged to pay them notice, so that London to them was populated only by men of their own class and education.

Mr Philpott was in his shirtsleeves outside his shop, supervising a man with a pail of whitewash and a ladder, and prattling away, quite oblivious to the builders' wagons forcing their way through the crowds around Temple Bar and swaying up the street shedding dust and rubble behind them. There were always new houses going up in the courts behind Ludgate Hill, and the appetite for building supplies was insatiable. I was overcome by a cloud of lime as they passed, and fell into a dreadful fit of coughing, whereupon Philpott broke off in mid-sentence and discovered me. He didn't seem to notice my workaday clothes. 'Laurence, upon my life. I have all manner of interesting news from America. Will you take a glass of ale with me?'

'Perhaps later, if I may.' Mr Gibbs was whining, looking longingly along the road towards Fleet Market. His nose twitched, savouring the noisome smells that wafted down the street from the grating to the subterranean river.

'Well, if 'ee say so.' Philpott followed me along the street a pace or two. 'I shall be in the Globe for the loyalist meeting later on. Come and find me.' He waved his hat jubilantly. 'And the *Cannon* shall have the finest display in Fleet Street tonight, did I not tell 'ee so?'

I had forgotten all about the illuminations, but they were throwing up a bonfire outside the Mitre as I stopped in for a dish of soused hog's face and a pint of ale. From its window I could see my lodging and Mr Philpott, who had returned to his workman and the paint pot. I waited for the arrival of the search party, my heart thrumming.

I NURSED MY PINT FOR so long the landlord began to turn black looks in my direction. What the devil kept the search party from appearing? I tried to make sense of it as the inn filled to overflowing, the bonfire was lit and still no one came to my door across the street. As the minutes turned slowly to hours, I grew surer than ever that Grenville knew I was innocent. If he really thought me guilty, I would be in irons already, and he certainly would not have forewarned me of the search, or forborne to send it. As far as he knew I spoke no French and could hardly have known the paper would be of use to Paris. Was it possible that Grenville had since reflected on my story about Canning at the art gallery? I began to fancy that even now they were arresting him, lulled into arrogant complacency by the unfounded suspicion that had settled about me.

But it was a wish more than a hope, and I could not go home yet. Mr Gibbs had licked my dish quite clean and gone to sleep when I gave up my vigil and we set out again into the streets, passing under Temple Bar and out towards Westminster. I could feel the heavy pistol in my pocket, and knew if I was wise, I would be rid of it directly. But the smoke, the crackling flames and the rough shouts from tavern doorways gave a violent edge to the hot evening that made me glad to have it, while Mr Gibbs found the atmosphere quite delightful, setting off his own enthusiastic volley of barks at every bonfire.

Perhaps in the back of my mind I was thinking of Anne and her father's party for the illuminations. At any rate, I was unconsciously heading west towards Kensington. All along the Haymarket the crowd grew thicker, until I found myself all at once in the middle of an eager heaving mob, all men, many carrying brickbats in their hands. Ahead was Piccadilly, with its grand thoroughfare of imposing stone and stucco mansions, and a huddle of timber buildings that lurked on the corner. Thomas Hardy's workshop was said to be among them. I did not put these facts together at once, carried along quite against my own will. Then there were women pushing towards me against the tide of bodies, pulling crying children behind them. I didn't like the look of any of it, but Mr Gibbs did. He gave his warbling ululation and quickened his pace, suddenly sensing a scrap.

It was only when I was swept into the courtyard of timber workshops like a piece of flotsam, that I realised what was happening. The mob was tearing down the cobbler's sign above Hardy's door and working at the closed shutters with crowbars. Two women were leaning out of the upstairs window imploring them to stop. Someone threw a stone that missed the elder of the two by a whisker and smashed into the wall beside them, sending down a shower of moss and soot. I flinched, and the women retreated, but they were braver than I was, or else they were desperate. As they came back to the window, I remembered that Mrs Hardy was supposed to be with child. I could see the curve of her belly pressing against the windowsill as she looked about for help.

The crowd had embarked on an ugly chant about the French and what became of filthy traitors, as the men started on the old wooden front door. There was a loud crack, the door splintered, and with one or two more blows gave way. The women upstairs screamed, alone in a sea of hatred.

Hatred and greed. A gang of young boys pushed inside as soon as the door came down, and reappeared a moment later clutching prizes to their chests: shoes, awls, hammers and chisels. They made off up the neighbouring alley, and Mr Gibbs took off after them joyfully. Meanwhile, the contents of Hardy's shop were being systematically thrown out on to the street. Someone shouted that the men were working on the inner door and would soon be in Hardy's private quarters. A group of ragged women appeared from around the corner and called to the women at the window to get themselves out. I was glad to see help coming, however feeble.

'We can't get out!' Mrs Hardy called back, her knuckles white and knotted on the sill. 'There's no other door!'

'The winders! Ain't there a winder you can climb through?'

Mrs Hardy spread her hands. If she jumped from where she stood, she'd be in the arms of the mob. She pulled her head back inside, then reappeared at a small window around the corner of the building, above a quiet narrow alley between the houses.

She seemed to be in some kind of argument with her companion, disappeared for a moment, and then the other woman's leg and skirts came out through the window. The group of women milling around beneath reached up, trying to seize hold of her dangling ankle. Then the woman came with a sudden rush into their arms, and they set her down on her feet. A couple tended to her, while the rest turned back for Mrs Hardy.

'I can't fit through,' she was calling, white-faced. 'I'm too big with child.'

'Try!' The women below were almost weeping with anxiety, and I found I was digging my nails into the palms of my fists. 'You'll come to worse grief when they reach you!' As if to confirm it, another crash came from inside the shop and someone shouted, 'The inside door's down!'

Mrs Hardy turned her head to listen, then screamed. She thrust herself at the narrow window, first one leg, then a shoulder, an arm. It was all very quick, for the men inside were racing up the stairs and she was desperate now. There was a rending of cloth, she gave another shriek, and suddenly was through and in the women's arms. There was blood on her dress as she lay insensible on the floor. The women pulled at her, but she seemed to be unconscious.

I would like to say that I hastened over to help. That I carried her tenderly to safety. But the fact is that one of the attackers appeared at the small window, there was a burst of laughter, a great crash, and a faint smell of burning. Within moments an orange glow was growing at the windows – those old timber buildings ought to have been torn down long ago. The crowd nearest to the shop fell back, afraid it would collapse on their heads, while others, more brave or foolhardy, pressed forward, pushing me towards the flames. I had seen enough. I shoved my way sideways out of the mob and made for the narrow alley where the boys and dog had vanished. I had no idea what had happened to Mrs Hardy. But I was glad to find Mr Gibbs almost at once, peacefully nosing among rubbish.

Danger lies in these dark alleys, where chickens scratch in the litter and tribes of cats patrol the shadows. Here you might easily lose your pocket watch – and if you took exception to the theft you might even lose your life. But now I was glad of its silence and darkness, for I had never before seen anything like this riot. Had the men who beat my brother worn the same maddened look? And how could they treat a woman so, a working woman like themselves, and with such trouble come upon her? As I squatted among the filth and rubbed the dog's ears for comfort, I remembered my mother's face in the firelight, in the days after my father died. Grace picking out a tune with one hand on the piano, and little Anthony lying on the rug with his marbles. I stood behind her chair and soothed her forehead. She closed her eyes and leaned back against me. 'Eh, Laurence, I be so tired.'

'You must leave off fretting, Mother. When I am gone to London you will have money enough, and the worst to be feared is that Grace drives you distracted with her tinkling.'

'Shall I leave off?' Grace asked, from the piano stool. 'Would you have me hold a skein of wool or darn a stocking?'

''Twould be a kindness. *Mes yeux sont tellement fatigués.*' When she was tired, her English deserted her entirely, and we slipped into French for the rest of the evening.

There were so many people in trouble in this city and who would help them? But now, as I straightened, whistled to the dog and turned towards home, at least my own predicament was momentarily forgotten. The orange glow was growing over the rooftops. It was certainly going to be the biggest blaze in the illuminations by far.

12

BACK IN FLEET STREET, the door to the Globe tavern was crowded, the Church and King loyalist meeting in full swing. They had lit their own bonfire outside, and every urchin for a half-mile had gathered to pursue their incendiary pleasures unchecked, as I pushed in through the bodies in search of Philpott.

I could hear his voice ringing out over the clamour as soon as I came inside. He was standing on a low platform at the other end of the room, apparently holding the stout timber merchant from the Treaty Committee by the scruff of the neck.

'If Mr Ransome will permit me,' Philpott was shouting, 'I should like to explain more plainly than he has done, the vital importance of peace with America.'

The crowd cheered obligingly. There was a gleam in Philpott's florid face as I pushed closer, waving away a serving maid who approached me with a jug of ale. 'Gentlemen, trade is all very fine, but it ain't the nub of this affair, not by a long sight. Mr Ransome owns vast forests in the West Indies, and if he don't mean to line his own pockets from selling the Americans his mahogany at a good price, I'll show my arse in St Paul's.' Another cheer.

Ransome was looking at his captor with venom, and then, pleadingly, down into the crowd. I followed his gaze. I had hoped him confined in the Tower, but no, George Canning was there, tankard in hand, laughing, without any apparent sympathy for his friend's plight.

'Now you may say, "Mr Philpott, what is America to us, so weak and so far away?"'

I pushed through the boisterous crowd towards Canning without any clear plan, as Philpott expanded on his theme. 'If America falls behind France it will give a damnable encouragement to traitors and revolutionaries here, like that Thomas Hardy and his crew from the Corresponding Society.'

'Mr Canning.'

The damned blackguard eyed me over the rim of his tankard. It was clear he knew me, but he only turned back to the entertainment, looking all superior disdain at Philpott, who was bellowing out that Hardy was in the Tower, thank God, and would soon be hanged, drawn and quartered like the traitors of old, his head stuck on a spike on Temple Bar.

'I suppose you know, gentlemen,' Philpott's voice dropped to a low and thrilling whisper, 'what that beastly punishment entails?'

More heads on spikes. God damn me, would they never tire of it? Ransome looked as enthralled as anyone else, until Philpott clutched him suddenly and unexpectedly by the throat and he bucked like a startled sheep. 'First the poor beggar is hanged. A short drop and a gallows dance. He's squeezed—' He squeezed. 'And choked—' Ransome turned purple, and Canning put down his pint and guffawed.

'His tongue turns black and his eyes bulge out of his skull. And then, gentlemen, then he is cut down.' Philpott snatched his hands away, and Ransome swayed on his feet, looking as though the evening had taken a decided turn for the worse.

I hadn't time for Philpott's games just now – or Canning's. 'Sir, I need to speak to you about this misunderstanding in the Department. That message I gave you—'

Canning finally looked at me, a smile still lingering about his mouth. 'A message? Oh – I dare say. But I hardly think this the time. Do you not know how many cross my desk?'

'But this is the one ended up in the *Observer*.'

Up on the platform Philpott was miming a dagger, slitting Ransome open from cock to gizzard, while Canning looked suddenly cagey. 'Hardly talk for a tavern, Mr …?'

'Then comes the drawing, and out spill his guts on to the table where he lies watching, poor devil. A flame is struck, and they sizzle like chitterlings in the pan.'

'Jesu,' someone said and made a hasty exit for the privy.

'My name is Jago, sir.' I was pretty sure he knew it too. 'I thought if you saw me, it might jog your memory about the note.'

'Off comes his head!' Philpott slammed his hand down on the table and someone else yelped. 'And the rest of him chopped into pieces, so that his bloody remains may be sent to the four quarters of the kingdom, as a warning to others.'

'I'm truly sorry, Mr …?'

'Jago, sir. I am being blamed for the business, but you must tell Grenville I gave the note to you. You know I did. For God's sake, on your honour—'

Philpott was rising to his climax. 'The French are run mad, gentlemen! Thousands are being sliced through the neck daily by their monstrous guillotine machine, even as we sit here drinking our porter in peace. Lose the war, and we'll find a guillotine set up at Temple Bar and *sans-culottes* in Downing Street. I bid you adieu, sirs, and God save the King!'

There was a tremendous cheer, and Canning wasn't even looking at me as Ransome fell down the steps into his arms. 'Get me out of here,' he said and, before I could say any more, they had left the tavern without a backward glance. Philpott bellowed a toast to George Washington, and confusion to his enemies, and then jumped off the platform and slapped me on the shoulder.

'Shook 'em up a bit. No one's had a sensible word to say since I arrived. And that man Ransome? A damned fool.' He whistled loudly to the serving maid. 'What's your pleasure, my dear sir?'

I had been staring after Canning, but now turned back to Philpott, remembering my mission. 'Nothing just now. I came to tell you there is a dreadful riot at Thomas Hardy's shop and his wife injured. A Church and King mob, quite out of hand.'

I hardly knew how he would take it. Pleased to sniff a story, as he had been with a dead clerk? Happier still to hear of loyalist fervour to match his own? In fact, he only looked serious.

'How long since?'

'I came straight back, when I could escape the mob.'

He pulled off his wig and shoved it in his pocket. At once he looked a man of the streets. 'Damn, I must see it for myself.' He was gone, pushing through the crowd with his usual stirring activity.

A FTER ALL MY FEARS, my room was still untouched, and Dora had had no visitors. But I slept badly, too aware of those damned spikes atop Temple Bar so close at hand, and still wondering what had kept Grenville from his search if neither I nor Canning were in chains. Philpott did not sleep at all. The candles were alight in his shop as I came out the next morning, and when he hailed me strenuously through the window, I realised he was half-drunk and dishevelled from a night at his desk. The riot had been still in progress when he reached Hardy's workshop, and he had spent the rest of the night scribbling his opinions on the affair, lubricated by ale and kippered by tobacco smoke.

'Hardy may be a scoundrel, but the poor woman ain't responsible for that.' Philpott was trying vainly to light his pipe, struggling with intoxication and damp tobacco. 'And if patriotism means woman beating, I find I ain't for it. Drink and fires and loyalism don't suit.' He gave up on his pipe and looked up at me. 'Mrs Philpott has gone in search of the poor woman to nurse her wounds, and I have been composing my paper all night.' He picked up a scribbled sheet and grinned at me ferociously. 'Quite the neatest thing, I assure 'ee, and you will admire it excessively. I have quoted Mr Burke himself, the most damned mad anti-Jacobin of them all, and turned his words against him.'

'I thought ten thousand Swords must have leapt from their Scabbards to avenge even a Look that threatened the French Queen with Insult. But the Age of Cavaliers is gone.' And so might we all lament, after the Events of Wednesday Night, when an innocent Woman was beset by Ruffians in the Heart of this great City.

He looked up at me for plaudits and I nodded. 'You will certainly vex my masters, if that's your intent. They would hardly compare their own ladies to Marie Antoinette, let alone a cobbler's wife. I thought you were hoping for Ministry patronage? You'll put paid to that if you publish such stuff.'

'I had no patron in America, and I find I want none here. If I cannot be independent, I shall be naught, I assure 'ee.' He was indefatigable despite his sleeplessness. 'The government looked a deal different from a distance of three thousand miles. Now I have the pleasure of a closer look, I find myself less enamoured. This business with the radicals troubles my mind, after all. I have spent the past five years telling Americans that all good things spring from the British constitution, and yet here they are locking up men without trial! And men not so very different from you and I, my boy.' His frown deepened. 'And this business with that poor hanged clerk! It fairly breaks my heart, believe me.'

'Business with the clerk?' There was something in his face that made me suddenly anxious.

'They have this morning fixed the blame for that damned leak on the creature. A man came to tell me of it shortly after six.'

'Fixed it! How?' To my shame, my first thought was relief, pure and simple. I could return the pistol to my drawer and return myself to Grenville's good opinion.

'They claim they found the key to some government safe in his room last evening, and a note that proves beyond doubt he was the culprit.' Philpott was scowling at me. 'Now, Laurence, you was with me in that boy's bedchamber. Did you see any such key, any such note?'

'No, sir.'

'Nor did I. We searched high and low, did we not? And found nothing.'

'Perhaps they were on his person when they took him down.'

'No such thing. They say they found them last night.' He was nodding. 'I tell you what it is. The paper was leaked to the press through some foolish mistake, and they seek to distract attention from the real culprit to save his political skin.'

No, the key could not possibly have been found last night, and now I remembered Canning's curious enquiries among the clerks as to Will's lodgings. Had a mere slip on his part caused all this trouble? Had he lost the message somehow, and invented the whole story of the missing key to cover up his own error? And then, increasingly afraid for his own neck, as I was, had he planted the key and note there himself, last night, to clear his name? He was a clever man, there was no doubt of that, and as vicious as the pike in the farm pond at home.

I straightened. 'Well, the boy is dead and buried, and well beyond their harm, I suppose, though it will kill his poor parents to see him further slandered.'

Philpott was still wrestling with his pipe. 'Beyond their harm! I'm afraid not. My informer tells me the boy never was buried at all.'

I had been turning to leave but was arrested. 'What do you mean?'

'They let his body go for dissection. Now they say it's just recompense for treason, for after all he'd have been chopped up for that, too.'

'Good God.' I clung to the door jamb. 'His poor parents. Will they be told?'

'Not by me.' Philpott gave up on his pipe and knocked it out on the empty fire grate before standing up stiffly. 'I'll not tell them their darling boy is to spend eternity on a shelf full of pickle jars.'

Were they still in town? I hadn't seen them since that day

in White's and felt ashamed of the self-absorption that had allowed me to forget them. I remembered Canning smirking at me over his tankard in the Globe inn. He had already known the whole story, already known that he and I were both exonerated at Will's expense. For the first time in my life I found out what hatred really meant.

13

'IT IS SO CRUEL! They now call him a traitor as well as a suicide. Doubly damned, for they think he killed himself to avoid punishment.' Mr Benson was valiant, but near to despair. We were in White's coffee house again, and their pain was almost too much to endure. 'They will not let us exhume the body and take it home. They will not even tell us where he is buried. How can we leave London without knowing, Mr Jago?'

'What will you do?'

If God was good, He would lead them home at once, none the wiser. But perhaps he was not good at all, for Mrs Benson was wiping her eyes. 'Ask everyone we can find. Friends, enemies. The coroner. Someone must know where he was taken.'

Everyone in Whitehall now knew he'd gone to the surgeon. If they had a shred of humanity, they would keep it to themselves, but there was bound to be some scoundrel who would enjoy inflicting pain on the old couple. I looked into their trusting faces. 'Let me find out for you. As Will's best friend here, I will ask. You need do nothing. Stay at your lodgings and rest until I come to you.'

It was a little more than three weeks since Will had died, and in this heat he would not have lasted long. Parts of him might already be in jars, as Philpott had said, ranged on an infirmary shelf, the leftovers tipped into a hole, along with the dissected corpses of cats and dogs. But perhaps by some miracle he was still in one piece – I thought I'd heard of corpses pickled in spirits, awaiting the leisurely attention of the surgeon – and if there was any chance of recovering him for his parents I ought to do it. There were only a couple of possible hospitals where anatomy was studied; only a couple of ghoulish museums of curiosities, where he could have found himself displayed. I would see him taken back to Kent for burial if I could. If not, I would find his poor mangled remains and tell them Philpott and I believed him innocent, even if no one else did.

THE CORONER TOOK MY word that I was acting on behalf of the Ministry without question. He directed me to Joshua Brookes' Museum on Great Marlborough Street, which happened by great good fortune to be open to the public each Saturday afternoon. Mr Brookes was an anatomist of considerable standing, the coroner told me, a student of the great John Hunter, and an insatiable collector of bodies.

I approached the door of the museum with trepidation. What manner of individual might visit such places for entertainment – let alone preserve and assemble the exhibits – was past my understanding. But it seemed I was alone in my squeamishness, for the room was full when I came in. It smelled strongly of spirits of wine and boiled meat. The crush of bodies hid the exhibits from view, for which I was profoundly grateful as I found an usher and asked for Mr Brookes. He was engaged at present, the usher informed me. But when I told him my business, the usher led me to a small door in the corner, and all at once I found myself in Mr Brookes' laboratory.

Mr Brookes was a pale-faced man, with fleshy red lips thrown into relief by his complexion. He was bending over a wooden frame as I came in, scraping delicately at a parchment with a scalpel. I drew near.

'I'm sorry to disturb you, Mr Brookes, but I'm come from the grieving parents of a suicide you lately acquired.' Was 'acquired' the right word? 'His name was Will Benson, a Downing Street clerk.'

'The traitor.' Mr Brookes did not look up from his work and I drew closer. The parchment was stretched across the wooden frame with pegs, and as he delicately scraped its surface, threadlike red lines appeared as if by magic.

'So they claim.'

'Yes, I have him here.'

I looked around at the room. There was a shelf of specimen jars, a bench behind us with a bloody saw, and a pot bubbling over the fire in the corner. It was hot and clammy, and my glasses were fogging up. Everything seemed to glisten as if with a layer of oil, and my fingers felt slippery.

'Then my search is ended. Thank you, sir.' I was backing for the door, in sudden need of fresh air.

'Young skin like this is delightful to prepare,' Brookes went on in the same leisurely tone, not noticing my sudden pallor, for he was still absorbed by his scraping.

'Young ...?'

He gesticulated with his scalpel towards the parchment on the frame. 'Oh, there is discolouration, and some regrettable decomposition, having been carelessly left to hang for a day or two. But his vessels are still marvellous well defined, and we can see exactly how the life blood is perfused through the epidermis, returns to the veins, and at last flies back to the heart.'

Brookes had Will there all right, just as he had said. He had him stretched over the frame, and was scraping the layer of subcutaneous fat from the inner surface of the boy's skin. Brookes straightened, put on a pair of spectacles, and looked at me for the first time. 'You're a relation?'

'No, sir.'

'Then you will not mind seeing to what invaluable use your friend is now put.'

Reluctantly, I followed him over to a shelf of jars. At first, there seemed nothing human there at all. There were vessels of increasing size arranged in a row, receding in a line from my sight. The nearest contained something akin to a walnut, as curved and fluted as a seashell. The next, a little bigger, a seahorse, I thought, remembering the creatures caught in the fishermen's nets at home. But the next disabused me of these comfortable notions. Still recognisably kin to the last creature, it was clearly a human child, the size of my hand. And behind it, lay the eldest of all, sleeping in a larger jar, almost ready to be born. But when I peered closer, my vision distorted by the intervening jars, there was something wrong with the shape of its head. What should have been inside, was out; a gnarled sail suspended in the liquid.

I turned my eyes hastily away, to a selection of smaller jars, then wished I hadn't. A tongue, ripped from its proper place, wallowed obscenely like a fat, grey crucifix. Toenails, curled and yellow, with matter still clinging where they had been levered from the flesh. And finally, where Brookes was just now reaching, an assault of human eyes, some brown, some blue, some blind and milky with cataract.

'Here, you see.' Brookes reached down the nearest vessel and Will Benson's empty brown stare confronted me. 'And here.' He took down another jar containing a different eye, improbably golden, with a slit for a pupil. 'Do you see? So like the eye of the cat in almost all respects, as I tell my students. If deprived of human specimens, a cat or dog will suffice for so many routine examinations.' He moved to the pan over the fire. 'And here are Mr Benson's fibula and tibia in preparation for articulation into their natural relation once more.' He smiled at me pleasantly. ''Tis a happy chance you find your way here today. Your friend has been sitting in a barrel of spirit ever since I took delivery of his corpse, and I am only just begun, as you see. I am excessively busy with my teaching and have far less time for study than I would like.'

I was retreating towards the door again as he talked on easily. 'Yes, a prime specimen, in full health. 'Tis a dreadful pity he was left to hang so long, but there, there, it can't be helped. The only real disappointment was the skull, of course.'

My lips seemed to have been glued together by the human fat that I realised now coated every surface in the room. But I managed to croak a reply. 'His skull?'

'The contusion made it quite useless. Split quite across the crown. The brain itself was damaged inside the cranial cavity.'

'Damaged?' I could barely speak above a whisper. 'Damaged how?'

But Brookes was coming back from the fire looking suddenly shifty. He had let his tongue run on in his enthusiasm and it was clear he had just regretted it. 'My dear sir, please forgive me. I am talking arrant nonsense.'

'There was damage to his skull?' I ran my tongue over my lips. 'No one mentioned *that* at the inquest.'

'I dare say no one looked.' Brookes appeared mighty uncomfortable. 'He was hanged, that's all they saw.'

'But the damage?' All at once I understood his unease. 'Good God, sir! Was it before or after he was hanged?'

Mr Brookes grasped me suddenly by the elbow and propelled me back through the museum towards the front door. 'A misunderstanding, my dear fellow. I find I am thinking of another corpse entirely.'

He had managed to get me out into the street, but I took hold of his sleeve and would not let go. 'Are you telling me Will Benson was killed before he was hanged?'

A pleading look came into Brookes' face. 'I did not even notice, until the body was quite dismembered. You'll not inform on me now? My work is so valuable—'

There was blood under his fingernails. I broke away and ran down Swallow Street through the Saturday-afternoon crowds. I didn't stop running until I reached St James's Park with its stately pelicans. A gang of workmen were dredging wreckage out of the canal, sunlight playing on their unclothed backs, and for a moment I thought about throwing myself fully clothed into its dubious waters beside them. Instead, I sat down, panting, on a stone bench, and put my head in my hands.

How could a man ever fancy himself a spiritual being, with the knowledge that he was in fact no more than a butcher's carcass? The food he savoured on his fat tongue turned to paste in his worm-like guts to pass out as stinking ordure. Good intentions, self-conceit, they were all a mask on the face of a rotting corpse.

'Fine day,' Philpott said from above my head. He was smiling down at me complacently, in a way that simultaneously confirmed and undermined these ruminations. 'God damn me, you look as sick as a dog.' He sat down on the bench beside me and produced a bag of pickled eels from his pocket. They smelled horribly reminiscent of the spirits of wine in the anatomy museum as he began throwing them to the nearest pelican. It seemed to know him, and approached with humorous enthusiasm, baggy beak gaping.

'Look it and feel it, seemingly,' he said, as I gagged and then wiped the back of my hand across my mouth where the oleaginous grease of the laboratory still lingered on my lips. 'What the devil have you been up to?'

I put my head back in my hands. 'I have just come from Joshua Brookes, who has Will Benson's corpse. He was dissecting him as I came in.'

Philpott turned an indignant face upon me. 'Damn it, Laurence, why didn't you take me with you? It would have been a fine story.'

He probably wouldn't have been squeamish either. 'I have a story for you anyway.' I looked away as Philpott turned back to his pelican and an eel slid unpleasantly down the grinning creature's throat. 'Will Benson was bashed in the head before he was hanged. He was no suicide at all.'

'No suicide!' Philpott was arrested, one hand in the bag of eels. 'What exactly did Mr Brookes say?'

'That the head was quite useless from a contusion to the skull. The crown split across. Someone murdered him and hanged him after.'

'He said so?'

'Not in so many words. But when I asked him, he didn't deny it.'

Philpott frowned at me, the pelican forgotten. 'You have lost your mind, boy. If someone had murdered him, he would have been found in an alley, smashed in the head. Why should anyone go to the trouble of a pretended hanging?'

He was right. Such an undertaking would have been as planned and pitiless as the guillotine. Was it possible, after all, that Will Benson had been Aglantine's *other eyes* in Whitehall and had somehow displeased her? She could hardly have carried out the attack herself and must have had some accomplice. But then I remembered Will's ingenuous smile and steady background, so unlike my own, and realised it was all nonsense.

Nevertheless, I had remembered something else. 'His wig was missing. I noticed it particularly. If he had died in that room, it would have been with him.'

Philpott wasn't willing to rearrange his thoughts merely at my bidding. 'Nonsense. If his head *was* cracked open, 'twas infallibly when they took the body down off the hook, I assure 'ee. A body is surprising heavy, and easy enough for it to tumble down with a dreadful thump.'

It would have to have been a dreadful thump indeed, to smash open a man's skull. But now the neglected pelican, which had been regarding us with a hungry eye, began suddenly to complain, with a sound somewhere between the rending of metal and the bark of a dog. It had lost its sense of humour and was advancing on us menacingly. Philpott threw the last of the eels at its huge webbed feet, grabbed me by the sleeve and, feeling ridiculously comforted by his large presence, I ran after him across the gravel walks towards home.

14

PHILPOTT'S DISBELIEF – his reasonable observation that the whole business was absurd – haunted me over the next few nights. Who, as he rightly asked, would murder a clerk and disguise the murder with a hanging? But even the Godfrey's Cordial would not soothe my disquiet, and on the Tuesday morning I found myself turning down Northumberland Street before work, to Will Benson's lodgings again. As before, there was a very long pause after I knocked. Eventually the door opened, and Will's landlady revealed herself, hair bundled under an old bonnet, broom in hand.

She knew me at once and embarked on a long tale of woe, concerning the re-letting of Will's room, as if I was an old acquaintance. No one quite liked to take it, she said, with the death so recent. She eyed me speculatively, perhaps hoping that was my purpose in coming there, but I could hardly lie in that bed without remembering the hanging corpse, the flies. 'I remember you said folks were bothering him,' was all I said, when she finally drew breath. 'Once, when I came in search of him, you thought me someone else. You were on Will's orders to send them away. Will you tell me who these visitors were?'

'Well.' She looked at me meditatively, perhaps wondering if I was good for a half-crown if she told me. 'There was a ruffianly fellow came once or twice, but I sent him away without bothering poor Mr Benson, for he'd have no cause to deal with a man like that. And then there was Mr Canning, of course. Mr Benson always implored me to say he was out, but he was surprising persistent.'

This was impossible, for Canning had not known where Will lodged, even after his death. I had heard him say so, in the back kitchen, among the clerks.

'I think you must be mistaken. Mr Canning is a handsome man, with quite a superior manner. Haughty, you might say.'

She nodded, unperturbed. 'Oh, dear, yes, I know Canning *very* well.'

'Then when did he call?' Perhaps I had misunderstood her. It was absolutely impossible to imagine Canning at this door, conversing with this benighted creature and her broom.

'Several times, that week before Mr Benson hanged hisself.'

And therefore long before he pled ignorance as to Will's lodgings. *Feigned* ignorance. I was perplexed. 'You did not say *that* to the inquest.'

She only smiled and rubbed her fingers together meaningfully, as if fondling a coin. But then her expression changed, seeming to realise she had therefore spoken out of turn and betrayed Canning's confidence. Did she fear the loss of her money? Perhaps something worse than that, for she made to shut the door abruptly in my face.

'You are afraid of Mr Canning?' I forestalled her by grasping hold of the doorknob. 'Why?'

She paused, regarding me through the crack of the door.

'Was it something Will said?'

She laughed hollowly and slammed the door so hard it rocked in its worm-eaten frame.

Canning had been here himself. Several times, in fact. And Will had been afraid. But though he might have hounded the lad, and even brought him to suicide and the anatomist's laboratory, he could hardly be a murderer. More likely was the *ruffianly fellow* she had also turned away. Had he been Aglantine's emissary? I should go to the coroner, or to Grenville, and tell them the story. Not the whole story – not my thoughts on Aglantine, of course – but I could at least tell them what Brookes had said, and mention the unwelcome visitors at Will's lodgings.

But then I remembered the look on the anatomist's face, his hand on my sleeve. *You'll not inform on me now? My work is so valuable.* Will's landlady had looked no less frightened. They would likely both deny everything. And where was the broken skull? In an unknown pit with all the rest, and beyond identification now. As I walked through Charing Cross and Whitehall, I remembered Philpott's disbelief and my fervour cooled.

But at the very least, I should somehow get the Bensons out of town before the news reached them that their son's eyes were on display in Brookes' museum. I should make up some story – concoct a burial place for them to visit and say their goodbyes. It would be easy enough to do it, after all, a suicide's grave being unmarked and unrecorded.

A SUDDEN MARTIAL FRENZY of bulletins arriving almost hourly from General Moira in Flanders had made Downing Street intolerable and, on Friday, Grenville and I escaped them by meeting Mr Jay at Aust's house in Kensington. It was peaceful in the garden square, birds chirping in the bushes outside Mr Aust's study window. Anne was out on the lawn with an easel, her face shaded by a straw bonnet, her expression absorbed. It ought to have been a good place for measured discussion, but instead this meeting was even less civil than the last. Jay's face was pinched into a scowl, while Grenville held Jay's paper of grievances with fastidious fingers, going straight to business without preamble or politeness.

'I see you protest our freeing those slaves that came over to the British lines during the late war. As I understand it, you claim they should have been returned on conclusion of the peace.'

Jay jumped to his feet and began to pace the short interval between the door and the fire grate. 'That is quite correct, Lord Grenville. You carried off near a hundred thousand Negroes during the war – property of immense monetary value – and my countrymen remain justly aggrieved.'

Grenville remained seated, his pale gentlemanly fingers clasping the brandy glass, his fingernails well tended. Money and a secretary to do your writing for you was what you needed for hands like that. I wasn't sure I had ever seen him hold a pen. I looked across at Theodore, who was supposed to be taking notes, but he was gazing out of the window, rapt in his own thoughts as usual.

'The freedom proclamation was made in '75 and was at that time the legitimate law of the land,' Grenville observed. 'When you rebels rose against us, we were well within our rights to seek allies where we could. We could hardly ask the Negroes to fight as Englishmen, if they were still enslaved.'

'My countrymen would contend that the slaves had no

business enlisting. They were property, not men.'

At this I forgot to write, staring at Jay's face as I remembered his strong words to Philpott on the same matter. And then at Grenville, who was smiling as if a pleasing thought had struck him.

'Very well. Let us make it so. But then, what of the many horses run or strayed into British lines, during those years? They too were property, but became spoils of war, along with captured guns and muskets.'

'I believe so.'

'As so much property, the same must be true for slaves strayed into our armies. And how could we return them in any case? How could we determine their former owners any more than those of a horse?'

'Many are branded, my Lord.'

'Ah! Very like a horse, would you say?' Grenville looked mischievous, and Jay looked pained. 'And the ones not branded? How were we to find *their* owners?'

'The slaves could have told you, my Lord.'

'Because they are rational, thinking men, and not horses?'

'Yes, my Lord.'

Grenville looked triumphant, Jay almost silly, but the exchange was odd enough to distract me temporarily from my own worries. Quite apart from Jay's vocal abolitionist beliefs, Grenville made no secret of his own personal wish to end the slave trade. Jay might merely be parroting the words of his masters at home, but the two men were in agreement on this, if nothing else, and to play at such discord seemed senseless.

As we came out into Aust's drawing room, Peter Williams appeared and spoke a few words in Theodore's ear. The boy flushed and let himself be led away. I wondered how soon Jay's apparently heavy investment in Peter Williams's education and genteel demeanour might be paid off. I too had received an education and a career above my station, and like him, no one thought much the better of me for it.

Except, perhaps, for Anne. She was still in the quiet square as I came out of the house, sitting under the plane tree, her straw plait sunhat casting a chequered shade over her face as she bent over her painting. There was a table beside her, holding water, paints and brushes, and a bored maidservant in attendance, exchanging flirtatious glances with the passing delivery boys and footmen from the neighbouring mansions.

Anne looked up at me and smiled without surprise, as I trudged towards her across the crisp grass. I took her hand and then bent over her painting with my customary obedience. It was all background – no, not even that, all grass. She was painting the close-scythed lawn where she sat, and the feathery edges where the plants had gone to seed. She frowned at the baffled look on my face.

'I call it a *paysage botanique*.'

'Do you?'

'Which means, for your ignorance, a botanical landscape. Do you remember how I used to send you notes in French?'

'Vividly.' I had to pretend not to understand, of course, though her dreadful blunders had pained me. I sat down on the grass and leaned against the tree trunk. It would have been pleasant, but I was too aware of Anne's dusky opal skirt, which brushed the grass by my right hand.

'I heard about the trouble in the Department. But Mr Aust says you are quite exonerated.'

'Only because some other poor devil got the blame. Someone too dead to argue.'

She looked at me. 'You should not be so surprised. They

blame Pitt for every setback in the war, every trouble at home. There must always be a scapegoat. Remember the poor Marquis of Bath my stepfather was so fond of.' I could see an ink stain on the pad of her thumb, and there was a smear of burnt umber across her nose that made her look like a gypsy. 'Mr Aust still sees you as his heir, I assure you.'

She spoke of the business as if it had been a mere misdemeanour, not a hanging offence, and I shifted restlessly. 'Oh, Mr Aust exaggerates. There is no automatic right to advancement, Anne. Grenville will have some man of his own in mind.'

She looked jealous. 'Who?'

'I don't know. Some rising man with Pitt's good opinion, I expect. Perhaps George Canning. Certainly not me.'

'George Canning!' She had caught the infection of my bitterness, but she was already pursuing another thought, I could tell, from the set of her mouth and the absent look in her eye. A thought formidably single-minded, if I knew her at all. It would have pleased me, in my vanity, to imagine she was thinking of roses and lace and wedding days, but I knew her too well for that. She might contemplate a rose, but if she did it would be a specimen to be sketched. If she contemplated me, it would be with the same ruthless attention. If she married me, and took my concerns as her own, she would pay them the same calculation. She would act the Under-Secretary's wife, entertain the Foreign Secretary and whatever envoys he produced with unfailing grace, give luncheons to their ladies, and do it all supremely well. She would do it for me, but still more she would do it for herself.

I hoped she was meditating some accident to Canning's glittering career, but when she finally spoke, she knocked the wind from my sails entirely. 'In any case, it was all false, you know.'

Not roses or lace. She had been contemplating whether to

let me into the secret of state she had in her possession. I was silenced for a heartbeat or two.

'What was false?'

'The whole business. The army never was anywhere near Ostend. The message was a lie.'

'The message?' I was stupid.

'The message leaked to the papers.'

I scrambled to my feet and brushed myself down, my blood rising. 'Anne, I know I am a mere fool, and you as political a woman as the Duchess of Devonshire, but will you please to explain exactly what your stepfather has told you? God damn me, I have had my head half in a noose over the business, and now you tell me it was all nonsense?'

She looked pleased to be bracketed in the company of such an illustrious female politician. 'Sit down, Laurence, and I'll tell you.'

I settled once more at her feet, and she arranged her skirts. 'The message came in while you were with his Lordship?'

'Yes.'

'It seemed serious, you recall. The army split and defenceless to a French attack.' She shook her head. 'None of it was true. Where the message came from, they do not know. None of our agents in Flanders admit to sending it.'

'But what possible purpose could it serve?'

She shook her head again. 'They do not know that either. Perhaps mere mischief, to sow confusion between London and the front. Or perhaps your poor dead scapegoat was paid by the French to leak it, in order to embarrass the Ministry.'

Before I could stop myself, I was telling her about my visit to the anatomist's museum, and the cracked skull. My visit to Northumberland Street and Will's strange visitors.

She looked at me quite unmoved. 'Don't be a goose,

Laurence. Do you not know politics is all about reputation? If even a gutter journalist like Philpott disbelieves you, what makes you think the Ministry will listen? If you run to Grenville with this story he will never look at you the same again, and all our hopes will be at an end.'

She did love me. But still I struggled, unwilling to listen. 'If he was murdered—'

'*If!* Where is the proof? The boy is in pieces, the body gone, and Mr Brookes at the museum will deny it all.'

Hearing my own thoughts spoken back to me, I knew she was right. 'But Mr Canning's visits – his lie to the clerks ...'

'I'll grant you one part of your fantasy. I can quite imagine Mr Canning might seek to save both your skins by leaving evidence in Mr Benson's rooms to cover his own mistake. If so, I rather think it was a sensible solution to a delicate problem.'

Yes, how much more she understood politics than I did, and I began to see there was absolutely nothing I could do. Unless something new came to light, to identify the *ruffianly fellow* or Will's skull miraculously returned from the grave to avenge him, it was over. I watched a party of gardeners crossing the road to the palace, armed with scythes to mow the vast sweeping lawns. *All our hopes.*

'Why are you smiling, all of a sudden, Mr Goose?'

'I was remembering how I took you to look at the cows in Hyde Park when you were young. I believe you even carried a bucket.'

'Nonsense, I was fourteen at least, and far too dignified. But I should have liked to, above everything!'

'Then tomorrow we shall perambulate the palace grounds. I shall wear my farm gaiters, and you must wear a suitably agricultural bonnet.' They would never let us inside the gate if we did. But now Anne was smiling too.

'Like Marie Antoinette? Oh, do say so. *She* was very fond of playing milkmaid, poor dear.'

15

'ELEPHANTS? ELEPHANTS UPSTAIRS?' Philpott demanded loudly. I had come upon him the following afternoon perusing a notice pinned to the wall outside Pidcock's Menagerie, announcing the imminent arrival of 'Three of the largest Elephants ever known to these Isles'. I was on my way out to Kensington, but was prevailed upon to delay my visit to Anne and step in for a moment. Mrs Philpott was entertaining poor Mrs Hardy to dinner, and had no desire for her husband's company, so he was at large on the street somewhat like an escaped elephant himself.

'God damn me, the floor will cave in. Are they out of their minds? And how the devil do they intend to get them up here? Philpott's eyes gleamed as we arrived in the crowded exhibition hall. 'Will *they* climb the staircase, do you suppose? I must seek an interview with Mr Pidcock directly.'

But he had never visited the menagerie before, and was arrested at once by the pens running in a line down one wall, and the chimps in high cages on the other. A wicked-looking specimen was squeezing its arm through the bars, reaching for the bonnet perched atop a lady's tall headdress. The lady's child was ill-advisedly reaching out a dimpled hand to a blue-faced monkey, one of a number chained to a bench below, watching the human crowd resentfully. If these were supposed to be pet animals, they had tired of their occupation. The odd adventurous dog wove through the forest of legs, while one of the keepers was putting his head inside the lion's mouth for the edification of the large crowd of onlookers.

'God bless me,' Philpott said with some admiration, before pushing his way into the throng, only to be brought up immediately by the sight of the rhinoceros, which was rubbing its horn thoughtfully against the bars of its prison and eyeing the crowd with apparent disgust. It filled the small compartment to overflowing, its ridged grey flesh bulging through the grating.

Philpott turned back to me in great good humour. 'What is that thing, Mr Jago?' he shouted over the din, the crowd breaking around him. I was quite hemmed in.

'An ill-tempered creature that would cheerfully run you through. The lion would then finish you off, and the hyenas would eat the scraps. Pleasant, ain't it?'

'A veritable parable of the French, I would say. But which is Mr Robespierre, I wonder? The lion or the hyena?'

'I imagine that depends upon your point of view.'

'Oh? And what is yours, Mr Jago?' He fixed his cheerful blue eye upon me as the crowd flowed suddenly and almost pitched me into his brawny arms.

'Mine?' But just at that moment I saw, over by the tiger, a small figure tightly laced in black, a figure I knew quite as well as my own reflection. God damn me, Aglantine had followed me again. I had often met her here, for she favoured the cheerful anonymity of a crowd. 'Oh, I serve Mr Aust, you know,' I answered abstractedly. 'He tells me we are not required to hold opinions.' Aglantine was in conversation with someone, scowling up at a man whose back was turned to me. Perhaps it was coincidence and not design that had brought her here after all. Then the man turned, and I saw his face. It was George Canning, smiling down at Aglantine with his customary scorn.

'Aye, aye, I dare say.' Behind me, Philpott was still speaking cheerfully. 'But – Laurence? *Laurence!*'

I had broken away from him and was fighting my way through the crowd towards Canning. Aglantine saw me coming and fled into the throng, but Canning was slower. By the time I reached him he had only turned, taken out a coloured handkerchief, and was mopping his brow with exaggerated unconcern.

'You.' I arrived at his shoulder but seemed to have left my words behind me. '*You!*'

'Help you, sir?' His grey eyes were quite cool as I floundered.

'You have acted most dishonestly.'

My brain, rapidly catching up with my tongue, flickered in alarm at my last word, but I was more preoccupied with the fact that he had been speaking to Aglantine. I remembered his sudden change of party, which had brought him closer to the source of power, and I knew at once and without a shadow of a doubt that he, not Will Benson, was her other spy in Whitehall. Canning had imposed upon Pitt and Grenville with his smooth deceit and had accused poor Will of his own wrongdoing as I had always thought. But for worse – far worse – reasons. Grenville should know.

But, in the time it took for Canning to curl his lip, I realised that at all costs I must keep these thoughts to myself. I could never tell Grenville. For the only proof was Canning's acquaintance with Aglantine, and my only proof of *that* was my own. What then, could I say?

'That business with the leak – I demand that you tell Lord Grenville the truth of the whole transaction.' My mind was racing. I had not thought it possible Canning could be a murderer – had blamed the *ruffianly fellow* for Will's death – but was it possible Will had discovered this secret of Canning's? His supercilious urbanity had always been cold, cold as the blade of the guillotine, worthy of the French, in fact. 'That poor clerk – his mother—'

Canning was now positively glacial. 'Forgive me, sir. Am I to understand you are calling me a liar?'

Philpott was at my elbow. He could have gathered nothing, except that I was making a scene, and he only put a restraining hand on my arm. I ignored him, raising my voice so that everyone could hear. 'Mr Canning, you may take my words in whatever way you will.'

'No, no,' Philpott flapped anxiously. He could see where the argument was tending more clearly than I could. Even the animals were transfixed. The blue-faced monkey bared its teeth; Philpott raised a hand to protest. Canning slapped my face, I heard myself demanding satisfaction, and the tiger, excited by such high emotion so infrequently encountered behind the bars of his cage, launched himself at the grating, all in the space of a blink.

A MISHAP AT
THE MENAGERIE

*Minding my own business in the crowded hall of Pidcock's
animal kingdom t'other day, I was the subject of a dreadful misfortune. Provoked by some hullabaloo, the tiger
made a sudden leap at the bars of his cage, causing me
to start backwards. This start brought me within reach
of the small monkeys suffered to remain at large, chained
only to a sort of table. The nearest of them instantly
seized hold of my hair, and began pulling with his utmost
strength, endeavouring at the same time to scratch out
my eyes. Nothing could have saved me from suffering the
severest injuries but the stout resistance I made.*

*My first scream was the signal for a general burst of
the wildest uproar throughout the whole menagerie. The lion,
with his mane erect, darted with surprising activity from
end to end of his prison, lashing the bars with his tail, and
thundering out his rage. The tiger sprang in all directions,
repeatedly turning head over heels against the gratings,
and making every effort to catch hold of me by thrusting his
fore-legs out to their fullest extent, and evincing his severe
disappointment on perceiving that he could only grasp the
air with his claws. The leopards and hyenas in like manner
manifested their eagerness to partake of the good fortune which
they imagined had befallen the monkeys; whilst immediately
facing the spot where I was struggling to escape, was an
immensely large black monkey or baboon, leaping from the
bottom to the top of his cage, and exhibiting a state of rage
which no one had on any former occasion witnessed.*

'GAWD ALMIGHTY.' The head keeper, a jovial man of fifty named Mr Grant, was tending to Philpott's head in the back room, while some of the others went in search of his wig, though I could hardly suppose it would be worth rescuing by now, having seen the insolent way the monkeys were using it. 'Mr Pidcock will have my guts, Mr Philpott, he really will. He's been complaining about them monkeys for weeks. They always try for him, too, you see, while they're fond of me and don't make no fuss. There must be something about you, sir, what reminds them of him. Or something else they don't like.' Grant studied Philpott as if looking for the point about him objectionable to monkeys, before continuing to poke at his wounds. 'Holdfast' was tattooed across his knuckles. He must have been a sailor before he found this billet in town, safe from the press gang.

Philpott winced. 'Don't fret yourself, my dear sir. Tell your master it will be the best publicity he shall ever have. I shall write an amusing report of the whole business in my news-paper, and folks will come flocking to see the ferocious beasts for themselves.'

'Very good of you to take it so, sir. But I'm afraid they'll be disappointed. Once the elephants turn up, we're off on a tour of the north for the whole summer.' He tapped Philpott on the scalp. 'Shipshape as I can make it, sir. Shall I bind it up for 'ee?'

'My wig will be enough, I think.' It had just been returned in a state of terrible disrepair, and Philpott looked at it doubt-fully. 'At least until I can get home to Mrs Philpott.'

Philpott leaned on my shoulder heavily, with the air of a man escaped from a shipwreck, as we made our way back through the exhibition hall, the chimps shrieking down at us from their high cages. The other spectators had been turned out, and I looked for Canning but there was no sign of his handsome figure as we staggered along the Strand towards Fleet Street. As my pulses slowed, and my mind cleared, I began to realise what folly I had done. How much wiser it would have been to have kept my own counsel, watched Canning, and found him out in some treachery I could safely expose without exposing myself.

I glanced at Philpott, who was muttering to himself as if he had lost his wits. 'Mane upright? Mane a-tousled? No, no, mane *erect*. That's it. That's right.'

'Sir—'

'God damn me, Laurence, I am about to faint, I do believe.' Philpott swayed, and his grip tightened on my arm as we paused outside Somerset House. 'Did you ever see such a thing? 'Twas the most shocking business I ever saw in my life.'

'Mr Philpott—'

'Should not be at all surprised if I lose an eye like that fellow Nelson.' He put his fingers to his swollen face and spoke broodingly. 'A nasty business, I imagine.'

'This affair with Canning—'

'Nancy will be most displeased. We had high words this morning, for young William will not mind the pig and she is obliged to do it. "Let Margaret do it," I said, but as she observed, Margaret is scarcely three feet tall and cannot manage the bucket. She will feel herself still more put upon to see me thus disabled—'

'Mr Philpott,' I was desperate and spoke loudly. 'For God's sake, sir, will you not help me?'

He stopped again and squinted up at me out of his one good eye. The other was already as swollen and shiny as a duck's egg. 'Help 'ee, my boy? God damn me, did the devils get you too? Art hurt?'

'Not yet.' I had finally got his attention as we began walking again. 'But I am likely to be dead within a day or two, and I know nothing of how these affairs are managed.'

Philpott looked quite blank. Recent events had obviously driven remoter ones from his mind. I reminded him.

'Challenged Canning?' He slowed to a crawl. 'In the menagerie? By God, my boy! George Canning!'

'Yes, sir. I will need a weapon – a meeting place – a second … Will you do it?'

'Be your second?' He grasped my sleeve, the gleam coming back into his ravaged face. 'I will!'

'I have a pistol.' I saw his surprise but didn't trouble to elaborate. I was glad, after all, that I hadn't thrown it in the river. 'Pistols are quite customary now, ain't they? I can't use a blade.'

'A damned effete weapon, in any case, I assure 'ee.'

I was now pretty sure Philpott knew little more of the business than I did. For my own part, sharpened steel in the hand of an expert seemed anything but effeminate. The one hope with a pistol was that it would miss. I wondered how well practised a marksman George Canning might be.

'Will you talk to him? Find out where and when?' I looked at Philpott doubtfully, wondering if he was capable of anything at all in his present state, but he seemed to have momentarily forgotten his wounds as we came up to his shop and paused in the doorway.

'Wonder what sort of a shot he is reputed to be? You'd not have me apologise? There'd be no shame in it.'

'I can't apologise, sir.'

'Well, I'll see what I can do.' He came to rest at his desk, called plaintively to his wife, then threw his battered wig in the wastepaper basket with a dead aim that made me wish he could stand in for me at the coming duel.

Dejection seemed to be returning rapidly upon him. 'Do I look very bad? I feel uncommon faint of a sudden.' He was unnaturally pale.

'Dreadful, sir. Shall I call Mrs Philpott again?'

'I think you better had.'

I ventured up the stairs from the shop, into their private quarters, which were a good deal shabbier than I expected. A young fellow I took to be William Philpott junior, reluctant pig-keeper, was dragging his younger brother under the kitchen table by the hair, while a small plump girl with eyes exactly like her father's examined me over the thumb that plugged her mouth. In the window seat, two further infants were locked in some kind of struggle.

Mrs Philpott was fanning herself against the extreme heat of the fireplace, in conversation with another woman whose loosened stays and curving belly told me it was the same Mrs Hardy I had glimpsed at the riot. Then, she had been a distant shape, no more, and I had thought her only a pitiful victim. But the tanned face she turned to me now was crinkled with laughter lines that radiated from the corners of her eyes. She was made for smiling, not sadness, and I saw at once how her fundamental good humour was at war with the dreadful griefs that had come upon her.

She was smiling now, despite everything, as Mrs Philpott, fanning vigorously, was apparently remarking on the shortcomings of her scullery maid. 'She will insist on spreading the linen before the fire, so that all the children smell faintly of bacon. And though I am fond of a piglet I would not have the world call them porkers.' She raised her eyes to me enquiringly.

'Mr Philpott has had an accident,' I ventured. 'Nothing too serious, don't be alarmed. But he needs some attention.'

She stood up briskly, fetched water and linen, and followed me down to the shop. Philpott winced as she dabbed at his head. 'My dear girl, can you go at it with a little less gusto?'

'Mr Blake the printer has left me the proofs of next week's paper,' she answered, 'and I must get through them before nightfall, your ridiculous capers notwithstanding.' I was surprised for a moment, and then less so as I examined her capable face. 'I have been in conference with Mrs Hardy, and for all his nonsense her husband has at least taught the good woman a fine hand and a clear understanding of grammar. She was his amanuensis in all his *correspondences*.' She frowned at the last word as if it offended her. 'If you like, I shall employ her about the proofs and give her an honest wage.'

'Just as you say, my dear.' Philpott was meek.

'The members of her husband's society try to help her, but they have little ready money of their own.' She tightened the bandage with a flourish. 'Will I bring her down to meet you?'

'By all means.'

I left before the introductions were made. Amid their family harmony, death grinned at me from behind Philpott's chair. Perhaps he tapped Philpott on the shoulder too, for as I opened the door he called after me in sepulchral tones. 'Come back tomorrow evening, my boy, and I'll have settled the whole matter with Canning, I assure 'ee.'

16

I STRODE BACK UP THE Strand towards the menagerie, thinking to ask Mr Grant if he had seen Canning and Aglantine meet there before, but the doors were still locked, the keepers no doubt restoring order after our rumpus, and though I hammered loudly, no one came. The offices of the *Sunday Observer* were only a few doors away, and after a moment's hesitation I turned in there instead. Someone must know something more than they had told.

The newspaper offices were attached to the print works, and if anything the atmosphere within the old building was sootier than the streets outside. Ink seemed to have worked its way into the fabric of the building, and to ooze from its surfaces. A sallow youth with black-streaked hair looked up and informed me cordially that Mr Bourne was out on business. 'Mr Johnson will see you, I'm sure.' He nodded to another clerk who got down from his stool with a sigh, returning moments later with a man of astonishing girth and an air of overwhelming fatigue likely brought on by the heat.

'Help 'ee, sir?'

'I hope so, Mr Johnson. I'm come from Downing Street, for more information concerning the leak you published.'

He looked glum. 'The press cannot be muzzled, you know.'

The clerks were smirking behind him, though which of us was cause for amusement I didn't know, as he beckoned me around the desk and into his office, which smelled strongly of damp and gin.

'I dare say you have been asked this question before, sir, but can you describe the person that handed in the message you published?'

He shook his head. 'I told the others I'd like to help you, but I know for a fact it came in as an anonymous note.'

'How was it delivered?'

'By a passing rogue of some description, I believe. But we could see it was genuine from the contents and the hand, so did not scruple to publish.'

'And who took delivery of the note?'

'It was lying on my desk when I came in. And then it was all such a terrible hurry, for we only received the paper on the Saturday morning, and it was the devil of a business to reset the type and get the news put in for the next day.'

I could see the man had indeed been asked these questions before, and answered them just as unhelpfully, and that he meant to defend his actions by claiming want of time to consider. I could hardly blame him for caution, but if I had hoped for a damning portrait of Canning, I was disappointed.

It was only as I left that I realised I had just been handed the final proof that Will was innocent of the leak, and the whole story of note and key invented. He had been sacked the day of the executions in Newgate Street, which was always a Wednesday, and I had found him hanging eight days later, on the day of the Foreign Office dinner. The Ministry's story was that he had stolen the note and leaked it to the press during the interval, but if Mr Johnson remembered rightly, that wasn't true. The message had reached the *Observer* only the day before it was published, he'd said, and that was a full ten days after I found Will hanging. Mr Johnson had likely told others the same story, but Canning was Pitt's favourite, and if the Ministry believed he had made an honest mistake, it seemed they were willing to protect him by overlooking inconvenient facts. How Canning must laugh at their simplicity.

T HE NEXT DAY WAS SUNDAY, and the menagerie was peaceful in Sabbath repose, still oblivious to my pounding at the door. I should have gone to church myself, to plead for the good will of my maker, but instead I examined the pistol with some sudden anxiety as to its working order, then put it in my pocket and set out for a hike into the parched countryside. Mr Gibbs ran ahead of me across the brown grass, in a manner more proper to a much younger dog. I wished I might share his joy, but the weight of mortality hung on my shoulders. I was a farmer's boy, no duelling gentleman, and how likely it was that I would join Will in shadowy blackness, his murder unavenged. The heat felt suffocating, and it caught my breath as if I was already in the grave with Canning exulting over me. I felt dizzy and was obliged to stop and lean my head on my knees.

'You in pain?' a voice said from above my head, with a strange inflection I thought I recognised. I looked up to see Peter Williams stooping to examine me. He wore a wide-brimmed hat instead of a formal wig, his own hair powdered, and I judged that he was at his Sunday leisure.

'Not at all.' I stood up and brushed myself down. 'Not yet, at any rate. Where are you going in this heat?'

'I ain't entirely sure.' He looked about him with a lack of curiosity I thought rather admirable, apparently unperturbed by the bad-tempered man doggedly flogging a donkey behind us, which had shed its load of early potatoes on the road. His eyes settled on me again. '*Not yet?*'

'I beg your pardon?'

'When will you be in pain, if *not yet?*'

'Oh.' I looked at him and wondered whether he would report me to the constables if I told him the truth. From the look in his eye I thought he would scarcely take the trouble. 'The fact is, I'm to fight a duel and have never yet shot a pistol in my life.' I produced the article from my pocket and looked at it unhappily. A flicker of something – could it be interest at last? – glimmered across Peter Williams's face. He held out his hand. For a moment I thought he meant to take the pistol, but then understood his meaning and swapped the gun to my left hand so I could shake hands with my right.

'They call me Peet,' he said. 'If you like.'

'Do you like it?'

Another flicker of interest. 'Not so much.' His eye fell back to the pistol. 'You mean to take a turn with that thing this afternoon?'

'Well.' I shook my head. 'I did think—'

'Come on,' he said. 'I'll lend a hand, if you're so inclined.'

We went to Hyde Park, coming in from the uncultivated side, across the water from Kensington and its formal gardens, and then struck away across the parched ground towards a lonely stand of trees in the distance.

I had shot my father's fowling piece at pigeons, and nabbed

a few by virtue of its spray of shot, but this pistol with its single ball was a completely different matter. It would take aim and cold-hearted detachment to hit a man, and I wondered if I had the stomach for it. Peter Williams had gathered a pocketful of the fallen potatoes from the dusty road and I saw now he meant to make me fire at them. Ridiculous. I could hardly hope to shoot Canning in the heart. I would wing him if I could, and for that I only needed a target the size of a whole sackful.

'You are fond of your guns in America, I recollect.' I was watching him lay out the potatoes along the top of a broken fence. He cocked his head in answer but didn't trouble to speak. He only stood to one side and bowed.

My first effort took off his hat, emanating from the muzzle of the gun at a forty-five-degree angle that seemed to defy every one of Newton's laws of motion. We stared at each other with some alarm. Then he bent slowly in half, and after a moment I gathered he was laughing silently at his own knee buckles. I was mighty glad not to have killed him, but it was no laughing matter. I would almost rather Canning murdered me directly than witness such an exhibition.

I went to fetch his hat while my cheeks cooled. It had a hole clean through the crown and must have missed his head by less than an inch. We sat down on a rock and examined the damage together.

'Ten shillings, minimum.' Peter Williams looked bleak now, instead of tickled.

'Let me pay you.' I fumbled in my pocket, but he had already raised his hand.

'Mr Jay will only add it to my account. Don't trouble.'

'Your account?' I remembered again Jay's words the night of the Downing Street dinner. 'He doesn't truthfully weigh up the money you cost him, and make you work it out?'

'He does. How else would he calculate?'

'And what is your hourly rate? How long will he add to your servitude to pay off this hat?'

He computed. 'Almost a month, I reckon.'

'A month!' A month of my own wages would buy near ten hats at the sum he had mentioned. 'But your labour must be worth more than fourpence a day! You read and write, do you not? And run Mr Jay's errands about Whitehall.'

'And more.' He looked as unperturbed as ever. 'But the worth of a slave's labours is notional, sir. There's no guild can decide it.'

I still felt the need to offer him something. 'You do know you are free, Mr Williams?'

He turned his head to look at me.

'You have heard of Lord Mansfield's judgment?' I rummaged my brain for the old case law I had learned as a lawyer's clerk. 'Having brought you hither, Mr Jay cannot take you back to America against your will. If you leave his service, he cannot make you return to him.' I was studying his expression, still frustratingly cool. 'Yes, now you are in England, you are assuredly a free man.'

Again, emotion crossed his face, but I couldn't tell exactly what it was. 'Very kind of you, sir. Will you get me a place in your Foreign Office, if I leave Mr Jay's household?'

I had nothing to say to that, and he smiled without amusement. 'Will you arrange me comfortable quarters?'

'There are many Africans in London,' I answered uncomfortably, remembering that I had seen them mainly down by the river in circumstances I would not wish to share.

'And suppose yourself now in Philadelphia, sir.' He was inexorable. 'Would you consent to remain there for ever, without the means of getting home to your family and friends? Being ever so free?'

'No,' I said. 'No, God forbid, I would not.'

He stood up again. 'Shall you make another attempt?'

'Perhaps you might demonstrate.' I offered him the pistol. 'You must know more of the matter than I.'

He raised his eyebrows. 'You think Mr Jay would furnish me with a gun?'

17

THE SUMMER EVENING was coming on, and though it was not yet dark Philpott's shop was cosy by lamplight. The old tabby was lying on the desk as usual, and she flexed a claw as Mr Gibbs sniffed at her.

'Well, I have spoken to the man.' Philpott was pottering about, finding tobacco for his pipe. 'We are to meet in the morning in Moorfields.'

'Moorfields!'

'The sodomites are quite departed from the place, I gather, and new houses gone up where they used to tryst. Bedlam will be asleep at such an early hour and no prying eyes over the expanse of moor between.'

I had thought to die in the picturesque precincts of Hyde Park, not in a bog between a by-word for bawdy jokes and a madhouse. But the matter had apparently been settled, and it was too late now.

'He agrees to pistols and will bring his own second.'

'Thank you, sir.'

'They will be there at five.'

'Then I had better make my will and go to my rest.' It was mere bravado. I had nothing to bequeath, and though I was worn out from the long walk in the sun, my mind was racing again. It would take a prodigious dose of Godfrey's Cordial to send me into slumber tonight.

'There is one matter remaining,' Philpott said, his battered face uncharacteristically grim in the candlelight. 'If things go badly, I'd like to tell your mother what possessed you to challenge the man.'

'He lied about the message. You know that. Would have seen me hanged for it, when I believe he did it himself.'

'Nonsense. Why should he?'

'I can't tell you.'

'You can tell me anything. I'm no blabbermouth. Not when it matters.'

I glanced at his plump face, and thought it was probably true. But he'd have no sympathy for me, if he knew my secrets, and I had no intention of disappointing him. On the other hand, if I died on the morrow, Canning would escape justice. 'Well then, sir, I'll say this much. I'd wager my life – I *have* wagered my life – that Canning is acquainted with persons even more objectionable than Mr Bourne of the *Observer.*'

Philpott looked at me enquiringly, but I only shook my head and left. I envied him his righteous slumber, his wifely bed-companion. There would be no peace for me tonight, unless I emptied the bottle of Godfrey's Cordial on my washstand. By tomorrow night I might no longer need it.

I almost tripped over a shadowy figure sitting on my doorstep. It was Theodore Jay.

'Good God. You find your way around the city admirably.' I had my latch key in my hand, but found I was glad enough to sit down beside him on the step. 'What are you doing here?'

'I have an idea you might help me with,' he said matter-of-factly, as though it wasn't the middle of the night at all. To do him some justice, he couldn't know my own problems. 'You *did* say you'd be my guide to the city.' He fumbled in his pocket and produced a dog-eared copy of *Harris's List of Covent Garden Ladies*. 'This fellow talks of respectable harlots in Newman Street, fallen gentlewomen in the main.'

He was proffering it to me, but I waved it away. 'I have read it.'

'They, too, deserve to hear God's word.' God damn me, he was smiling furtively. Was he as pious as he pretended, or was it all an excuse for a glorious lark? 'I can pay handsomely for an audience with them. Will you take me there? I have escaped Peet tonight, thank God, after a very tiresome chase about Pall Mall, and shan't waste the opportunity. He is so very hard to shake off.'

I glanced down the street. Philpott had taken himself to bed, for the candle was gone and the shop was dark. But how could I possibly sleep, with what awaited me in the morning? And there were still too many dreadful hours until dawn.

THERE WAS AN AWFUL stench from Cleveland Street poorhouse and its cemetery that brought Will Benson's corpse and my own impending death to mind as we turned up Newman Street. Theodore kept pace beside me, eager but reserved, looking about with an owlish solemnity rather reminiscent of his father, at the carriages drawn up outside the handsome doorways, their drivers apparently asleep. Lights spilled down a set of broad steps, along with the sound of a string ensemble. Amusement and interment within fifty yards of each other. Life in the midst of death.

The lobby, furnished lavishly with gold brocade, was mercifully empty, but there would always be customers of some sort or another. 'You're in august company,' I said. 'If you bump into Mr Pitt, for God's sake pretend you don't know him.'

'He frequents such places?'

'On second thoughts, no. He's more likely gone on a trip up the Windward Passage in Moorfields.'

'Is that in the West Indies?'

'No, Mr Jay, it's somewhere a deal more sensitive. Sit yourself down in this comfortable armchair and I'll find someone.'

The lady of the house was polite but incredulous. '*How* many does he want?'

'As many as ten guineas will buy him for an hour.'

'He can't screw that many, you know. Can't he be a little more reasonable and leave some free for the other gentlemen?'

'As I explained, ma'am, he does not wish to screw them, merely talk.'

'Oh – talk!' She understood that by her own lights. 'Well, I still think it's greedy, but it's his money. He'll have to wait, mind. They're all engaged at present.'

A girl walked past in her shift, barelegged to the hip, but Theodore had taken out a book and begun to read, apparently oblivious. I sat down beside him, my mood darkening. Was I really to spend my last night on earth in a bawdy house without the means to enjoy it? 'You can spend a week's wages here for a mere spurt, easily to be gained elsewhere at a lower price, and by your own hand entirely free. But the spurt will, of course, be so much more satisfactory.'

Theodore's ears reddened, but he didn't reply, and at this juncture the lady of the house reappeared and took charge of him at once, leading him off into the shadows. I could see him talking earnestly, and the lady nodding briskly. She said something to a girl in passing, and a moment later a door opened close at hand to reveal a female of ample proportions, her petticoat hitched to her knee.

'Ready, my hearty?'

She held out a hand to me invitingly, and I glanced back at Theodore's retreating figure. Had he somehow contrived this? I couldn't believe it, but the woman was still waiting, hand outstretched. I took it doubtfully, and she pulled me into her chamber, closed the door, pushed me down with arousing force on to another gold brocade sofa and plucked off my spectacles.

She was something of a blur as she took a pinch of snuff from a box on the mantelpiece, sneezed, coughed, and spat discreetly into the fire grate. 'I must tell you I am excessively particular, sir.' She put back the snuffbox and grasped her hem. 'Fair exchange. Show me yours and I'll show you mine. Then if we're both satisfied, we may proceed to amusement.'

This ought to have dampened my ardour, but I was going to be dead in the morning and my whole body was suddenly on fire. My hands were fumbling at my buttons when she added, 'Two guineas on the table first, if you please, sir.'

I was back out on the landing directly, looking down wearily from the front window on to the street. The lamps were going out, and the horses only restless shapes in the darkness. What light there was reflected off the wheel of a carriage, the brass of a harness, the white face of a small figure leaning against the lamp-post directly below, looking up at the windows. Another more shadowy figure stood apart, and I wondered if it was Peter Williams back on Theodore's trail. I could hardly imagine he would like such work, a good deal beneath his dignity.

The whole affair seemed a parable of my short life, where

every solemn moment turned to farce. I remembered the only time I tried to kiss Anne. She was seventeen, no longer a gawky child, and we had found ourselves alone in her step-father's drawing room. Evening sun was pouring in the big windows as she gazed out at the distant view of cattle grazing in Hyde Park. Too short-sighted to see more than a blur at that distance, I contented myself with studying her. I touched her hand and then took her by the waist. For a moment I thought she was willing.

'Oh, Laurence,' she said mournfully. 'Don't you know I can't?' She meant my money, of course – or lack of it – and my lowly position in the Department. But if she'd loved me at all, I thought afterwards, she would have kissed me first and repented later. Now I reflected that if the next day went badly, I would never kiss anyone again.

It would soon be dawn, and my appointment awaited me. I left Theodore there and walked home alone, tired but still wakeful, down Drury Lane, past another stinking graveyard. I held my handkerchief to my nose with a hand that trembled, looking at the houses around the burial ground, waist deep in graves. Silhouetted by a solitary rush light, an old man leaned on a windowsill looking down on his likely resting place, while quicklime lay in the corner, a pure, blistering white.

18

BY FIVE O'CLOCK THE SUN was already shining on the tiles and leadwork of the roofs. Gulls and pigeons were making their raucous din, and the pigs penned behind every tenement were stirring, exchanging news in low muted grunts. It was full day as we passed the entrance of the old Sodomites' Walk, a path that had once led across the boggy heath of Moorfields, but now formed the south side of a square of new houses. We left the habitations of men, striking off the path, and walking over crisp grass and heather between gorse bushes. Their scent filled the air and insects rose in clouds from under our feet. It was already another hot day. I could see Canning and his companion waiting in the middle of the moor, the mad hospital behind them. Its walls leaned crazily, and its stonework crumbled, as though it had taken infection from its inmates.

I gave a letter into Philpott's hand as we walked towards the two figures. 'For my mother. Will you take it to her?' If I was dead, there would be no harm in Philpott learning the secret of my French ancestry after all.

'I will.'

'And try to get some money out of Aust. I'm owed my salary for July.'

'I will take it to her.' Philpott looked suddenly serious and cast me a look from under his sparse fair eyebrows. The wounds the monkey had inflicted at the menagerie were maturing. Livid colour now suffused the whole right side of his head, as if he had been coshed with a cricket bat.

'And for God's sake, get the Bensons out of town. I had thought to invent some story – some peaceful grave – but events have overtaken me.'

'God damn it, Laurence—'

But now I only had eyes for Canning, who was fully dressed as we came up, and had made no preparations for battle. His second held his pistol unloaded. The mad hospital was closer now, and I could see white shapes at the windows – faces of the unfortunate creatures confined within. They would witness our unlawful proceeding, but no one would ever believe them.

There were no pleasantries, but it seemed Canning was not ready to launch either of us into eternity without some of his usual unpleasantness. His second came up to Philpott and raised his hand.

'Before we proceed to the business, my client has some questions to put to Mr …?'

'Jago.' Philpott was gruff. 'He may put his questions through me, sir. My client will not be confused by interrogation when he holds his life in his hands. Unless Mr Canning wishes to apologise for striking my client t'other day?'

'Not at all.' Canning's second bristled before turning back to his principal. 'Very well then, sir. Make your enquiries through Mr Jago's second.'

Canning looked in two minds at being obliged to confer with a fellow such as Philpott, but he cast me a glance and seemed to resolve to bear the ignominy. For myself, I was shaking, and only wished the business to be over.

'Just a couple of questions, Philpott.' Canning was still looking at me. 'Mr Jago seemed to suggest I had behaved with impropriety regarding the leaked message to the *Sunday Observer*. As the blame was fixed firmly and fairly on Mr Benson, I fail to understand his animus.'

I didn't wait for Philpott to relay the question or answer it on my behalf. 'Not firmly. Not fairly. You know as well as I do that the boy was innocent.'

Canning studied me. 'You were acquainted with Mr Benson? You know something I do not?'

I paused. His eyes were on me, cool and calculating, and I suddenly wondered if he had goaded me into a challenge in order to kill me and my suspicions as ingeniously as he had feigned Will's hanging. If, by some miracle, we both got out of this alive, I should by no means give him further grounds for distrust. Though I felt like St Peter denying Christ to save his own skin, I shook my head. 'No. I did not know him well.'

'Then the grounds for your accusation?'

I saw you in conversation with an old acquaintance – a French spy. You are the traitor and a murderer. I could not say any of it. I only waved my hand helplessly and wished he would turn his eyes away.

'We are done?' Canning's second had apparently grown tired of the conversation. 'Twelve paces apart, sirs, if you please. One shot. No aiming, I beg you, but a good quick fire on my signal.'

'Both fire together?' Canning looked pale but quite composed. 'If Mr Jago will not tell me on what grounds he impugns my honour, I think I am the injured party after all, and might have the first shot.'

I had been watching Philpott load my pistol, but looked up, provoked, as he probably intended. '*You*, the injured party!'

'I beg you, sirs, be seemly. We may toss a coin, if you wish it.'

Philpott had taken the measure of Canning's calm manner, steady hand, and expensive pistol, and of my trembling fingers and the sweat that made my hair stick to my neck and my glasses slide down my nose. Canning wore a good suit and a powdered wig. I was bare-headed and wore only my waistcoat. Philpott evidently concluded if we fired together, or Canning first, I was a dead man. 'Let's toss for it.' He grimaced in my direction. 'We call tails.'

Heads, I thought, *it should be heads*. And I was right. Canning won, and his second began methodically loading his pistol.

Mine was already loaded, but Philpott checked it again. His own hand was unsteady now. 'Stand sideways,' he muttered, as Canning's second began to pace out the distance. 'Duck. Run.'

'He'd be as likely to hit me anyway.'

'I reckon not. He looks like a man used to the business.'

'Fate will decide.'

Aglantine's voice came into my mind, from long ago. 'We no longer believe in fate, Laurence. Men make their own destinies.' Well, I was about to make mine, but if George Canning really was her other spy in Whitehall, then she would have had a hand in it too.

Canning turned at his twelfth stride and stood looking at me. I think I was fluttering as feverishly as a lunatic from the asylum behind us. I admit now that I can have struck no heroic figure. I could hardly bear to look at him, still less the pistol in his hand. He raised his arm. I am afraid I shut my eyes. Terror flooded me.

A bee buzzed past my ear. A cock crowed somewhere far off.

When I opened my eyes again, wondering if I was dead without knowing it, Canning was walking away across the moor, with our two seconds running at his heels, expostulating. I sat down heavily among the rough grass and heather, put down the gun, and thought I might be sick. Someone in the asylum screamed.

Philpott returned with a heavy tread. He was purpler than ever. 'God damn the bastard.'

I raised my eyes, surprised at the profanity, which was not like him. At first I thought he was merely shaken, as I was. 'Why did he run?' I was woefully ignorant of the protocol of a duel. 'Is he satisfied?'

'Satisfied!' Philpott flopped down in the grass beside me. 'It's you should not be satisfied, Laurence. Should challenge him anew.'

I thought that was very unlikely. The trembling of my hands was so bad I had to clench them between my knees. 'What the devil …?'

'He declines to give you the satisfaction of a bullet in the heart. Duelling is the preserve of the gentleman, and you ain't one, he says. He should as soon duel with Jay's darkie, as meet you on equal terms.'

'What—'

'Only came for the satisfaction of seeing you squirm like a beaten dog. *He* is now quite content.'

'Oh.' I took my hands from between my knees and observed their quivering with disfavour. '*Oh!*'

Philpott pulled me to my feet. 'Come, let's be away before the constables find us with this damning evidence.' He unloaded the pistol and put it in his pocket, before setting off across the moor with surprising activity for a man so beaten and battered.

I took the gun and the letter from him as we reached town and declined his offer of chocolate at Dick's. Instead, I walked down to Blackfriars, past the *Times* offices, where the morning papers were being loaded on to carts for distribution about the town. The clocks were chiming eight, and the streets were filling.

I leaned on the balustrade of the bridge and looked down. It had only been standing twenty years, but like Bedlam hospital, the stonework was already crumbling. I took out the pistol, wrapped once more in its silk handkerchief, felt its weight in my hand for a moment, then let it slip from my dangled fingers into the black water below. The handkerchief floated for a moment, then turned an evil brown and was caught up with some passing wreckage and was gone. I imagined the pistol lying on the bottom, its ornate metalwork turning to rust and then to nothing. It would take a long time. It would outlast the shoddy workmanship of the bridge I stood on, and the ramshackle buildings on the wharf. It would outlast me. It was hard to confront the humiliations of the morning. Canning was right, he had made me cower. I was a country lad like Will Benson, quite out of my element in London, defeated by its monstrous indifference. Instead of going back to Fleet Street, I headed on, across the bridge, into Southwark, with its squalor and luxury side by side. At home in Cornwall the inequity seemed less wrenching, less cruel. As farmers we were respectable enough, on an easy gradation somewhere between the gentry and the cottagers, fishermen and tradesmen. Would I ever have espoused the cause of liberty so loudly, if I hadn't had London's ugliness before my eyes on returning from France?

It had only brought me grief, and with this duel reminded me how far I had risen above my proper place, to mingle with the likes of Lord Grenville and Sir James. I thought about the young gentlemen in the garret of the Foreign Office, and pale Pitt over the road in Number 10. Then of Aust being derided by Canning, Will Benson his scapegoat, and Peter Williams, whom Canning would not meet on equal terms, though I would back the slave's coolness under fire as much as his own.

There was a painful tightness about my heart, and on the way home I stopped for a new bottle of cordial at the apothecary shop, with its row on row of small drawers, earthenware bottles and mysterious instruments.

'For yourself?' The apothecary pushed his mortar and pestle aside and shook his head. 'Godfrey's Cordial, now! 'Tis entirely for infants, sir, colic, and teething and what have 'ee – a quite contemptible amount of opium, barely a grain in an ounce. You should try my Kendal Black Drop. 'Tis a hearty medicine, much more suited to a man like yourself.'

I took the bottle he offered me. 'But it has the same effect?'

'Yes, sir. Very tranquillising, very soothing, and yet invigorating if taken in sufficient measure. And almost four grains of opium in every ounce.'

'It is more costly than the other, I suppose, if you recommend it?'

'Well, sir ...'

The Godfrey's tincture had proved feeble enough against despair. I had money in my pocket, and I was alive, with nothing yet resolved. 'Never mind. I'll take it.'

19

BACK IN DOWNING STREET at ten o'clock, the clerks' day was beginning as usual, just as though the world had not shifted on its axis. There were preparations in motion for yet another reception in the Foreign Office lobby that evening. General Moira was returned from Antwerp, and the army's ignominious escape must needs be celebrated as a great victory – not least to prove the *Observer*'s message entirely mistaken in painting our forces lost and helpless. Anne would also be there, and just now I needed the touch of her hand more than ever.

I took refuge in a liberal dose of the new Black Drop in my office and half-slept through the afternoon, while Aust fussed about with the Chamber Keeper, his voice coming and going like the tide as he bustled from room to room. The Black Drop was far more potent than my old Godfrey's Cordial, as the apothecary had promised, and the events of the night and morning lost their clarity, seeming like a dream to be superseded by a delightful peace of mind, and then a patchwork of memories.

First Roscoff, and myself a taut string waiting to be played, the news from Paris providing the melody. The sun hot on my back, and my uncle looking out across the rocky beach, as if, for the first time, the old man felt he owned his own country, his own town, his own future. It made tears come to my eyes, for I myself felt so powerless that I was as emotional as a babe, and wept in my stupor.

Then my sister Grace, sitting on the bench under the apple tree at home. Rain hanging in the air, and the old collie's coat damp under my hand, its head on my knee. Perfectly dark and perfectly still, and the mist on my face. 'I wonder when I shall have such peace again?'

'Whenever you come home. You'll not leave us for too long, Laurence?'

The scent of oranges, and Aglantine was there. I never knew where she hailed from, or who her father, husband or brother might be. I dreamed I asked her, 'Aglantine, do you not love the people?' and she answered, 'Oh, yes, perhaps, but only as one might love a flock of sheep.'

'You wish to protect them from wolves?'

She only looked at me, with her small pale eyes amused in her monkey face.

L IGHTS DANCED BEFORE my eyes when a knock at my door roused me and Aust came in.

'His Lordship wants you.' He was quite the greyest I had ever seen him.

I followed him into Grenville's room, still dazed. Hard to think this scowling Lord Grenville the same man who had filled my office with flowers, or to remember that I had once thought him a good-looking fellow. Now he was yellow and lined, his large brow and prominent eyes bulging.

'Canning has been here.'

'Yes, my Lord.' Of course he had. He would only wish to make my sorrows complete. I straightened my shoulders, made some attempt at dignity.

'Duelling is, as you know, of particular abhorrence to the Ministry, not to mention in contempt of the law of the land. Mr Canning tells me he refused your challenge on both these grounds.'

I think, at that moment, I might have told them everything, except that I saw clearly, even drugged and foolish as I was, that Canning had forestalled me. He had taken my reputation instead of my life and, as Anne had warned me, by doing so he had silenced me entirely.

'This puts a very different complexion on things, Mr Jago. I would dismiss you at once, if Mr Aust did not keep some lingering regard for your person. Instead, you will vacate your office and return your belongings to the garret, where you will stay until I decide what to do with you. From this moment your pay will be docked below that of the meanest clerk. And if any other document finds its way to the papers, I will hang you directly.'

Aust put a packet into my hand. 'Your pay for July,' he mumbled. 'To tide you over, my lad. He means what he says. You'll be lucky to have six shillings next month.'

I stumbled out and took my things up to the attic as well as I was able, numb as I bid farewell to the bookcase, the wine cooler, the comfortable chair. I had hardly been in the garret a half-hour when Aust came gasping up the narrow stairs, to the consternation of the young gentlemen across the landing, whose room was a disgraceful litter of empty porter bottles and peppered snuff. I had already put my head down to a message from the diplomatic bag, as an antidote to misery. Something about a shortage of tents and kettles in one of the Duke's divisions.

'A blessed bad business.' Aust sat down on an empty stool, his small feet at the end of short flabby legs suspended above the floor, and I raised my head and looked about me. The garret looked more than usually squalid after my little office downstairs. The roof was thick with cobwebs, and the grate needed polishing. 'Whatever possessed you to challenge Canning?'

I would have given anything to expose Canning for what he was. Instead, I said, 'He lied about the message, sir. He did take it from my hand, whatever he claims.'

'Well, perhaps he did, but the true culprit was swiftly found, and the whole matter explained.' Aust frowned at me. 'You have behaved most unaccountably and brought your own ruin upon your head.'

If he was only here to reproach me, I wished he would leave. But his grey old face softened. 'I cannot say I am much enamoured of Mr Canning, myself. A spiteful sort of fellow with a cutting tongue.' He took out his handkerchief and dabbed at his neck. 'But Lord Grenville is quite adamant against you. I will speak to him, but I'm afraid it will do no good.'

'Thank you, sir. I'm sorry, sir. I have been a fool.'

There was a hum of conversation in the lobby as I came down from the attic at the end of the day, and I remembered the reception for Lord Moira. I leaned over the banister and looked down. I could see Pitt below, the top of his head bowing coldly to the top of Grenville's. George Canning was there, taking a glass of sherry from one of the clerks, and Anne was standing between the Home Secretary and a junior clerk. My knees were trembling, and I clung to the handrail as I trudged down the steps. Canning was bending Aust's ear about something as I passed them at the foot of the stairs. I suppose I intended to make straight for the front door and remove my objectionable person from Grenville's sight, but I felt a violent disinclination to be recognised by Canning, and allowed myself to be funnelled away by the crowd instead, in whatever direction it wished to take me.

'What does your grandfather tell you of the battle?' the Home Secretary was asking the young clerk as I arrived beside Anne.

'Very hot, my Lord. I think he has some new scars to add to his collection.'

The Home Secretary turned as I fetched up at his elbow. 'And you are ...?'

'Laurence Jago, my Lord. Clerk to ... to Mr Aust.'

Lord Grenville was beckoning the Home Secretary. Aust had freed himself from Canning and was summoning the young clerk, and in another minute I found myself alone with Anne. The effects of the opium seemed to be intensifying instead of receding. I must have taken far too much. She was looking at me, but I was too dazed to read her expression.

'You should have called yourself "chief clerk". Or chief secretary. Remember, you are a coming man, Laurence.'

I couldn't bear to tell her that far from coming, I was back in the attic. I was saved by a sudden banging of spoon on glass, and Sir James becoming visible upon the staircase, waving his arms.

'Gentlemen – ladies! We are here to welcome our conquering hero, General Moira, on his return from the bloody fields of Flanders!' A dignified, self-conscious cheer rumbled around us, but Anne was still looking at me. I couldn't meet her eye, and kept my gaze fixed on Sir James's round face.

'Having foolishly owned to a poem on the solemn occasion, Lord Grenville has been good enough to desire a hearing. I am conscious of a certain reluctance – a sense of impropriety—'

'Get on with it, Sir James,' Lord Grenville said from behind him, and the crowd laughed. The noise buzzed in my ear, and I felt suddenly hot. I pulled at my neckcloth for air, and longed to tear off my vile wig. Sir James was still talking, apologising for his poem instead of reciting it, and the buzz of laughter was growing.

Anne was close at my side, her dress touching my leg, and I could smell her scent. 'Anne … I need to tell you …'

But Sir James had begun reciting, and someone turned to shush me. I must have been talking too loudly, and Anne's shrewd dark eyes were large as damsons in her pale face.

There was a commotion at the door, and Sir James broke off his recitation. A crowd was bursting in, with the Chamber Keeper in their wake. For a moment I thought they were coming for me. What especial crime I thought I had committed escapes me now, but emptiness sucked at my chest, leaving me light-headed and gasping. The new arrivals eddied into the crowd and the whole room surged. There was no way out. I was trapped almost under the staircase, with the whole company between me and the door. But no one was looking at me. Someone was waving a piece of paper and making straight for Pitt.

'Great news!' the fellow cried, so that everyone could hear. 'Great news, Prime Minister! The tyrant Robespierre is dead!'

There was an intake of breath, like the ebbing of waves over shingle, a moment's pause, and then a great crashing cheer. People were bowing, shaking hands and kissing all around us. The whole world was run mad, all common courtesies abandoned. 'Guillotined by his own people!' the same fellow was exclaiming. 'Champagne! Mr Pitt, I congratulate you!'

'Laurence!' Anne had my arm and was guiding me back to a knot of deserted chairs under the staircase. 'You're white as a sheet.'

I took a deep gulping breath and my head swam. The excitement had sent another pulse of opium to my brain and I found I could barely stand. 'Forgive me. It is a great event—'

Anne's fingers were cool, but her eyes were not, and shielded from view by the staircase she pulled down my face to hers and kissed me. *I should tell her*, I thought, through waves of stupefaction. *Tell her now or repent after.* But it was so long since I had touched a woman – so very long that I had loved her – and she was eager too. In the frenzy of celebration no one was looking. In the deep shadow of the stairs, I touched her hair, her face, her breasts, slipped the shawl from her shoulders and kissed the tender point where her spine disappeared under the neckline of her dress. Her eyes were dark and wide and, for the first time I could remember, there was no teasing in them.

20

I HAD BEEN A KNAVISH FOOL to kiss Anne when I knew she would turn her old face to me, aloof and unobtainable, once she heard of my demotion. Of course, that was why I'd done it, urged on by the new laudanum. When I woke the next morning, ill and ashamed, I resolved to take no more or, if that proved impossible in these troubled times, to take a good deal less. A resolution strengthened when I reflected that the headlong plunge into laudanum had also muddled my mind.

I had been so busy rushing my head into danger by challenging Canning, I had failed to ask myself any further questions. Canning might be Aglantine's accomplice, but what had possessed him to give the leaked message to the *Observer*, when he could have put it quietly into her hand, and thence to the French military without fuss? That was strange enough, but paled to nothing when you considered that the message had proved false.

Where had the story come from in the first place? I

remembered the clerk clattering down from the attic; Grenville handing me the note, his face a picture of concern. None of it made any sense. All I was sure of was that Will had been as innocent as I was, and Canning the author of all atrocities. Somehow, I would find him out, and in the meantime I would see Anne if she would receive me, and beg her mercy. There would be no calling at Aust's house now, for Mrs Aust would likely pretend the whole family was out, rather than receive me. Instead, I followed the fashionable world out to Kensington Palace the following Saturday afternoon, and loitered outside the gates, hoping to see Anne's figure emerge from Aust's house into the garden square, to paint at her easel.

Instead, she came upon me unawares, from behind, with a grave 'good day', coming out of the palace's gravel walks on the arm of George Canning himself. A good-humoured smile lingered on his face until he saw me, whereupon he recoiled as swiftly as I did, white-faced and aloof at once. A terrible sense of dread came upon me.

'Your father sent me for you,' I said to Anne, with a presence of mind that surprised even me. 'Good afternoon, Mr Canning.' I took Anne's arm and walked her away from him across the street to the square of houses and the shady lawn. Somehow, I should warn her to avoid his attentions.

'My father sent you?' She was as stiff as a starched collar, half glancing back at Canning's retreating figure.

'No, of course not.' We had paused under the plane tree. 'I need to talk to you, Anne. Will you come back to the park with me? I know I've behaved like a dog, and I can't come in. Your mother would not approve.'

She was looking at me coolly, just as I had known she would. How rarely she lost her self-possession! But we had crossed some Rubicon with that kiss under the stairs, and after a moment's hesitation she nodded, though her hand was steely on my arm as we walked back over Kensington Road and into the palace grounds once more.

Neither of us spoke for a long time. We had come as far as the Round Pond, with its collection of tame geese and squirrels, before she even looked at me. Yes, I had offended her quite as much as I had feared. If either of us was to break the silence, it seemed it would have to be me. 'You know I have always loved you, Anne.'

'So Henry told Anne Boleyn as he shooed her off to the axeman.'

'I would never harm you.'

'Except with discourtesy, and your own self-ruin.' She was taut as a wire, so that the ribbons of her bergère bonnet trembled and sunlight flickered through its straw brim across her cheek. 'I relied on you to be sensible, Laurence. With all your new advantages.'

'I see you don't require the same of George Canning. What was he doing here?'

'Attending a meeting with Mr Jay and Lord Grenville.'

The world was going on without me, and though I did not like it, I could hardly make this the grounds of a quarrel. 'Did you find *his* company sensible?'

'He made sure not to be blamed for your foolish duel. I call that prudent enough. We spoke of you.'

'Spoke of me! What did you say? You didn't tell him any of my suspicions about Will Benson?'

She didn't answer. Christ in heaven, he would likely kill me too if he knew I'd guessed his secrets. 'Anne? What did you say?'

'Only things to defend you. That you were grieving for Mr Benson, whom you had thought a pleasant fellow. That you were not quite yourself.'

We had passed the basin, and by mutual consent, we left the busy path and the formal gardens for a mown byway that led off towards the Serpentine. Anne's skirts were stuck with goose-grass and pollen, but she didn't seem to mind it. It felt like an eternity since I'd called her a milkmaid in jest under the plane tree. 'I know I have disappointed you with this business and especially with the duel. But there were good reasons.'

'Good enough to cast aside a respectable career?' She sounded disbelieving.

'It's only money, Anne. I'll find some other way to make it, if you'll wait for me.'

She stopped and confronted me. We were almost alone. 'Only money! Do you really insult me by believing that's all I want?'

'I once hoped you wanted me, too.'

'Money! Love!' She was withering. 'God damn me, Laurence, you have poor ambitions. And don't look so shocked to hear me swear. I am a widow, not a maid, and could reel you off half a dozen curses that would make your toes curl.'

'I should be delighted to hear them at a later date.'

'And don't take refuge in raillery, neither. When will you take me seriously?'

That was unfair. 'I joke because you joke. Believe me, I could be lyrical if I thought you'd let me.'

'Poetry!' She took off her bonnet and smoothed her hair as if she could rid herself of troublesome emotions in the same way. 'Life is too long for sentiment, Laurence. Don't you feel it so? And how are we to fill it? Tea parties? Embroidery?'

I opened my mouth to observe that these were not my ordinary pastimes, but then remembered her injunction against teasing. 'You paint beautifully.'

'So I should hope, with all the hours I've devoted to the

practice.' She settled her hat back on her head and struck off back towards the formal gardens. 'I married Ned, thinking the wife of a Navy officer would have something to do. Instead, I sat in lodgings in Plymouth and played loo with the other wives until I feared for his salary and my reason. Nor did I ever know a broad from a beam reach, or a mizzen from a mainstay. Politics is the only business I understand, and it's the finest, after all. Real power for a woman if she chooses wisely.'

'If that's all you desire, Mr Aust will serve your purpose as well as a husband.'

'Mr Aust is old. He begins to talk of retirement.'

I began to see her walk with Canning that afternoon in a new light. Perhaps it was she doing the wooing, with the usual single-mindedness that would brook no interference. If Canning was unmasked as a spy, and Anne his intended bride – still worse, his wife – she would be brought down with him and all her ambitions destroyed for ever. But I knew if I told her my suspicions, without revealing my own secrets to support them, it would only make her more obstinate. I admitted defeat, at least for the present, and changed the subject. 'How do the talks go on? Is Mr Jay as bad tempered as ever?'

'Bad tempered?' She turned her eyes to me with innocent puzzlement. 'I have always found him a most agreeable man.'

I MET THEODORE ON THE way out of Downing Street, and remembered that, demoted and debarred from Grenville's meetings, I hadn't seen him since our night at the brothel in Newman Street. 'Well?' I was faintly acid. 'Did you resist the fallen women's wiles?'

'Wiles?' Theodore smiled serenely from his rosy lips. 'You

quiz me, Laurence. They wept for their sins and it was very affecting.'

'I'm glad you enjoyed yourself.'

'I have learned a good deal about womanhood, too.' He held me back. 'Do you know that some of them sell their bodies for the sheer pleasure of it?'

I looked at him. 'So they say. I dare say they would not do it *gratis*.'

'Oh – yes! One of 'em offered me, I assure you.'

'An investment with an expected return, I fear.'

As I came out of the shadow of Temple Bar on my way home, and into the blinding sunlight, I bumped straight into Philpott, emerging from his shop backwards in full flow of conversation with those within. He turned and grasped me with delight. 'Laurence! Exactly the man I have been longing to see!'

I hadn't spoken to him since the previous Monday morning, and the mortifying duel. I felt ashamed of the whole affair, but he himself seemed to have forgotten about it already and was pulling my sleeve with a brawny hand. 'Come in, come in, and meet Mrs Hardy. What a woman! You will be delighted, I assure 'ee.'

I allowed myself to be propelled into the shop, where his wife and Mrs Hardy were sitting at the desk in ink-stained pinafores, bent over a scatter of printed pages. Philpott eyed them proudly. 'What assistants! The finest in London, by God, with a finer grasp of grammar than I could ever have supposed.'

Mrs Philpott looked up at me with a shade more interest than formerly. She had probably heard the whole sorry tale of my meeting with Canning. 'Mr Philpott taught English to Frenchmen when we were in Philadelphia – did he ever tell you?'

'No, indeed.'

'I sat nursing our eldest, in the corner, while he taught, and learned as much as any of his pupils.'

'And I copied out Tom's minutes for the chapel.' Mrs Hardy's voice was soft, but sensible, and Philpott goggled at her admiringly before dragging his eyes back to me.

'I find Mr Thomas Hardy has been as active in his chapel as his society, Laurence. A born organiser, like myself, no more. Never in life a revolutionary, Mrs Hardy tells me.'

'Mr Erskine must have also told you so.' Mrs Hardy was a little reproving, not quite so enamoured of Philpott as he of her, but perhaps that only added to her allure.

'So he did, so he did, and I find Mr Erskine also improves on acquaintance. But I must leave these able assistants in charge of my affairs for a week or more.' He saw my look. 'I am called home, to my father at last. He is poorly, poor fellow.'

'I'm sorry to hear it.' And sorrier still that he was leaving town. He was the best antidote to despair I had ever known, and I found I had relied on his brisk sympathy for my demotion and exhortations as to my future – perhaps another consultation concerning my suspicions – but instead I was to be left alone with my troubles. Perhaps it was for the best. There was so much I couldn't explain.

There was another letter from my mother behind the flat iron in Dora's kitchen. She was *désolée* to tell me that the family was about to be ruined. The mortgage was due, and the bank was absolutely refusing to renew it on the former easy terms. Moreover, she had just begun new works to the farmhouse on the strength of my promotion and higher salary. There were holes in the walls that must be filled before the autumn. There were bills to be paid in the town and she was even contemplating sending my sister to London, to earn something as a servant, a barmaid, or perhaps a market woman.

Crowds of country folk flocked through Temple Bar every day. Waggoners with foodstuffs for the hungry city; journeymen carrying the tools of their trade and stepping out briskly in search of work. But among them there was always a handful of girls, alone, with ribbons in their hair, carrying their worldly goods in wicker baskets. What did they imagine they would become? Servants, barmaids, market women, with nothing but their pretty faces to recommend them? I took out pen and paper and scribbled furiously. *For God's sake, keep Grace at home, and I will provide.*

But how could I? The packet of coin Aust had given me was all I had, for next month I would scarcely be able to pay my own rent. I could raise a bill with the moneylenders but, if Grenville meant what he said, my pay would barely cover the interest. And if Aust was my only ally in Whitehall, there was hardly a chance of reinstatement.

I took a small dose of Black Drop to steady my hand, opened the packet of coin, took out just enough to pay Dora and buy a chop or two, then wrapped the remainder in the letter for home.

21

WITH MY NEW POVERTY THERE were few comforting treats at Dora's table, and Philpott's shop was oddly quiet without its ebullient master. Even Mr and Mrs Benson were finally going home, for I had arranged to take them to Hyde Park to display Will's invented grave. With its cattle and quiet landscape, the park was a peaceful resting place, I had decided, for a young man from the provinces.

We left the hired hackney carriage and walked across the rough pasture towards the sunken ditch that separates the park from the grounds of Kensington Palace. On the far bank, the gardens were in full bloom, and I could see the gravelled paths where I'd walked with Anne. On our side the grass was longer, the scenery more wild. A group of twisted sallows leaned over a dried-up spring that would fill the ditch in winter and find its way to the Serpentine. It was the same spot I had fired my pistol and almost killed Peter Williams. Since then, cattle had been sheltering under the trees, and the ground was disturbed and muddy, which made my story more plausible than I'd even hoped.

'Here,' I said. 'This is where he lies.'

Mrs Benson had been quiet since we left their lodging. Now she staggered, and her husband took her arm. They moved away together, under the dappled shade of the grey-green leaves, the twisted branches groping out over their heads towards me.

'In sight of a palace!' Mrs Benson smiled up at her husband and watched as he placed a nosegay of flowers on a low-hanging branch. 'Will would have liked that.'

Mr Benson shook his head at such whimsy, then turned and gazed out across the rolling parkland. 'My dear, I would take him home, if I could. But of all possible spots, this is by no means the worst.' His measured voice broke, and he passed a hand over his eyes.

'What will you do now?' I asked.

Mr Benson shook his head. 'Return to Kent. My practice needs me, and Mrs Benson misses our other children. But you have been a good friend to us, and a good friend to Will. We'll not forget you, Mr Jago.' He took one last look at his son's supposed resting place and walked back with me towards the carriage. Mrs Benson lingered behind, her lips moving. She was talking to thin air, gazing down only on cowpats and mud, but wherever Will's soul really was, I supposed her voice would reach him well enough. And wherever he was, he was beyond caring about Canning now.

I had no such luxury. From the look in his eye when I met him in the park with Anne, Canning would do me further harm if he could. And the pain he might bring Anne was beyond enduring.

I strode back up the Strand towards home with new activity, trying to remember Canning's movements these past weeks. I had thought Aglantine had been following me that day in the art gallery, but now I wondered. When Canning disappeared into the unfrequented part of the gallery, had he been meeting her there? I had bumped into her soon after. But the place had been thronged with the fashionable world, coming and going about their business oblivious, and it seemed hopeless to find a witness among them.

'*Bonjour, bonjour*, old cock!' It was the mynah bird outside the menagerie, who then added as an afterthought, '*Vive la France!*' in a basso profundo. A keeper was sweeping down the staircase apparently preparatory to closing. I recognised him, for the same keepers were there day in day out. Chief among them was Mr Grant, of course, who had bandaged Philpott's head so obligingly after his mishap and might therefore remember me. Might remember Aglantine and Canning, too.

'All aboard, all aboard. Sixpence a go.'

I took up the bird's invitation and bounded up the stairs into the exhibition hall. They were sweeping here, too, clearing the filth left by the visiting throng, while other keepers were feeding the animals. Man and beast alike looked tired as I hurried through in search of Mr Grant. 'He's in the barn,' someone told me, jerking his head towards a door that gave on to another flight of stairs, leading down to a ramshackle outbuilding which ran along the back of the genteel shops on Exeter Exchange and the Strand.

Grant was there, engaged with a hayfork and a large bundle of straw, using the one to toss the other into the air to cover the uneven mud and cobbles of the old floor. There was a massy hayrack, made of raw new timber, affixed to the rough wall behind him, and a couple of immense half barrels, brimful with water. 'Elephants,' he said briefly, in answer to my enquiring look. 'Coming tomorrow.'

Philpott would be exceedingly vexed to miss another spectacle. Mr Grant paused, leaning on his hayfork to drink from one of the barrels, apparently waiting to hear my business. He looked like a living scarecrow, straw behind his ears and in his eyebrows. He was genial enough, and certainly not a man to be afraid of, despite his tattooed knuckles.

'Do you remember Mr Philpott's accident?'

'Remember!' He wiped the back of his hand across his mouth. 'I should say so. Could have shut down the whole concern if he'd cut up rough about it.'

'He is a very amiable man.' I hesitated. 'There was another man here that same day. A Mr Canning. Do you know him?'

'Government chap?' Grant sounded offhand and picked up his fork again.

'The very same. I'm afraid it was our fault Mr Philpott came to grief. We were arguing and upset the tiger.'

'Ah.' Mr Grant betrayed no special interest, which told me he was wary. Surely anyone would enquire how exactly two stringy government fellows had contrived to do so. Instead, he only plunged his pitchfork into the strawbale and began tossing it about again.

'There was a woman there too. Small, ugly and old. But fierce. Very fierce. Dressed in black. Does she come here often?'

'Couldn't say.'

'She is French, I think. Does she meet Canning here?'

He didn't answer, but instead threw the straw so vigorously into the air that chaff showered everywhere. 'Mr Grant?' I drew nearer to him and laid a hand on his sleeve, probably looking as hedge-pulled-backwards as he did. 'I think there may have been some mischief happening here, under your nose. If you know anything, it would be in your best interests to confess it now.'

He turned, the prongs of the fork bent towards me, though whether in attack or self-defence was hard to say. I took a step back. 'Ministry heard I go to the cobbler's society, did they? And sent you along for information? Run along, son. I'm no traitor but no snitch neither. You'll get nothing from me.'

The cobbler's society! This cast a whole new complexion on affairs. The Corresponding Society loved nothing more than the French Assembly, for all its murderous excesses. Grant could be in on everything. But just now I was only concerned with Canning. 'You misunderstand me, sir. I have no interest in your own affairs. However, Mr Canning may have acted dishonestly. Do you know anything of him? Did he ever say anything to you?'

'Only that he'd feed me to my own lions if I opened my trap.'

'He said *what*? Nonsense. He is a—'

I was going to say, 'gentleman', but Grant was definitely afraid of something more than arrest. He was prodding me inexorably towards the door and I left the word unsaid as I fled back into the Strand.

Will's landlady afraid, Grant too, Will like a ghost that last day I saw him, and Canning certainly a French spy. I remembered the look on Grant's face and I was more than ever certain that I had been about to defend a murderer. What had Anne really told Canning about me, that day in the park? It came forcibly to my mind that – with the possible exception of Mr Gibbs – no one in London cared whether I lived or died. Alone in the city, without friends, I kept to wide streets and came home early to my rooms.

FIRST THING ON MONDAY MORNING I found myself in the lobby of Erskine's legal chambers in Lincoln's Inn. The sounds of the city were faint. A thrush hopped about on the lawns outside the window, and peace hung over the cloisters, where so many men were poring over documents in search of precedents.

Erskine was the cleverest man I knew, and it had seemed to me, in the depths of the night, that he was my best hope. Alone of anyone in London, I thought I could confess to him my dealings with Aglantine. Had he not defended every so-called traitor these many years? Was he not defending the shoemaker? Once my secret was out, he might believe what Philpott had not, for there would be no need for dissembling, and he could tell me what I should do.

Erskine's voice rose loud and impatient from beyond the door. 'I tell you, the people are waking up to their power! Whether that means political organisation like Hardy's or the mob that attacked his wife, the Ministry cannot cow them into submission any longer. If you push them, they will rebel.'

Another speaker seemed stung into protest, and as he raised his voice in turn, I realised with a shock that it was Lord Grenville himself on the other side of the door. 'Mr Erskine, I admire your principles. I am glad you defend Hardy – no one will be able to call his trial unfair. But after he hangs, no mob will dare assemble for fifty years.'

Erskine again, unabashed. 'My Lord, we are both Whigs, but I gravely fear what the world will say if you destroy my client.'

'Never mind the world,' another voice put in. 'What America thinks is more germane.' It was Philpott, and I wondered what the devil he was doing there, for I had thought him still in Hampshire. 'If you murder Hardy for his opinions, my Lord, you'll murder the treaty in its cradle.'

The door opened, and I jumped to my feet as Grenville came out. In his surprise he almost bowed, before stiffening and sweeping past without a word. Then Erskine beckoned me in. Toss was asleep under the desk and the air was thick with tobacco smoke. Philpott was in the corner, examining the contents of his pockets in an absentminded sort of way, and I hesitated in the door. I had been afraid enough to lose Erskine's good opinion by confessing my secrets, but I now saw I had relied on keeping Philpott's benign regard.

'I begin to think your masters are losing their minds.' Erskine waved me to a chair and sat down across from me at the desk, as I failed to come to any conclusion and sat down obediently. 'Mr Pitt has taught himself to forget that he supported reform not ten years ago, and the whole lot of 'em seem entirely oblivious to the risks of their situation by bringing this action against Mr Hardy.'

Philpott nodded cordially to me, but he was too full of other matters to ask me how I did. His wounds were fading, though some lingering redness made him look fiercer than he really was. 'The bare-faced effrontery of the man is what sticks in my throat. We know full well the radical meetings are stuffed with Government spies, but he denies it point-blank.' He looked at me. 'What do you know of the Government case against Hardy, my boy?'

I dragged my mind away from my own concerns. 'Almost nothing, now I'm back in the garret. The Cabinet meets to discuss it, and Lord Grenville goes to the Secret Committee—'

Erskine waved his hand. 'For God's sake, Laurence, I won't have you locked up for passing secrets. But Philpott's right. We know nothing at all of the Ministry's case, except that they have not yet found any overt act against the king or his ministers, and will rely entirely on the evidence of the Government's spies in the Corresponding Society. The radical meetings are riddled with informers, of course, as Philpott says. But being paid in direct proportion to the usefulness of their reports, their testimony is worthless. Always looking for treason, naturally enough, where there may be none.'

I remembered Grant's caution. Perhaps he had taken me for a Government spy myself. 'Who are they? The informers?'

'We don't know, and must find out, so that when they testify in court, we may reveal them for what they are.'

'A strange, precarious life, I imagine,' Philpott observed.

'Not if you are spying on the Ministry's orders – quite lucrative, in fact. Nothing like spying for the French against us, for that's a narrowing ledge with only a hangman's noose at the end of it.'

'I thought you defended traitors and Jacobins,' I said faintly.

'*So-called* traitors, Laurence, hardly real ones. Mr Hardy is no more a traitor than you or I.'

I had hoped for salvation, but there was none to be had. Murder I might yet contrive to avoid, but if I confessed to Erskine, I would not cheat the gallows. It became quite clear to me that I could not speak of what I had come to say. All I could do was listen, as Philpott went off at another tangent.

'So, as I was telling 'ee, Erskine, before his Lordship burst in upon us, Lydia Hardy is exceeding well, and Mrs Philpott keeps her body fed and her mind employed admirably. And I am come to ask if Hardy has thought of speaking to the press at all.'

'He has not. The quality papers eschew him, and he eschews the gutter press. An ill-written broadside could ruin him.'

'I should like to meet him, nonetheless.'

'I cannot allow it, for the reason I have just given.'

Philpott whistled and raised his eyebrows in mock offence. 'I shall disregard the suggestion that my *Cannon* is a species of the gutter press, and will only remind 'ee that a newspaper man is a kind of historian, and his paper a record of events. Let me meet Mr Hardy and he'll get the account he deserves. I promise I shall set him down a dignified man for posterity, if that is how I find him.'

'You assume he'll hang,' Erskine said.

'I do.'

They looked at each other for a moment. Then Erskine smiled. 'Well, well, let me speak to Mr Hardy. He's seen your piece on his wife and was grateful. If he'll agree to receive you, I find I shan't object. Curiously enough, I believe you would write him up fairer than any other man I know.'

'I should hope so. I'm a man of his own class, and immune to the general infection of yours.' Philpott began to stuff his pipe with tobacco. 'You defend him in the belief he knows his place. You think he wants the vote for the same reason you do. But what if he has his own thoughts – goes his own way? Well then, you will say he is unruly, ignorant – dangerous.'

Erskine looked surprisingly unconcerned by being so maligned, and I realised he had begun to like Philpott as much as I did. 'My only chance with Hardy is to show that the desire for reform is entirely respectable, and little threat to the established order. As for the unruly poor – say what you will, but they have some very reprehensible habits. Half of 'em are entirely addicted to gin, the other half to opium. They dose up their children with both to give themselves a bit of peace, and too often send them into a sleep everlasting.'

'Reprehensible habits! And so do you, Mr Erskine. You have the reprehensible habit of gathering to yourself all the good things of this world.'

'You are converted,' I said, somewhat astonished to find that in less than a fortnight, Philpott appeared to have turned his coat quite inside out and abandoned all his old Toryism. 'You did not used to talk this way. Mr Erskine has got you hooked, and you are become even more radical than he is.'

'No such thing, I assure 'ee. It is not Mr Erskine's doing. I am my own master and make up my own mind.' Philpott frowned. 'Doubts have been growing in my mind ever since I reached England – the arrests, the Ministry's contempt for the people, those poor abandoned urchins at Temple Bar. I confess I thought they were merely London troubles, as such things have always been. But when I went down to see my father in Hampshire last week, I endured the dreadfullest shock of my life, Laurence. 'Tis that has brought me straight to Mr Erskine to offer him my help.'

Philpott came to the desk and sat down heavily beside me, studying his pipe as if for once he was lost for words. Erskine had looked up from his papers and was listening too, as the editor of the *Weekly Cannon* arranged his ideas with unusual restraint. On the whole, I was glad to be forgotten, and my presence here unquestioned.

'I have been pondering what I saw these past days, and 'tis no matter for amusement or even common-or-garden political disputation, I assure 'ee. When I left Hampshire, ten years ago, life went on as it always had, time out of mind. I always knew it was a thing to be prized, but I was young – chafed at the old ways, longed to see the world, and left without a backward glance. But I come to see that it mattered to me to remember it, as I wandered from place to place. 'Twas good to know I could go back, when I was ready, and find all unchanged.'

He put the pipe in his mouth and wagged his head dolefully.

'But when I got home last week, all had been swept away. A thousand years of custom gone in a decade. The land enclosed, the commons drained, and the cows and pigs and vegetables all gone. The men entirely dependent on their wages to buy food and drink, and my father's produce undercut by the cheap stuff the big farmers fling out with their new methods and their new machines. He cannot go on much longer, and like his men he will be landless. Within a generation I predict half the labourers will have left the countryside for these damned cities to rot neglected in the streets or labour in a damned manufactory.'

'And what has this to do with Thomas Hardy?' I could scarcely believe he could have changed his opinions so completely.

'Oh, with the link of kindness between master and man quite gone, I begin to see that Hardy is right after all. The vote is all that can give us a voice among these men of wealth and power. They treat the poor like mere machines, left to rust when no longer of use. What kind of life is that? Independence, Laurence, and a dignified freedom. That is what all men seek.'

I turned my eyes to Erskine, who was listening with sober attention. It seemed an unlikely alliance, but it was undeniable that they were delighted with each other, and were in a fair way to becoming fast friends. Erskine raised his eyebrows at me and smiled. 'Forgive us, Laurence. Was there something particular you wanted?'

I began to say no, then saw it would look strange, and told him about my mother's money troubles, the first thing that came into my head. Erskine heard me out kindly. 'Do you wish me to intercede with the mortgagee?'

'No, sir. I fear you'd never succeed.' My mother knew for a fact it was sheer prejudice against her on the grounds of her nationality – Reverend Willoughby now preached against all things French from his pulpit each Sunday.

'Did Grenville see you here?' Erskine stood up to close the window against a hot breeze that had suddenly sprung up and lifted the careful piles of paper on his desk.

'Yes, sir. He almost bowed but changed his mind.'

'I'm afraid your foolishness has displeased him more than I could have possibly imagined. Someone is spreading rumours that you are in debt, or in disgrace with some nobleman's daughter, or even that you are a common thief.'

'It's the most devilish thing I ever heard in my life,' Philpott said. 'And exactly the kind of scandal I have been complaining of for ever. A rogue, entitled by meaningless birth, to call an honest man a reprobate, and get away with it!' He re-lit his pipe at the candle and puffed vigorously, eyeing me through the blue smoke. 'I am minded to write a piece about it.'

'I wish you wouldn't.' I had no desire to be Philpott's cause, for it would inevitably raise awkward questions and discoveries that now seemed more than ever to be avoided. I could not speak of any of the dread that really gripped me, and all I could do was thank them, and take my fears and my evidence back to work.

22

IT WAS NOW LATE AUGUST, and the summer heat was more tired than fresh, more brooding than brilliant. The gentry were at their country estates, and if there was to be sickness it would come soon, breeding in the stifling air like midges in a dank ditch. As I came to Charing Cross, they were clearing up after a pillory, raking together the shit and vegetables and rocks the crowd had amused itself with throwing, pitching the blood-soaked straw into a cart. The throng had passed on, though there was a knot of bodies ahead of me on the Strand, and I hoped fervently that it was not to be another riot. I was looking about for a side street that might safely take me home, when Peter Williams appeared at my shoulder. 'Thought you were dead, for the longest time,' he said, with his usual abruptness. 'Thought Canning had got you for sure, when I didn't see your face at the talks.'

'Well …' I gesticulated about at the rising chaos. 'Here I am.'

He didn't express any particular joy at my continued existence. 'Wished I'd asked you for those green glasses,' he said.

'When I thought you was dead.'

'I should have bequeathed 'em, if you'd asked me.' I took them off and proffered them for his perusal, but he didn't take them, likely having had second thoughts, perhaps reflecting he'd look as outlandish in them as I did.

Ahead, the traffic had ground to a standstill. But I now saw that the crowd was, in fact, excessively cheerful, and my fears began to subside. For his own part, Peter Williams was scanning the crowd with a look of mere irritation.

'You're not in search of Theodore again? What has he done now?'

'What *ain't* he done?' Theodore was one of the few topics that could disturb his equanimity.

'Is he still preaching?'

'You'd hope.'

I stopped and looked at him, while people cursed and walked around us. 'He's not …?'

'Damned if I know. But if he is, I'll be blamed.'

'But that's not fair.' I remembered his hat, his hourly rate, and Jay's methods of reprimand. 'Jay won't penalise you further, I hope?'

'He made me an offer.' We had begun walking again, Peter Williams's eye ever busy over the gathering bodies ahead. 'If I can keep Theodore in check, he'll count it a blessing and take a full year off my service.'

'And if not?'

He looked at me expressively, and I remembered with some guilt that I had already added a month to his servitude. 'Well,' I said, 'Mr Philpott gave me the same task weeks ago. He fears for the treaty if Theodore makes a fool of us all. Perhaps I'll make amends for the hat if I keep my eye out for him. Is he here, do you think?'

'I saw him back in Whitehall. Lost track of him at the pillory.' He bowed. 'I'll search up among the bawds in Covent Garden, but if you see him, I'd take it as a kindness if you'd send him home.'

It was only a minute after he vanished into the swelling crowd that I came upon his quarry myself. Theodore had got himself wedged between the threatening hindquarters of an anxious horse and a costermonger's barrow, and I extricated him with some difficulty. I had to shout above the ruckus. 'What's going on, do you know?'

'Something about the menagerie.' He wiped the sweat from his eyes and bowed gratefully. 'That's what I heard, anyway. Do you think something's escaped?'

This did not seem a comforting thought, and now I looked about me it seemed that every animal on the street was restive. But as we drew nearer, we saw that the street was full of wagons, and the whole concern embarked upon its advertised summer tour. The rhinoceros was dangling in a harness from the upstairs window, apparently insensible, and behind it Philpott's face could clearly be seen, lit up with glee like a gargoyle. 'Done it a dozen times, my dear fellow,' he was booming to someone behind him. Probably Mr Grant, and I felt a twinge of something between regret and irritation that he was taking himself and his knowledge beyond my reach. 'I have kept cows, man and boy, and rescued them from pits and lakes often and often in this way.' His unseen interlocutor apparently asked something else, for Philpott began to chuckle. 'Alcohol, my dear sir, only alcohol in copious quantity.' A reply from within. 'Yes, drunk, sir, quite drunk. Drunk as a lord.'

The unconscious creature hit the ground with a thud, just as we drew level, and a crowd of workmen gathered round it in apparent discussion as to how to hoist it into the waiting open-sided wagon. Across the street was another waiting cart, the horses in its shafts nervous and sweating. 'Lions,' somebody said. 'There's lions in that one. Been there since last midnight. Didn't dare bring 'em out in the daytime.' A roar from the wagon confirmed this story. 'Terrible hungry and thirsty, I don't doubt, poor critters,' a woman said sorrowfully, as we squeezed on past the crowd, who were now looking back up eagerly at the windows, perhaps hoping to see the elephants dangle out in the same manner as the rhinoceros. We could still hear Philpott.

'Fine work! I shall write you up a splendid piece, sir. Where is your first stop again? Ah, yes, Northampton. Yes, I shall remember. What a spectacle! Words might fail to do it justice, but fortunately I have a prodigious turn for the sublime.'

'What a singular fellow he is,' Theodore observed, as the crowd thinned between the Royal Academy and Temple Bar but began to thicken again as we came into Fleet Street. The whole world seemed to be taking its recreation, and here the promised 'Death of Robespierre' had opened its doors to the public at Mrs Clarke's waxworks, amid an eager crowd of journeymen, labourers and whores, and a good deal of hilarity.

'Shot his own face off!' someone was bellowing as we came up. 'Wait till tha' sees the blood!'

We exchanged a look, and by common accord turned inside the shadowy premises. There was a huddle of admirers four deep around the new exhibit, so we lingered by the door and examined Mrs Clarke's idea of the Mutiny on the *Bounty*. A noble-looking Captain Bligh rowed away from the desert island, while Fletcher Christian and a band of Tahitians stood among palm trees, blowing poisoned darts in his direction from elaborate and impractical-looking native weapons. From what I remembered reading in the papers, this seemed inaccurate on a number of levels and boded ill for her imagination of the guillotine.

Praying, for once, did not seem to be on the boy's mind as he turned to me with a pallor I had attributed to the proximity of the horse's hindquarters but now saw was more profound.

'That bawdy house in Newman Street?' he ventured, after a pregnant pause. Christ Almighty – was I to be called upon to explain the causes, progress and treatment of gonorrhoea? It wasn't that bad. Theodore's mobile face was contorting itself with the effort of confession. 'Nothing at all improper occurred, I assure you. We discussed only religion until dawn.'

But there was obviously more to the tale than that, and I tried to help him, for Peter Williams's sake. 'But then ...?'

'I think I may have been foolish.'

'Are you sure you want to tell me? You may regret it later, you know.'

A great hullaballoo broke out behind us around the guillotine. Some wag had got hold of Robespierre's head and was running about with it by the hair, acting the executioner. The customers were laughing, while Mrs Clarke herself emerged from her private quarters to remonstrate.

'Let me begin for you,' I said, taking pity on him after all. 'You returned another night, and another, and are now quite enamoured of one of the girls you've been preaching to.'

'Yes.' Theodore looked at me sideways, under his lashes.

'Perhaps, I surmise, the one that offered you a tumble *gratis*, and therefore changed your opinion of womankind?'

He coloured. 'She's a good girl and I never touched her.' There was something galling in his prudery, as he looked at the comely, naked Tahitian women, hanging about the necks of the mutineers.

'The root of all evil?' I suggested, thinking I could read his mind.

He only turned his eyes away, as if afraid the figures would distract him with their loveliness. 'Do you think the sailors would have mutinied without them?'

'Yes, of course, for their freedom, surely? Bligh was a tartar, by all accounts.'

'Freedom!' Theodore looked perplexed.

'You remember. Life, liberty and the pursuit of happiness. You, of all people, should understand that.' But then I remembered Peter Williams; remembered that Theodore came from a world where the idea was, despite everything, problematic. 'Thomas Hardy does not risk his neck for anything less. Can you imagine how it feels to have no liberty? To wonder where your next meal is coming from? And, all the while, to see men like us, well fed and content? How else are they to get a voice, but by rebellion?' I had wandered rather far from Tahiti or Newman Street, I own, and it was stretching a point in my current pecuniary distress to say I was 'well fed'.

Theodore sighed. I had also wandered rather far from his own concerns. 'Well, I shall have to leave off, in any case, for I begin to fear something is amiss. There is another lady always in evidence. I used a false name, you recollect, but I begin to think she knows me – even asks questions in a roundabout way, about my father's work.'

'You think she's a spy?'

'I begin to think so and am very much afraid. What shall I do?'

'I'd be inclined to keep your mouth shut. Leave well alone, keep away, and hope the thing blows over.'

'You don't think I should tell my father?' He looked at me earnestly. 'In honour, I ought to do it, you know.'

Again, I thought of Peter Williams, and reflected that Theodore's confessions would do the slave no good at all. 'Oh – honour! If you never go back, there's no fear of your doing further damage, and what's done is done.'

We finally had a sight of the new exhibit, for while we had been speaking the revellers had been summarily ejected from the building and told not to return. We penetrated further into the gloom, where Theodore looked down pensively at Robespierre's shattered face, now restored to its proper place in the basket. 'Never go back? Well, never mind. I must bear it somehow.'

'I'd take it as a kindness if you'd bear it in your own lodging. Poor Peter Williams is in search of you at your father's bidding, and he has no choice in the matter.'

'Peet? Looking for me?' He wilted. 'Well, I'll go home then, or he'll only complain to my father. I am ill used, Laurence, I assure you.' He trudged out, and I went back for another look at the guillotine, the room now entirely deserted. It was a relief to be alone after the boy's idiot foolishness.

How lifelike the figures seemed, and how red and glistening the blood! There was an old crone sitting by the steps to the guillotine, and I almost thought she moved as I turned my head. Ridiculous. The uncanny reality of the figures is part of their appeal and, at one time or another, everyone has mistaken them for their human attendants. But I couldn't help another look, a step closer. She was dressed in black, of course she was, and was there a scent of—

'Good afternoon, Laurence.'

'Good God!' I had put out a hand to touch her shoulder and now snatched it back. She smiled, more amused than I had ever seen her. 'Aglantine, how long have you been there?'

She didn't answer. The dreadful smile faded, and she sighed

as she looked at Robespierre's cat-like features. I felt constrained to help her to her feet as I recovered from my shock. 'Poor Max.'

'What are you doing here?' Her ability to follow me, to find me out, was disquieting, but in fact I was glad, for despite everything she was the only person I could talk to. I realised now she was the only person who might help me, or have answers to the questions that had been revolving in my mind. She was moving towards the door and I found myself following. 'Is George Canning your other spy in Whitehall?'

She stopped and turned to me, but didn't deny it, and I flushed. 'Between you, you have ruined me. My mother is in trouble, and I can't help her.'

'Ah yes, your mother, in Cornwall – a Frenchwoman, and the papers tell us all Frenchwomen are spies, in receipt of French gold.'

'Just at present I sincerely wish she was.' We paused by the Crowned Heads of England, who looked down at us from their platform with thoughtful eyes. 'I suppose it was Canning who gave you the leaked message and started the whole business. But I cannot understand why either of you would give it to the *Observer*. I know for certain it was not the poor Downing Street clerk.' What I had learned at the *Observer* offices exonerated Will of that charge, but I was also sure he had somehow discovered Canning's secret and was now dead. I was about to say something more, but found I was afraid after all. I always thought of Aglantine as small – old – a woman – but in the flesh she still scared me.

Her pursed mouth twisted. 'There are stupid men in Paris as well as London, Laurence. I give them information. How they act on it is their own affair.'

'But you call it stupid.'

I hardly expected her to explain herself to me, but for once she did. There was that look of defeat again, and, of course, I thought, now Robespierre was dead her circumstances might well be precarious. 'Our forces went to Ostend and your royal Duke and his Irish saviour slipped by to Antwerp. Paris was most displeased and took its foolish revenge.'

If there had not been a sudden screaming from the street outside, I think I might have understood a great deal at that moment, and saved myself and other men much grief. But there was a great roar of excitement coming up through Temple Bar like a wave, and we hurried back out into the humid heat, past the *Bounty* mutineers. There was a fierce human gladness in Fletcher Christian's lifelike eye as he raised the blowpipe to his waxy lips.

23

WHEN WE TRACED THE hullaballoo back up the Strand to the menagerie, Philpott was flat out on his back in a state of quivering prostration, with a crowd gathered around him. A hapless keeper, I soon gathered, with Philpott in cheerful attendance, had been sent out to feed the suffering caged lions in their over-heated wagon.

There was no practicable way in which to safely open the grating, so the keeper had begun to introduce morsels of meat through the slats of the cart, while Philpott had gone around to examine the creatures through the back door, which had a six-inch gap at top and bottom. As the keeper introduced fresh meat in at one end, the lions took it upon themselves to pass out the remains of their previous meal through the opening at Philpott's feet. First to emerge was a mangled leg bone of a species disturbingly familiar. The next, a gnarled forefinger, tattooed with the letter H.

'Poor fellow.' Philpott was allowing himself to be supported to a sitting position by the solicitous crowd. 'Poor fellow. He mended my head, you know. That finger.' He shuddered. 'In my very hair, not three weeks since.' At this juncture he caught sight of me and held out his arms plaintively. 'Laurence! What horror! I have just had a terrible shock, I assure 'ee.'

Contrary to my previous assumptions, I now saw he would have been a hopeless companion in the anatomist's laboratory. A woman was soothing his brow, while another had just appeared with a jug of fortifying ale. Worse, much worse, remained in the wagon, people were saying behind us. It could only be hoped that the lions themselves would, with tactful efficiency, clear up the nocturnal tragedy they had enacted.

'It's Mr Grant?' I already knew the answer to that. *He'd feed me to my own lions if I opened my trap*. I hadn't expected Canning to be so literal.

'Of course it is! God damn me, Laurence, you're very cool. A good deal heartlesser than I took 'ee for.'

Heartless! On the contrary, I felt sick. Had Canning found out I'd questioned the man and carried out his threat so ruthlessly? And if he would do this to a man on so little grounds, what might he do to me? There was a keeper, wilting by the steps to the menagerie, and I hastened over to question him. 'Does anyone know how it happened?'

The keeper straightened and blew his nose on the rag he apparently called a handkerchief. He hadn't been there himself, when the lions were loaded, but no one had seen Mr Grant since. In fact, there was some doubt among the keepers as to whether Mr Grant had even been there when the beasts were brought out. He'd been off at some meeting in Shoreditch.

'Meeting?'

The keeper looked shifty. 'He had other fish to fry, sir, in his spare time.'

'The Corresponding Society?' I waved a dismissive hand at his cautious look. 'Don't fear. He told me about it himself.'

'Well then, yes, sir. He was very hot for the vote, and a great enemy of the press gang from his Navy days. There was a meeting last night.'

'A strange going-on for the head keeper to miss such a dangerous business as moving a pack of lions.'

'Pride, sir. We call it a pride.' He blew his nose again. 'There was some bad trouble, at the Society, he said. But it seems like they're always fighting among themselves. He promised to come back as soon as he could.'

'What were they fighting about?'

He spread his hands. 'Couldn't say. He belonged to Mr Hardy's branch, and since the poor devil was arrested they're always in some ferment. But there was a fellow had been bothering him especial there.'

Was it possible that Canning went to the radical meetings in disguise? At this moment he seemed capable of anything. Where had he been last night, and how could I possibly find out? If I went to the meeting in Shoreditch I could question the other members – even catch Canning red-handed. But Erskine had said the meetings were riddled with Ministry informers, and it would look bad in Downing Street if my name was mentioned. It would only give Lord Grenville cause to doubt me again, and make my own precarious position even more perilous.

ANOTHER LETTER BEHIND the flat iron, and although it was not from my mother, it was still news I would rather not have received. Or at least, that was my first thought.

My Dear Jago,

After so many weeks, Mrs Benson was prostrated yesterday by the receipt of a letter from Will. How could she not wonder – hope – fall into a sudden fainting fit? But in fact, it was merely the fault of the post office, for of course the letter was sent before his death, and only now finds its way to Kent due to the dilatoriness of the times.

I am afraid it casts more light on Will's despair, and that too has grieved his mother beyond words. He writes wildly. People following him about the streets. He blames Mr Canning for some unspecified fault and calls him a lying devil – seems quite terrified of Canning, in fact. No mention of the leaked note, of course, but I do not think he was in a state of mind for treason. I very much fear his reason was deranged – he was falling into madness – and that is why he took his own life.

Well, at least the matter is closed, as much as it ever can be. We shall always remember your kind attentions in the time of our grief.

Mr William Benson, Snr.

Yes, if my first thought was sorrow, my second was a sudden rising hope. Mr Benson might think the matter closed, but in fact his letter opened it up again. At last, I held something in my hand that was evidence independent of my own, forbidden knowledge.

I went back to Erskine, with new determination, to find Philpott once more ensconced in his office amid an explosion of law books and papers in precarious piles. I laid the letter before Erskine and told my tale of Brookes' laboratory, Mr Grant's hints about Canning, that day when I quizzed him in the elephant house, and the dreadful death that had since overtaken him.

'I came to tell you this before,' I said, 'but then I had only conjecture. Mr Canning blaming others for his own fault, Will Benson's head smashed in – I feared my own resentment made me suspicious. But see! Will's father now points a finger at Canning. And poor Mr Grant told me Canning had threatened him, too.'

Erskine was frowning, as he cast his eye over Mr Benson's note and then passed it to Philpott. 'I'm afraid I don't rightly follow your meaning, Laurence. You don't mean to say you think Canning bashed his clerk's head in and then hung him from a beam in his room? That he threw the burly Mr Grant into a den of lions with his own hand?'

I saw Canning in my mind's eye, in his usual immaculate clothes and with his usual laconic air.

'He might have *hounded* the poor lad to death,' Philpott said. 'I have no liking for Mr Canning and can well believe he would bully a poor lad into suicide. But that poor devil in the wagon ...' He shuddered so hard his cheeks quivered. 'That was a terrible misadventure, I assure 'ee. I have a whole column about it in the *Cannon*.'

'You misunderstand,' I said, but already I was losing hope. Unless they knew him a spy, as I did, why should they believe me? 'Will Benson was no suicide at all. Grant's death was no misadventure.'

Erskine frowned. 'Believe me, Laurence, I like Mr Canning as little as you do, but I'm afraid he is merely repellent in his manners, not his actions. Anyone less like a murderer I confess I have never seen in all my time in the law.' He stood up.

'You have taken your disgrace at his hands too much to heart. Pull yourself together. I have no doubt you'll work your way back up the ladder through your own native wits. But you look tired and thin, my boy. Does anything else ail you?'

'Oh.' Coming here had been a terrible mistake, and I only wanted to take myself away again. 'I'm a little hungry, that's all. I'm penniless at present, having sent my mother all my wages for July. But I shall soon have whatever stipend they see fit to bestow on me for August. I dare say it will be small enough, being such a disgrace to the Department.'

Philpott perked up at my bitterness, charmed to have a practical outlet for his benevolent impulses. 'Then come home with me, my boy, and Nancy will feed you. She delights in company.'

Erskine was watching me thoughtfully. 'As it happens, I can give you a few small coins if you really need them. Philpott and I were just discussing a use we might have for you. It might not sit well with your employers, but as they have already washed their hands of you, it hardly signifies.'

'You might positively enjoy the chance to put one in their eye,' Philpott added helpfully, and took up his hat. 'Come home with me, and I shall tell 'ee everything over a good meal.'

M RS PHILPOTT SUMMONED US to the table in quite the same tone of voice I had often heard her address the pig. She also appeared to have taken Mrs Hardy under her wing, for the poor woman sat quietly at the other end of the table, helping young Margaret arrange her pinafore, while Philpott presided over the family board.

'Take it, boy, take it,' he threatened, forcing a desiccated chicken wing on me.

Mrs Philpott looked displeased. 'William, don't browbeat the lad. I dare say he is used to finer fare than this.'

This was undoubtedly true, and I pitied her children, who were looking at the stew of some highly doubtful provenance with quiet dismay. For my own part I found I was not hungry enough to do more than toy with the gristly slime, and hide the chicken of inedible toughness beneath it. I settled to nibbling at a piece of bread, while the women nattered at the other end of the table, and Philpott talked and smoked and wisely seemed to eat nothing at all.

'Tell me more about your mother's troubles, will 'ee?'

I had had another letter that morning. 'Not much to tell. The bank has raised its rates well above five percents on the renewal of the mortgage, they are mired in building works, and they need rain. The barley's wilting in the fields.'

Philpott nodded. 'Aye, aye. And when the rain does come, it'll come with a vengeance, I dare say, and finish the job entirely. There'll be much hunger, many deaths, and more anger before the winter's out.' He piled more stew on my plate. 'But it passes my understanding why a Cornish farmer should need a mortgage at all. God damn me, my father eats off the same wooden plates his father left to him, and drinks from the same old tankard.' He sighed, perhaps remembering his visit to Hampshire. 'But how many folks keep to the old ways, in these changing times?'

Certainly not my own father. I myself was the living embodiment of his ambitions, and he had desired to better us in many other ways. I remember the commotion as my sister's new piano came off the wagon, my mother watching from the kitchen door, her face rather drawn. 'I am wishing that thing at the devil,' I remember she said, as we watched my brothers sweating and straining. They were half-grown boys, all elbows and knees. 'James will infallibly break his foot for he's as clumsy as an old sow and has dropped his corner three times already.'

But she warmed to the instrument, as Grace slowly learned. That last Christmas of '90, I had come in from visiting Reverend Willoughby to find my sister plinking away in the dusk. I sat down in my father's armchair, listening to her tentative notes, watching her pink face furrowed with concentration as she picked out the melody to 'Sweet Nightingale'. How dearly I loved her! It broke my heart to imagine Grace poor and destitute at home; it would have killed me to think her in Newman Street or Covent Garden.

'Your mother never remarried, I think you said, though tolerably young when widowed?'

I came back to the present to find Philpott examining me. 'No, sir.'

'A decent-looking woman too, if you are her son, and a fine farm to boot. Was she not besieged by suitors?'

She might have been if her foreignness hadn't deterred them.

'And a falling-out with the bank. It's an unaccountable business.'

I didn't much like this curiosity. 'She has a home of her own, and I dare say she likes her independence. My father was a difficult man, and she'll not quickly choose to put her neck under the yoke again.'

'You resemble her, I think.'

'Do I?' I thought of her dark Gallic face, so like my own.

'A well-placed request to empty the chamber pot answers admirably, I find,' Mrs Philpott was telling Mrs Hardy at the other end of the table, as the poor woman played with Margaret's hair ribbon and then, unconsciously caressed her own belly. 'It is hard for a man to remain enflamed when confronted with the contents of the piss pot.'

Philpott was not listening to this domestic wisdom. 'Yes, you have an independent streak, my boy,' he was saying in my other ear. 'Tramping the streets dressed like a peasant, choosing yourself a rascally dog for company.' His purple countenance turned rosy pink and broke into an approving smile. 'You're just like me.'

He stood up and began to pace as the women stacked the dishes. 'Yes, much like me in many ways, Laurence, with the inestimable advantage of anonymity in your old rags. You mind those spies we spoke of, in the Corresponding Society meetings? Well, Erskine thinks we must find 'em out. We've still no inkling of the Government's case, though we may learn something of their methods next week, with the trial of the Scottish traitor.'

'Sir?'

Philpott wagged his face at me. 'For God's sake, you must have read about Robert Watt in Edinburgh, to be tried for insurrection and treason? The papers are full of nothing else.' I'd seen something, but it had only buzzed in the background of my affairs. 'Mind 'ee, Robert Watt is a different kind of man to Hardy. Was a government spy himself, like these devils we'd have you find. Sacked by the Ministry, he turned a real revolutionary in revenge. Planned to seize Edinburgh with fire and arms ...'

I stopped listening to Philpott's observations on the Scottish case, for I realised he meant to send me to Mr Grant's own branch meeting in Shoreditch to look for government spies. If I could claim Erskine had sent me, I need not fear to go. The evidence I had just laid before Philpott and Erskine had been too thin to convince them that Will's fears had been well-founded, but if I could find proof among the radicals that Canning had murdered Grant, then justice might still be done.

I smiled up at Philpott as he produced a handful of coins and pressed them into my palm. 'Well then, my boy, will you go? See what you can find out? All we need are the informers' names.'

24

THE DARK-PANELLED TAPROOM in the Fountain was a fug of smoke, and smelled of stale beer, as the members of the Corresponding Society arrived from their various labours about the city. There were shop men in cheap suits, shoemakers wearing leather aprons, a tanner from Spitalfields, orange from piss. I was wearing my own dark hair unpowdered and a coarse linen shirt. My fustian jacket hung over the back of my chair and I sucked on a clay pipe. In the mirror hanging over the fireplace I looked just like my father. Mr Gibbs lay at my feet, adding to the agricultural effect, his eyes fixed on the tanner who was eating a mutton chop. To my disappointment – or perhaps relief – there was no sign of Canning, but if I kept my ears open I might still learn something useful.

The meeting was more like a clerks' debating society than a revolutionary conspiracy, an impression confirmed when a new fellow staggered in as the minutes were being read. He was in drink and boastful, eager to see the King's head on a spike on Temple Bar. The others shouted him down, to the enormous delight of Mr Gibbs, and in the end he was led out into the street and left there.

'Let us remember, citizens, we are a respectable body of men,' the chairman said as they returned, and Mr Gibbs came back to me with an insolent air of independence. 'And that fellow is no friend to our cause, whatever use he may be to the Government. Argument and persuasion are our weapons, not violence.' He looked about him. 'Now, citizens, to business. Shall we have a moment's silence for our poor Citizen Grant?'

We stood, caps in hand, for a sober spell. There were no prayers for, after some squabbling as to Grant's religious preferences, it seemed that he had been a sceptic. After we sat down again, the chairman called on a Mr Higgins to report what was known as to the man's death.

Higgins was a middle-aged, thickset man. 'He was here, citizens, the previous evening. Had a letter he showed me. Some Ministry chap he'd met at the menagerie had turned out to be sympathetic to the French, and to our cause. Said the letter was from him. Wanted to meet up at midnight by Blackfriars Bridge.'

There was a shifting, a low whistle. 'And did he plan to go?' someone asked.

'He wasn't sure. Seemed afeared.' Higgins hesitated a moment, then produced a paper from his pocket. 'He gave me the letter. Said if aught happened to him, it would be evidence.'

'Evidence!' I couldn't keep quiet. 'Then why haven't you produced it to the Runners?'

A low laugh rippled around the room.

'You're new to this game, I see, citizen. Who's not for us is against us, and especially the Runners.'

His neighbour was beckoning impatiently for the paper

and it passed round the room from hand to hand. Some could not read and only nodded sagely before passing it on, others pored over it laboriously. When it came to my turn, I nearly spat my beer over the sticky floor. It was the same hand as had written the false news of the British army's plight in the message that Grenville had given me all those weeks ago. A message purportedly come from one of our informers in France. A message, Anne had since told me, they had been unable to trace back to its source.

This new letter had come to Grant from *some Ministry chap he'd met at the menagerie.* If the handwriting belonged to Canning, the message and all its evils had been conceived in Downing Street and birthed by Canning's own hand at the *Observer.* No wonder they had failed to trace the source back to France. But I couldn't imagine what it meant. Why would Canning start a rumour of British peril in Europe?

There must be more to all this I couldn't see. At present it was a fragment of a picture, a shard of broken glass reflecting only my own understanding back at me. My mind was racing, so that I hardly listened as the letter went back into Higgins's pocket and the meeting moved on.

'Now, as to Citizen Hardy, and the efforts for his comfort. Higgins?'

'We've collected a goodly sum this week, and sent in meat and bread, and a new shirt.'

'Anything for his wife?'

'Some fruit, for she's near her time and craving.' Higgins shifted uneasily in his chair. 'But there's a difficulty, citizens, with Upton.'

It would have been hard to follow even if I had been listening with full attention. A fellow named Upton was on the committee to aid Hardy, but had some scandal against his name, involving old women and their wills, along with a dubious insurance claim that might injure Hardy's reputation if Upton figured too largely in the effort to succour him. The Chairman shook his head. 'We must be careful, citizens. The Ministry will use anything against Hardy they can find. Perhaps you had better write to Upton, Higgins, and ask him to stand down.'

The meeting went on after that, very much like a night in the Angel at home, where farm labourers gathered every evening after work. Jokes and laughter. Women, the weather, the price of bread. What else would working men talk of, anywhere in England? I had held myself aloof from common men at home, conscious I was on the rise, but I understood men like these far more than I would ever fathom Sir James or Lord Grenville. And yet, haunted by my own concerns, I was not one of them either. Instead, as I look back now, I see these men – even Thomas Hardy and his wife – were not real to me. They moved past me without substance, like the crude parade of images in a magic lantern show at Helston Fair, while my mind went back to the elder Mr Benson's letter, and Erskine's disbelief that Canning could ever have been involved. Like no murderer he had ever seen, he had said, and indeed I myself had first imagined a paid shabby figure or two. But Will's fears and Grant's death had changed my mind. Both had feared Canning. Will had heard footsteps behind him in the street. I now believed without a shadow of a doubt that Grant had heard them too, before he was thrust into the lions' wagon by an unseen hand.

After the meeting I held Higgins back. He looked at me suspiciously, and I remembered again that the meeting was riddled with informers. I hadn't identified a single one.

'That letter. Did Grant say it definitely came from the spy he'd spoken of?'

'He said so.'

'Did the fellow ever come here? To this meeting?'

'Grant asked him once. But the man feared exposure.'

Of course he did. 'Why did Grant deal with him at all?'

'Because the fellow supported the French, as we all do. Because an ally in the Ministry might be a help to us – to Hardy, too. We live precarious lives, citizen.'

'I am a lawyer's clerk.' It was almost true. 'I know Mr Erskine, who defends Hardy. The letter might be useful to him.'

If I had the letter, it would be another piece of proof to show Erskine and Philpott. Another proof that did not rely on betraying my own former misdeeds.

But Higgins looked doubtful, and I remembered he didn't know me. Here, at the Corresponding Society, no less than in Downing Street, every man might be a friend or a deadly foe.

WHEN I CAME INTO Sir James's room a couple of days later with a bundle of transcriptions, Mr Jay was engaged with Lord Grenville in his office beyond the tapestry and I could hear the quiet hum of voices. Theodore Jay would be there, supposedly taking notes but no doubt wild-haired and dreamy-eyed, absorbed instead by his own peculiar fancies. Perhaps soon I would be with them too. I hadn't yet found a specimen of Canning's handwriting, but I felt more hopeful than I had for weeks. It seemed only a matter of time until I would lay the proof of Canning's betrayal before them all and see them draw the right conclusions.

'His Majesty is full of some foolish plan to win the envoy's favour,' Sir James was telling Aust as he beckoned me in, and I laid the papers on the desk. 'American or no, the King believes it quite within his powers to reward Mr Jay for a successful outcome with a baronetage.'

'Bless me, that would look like nothing so much as a bribe.'

'Precisely, Mr Aust.'

'Do we know what exactly is in the King's mind?'

'He has had the happy thought to bestow the honour only on the conclusion of an agreement, which makes it worse, of course. A bribe and a reward all at once. It would kill any treaty stone dead in their Congress – if the talks ever get that far.'

'Has Lord Grenville explained …?'

'At some length.'

'He has represented to his Majesty the consequences should the idea get out?'

'Yes, yes. Lord Grenville believes he got through at last. The King will keep the royal mouth shut, at least for now.'

I could tell Mr Aust did not quite like this levity at the King's expense. He jumped up to run his finger along the frame of the royal portrait which hung over the desk. There was no dust, and he nodded to himself. The Necessary Woman, at least, had shown due deference to his Majesty.

The voices in Lord Grenville's room rose for a moment as I turned to go. The creaking of the door half hid the words, but I could swear I heard Grenville cry out, 'A peerage of the realm, God damn me!'

And then someone laughed.

I had heard Lord Grenville laugh often enough. Had heard Theodore Jay laugh once or twice, when he was not being too pious. This joyful peal belonged to neither of them. I looked from Aust to Sir James, but they seemed quite oblivious, engaged in discussion again, and myself quite forgot as I lingered shamelessly to listen.

'That new clerk of Canning's is an idiot and a fool. Doesn't know when he's wanted, or when he's dismissed. I shall be glad when Canning comes back to town.'

'Mr Canning is away?'

They remembered I was there, and Sir James wasn't pleased. 'He has been down in the country this last fortnight, I gather, seeing his mother. But I advise you to put him from your mind, Mr Jago. This regrettable enmity is best forgot for your own sake.'

Canning had been missing two weeks! It could be either a certain alibi against any part in Grant's death or proof positive he had been the murderer and had taken steps to disguise his presence in London at the time. Only proof that the note sent to Grant had been his would show which of these was true, and that, at least, seemed possible, for memoranda flew about Downing Street every day, and surely one written in his hand would be easy to find.

I loitered on the landing, lost in thought, looking down on the alley into Fludyer Street through the arched window. It was littered with cherry stones tossed out from the clerks' window, and clouds of late-summer wasps were buzzing about the oozing piles in the shade. Grenville's door opened behind me. Theodore came out first, his colour rising in his cheeks as he smiled at me. Behind him, Jay senior and Grenville were bowing to each other with elaborate coldness.

'Mr Jay, I regret this hostility,' Grenville said. 'Believe me, the whole phalanx of Government wishes you well.'

John Jay only frowned icily. 'And I regret your arrogance, my Lord. I will let it be known at home that you rebuff me at every turn.'

No one else came out to account for the good-humoured laugh I had heard, and now, despite all appearances to the contrary, I remembered Anne looking at me with mild surprise that day in Kensington Palace gardens. *I have always found Mr Jay a most agreeable man.*

25

IT WAS THE MIDDLE OF September, but every day the heat seemed to get worse. Coming along Piccadilly, I found Philpott in negotiation with an impressive woman with strong arms and a large straw hat, a fruit seller, haggling over the entire contents of her basket. In fact, he wanted the basket, too. I came up to his elbow and watched the proceeding develop, until an arrangement was reached agreeable to both parties. The sun beat down upon the three of us. Sweat trickled down the fruit seller's cheek like a tear.

Philpott saw my questioning look as he hung the heavy basket over his arm and set off along the street. 'Mrs Hardy has been taken ill, poor woman. Nancy is with her, at her lodging, and has sent me out for fruit.'

'Ill?' She had seemed well enough when I saw her that day at Philpott's table. 'What is it? A sudden sickness or the child?'

'Both, I fear. She has not felt it move these past three days, and there is a feverish pallor about her face.'

'When is her time to be delivered?'

'Not long, I believe. But if the child is already dead ...'

'God help her. Can she not get it out?'

'How do you propose she do it? Charm it out like a snake? Cut her belly open?' He frowned as we came up to the charred remains of the cobbler's shop. It seemed Mrs Hardy was lodging with a neighbour, for he rapped at another door. 'Poor woman, poor woman. Nancy tells me that every child she has borne has died at birth or in early infancy.' I remembered Mrs Hardy stroking Margaret's hair, and then her own belly. 'A healthy child would comfort her – and her husband – in their troubles. By God, I hope she mends, and the child kicks.'

When we came in, Mrs Hardy was sitting up in a basket chair by the dirty window, but she looked poorly, and Mrs Philpott hastened over to take the basket from Philpott's arm. 'She should be in her bed,' she said quietly to her husband. 'But I think she fears she won't leave it again. I'd take her home, but there's no time. The pains are coming, which may prove a mercy.'

Mrs Hardy was watching, though I didn't think she had heard. She smiled faintly and held out her hands to us. 'Lord, Mr Philpott, what have you done? Such profligacy!'

'Nonsense, nonsense,' Philpott said, sitting himself down beside her with a handful of berries for himself. 'It's a token of esteem, ma'am, for you and your husband. You must get well, you know, for he needs you.'

'You are so kind.' She turned to a cluster of women and children, who had materialised from the inner room. They looked respectable enough, but the place smelled of drains and unwashed bodies. It was really no place to be sick in. Mrs Hardy beckoned to them. 'Come, friends, have a taste.'

Though she was sitting up she looked pale and exhausted. A spasm seemed to pass through her and as she clutched her belly, the stain of berry juice around her mouth only made her look more ghastly. 'God forgive me, to enjoy 'em, when Tom is languishing in the Tower,' she said, pushing away the basket and closing her eyes.

'Don't fret your mind with such ideas,' Philpott said. 'In fact, I shall send him half the basket if you wish it. They will pass it on, I assure 'ee. Want him fit and healthy for his trial, whenever that may come on.'

It wasn't an entirely happy thought, but Mrs Hardy looked pleased, and nodded faintly. 'And give him my dear love – poor Tom!' But then another spasm took her, and Mrs Philpott exchanged an anxious look with the other women. By common consent Philpott and I moved to the door, our presence no longer required or desirable.

D EATH WAS IN THE air as the week wore on. The traitor Watt in Scotland had been found guilty of treason, as everyone had known he would, and was bound for the scaffold. I had not found a sample of Canning's handwriting, nor did I know how to persuade Higgins to give me the message Grant had left him. But there was another meeting of the Corresponding Society the next night in the Fountain, and I had resolved to go back.

All this seemed far away from the comfortable confines of Sir James's room in Downing Street as Aust watched Jay and his son walk away across Horse Guard's Parade, Peter Williams a step behind them. Mr Jay was stiff with ill humour, and Theodore's head was bowed as they crossed the empty parade ground.

'What has become of Mr Theodore Jay's eye?' Aust asked, turning to take the raft of messages I had brought down from the garret.

'He went to Jackson's, for a boxing lesson.' Sir James had just come in. 'Not a proceeding at all agreeable to his father. I gather he puts the slave to mind the boy, but he is a slippery fish.'

This was a story not in any possible particular true, and now I remembered I had promised Peter Williams to keep an eye on Theodore. I called at the Jays' lodgings in Pall Mall on my way home and found Theodore within, resting on a sofa, with a poultice strapped to his eye. 'So, it's true,' I said. He obligingly lifted the poultice to reveal the damage and I admired it, as he seemed to hope I might. 'How the devil did you get it? Not at the boxing ring, that's a fact.'

'Of course not!' There was an eager brightness in his eye, and his lips were redder than ever, like bruised cherries as he looked fearfully towards the door. 'Hush, my father is in his study yonder.' He beckoned me closer. 'I went to The Grapes in Clements Lane. Just round the corner from your lodgings, you know.'

'Oh, yes, I know.' I think my face was probably a picture of exasperation as I sat down beside him. 'So, amid your father's delicate negotiations, and recognised for who you are in a bawdy house, you take it upon yourself to interrupt a molly meeting, offer salvation from sin, and get a black eye for your troubles?'

'Yes.' He looked a little disappointed. 'You knew about the men?'

'Everyone in London knows about the men, Mr Jay. A goodly number probably attend their meetings. What were they doing?'

'Dancing.' He was animated again. 'In most extraordinary costumes. I think they feared me an officer from Bow Street. I was punched square in the eye.'

'I expect you were. You do know they face the lash, or the

pillory, or even hanging, if they are caught?'

'And hellfire and everlasting damnation from God.' He looked prim.

'And imagine if you were discovered among men dressed as women! Your father would die of shame.'

Theodore actually smiled. 'I think he would! Though my father is never surprised by sin in other men – quite expects it, in fact, which is why he sets Peet to watch me. He says politics is the dirtiest business on earth and that politicians are all liars or rogues.'

I remembered Peter Williams again and sighed. 'For God's sake, Theodore, give up your adventures – or at the very least let me come with you.'

He looked at me and smiled again. 'What a friend you are, Laurence, to seek me out this way. Much more than I ever deserved.'

I SAW IT THE NEXT morning in Mr Aust's newspaper.

Last night died Mrs Hardy, wife of Mr T. Hardy, shoemaker, now confined in the Tower, under a Charge of High Treason. She expired in child-bed, and left a half-written letter, regretting the terrible events of recent months.

'Impossible,' I said, pushing my eyeglasses up on to my forehead as the tears started into my eyes, and later, in the quiet garret, I laid my hot face down on the desk and wept. She had truly never recovered after the Church and King riot at her house, a mob set on by the Ministry's illuminations. Will Benson, Mr Grant, now poor Lydia Hardy. There had been too many deaths, all unjust, and all, one way or another, emanating from within the street where I sat.

G RENVILLE WAS AWAY at the mysterious Secret Committee, while the usual members of the Treaty meeting convened in the Cabinet Room. Although I was no longer its secretary, I found myself moving about with refreshments after the talks had broken up. Canning was back from his supposed absence in the country, and was standing by the window with the objectionable Harry Ransome. They were talking of another Church and King meeting to be held at the Globe in Fleet Street that night. I was surprised Ransome would ever consent to go back, after his humiliation at Philpott's hands the night of the Hardy riot.

'It will be lively,' Ransome said with some relish, as he took a cup from me and gulped down his tea. 'I gather they begin to speak of a date for the shoemaker's trial. And now, of course, there's this business with his wife.'

'Indeed.' Canning took the cup I offered without looking at me. 'I imagine general satisfaction will be expressed, that Providence has thought fit to punish the scoundrel in this way. Most extraordinary accounts in the press. The woman was hardly above a drab, yet they claim she has left a note complaining of her state in a style strangely political.'

'Nonsense,' Ransome was saying as I moved away to prevent myself dashing the scalding tea in both their faces. 'How could such a woman write anything?'

'Well, well, let us hope her husband's grief loosens his tongue to the Secret Committee. Believe me, he's a tight-mouthed whoreson. Pitt won't waste the opportunity of prodding him now, until he sings.'

26

'WE DIDN'T EXPECT TO SEE you here tonight, Citizen Upton.'

I had recognised many faces when I came into the Fountain, but there were some new members present, for the main order of business was Mrs Hardy's funeral. The chairman was addressing one newcomer – a querulous-looking fellow sitting in the corner, arms crossed over his chest. I'd already noticed him limping in, one leg notably shorter than the other with a thick clumsy boot to compensate. He looked as if he expected trouble, and he was right, for the chairman added, 'Citizen Higgins has already written to 'ee, I believe, suggesting you—'

'Resign from the Society?' Upton grinned with painful fury, showing bad teeth. He had his eye on two men across the other side of the fire grate. 'Yon Higgins and his puppet Lemaitre have a grudge against me, and I'll not be dictated to by *them*.' I remembered now that Upton had been the name of the man Higgins had argued should be dismissed at the last meeting.

Lemaitre was also new to me. Naturally I wondered if he was French, but when he spoke, his accent was thick Cockney. 'It don't signify who wrote it, who thought of it or who meant it.' He was only young, long-haired and ready for a scrap. 'We're all agreed you should leave, Upton. The fire at your house and the claim you made about it stink to heaven. The insurance office issued a reward to find 'ee, and you put a friend up to claim it, and split it down the middle. Then there's the old woman and her will. We have heard about it all, and it ain't a very good reflection on your character.'

'It can all be accounted for.' Upton had folded his arms again and was now frowning as painfully as he had grinned. I looked around. No one met the man's eye, and I could see they all disliked him. 'Some devil has put it about I'm a spy for the Ministry an' all.' Upton looked pointedly at Higgins. 'Do you think you'll convince the rest to hate me with such a hail o' shot? P'raps you think summat will stick, if you throw shit hard enough.'

'Citizen Upton, we can't afford scandal.' The chairman, at least, was trying to be reasonable. 'Whatever you have done or not done, 'tis the appearance of the thing that matters. We can't risk the attention of Pitt's Secret Committee.'

'Secret Committee!' Upton evidently thought about spitting but refrained. 'This here is a damned secret committee designed to malign me.'

But Lemaitre was already looking at Higgins, who seemed to nod his permission.

'Chairman, I propose a motion of censure against Citizen Upton,' Lemaitre said.

'And I second it.' Higgins took his pipe out of his mouth and reached for his tobacco. 'Though God damn me, he don't even *deserve* to be called citizen.'

Upton jumped to his feet, furious, as best he could with his bad leg. 'I'll not stay to be censured.'

'Quick, citizens, a show of hands before he hops off.'

Then there was terrible confusion for many minutes, as Upton went for Higgins, his hands outstretched for his throat, Higgins punched him in the face, and the rest of the members did their best to separate them. Two men sat calmly by, one a fellow named Groves, the other Metcalfe, I remembered. I took my glasses from my pocket and put them on to examine the men more closely. They were looking at each other coolly, and imperceptibly nodded. If anyone in the room was a government spy, I thought, as George Higgins nearly landed in my lap, they were the likeliest candidates.

Mr Gibbs lent his assistance to eject Upton from the meeting, biting as many of the men as proved practicable amid the turmoil. At the door Upton looked back over his shoulder at the two men he seemed to loathe so much. 'I'll have you!' we could hear him shouting from the street. 'You'll be sorry!'

The meeting soon broke up after such excitement and I approached Higgins again. He remembered me well enough from the last meeting, but looked cagey when I asked once more for the letter. The chairman came over to see what ailed us, and I explained once again that I was acquainted with Mr Erskine. 'And my neighbour and very good friend William Philpott will vouch for me too,' I added. Higgins and the chairman looked at each other with new interest, apparently remembering that Philpott had now turned his *Cannon* on the Ministry, and I saw a way through the difficulty. 'I understand you can't trust me. I know the meetings are said to be rife with spies. But why not take the letter to Mr Philpott yourselves? At the least, he will print it in his newspaper and raise a doubt about the manner of Mr Grant's death.'

'Well.' The chairman nodded. 'Damned if we don't do it. The letter does no good here in our pockets, Higgins, and it may be of use to Erskine somehow, with his case. Give it me, and I'll see it delivered to Philpott's shop tomorrow.'

'MURDER, NONSENSE.' Philpott threw the letter at me the next day, with a look of long-suffering pity. 'You grow antic, my boy, and I begin to fear for your reason. The fellow who wrote this note probably wanted to meet Grant to sell him some bird, fish or fowl for his zoo.'

'At midnight?'

'An owl. Or a bat.'

I ignored him. 'I'm certain it is the same hand that wrote the message about the army.'

'A message you saw three months ago, for a mere ten minutes?'

'It's still filed among Grenville's papers, I dare say. I put it there myself, and it will be the work of a moment to take it out and compare them.' But there was no need for that. The illegible scrawl was as fresh to my mind as the day I saw it.

'And if you are right? How does that advance your case?'

'Someone wrote this letter to lure Mr Grant to his death. The same hand wrote the false message from France, that was leaked, and the leak pinned on Will Benson by the man who killed him and disguised his murder as a hanging. I only need to identify the writer, to know who killed them both.'

Philpott looked exasperated. 'Quite besides the wrong-headedness of your reasoning, how do you mean to accomplish that, among the quarter million literate men in London? I wish you joy of your search.'

But undaunted, and armed with Grant's letter, I wrote

Canning a note the moment I got into work the next morning. Mr Aust wished to know, I wrote after sucking the quill for a spell, whether the number of secret messages coming over from France had increased or diminished since the fall of Robespierre. It was arrant nonsense, and Canning would indubitably raise his immaculate eyebrows over it, wondering what business I had writing on behalf of Mr Aust in my degraded position. But the note's very temerity might provoke him into a response, and a response was all I wanted.

I put the paper in the hands of a clerk who came up, mid-morning, with the day's diplomatic bag of messages for decoding. By the time I had shared out the contents with the young gentlemen across the landing, the clerk had returned, with not one but two papers in his hand.

'Compliments of Mr Canning, though I don't think he meant it,' he said, laying the first, folded paper before me on my desk. 'And another message for copying.'

The clerk strolled back across the landing while I took Grant's letter from my pocket and set it down, smoothing the creases, heart thudding and my hands trembling. I opened the reply from Canning and laid the two papers side by side. I stared for a moment, then called the clerk back from the landing.

'This can't be Canning's own hand,' I said.

The clerk was still half-listening to the conversation next door, about Mrs Siddons at Drury Lane theatre. 'Watched him write it with my own eyes, didn't I?' he answered without interest.

My pulses slowed, the sweat on my palms turned clammy, and I sat down heavily on my stool. In neat copperplate script, almost worthy of a clerk, Canning informed me the confidential matter I raised was only for the ears of Lord Grenville, and Aust should know it. I felt sick with disappointment, and hardly conscious of my actions, mechanically opened the second paper the clerk had brought me.

'Whose hand is *this*?'

Here, against all the odds, was the script I had been expecting to see in Canning's note, dropped into my hand by God's will. The same hand as on a message supposed to have come directly from the battlefields of Flanders. A false message, that had tricked the French into allowing our army to escape. The same hand that had lured Mr Grant of the menagerie to his death.

But whether it was God's will, or the Devil's, it was only the timing that was providential. The answer was prosaic enough.

'This?' The boy looked vague. 'Oh, Lord Grenville's, I believe.'

27

THE HEAT WAS OPPRESSIVE, even before mid-morning, on the day of Mrs Hardy's funeral. But the sky was an unnatural steely grey, and the light was curiously dull when Philpott came to fetch me. 'Erskine believes the funeral will tell us much about the general mood,' he said. 'If there's to be trouble, this will be a good excuse. I am going, and *incognity* as the macaroni-eaters say. Men will comport themselves vastly different when unobserved. I shall write a piece, too, of course, describing the affair for the *Cannon*.'

It seemed Mrs Philpott had not clearly understood the notion of incognito, for her husband glowed conspicuously in an agricultural smock of starched pristine whiteness as we walked towards Piccadilly, through the unwashed crowd. He was sombre, but his busy mind was still at work under his broad-brimmed straw hat, and he quizzed me about the Corresponding Society meeting at the Fountain.

'Well, keep visiting the meetings, my boy. Erskine will look into these fellows Groves and Metcalfe and if they're called to testify, he will seek to prove their testimony is bought. Any doubt that can be planted in the jury's mind will help us. I myself have already smoked another spy among the Ministry's witnesses.' He smirked, despite the occasion, as smug as a choirboy in his white surplice. ''Twas a work of excessive genius on my part to find him out – the neatest thing you ever saw. It turns out the scoundrel, John Taylor, has a damned unsavoury secret – has one wife in his village, and another in London – and Erskine, of course, knows just when we should inform upon him to have him locked away during the time of the trial.'

'They will be preparing you a chair in Bow Street as one of their own,' I said.

'I believe they will.' But Philpott's complacency faded as we arrived at the workshops on the corner of Piccadilly, where a middle-sized crowd of working men and women stood outside Mrs Hardy's door, waiting quietly for proceedings to begin, and talking among themselves in subdued voices.

There was no sign of trouble yet. Some of the members of the Society I'd seen at the Fountain were going in and out of the doorway, but there were no political speeches or protests. Instead, the mourners behaved for all the world as though the funeral was taking place in a quiet country churchyard. Women fanned themselves with their shawls, men mopped their foreheads in the oppressive heat. The sky was greyer still. Further up the street a few Church and King loyalists were hanging from a window, shouting taunts to anyone that passed beneath, but no one in the crowd took any notice, and to give them their due, even the Church and King crowd were tolerably half-hearted. Their small numbers suggested that most loyalists had better taste than to mar the solemn moment with disorder.

After a long delay, Mrs Hardy's cheap deal coffin was brought out of the house and hoisted on the shoulders of half a dozen men. A handful of weeping women followed, and the procession began. I walked behind, marvelling that the human creature I had last seen smiling and talking, seen stroking a child's hair with a warm human hand, could now be contained in that box, no more than a lump of meat for burial.

The small crowd rapidly grew, as more mourners joined at every street corner, and men watched from doorways as we passed – Bow Street Runners or King's Messengers, most likely, perhaps looking for wanted radicals, but there were no arrests that I saw, and Philpott looked around approvingly. There was no chanting, no excitement, just a deep silence, broken only by the sound of many boots trudging slowly up Piccadilly towards the cemetery. But to my ears it sounded like an army, echoing back along the still, sultry streets.

We knew when we were getting close, from the smell. Some people fell back, their neckerchiefs clutched to their mouths, but most moved on, a slow river, crowding through the narrow gates into the burying ground and then splitting off into separate streams that ran around the edge of the confined space, making room for more to follow. Philpott nudged me and pointed to a man standing on the far side of the crowd. 'John Walter, editor of *The Times*.'

After the earth had been shovelled back into the shallow grave with a generous quantity of lime, the crowd began to disperse. Now, if at all, was the time for a riot, but my mind had gone back to Will Benson's pitiful end, deprived even of a funeral like this, and I was too preoccupied to look about me, until Philpott pulled me up into a doorway out of the way. We watched the people trudging past. Most of them were heading back to work, others for the tavern, to drink the poor woman's health.

'Do you see anything?' Philpott scanned the passing faces. 'Any hint of violence?'

'None.' It was a far cry from the night of the illuminations, but I wasn't sure it was any less alarming. Though the people were peaceable, there was a kind of terror in their sheer numbers, and in their solemnity. If they put their minds to rebellion, what could stop them? The Ministry was right to be afraid, I thought for the first time, watching the seemingly endless procession go by. If, as Burke had written, the people were like cattle sitting placidly beneath the branches of the spreading British oak, they were full of latent power, if they only knew it.

Philpott, too, was struck quite solemn by the whole occasion, but there was only a tear in his eye instead of my foreboding. Either he did not see the menace or he merely welcomed it as evidence of the people's strength and common sense. He sighed. 'Well, well, Erskine will be mighty relieved, and your masters disappointed. He feared there might be weapons somewhere, unknown to Hardy, and guessed today would draw the troublemakers out. But 'tis a very dignified affair, ain't it? Poor woman, poor woman.'

I hardly heard him, my eye drawn to another figure approaching in the crowd, dressed in black. The tilt of her head, the vigour of her step, and the set of her wrinkled mouth – yes, it was Aglantine. I had never thought her interested in our home-grown radicals, but now I remembered how, all those long weeks ago when she first reappeared in my life, she had listened with such interest to the men at the hanging. Men who had feared – or relished – the prospect of trouble, if Hardy were to face the noose and the knife at last.

Philpott stirred. 'Well, we had best get back to Fleet Street. God damn me, it's raining.' He was right, solitary fat drops were falling, the first for months. 'What a cloud! The purplest I ever saw in my life. I believe we are in for a storm, Laurence.'

He was right about that, too, for the heavens abruptly opened, and he scurried away across the street with sudden activity, his smock slapping wetly about his knees. Others who could afford it flagged down hackneys for a dry ride back to town. But I didn't run after him or make any attempt to get out of the rain. Instead, I turned to follow in Aglantine's footsteps.

She was doggedly trudging down Haymarket as I fell into step beside her. There was rain in my shoes and a steady spout of water poured off the brim of my hat, splashing on to my spectacles as I peered into her face. She looked frail, her black costume plastered to her bony figure.

'That message Canning gave you came direct from Grenville,' I said. 'It was his own handwriting I copied. It was a trick to fool your armies and allow ours to escape.'

I had understood all this in the night, tossing and turning in my stifling attic, with Mr Gibbs a disgruntled bedfellow. The first information I'd passed since war broke out tripped off my tongue without effort or misgiving, and Aglantine showed no surprise, only glanced up at me and scowled.

'I am disliked by these new men in Paris,' she said, after a moment, and there was that vulnerable look again, the look that made me think of my mother, and of poor Mrs Hardy in her grave. 'I was Robespierre's creature, and they will kill me if they can. But if I can give them some useful information, they may forgive me my *misguided* loyalties.' She smiled, and for once it was not in derision. 'Your news may help me, Laurence.'

'But I don't understand Canning,' I said. I was still more taken up by my own concerns than hers, still following the train of my own thoughts. 'Is he being used by Grenville? Taken for a fool?' I had been pondering it in the night, imagining the fading of his self-complacency if I told him that they had always known he was a spy and that he was only a pawn in Grenville's hand.

Aglantine's face twisted. 'Or he knows full well what he is doing, and passes me false information on Grenville's orders.'

We stared at each other as the rain teemed down steadily. We were both so wet already that it scarcely mattered.

'But then, in that case—' If Canning acted on government orders, how had Grenville let him whirl so out of control as to leave this trail of bodies across London? Was the customary law of the land suspended merely to serve his purpose? I found myself trembling. 'Aglantine, does he know about me? Have you ever told him?'

Aglantine had folded her arms across her scanty bosom, perfectly composed. 'Have I ever told you anything of my other agents?'

No, she never had. It was entirely my own doing that I knew Canning was also her man, and the sudden terror that had shaken me now subsided.

'I say nothing, in case a friend proves false,' she went on. 'But in this case, I would rather have it so. If Canning really acts for the government, he would be of great use to Paris, and I would make myself of worth again. We might use him as a back channel to feed the Ministry false news, just as Grenville used Canning to feed this lie to me.'

'You have no inkling, at all, of where his true loyalties lie?'

She shook her head.

'How long have you known him?'

Ordinarily I would have expected her to rebuff me, tell me to mind my own affairs and leave her to mind hers. But instead she took my arm and led me on down the street. 'He entered Parliament last year. It was not long after that I sought him out.'

'What made you choose him?' Again, I thought she would scold me but she did not.

'He fancies himself a gentleman, but his father long ago lost their estates, and his mother turned actress to support them. As he does not let *that* information circulate in Downing Street, I thought he might be ashamed of her, and easy to persuade.'

'Is that how you get your informants? By threats?'

'Not always.' She looked at me pointedly. 'Though men are often easy to entangle, being so full of cant and base desires. In fact, Canning was not ashamed of his mother at all, quite the dutiful son, and was not to be influenced that way. Nevertheless, he agreed to help me in return for money for her upkeep. He goes to the country every month with my coin.'

She stopped for shelter under the porch of the New Theatre and looked up at me. 'You could help me, if you're willing. If I tell Canning something, and it comes to Grenville's ears, I will know he is passing information in both directions.'

'What sort of something?'

She looked at me meditatively. 'Something notable. Something you will recognise as my message, something that cannot be mistaken, or obtained in any other way. Something concerning Hardy, perhaps,' she added, 'for they think of nothing else. Some morsel of information that will send them into such a spin that you will infallibly hear of it. This is how you may help me.'

I had thought myself immune from the seduction of the Devil. But he creeps into our affairs like a tick in a mattress, while we think of other things. 'A plot like Robert Watt's, perhaps? Except that there are always rumours of plots. We could scarcely know whether it was your information or another's.'

'An attempt on the King.' She looked quite phlegmatic. 'It must be on the King, for that is all they long for. They need an overt act for their prosecution case and would leap at any hint of one we could give them. But it must be so particular that we will recognise it as our own.'

The Devil itched me and spoke through my mouth. I cannot explain how else the idea came suddenly into my mind. 'A plot to kill the King with a poison dart. You remember Fletcher Christian at the waxworks with his blowpipe?'

She scowled furiously. 'Preposterous.'

'Exactly!' God help me, I laughed. 'It would certainly be notable and strange. And, best of all, entirely harmless. Imagine the absurdity of Pitt and Grenville searching in vain for a make-believe scoundrel with a non-existent weapon!'

'They would certainly look like fools.' Her scowl faded as she understood what I was proposing, and she even began to smile, her eyes busy.

'Fools? They would look like madmen!'

Perhaps it was then the Devil left me again, for all at once my teeth began to chatter and I noticed I was soaked to the skin. Even so, I did not flinch at the look of sudden comradeship she turned on me, or at her warmly extended, citrus-perfumed, hand. 'Well, I will do it. I will tell Canning I have heard a rumour of such a plot, and if Canning is acting for the Ministry the news will soon reach Lord Grenville. Meet me in Covent Garden, Laurence, at dusk, a week tonight, and tell me what you have heard.'

What possessed me to help her? I would have claimed a noble motive – honest incredulity that the government could willingly entertain a viper like Canning in their bosom. And then there was Grenville's letter to Grant. I hoped he'd somehow learned the poor devil was in danger from Canning, and wanted to warn him, for any alternative explanation was much worse. I had to find out the truth, or how could I go back to my quiet garret and toil dutifully in the Ministry's service?

But, in truth, I was overwrought by Mrs Hardy's funeral, and had felt so alone for months. I had seen too many deaths and, though I knew she was brutal, I thought Aglantine might be the only one who could save me from becoming another of Canning's victims. I freely confess our talk was treason, but it is a strange irony in the circumstances of my life, that of all my mixed intentions on that day, revolution was not one of them.

28

IT WAS SCARCELY THE beginning of October, but the streets were already full of Guysers, collecting money for Guy Fawkes Night. London's orphans had left their clandestine thieving and had taken to the age-old practice of extortion. Why the magistrates turned a blind eye was a mystery, but one so lost in the mists of time that no one even asked. A gang of dirty urchins with a stuffed sack – hardly a figure of a man at all, and with a charcoaled grin smeared clumsily across the hessian – followed me through Temple Bar on the way to work, demanding small coin, and satisfied their disappointment with a hail of pebbles aimed at my retreating back. But it was merely an opening salvo in the campaign. By Bonfire Night the streets would be practically lawless, and the Guysers would be old as well as young, with fiercer weapons and louder voices.

I was in the Cabinet Room, clearing up after another meeting of the Treaty Committee. Aust was there too, reading the newspaper reports of Robert Watt's execution in Edinburgh out loud to Anne, who had called in on her stepfather on her way home from her dressmaker in Cheapside, and now stood pensively at the window looking over the street at the door to Number 10. She was coming out of mourning little by little, a touch of colour now mingling with the grey of her costume. Was this for Canning's sake? I felt sick at the idea.

'I believe the Scots have bungled the whole business,' Aust said, as he folded the paper. The news of Watt's death was trickling south, along with his florid final confession made the night before his execution. 'Only hanged the traitor, then chopped off his head when he was already dead. And the crowd quite unmoved.'

It was rather as if a dormouse I had been nursing in my pocket had turned nasty. I looked up from buffing the high polish of the table where some careless visitor had spilled a glass of wine. 'You would have wished for more drama?'

'I would have wished for more terror. Merely to hang him – he may as well have been a common thief.' Aust padded to the window in his stockinged feet and stood beside Anne, looking out. 'But at any rate he is dead, and Hardy as good as dead, when his trial comes on.'

'Mr Erskine would disagree with you,' Anne said, with a smile of tolerant amusement at the fierceness that had disturbed me.

'I expect he would, but even he must know it.'

Anne brushed something from her stepfather's collar as though they were discussing the weather, and I couldn't hold my peace. 'Don't you think it a dreadful burden to take an innocent man's life?'

'Eh?' Aust looked back at me as if he had forgotten I was there. Sometimes I had wondered if his mind was softening with age, but now I only saw deceit and disguise everywhere.

'To infiltrate the radical meetings with spies and kill a man for his opinions. Does it not make us as bad as Robespierre?'

'Good God!' He stared at me. 'You would draw such a parallel?'

'Robespierre killed those who disagreed with him. Is ours not a Terror too?'

He came close and laid a hand on my shoulder. 'For God's sake, Laurence, don't say such a thing before Grenville, when I am taking such pains to bring you back downstairs.' He shook his head. 'You have been spending too much time with Philpott.'

Anne was also looking at me. 'The papers say they have knives and pikes,' she said reasonably. 'And Mr Pitt and Lord Grenville know far more than we do.'

'And you'd have their blood on your hands?'

'It's the law, Laurence. Hardy knew what he was about, just as Watt did. You don't pity Mr Watt, I hope?'

I tugged at my wig. 'Thou shalt not kill.'

'And you think we'll be damned merely for approving the operation of the law?' She looked offended, then laughed as I came up beside her at the window, and she squeezed my arm with almost her old warmth. 'For God's sake, don't turn into Miss More. Such moralising doesn't become you, any more than Mr Jay, poor dear. It is a terrible burden to him to appear so stern, when he is naturally so jovial a man.'

'Jovial?' I was startled out of my brooding for a moment, but then I remembered the hearty laugh I had once heard in Grenville's study, and another crashing wave of disenchantment broke over me. Was anything I had witnessed in the Department true?

'Oh, yes, indeed. But the Americans long to see him cross swords with Lord Grenville – cannot abide the idea of an amicable agreement – so they must feign some dreadful enmity for the public view. He finds it quite wearing.' She was smiling down at the street, and when I followed her gaze, I saw Canning emerging from the door of Number 10. He looked up, saw her at the window, and an expression came into his face that I hadn't seen before.

'Anne!' Aust said warningly. 'Be careful. Laurence is friend to Mr Philpott, you recollect. None of this must reach the press.'

She turned back into the room, something expectant in the set of her head, the thrill of her body. Good God, she was waiting for Canning to come to her, ready to take his bloody fingers in her own.

But she was still smiling at me, quite in her usual way. 'Laurence is perfectly sound, Mr Aust, you know he is. He would never betray our confidences.'

A UST HAD ME COPYING draft treaty clauses in the corner of Sir James's office on the day I was to meet Aglantine again. Perhaps he was a monster disguised as a dithering old fool, but his attempt to bring me back down from the attic seemed kind enough. And Anne had been right about the treaty, too. Whatever their bluster, and whatever their lies, Grenville and Jay had lost no time in agreeing the dullest set of clauses on God's good earth. They had wished to make America believe Jay was striking a hard bargain, while, from what I could gather now, he had in fact capitulated on everything. Until now there had been no word of the blowpipe plot, and I was beginning to think Canning a faithful Jacobin after all, when Lord Grenville called Sir James and Aust through into his office, beyond the tapestry. I could hear every word.

'I am just come from Mr Pitt.'

Sir James tutted consolingly, and I heard the clink of the decanter.

'A new piece of evidence has come to hand in the Hardy case. An overt act against the King at last. If it's true it will be a Godsend, but I own myself once bitten twice shy. Until now there's not been a shred of evidence good enough to finish him.'

'Until now?'

'Until now, Sir James.'

'Can I enquire …?'

'That's the devil of it. The story is quite preposterous.'

'My Lord?'

I heard the scrape of Grenville's chair as he stood up, and he began to pace. I held my breath, but he spoke so low I didn't catch what he said. Nor, it seemed, did Sir James.

'A *what*, my Lord? Forgive me, I believe I have misheard you.'

'A poisoned dart.'

I laid down my pen. Aglantine had done her deed, and Canning, it seemed, had done his. He had been acting on Pitt's orders all along, and Grenville was involved. But in what, exactly? How far did the collusion extend between the two most powerful arms of the government, and their vicious agent? The enormity of it brought black shadows in front of my eyes.

'Ah.' Sir James sounded suddenly cautious. 'I fear I heard aright.'

'You may well look incredulous, but our informant flatly asserts that the King was to be the target.'

'Good God. Does His Majesty know?'

'The Home Secretary has told him. The King is, as ever,

quite philosophical, only glad the thing did not come off.'

'Are you quite sure it was a – *dart*?' Sir James could hardly bring himself to speak the word. In my mind's eye I could see his baffled moon face.

'Quite sure.'

'Something akin to the weapons of the aboriginal peoples of Australia, I suppose?' Sir James was showing considerable acumen, God bless him.

Grenville sounded unhappy. 'Indeed so.'

Sir James had reached his decision. 'We will be a laughing-stock, my Lord. Where does Pitt get this fairy tale? Or should I say, *pipe-dream*?'

'I'm not at liberty to say, as yet. But no doubt 'twill all come clear in time.'

It certainly would, and they would be mocked as roundly as Sir James feared. Well, so I hoped, in among so many other racing thoughts. They say God damns us by granting our prayers.

'You are quite sure it was a blowpipe?' Sir James still seemed to be having difficulty getting past this point.

'I'm afraid so.'

'Perhaps we could call it an air-gun? The method of propulsion is, after all, the same.'

'I hope we will call it nothing until we know more, Sir James. I am to attend the Secret Committee tomorrow and may learn the truth of it.'

WHEN I ARRIVED PUNCTUALLY AT dusk in Covent Garden, Aglantine was waiting amid the wreckage of the market. The stallholders were all gone into the squalor of Seven Dials or, if they were lucky, out to the cow pastures and market gardens of Brompton. Apart from the litter of autumn marrows, tattered cabbages and wasp-damaged apples, the place looked like one of those engravings in the shop windows of St Paul's Churchyard. A dream of London, empty of the human life that clogs up the grand spaces and tarnishes the beauty of the stately buildings above our heads. Mr Gibbs ran ahead of me, nosing through the piles of debris, sending papers scudding in the curious draughts created by the open space of the piazza, and the innumerable dark alleys around it. Aglantine wrinkled her nose in disgust as he greeted her by pissing on a lamp-post.

'Canning passed it on.' I couldn't wait to tell her. 'Just today. I heard Grenville say so.'

She frowned at my excitement and only nodded towards the church. I followed her under the portico, where we sat down among a crowd of chattering drabs. 'What exactly did Grenville say?'

The lamplighter was working his way around the square with a gaggle of larking boys behind him, while from the dark graveyard behind us, I could hear the rhythmic wheezing of a man in the throes of passion. Suddenly my excitement evaporated. 'That it might be the overt act against the King they've been waiting for.'

'Did he believe it?'

'I don't know – don't think he does either. Sir James was horrified – realised at once that they would look like fools. He has more understanding than I ever gave him credit for.'

She waved her hand indifferently. 'What will they do next?'

'The Ministry? Discuss it at the Secret Committee. Look for the perpetrator, though they'll not find one.'

Aglantine poked Mr Gibbs with the toe of her pointed boot. 'Erskine has sent you to the radicals' meetings, I believe?'

'How did you know?' She only scowled at me. 'Yes, I've been a couple of times.'

'How do they prosper?'

'Well enough, in the circumstances, bedevilled by the odd hot-head or argument, but on the whole very dignified, like Mrs Hardy's funeral.'

'Dignity will not bring them what they want.'

She quizzed me a little about Upton and the men he hated, but I hardly listened, still thinking of the truths I had learned about Canning that week. 'The radicals fear for their lives,' I said. 'They fear the Ministry will crush them if it can.' They would do better to fear Canning, as Grant had done.

'Governments are cruel,' she answered, and then, slowly and carefully, she took off the gloves she always wore and laid them neatly on her knee. Exposed to the lamplight, her hands were raw, the skin flayed – or perhaps burned – her knuckles warped and swollen, her nails black. She studied them as if they did not belong to her.

Whoever had inflicted those wounds should be arraigned for monstrous cruelty, but they would no doubt blame the dreadful times, call themselves obliged to obey orders. Governments were not men, and war was not murder, after all. What did Grenville really know of Canning's ruthlessness? Something, certainly, or he would not have written Grant that letter. But the Ministry likely closed its eyes, thinking the information Canning passed and received too important to question his methods. And if I demanded of Grenville what Will Benson had done to deserve his fate in Brookes' laboratory, what Grant had done to deserve his in a lion's cage, would he only shrug and reach for another glass of brandy?

29

THERE WAS AN ATMOSPHERE of quiet industry in the palace, a watery autumnal sun slanting through the windows on to men's faces and sober everyday suits. Aust had brought me along to the royal Levée as a messenger, the following Wednesday, and I was able to draw near and listen, as the King paused at Jay's elbow and nodded cordially. I wondered if His Majesty knew what Canning had done – and knowing, if he could have possibly approved it.

'Well, sir,' he said to Jay, 'It seems we are to have an agreement at last, and you shall be quite the success.'

Jay bowed. 'I am gratified, Your Majesty, to find you think so.'

'And don't you consider it likely?' The King was cheerful, his benign expression so familiar from his portrait on the guinea, blunt faced as a good-natured axe.

'Some recent developments suggest it will be so,' Jay answered. A slight rise of colour in his waxy face seemed to show that he was pleased.

The King nodded and turned to Lord Grenville with a jovial smile. 'Well, my Lord? What news of the aborigines?'

A shadow of irritation crossed Grenville's face but was suppressed at once. 'Your Majesty is very droll. Sir James also fears we will be lampooned in the press.'

'I should think it a certainty.' The King looked tolerably unconcerned. 'Those damned Whig rags will twist all our words to ridicule.'

At that moment Canning came striding in, without much deference to protocol, and whispered in Grenville's ear. Everyone watched, in expectation of some military disaster, I suppose, but in fact, a gleam of satisfaction came into Grenville's face as he turned back to His Majesty. 'I am happy to be informed by Mr Canning that the Secret Committee has this morning found a man who will testify to the absolute truth of the blowpipe affair. There has been a falling-out between the guilty parties, I gather, and an informant has come forward.'

Canning nodded, Sir James looked from one face to another with candid disbelief, and the King looked grave. 'Any informer that comes voluntary forward ain't to be ignored, Lord Grenville, but remember he may only have the object of money in his eye.'

'Quite so, Your Majesty, and I am, of course, yet to be persuaded.' Grenville looked mighty relieved all the same. 'But Mr Canning informs me Mr Pitt will present the evidence this afternoon, and the man in question – a Mr Upton – will appear before the committee to be questioned further.'

'Well, well, I suppose I shall hear about it all, though I would rather forget such dangers. If a scoundrel will act at all hazard, there would be no stopping him.'

'No, indeed.'

'Have they found the weapon?'

Grenville looked to Canning, who spoke smoothly. 'Not yet, Your Majesty, but we know a good deal more about it. It is actually some kind of brass blowpipe, something akin to an air-gun, manufactured in Birmingham. What poison was intended is unclear, but one of the parties, George Higgins, is an apothecary's assistant with access to many drugs, while another, Paul Lemaitre, has a knowledge of instruments.'

'And who are these villains, do we know?'

Again, Canning was the one with information, the coming man. 'They are members of Mr Hardy's Corresponding Society and were, in fact, tasked with raising money for his comfort and defence.'

'The Attorney General will be pleased.'

'Yes, Your Majesty, it will be a Godsend to us if Hardy is implicated. Though with the trial about to come on, we have little time to make the case.'

It is quite easy to record this conversation on paper in the quiet of my room, the sleet turning to large soft snowflakes against the windowpane as the night grows colder, but much harder to describe how I felt as it unfolded before my eyes and ears. All I can really remember now is that a hot flush sprang up my neck, making my scalp prickle, and I began to gasp. There was a sharp pain in my chest, and I clutched at Aust's sleeve in defiance of all protocol.

'Your clerk appears to be indisposed.' The King's voice reached me, quite aloof and disapproving. 'Is it some sort of apoplexy?'

Aust had hold of me, keeping me upright at all costs. 'I fear it is. Will you excuse us, Your Majesty?'

'Yes, yes. We would not wish to have an unpleasant scene.' Now, under the displeasure, a note of curiosity had crept into the royal voice. 'If it is a nervous malady, bind him, sir.' The King knew all about that. 'Bind him and bleed him. 'Twill right itself with no more than a cupful, I dare say.'

Aust marched me away into the corridor, followed by Canning's grey gaze, and I heard no more. The old man sat me down against the cool stone wall, and the flush dissipated slowly, leaving my skin clammy. My vision cleared, and the sharp pain turned dull. Aust met my eye, which was probably very wild, certainly wholly bewildered. My legs were shaking, and I had a fit of the shivers.

'Better, my boy?'

'Yes, sir. No, sir.'

Aust produced a hip flask and put it to my lips. I sipped once prudently and then again with more gratitude. The brandy was fortifying, not tranquillising like the Black Drop, and I was finally able to look about me again, at a world turned dizzyingly upside down. My mind recoiled, and I would have downed the contents of the flask if Aust had not put it back in his pocket. Above anything, I wanted to distract my mind from what I had just heard.

If the Devil had possessed me in the rain that day with Aglantine I had not known it. But now the veil was torn aside, and like Faust pacing his laboratory in fear and trembling, I knew I had done a dreadful thing. The worst of it was that I had meant so well. I had only meant to unmask a murderer at the heart of Government. How could that have been wrong?

Perhaps not wrong, but so stupid it was as good as a sin. Upton had been a Government spy planted in the meetings as Higgins had claimed, and was now paid to turn fiction to reality, to secure Hardy's conviction.

G RENVILLE CAME IN LATER in the afternoon and stripped off his coat. Aust set it to dry by the fire. Since the weather broke on the day of Mrs Hardy's funeral, it had rained incessantly and it was growing cold. 'Upton is a fool,' Grenville said, pouring himself a brandy and coming to the fire. 'Changed his story three times in the space of half an hour. We sent him off to meditate on his tale and come back with one that makes sense.'

'And the others? The plotters, my Lord?' Aust looked up from the careful arrangement of Grenville's coat. I was still copying treaty clauses in the corner. As yet, Grenville had never acknowledged my presence, but now, for the first time in weeks, he turned his eyes on me.

'Runners have been dispatched to arrest them, and they will appear before the Secret Committee tonight. Pitt and I are meeting with the Attorney General to suggest he spins out the Hardy case in court as long as possible, while we investigate this plot. Canning will question the men in Pitt's stead, and I have offered you, Mr Jago, as my representative – but in the meanest capacity, I might add. You will do as Canning bids you, and only take good notes for me to read later. I am offering you a lifeline back to your old standing, and hope you'll not let personal feeling against Canning cloud your judgement at this crucial time.'

T HE SECRET COMMITTEE met in the Privy Council Chamber, a stone's throw from Grenville's window, an eight-sided old building that had once been a cockpit, and then a theatre. It retained a predilection for both drama and bloodletting, I discovered, when I followed Canning through its quaint doors, hung over with carved swags and foliage of stone. 'Keep your lips closed, Mr Jago,' he said grimly, as we came into the council chamber, which was achingly cold and damp. 'You would not wish to embarrass yourself.' Not for the first time, I wondered why he hadn't taken the chance to kill me at the duel. But perhaps not even Grenville could have saved him from the constable if he had. A table ran the whole length of the room, ablaze with flickering candles, but there were only a few committee members present, sitting at the far end of the table as near as possible to a pitiful fire guttering in a large grate. It was near seven o'clock as Canning sat down, and I found a place at the board as far from him as practically possible. I had only just arranged my papers when the door opened, letting in a dreadful cold draught which extinguished half the candles, and the first prisoner to be questioned, Paul Lemaitre, was led into the room.

The man had seemed at ease in the Fountain, but here he looked much younger than I remembered, dirty and dishevelled. He stood awkwardly at the far end of the table, his hands in front of him as if chained. They had not let him wash or change his clothes, and the gentlemen around me looked at him with distaste as he gave his name and occupation.

He was hungry, and they fed him. He was weary and they bade him sit. But he knew they were willing to hang him, and they knew he would lie to save himself. It soon appeared he would save others, too, if he could. No, he never knew Upton or Higgins, he said. Never to speak to, only by sight. Well, he admitted, he had called upon them a time or two for subscriptions to succour Mr Hardy in the Tower. And this letter, the committee produced, apparently written in his hand? A forgery, not his letter at all. Never in life had he written *brass is not ready, nor poison prepared, but enough of that hereafter.* No, he had never said, *royal game is best.*

'Did you ever see Upton, outside of the meetings?' Canning asked, as the echo of the incriminating words, read flatly by a clerk, dissolved into the shadows above us.

'Only once.'

'Where did you see him?'

'I will not say.' Lemaitre looked straight into Canning's face with a return of some spirit.

'What was the meeting for?'

'A thing quite indifferent.'

'I have heard it was on account of some quarrel.' Canning was smooth, and I remembered Upton shouting his threats as he left the inn, Mr Gibbs snapping at his heels. 'You had quarrelled with Upton, and he sent you a letter. A challenge.'

'Yes.' Lemaitre wilted under the force of Canning's stare.

'And did you accept?'

'No!' He passed a hand across his forehead. 'No, I wrote back and told him he was a bloody fool. *That's* the letter I wrote him. The only one. Not this forgery about brass and poison.'

'And you met to make your peace?'

'To discuss it.'

'Then is it possible that Upton seeks his revenge by fabricating this tale against you, Mr Lemaitre?' I asked. Perhaps Upton was not a Government spy at all, but only motivated by spite.

Everyone looked at me. Canning annoyed, the others only half comprehending – and Lemaitre with a strange look that I realised, with some confusion, was doubtful recognition. He passed his hand across his brow again, trying to place me. 'Well, I—'

'And do you call this fabrication?' Canning leaned over to a member of the committee nearer the fire and took something from his hand that gleamed. A brass tube, about two foot long.

'Did you ever see this?' Canning reached once more, producing a wooden contraption that he fitted neatly inside the tube.

'Nothing resembling it in my life.'

Of course he had never seen it, for it had had no existence before I conjured it into being. The deep shadows of the old building and the guttering flames of the fire grate made it feel as though we were transported back to Tudor times, and Canning some kind of ruthless Thomas Cromwell. When they took Lemaitre away, Canning turned to look at me measuringly and I arranged my face into indifference.

They brought George Higgins in next. He looked and smelled worse, with stubble on his face and a stench of the privy about him. He told the same story as Lemaitre because it was true. Upton was still changing his story by the hour, but it suited the Ministry only too well to call it guilty equivocation, instead of lies.

We had been at the business for half an hour when a clerk came in with a note for me from Mr Aust. Higgins' eyes followed him as he skirted the table to find me and bent to whisper in my ear. What Aust wanted I don't remember now, but there was the sudden scrape of a chair and Higgins was on his feet. His gaolers hastened forward to take hold of him as he stared at me across the table.

'God damn me, a spy after all!' He shook off the gaolers' restraining hands and put up his own to show he meant no harm. 'Not a lawyer's clerk at all, then, citizen?'

Everyone looked at me, as they had when I spoke up for Lemaitre, but this time with mild bemusement. Canning's eyes narrowed, but there was also the glimmer of a smile about his mouth as I adopted my most clerkish air and answered, 'I beg your pardon, sir?'

'Don't dissemble, citizen. I remember you. Dressed not quite so genteel as now, I do confess, and no damned wig, but I'll not forget them green glasses.'

I looked into Higgins' stubbled face, willing him to be quiet, willing him to see that I was in almost as much danger as himself. 'Not at all, I assure you. Never in life. You are quite mistaken.' But he saw only the well-dressed Government clerk. The enemy.

'A rascally dog – God damn me, you had a rascally dog with you, what near took my finger off in that scrap with Upton.'

'I have no dog,' I found myself saying. 'No dog in the world.' It was the second time I'd been frightened into a downright lie. But Canning had stopped looking at me. He was actually laughing, for which I found myself profoundly glad.

'Mr Higgins, I'll say this for you – you have a nose for a parvenu. But I'm afraid Mr Jago is not the only man in London in those ridiculous spectacles, and I am well enough acquainted with his spinelessness to tell you he is certainly not capable of what you suggest.'

30

I was standing in the doorway of Westminster Hall the following day, hoping to catch Erskine on the way out of the Lord Chancellor's Breakfast. A sketchy account of the blowpipe plot had already appeared in the morning papers, and I wanted to tell him what more I knew. I came to the door as the proceedings ended, to find my news anticipated by Mr Rose, the court Recorder, standing up to propose a toast to the King. It was drunk with a solemn excitement worthy of the radicals themselves.

'I am pleased to say the Ministry has given me a fuller account of the affair than has so far appeared in the newspapers.' There was a stir of silk and damask as every man turned to look at Rose. 'The culprits are two working men, betrayed in their nefarious design by another. I am sorry to tell you that all three are members of the London Corresponding Society, and particular friends of Thomas Hardy.'

'God damn me,' Erskine said loudly from his place on the far side of the room. Rose had made to sit down but was obliged to stand up again by a hail of questions.

'My Lord Chief Baron, I cannot tell you whether Mr Hardy was directly involved. Clearly, at this time he is in the Tower, but he has had visitors of course. His wife – his friends. The Secret Committee will determine his involvement. But in any event, it clearly shows his Society is disloyal to the Crown.'

Erskine raised his voice again, and a hundred heads turned towards him with a mixture of disapproval and curiosity. 'May I ask when the arrests were made?'

'Last night, I believe.'

'And the news reached the press already! Do we know how that singular fact came about?'

'I imagine that news spread from the men's families, or the King's Messengers.' Rose looked pious. 'We all know how unreliable these men can be.'

'Or from a member of the Secret Committee,' Erskine said, in a hard voice. 'Or from Mr Pitt himself. It's mighty convenient timing, with Hardy's trial at hand.'

There was a general growl of disapprobation, but Rose raised his hand peaceably. 'You are quite at liberty to see the case in that light, Mr Erskine, or in any other you please, but I hope you don't deny the terrible seriousness of this affair. Good God! The King almost murdered!'

Erskine shook his head. 'Mr Rose, I shall behave like a good jury man and reserve judgement till I have heard all the facts.' But his voice was drowned by the rising murmur of conversation.

Close to me, a bewigged judge was lecturing his neighbour. 'Just like Watt! Planned to take over every civil power in London, I dare say. Weapons secreted about the town, no doubt, ready to take the Tower. An army of followers ready to capture Pitt and seize the banks. The devils! I hear Hardy is a desperate-looking character, tall and thin with a pock-marked face and dressed like a damned Jacobin.'

I wondered how long it would be before such speculation became fact in the eyes of the world, and caught hold of Erskine as he came out, looking dark and troubled. 'It's not true, sir.' I followed him out into the street. 'I saw their informer, Upton, argue with the others at the meeting in Shoreditch and threaten them. He is definitely lying.'

Erskine grasped my arm and smiled through all this new trouble. 'You're a good lad, Laurence. Between you and Philpott I find I have two staunch lieutenants, admirably exercised by injustice.'

Philpott was waiting for us back in Erskine's chambers. I sat down by the fire, fondling the dog's ears for comfort, feeling as if I had tossed a burning cartwheel into a crowded street, and was doomed to watch its destructive path. Erskine's good opinion of my motives made it even worse, and having conspired with Aglantine to concoct the whole tale, confession was more impossible than ever. Not for the first time, I imagined my head side by side with Hardy's above Temple Bar.

'It's damnable, Philpott,' Erskine was saying. 'I swear it's got the Ministry's stamp all over it.'

'Everyone believes it, nonetheless.'

'Yet, God damn me, the tale is quite absurd. And now they have manufactured a link to Mr Hardy, a link that will no doubt appear in the papers tomorrow, as soon as the reporters get the news from my eager legal colleagues. I tell you frankly, Mr Philpott, that Hardy is quite undone. His wife's death and now this! I dread to think how he will take it. I tell him he must keep his spirits up, or the prison will have the better of him. By the by, he sends his thanks for your article on the funeral. Between that and your defence of himself, you have disarmed him entirely.'

'There is no need for thanks.' Philpott was uncharacteristically modest. The seriousness of the business had finally deflated him. 'The contrast between that solemn funeral and the histrionics of Mr Watt's trial in Edinburgh was clear for anyone to see.'

'Ah, yes, Robert Watt's trial. The papers are full of pikes and muskets, though Hardy had no desire to wield either, whatever some foolish members of his Corresponding Society may or may not have done with poisoned arrows. I confess I wondered today in Westminster Hall whether men had all forgot their own youth. Half of them supported reform ten years ago – by God, even Pitt did.' Erskine turned to me. 'I have looked into those men, Groves and Metcalfe, you thought were spies, and I think you may be right. And so it goes on, one step forward, and two back.'

'THEY SAID UNDER questioning they'd fallen out with Upton, and I believe he's putting their heads in a noose for mere revenge,' I reported to Grenville later, but without any hope he would listen. He probably knew the whole story already. 'Upton was on their committee to raise money for Hardy, but they asked him to resign. They didn't want him bringing Hardy into disrepute.'

'Disrepute? *They* talk of disrepute?' Sir James rolled his eyes. He was cheerful in a direct inverse proportion to how I felt, mighty relieved at the Ministry's escape from the danger of ridicule now the plot had proved real. 'Lord, how they do go on.'

'Upton refused to resign and challenged Lemaitre to a duel. He declined, and Upton promptly came to us.'

'A duel!' Sir James looked his disgust. 'What honour among scoundrels! I know we're to censure the practice, my Lord, but at least it used to be the recourse of gentlemen.'

'And fools.' Grenville had not appeared to be listening, but now looked at me reprovingly.

'And yet,' Aust sat down in the window and began unbuckling his shoes, 'the plot may still be real. You said the device – the blowpipe – does, in fact, exist?'

'An instrument was produced,' I said reluctantly.

'Well, we'll take our time about it,' Grenville said. 'Lemaitre and Higgins are in custody, and we'll not rush to decide their guilt with Hardy's trial coming on. Yes, this story is well timed. The first luck we've had in many months. If Jay returns home with a treaty and Hardy goes to the block, I believe we may call 1794 a satisfactory year, despite the war.'

M R GIBBS WAS BARKING so loud I could hear him from halfway down Fleet Street. Mrs Philpott was standing in the door of her shop, pen in hand, and an interested look on her face as I came up.

'What has happened?'

'Visitors at your lodging. You just missed them.'

'Was there trouble with the dog?' His high, excited bark told me he was pleased with himself and had probably sunk his teeth into someone.

'They did carry someone out.'

Dora was fortifying herself with gin in the kitchen. Mr Gibbs thrust his nose in my hand for praise.

'I'm sorry, Mr Jago, I couldn't keep 'em out. They went in your room, prodding and poking till yon critter took exception.'

'Who were they?'

'Men. Just men. Couldn't say.'

'Gentlemen? From the Ministry? Or Bow Street Runners?'

'Couldn't tell.'

'What did they say?'

'They asked me about a pistol. Asked if I'd ever seen one.' She was aggrieved. 'As if any lodger of mine would possess such a nasty thing.'

They had kept me in Lord Grenville's office, all courtesy, while their officers ransacked my room, and no one seemed much to care. Though Dora broadcast her resentment up and down Fleet Street and his wife had witnessed everything, Philpott was too busy with Hardy, and only dismissed the business as some arbitrary wartime safeguard dreamed up by Whitehall. Probably every clerk had suffered the same indignity.

But I didn't believe it, and could hardly ask them without confessing I was under suspicion. It proved the final straw that broke me. Over the following days, as I read the papers and listened to Erskine and Philpott making their plans for the coming trial, it all assumed the quality of a laudanum nightmare. How far things had strayed from Will Benson's suicide! And yet it was from that beginning that I now found myself confronting truths I had no wish to understand. I had thought the Ministry winked at Canning's murders, but now I saw it was as ruthless in its way as Robespierre had ever been. The manufacture of a brass blowpipe to lend credence to a made-up tale; the careful leaking of the news to the press ahead of Hardy's trial – these were not the actions of mild-mannered men, but cold assassins. They would kill Hardy, and these foolish members of his society, even though they knew they were innocent. Hardy's trial would be for show, a warning to others, with no regard to the strength of the case against him.

Erskine knew some of it, of course, but even he did not know the murderous depths to which the government would stoop to see French ideas stopped at the channel. What had Lord Grenville said in Erskine's study? That after Hardy's trial a mob would not dare assemble again for fifty years. Yes, they were single-minded in their determination to quash revolution. Their windows were tightly closed, as much against the disorderly world outside as against the pestilential air.

How much more likely, therefore, that far from being innocent bystanders, they had colluded to protect Canning from Will's suspicions and Mr Grant's indiscretions? I knew everything but could say nothing. I could not confront them with their crimes, or I would go the way of the other unguarded dead. Justice was a delusion, as intangible as the blowpipe plot I had invented. No one would help me – least of all Lord Grenville, Sir James and Mr Aust, for they were all implicated in Canning's falsehoods. I found myself like Will Benson, starting at shadows as the days rapidly shortened through October, the air grew cold, and I walked home by lamplight. Alleys and doorways frightened me, and my skin crawled. Black Drop and terror combined to floor me, and for a week I took to my bed, white-faced and trembling amid the sheets.

P HILPOTT ARRIVED IN MY room as a rattle of firecrackers woke me late one afternoon. It was already dark, and I had slept the daylight away. My mouth was dry, and my legs were heavy. He took in my appearance with a look of compassionate repugnance.

'God damn me, Laurence, look at you! Thin as a lath. Your eyes like saucers. I'd lay money you've been eating opium, only I hope you're too wise for that.'

I sat up. There was no hiding the bottle on the bedside for he'd already seen it. 'It helps me sleep.'

'Sleep? How should a healthy young creature like you be wakeful? By God, I am asleep before my head hits the pillow.'

I would have expected nothing else. 'You have no worries,' I said with some bitterness, cautiously putting my feet to the floor to see if I could stand.

Philpott purpled. 'Worries! When America teeters on the brink, and Hardy's neck is in the noose? God damn me, what worse troubles could possibly afflict *you*?'

I held my peace and went over to the washstand, where I splashed my face and took in the ill-effects of my dissipation in the mirror. 'As for America, you need not trouble. The treaty is quite agreed, I believe.'

Philpott stared. 'Agreed? When it's notorious that Jay and Grenville hate each other?'

I changed my shirt for a new one and pulled on my breeches. 'There are many notorious things, sir, that seem less clear on close inspection.'

I sat down suddenly, my legs folding under me, but Philpott was fetching my coat and hat and, taking me by the arm, lifted me to my feet again as Mr Gibbs scratched at the door. 'See, my boy, your dog is tired of this confinement, poor thing. I am to meet Erskine in the Salutation for something of a celebration. For God's sake, come out of this black humour and join us.'

Erskine was sitting in the window of the Salutation and Cat, among a crowd of Bluecoat boys let out of school. The inn smelled faintly of wood mould and gunpowder, the boys no doubt fresh from the building of their bonfire and the testing of their squibs. We sat by candlelight, our faces reflected in the small panes of window glass, and I watched Philpott guzzle down a plate of tripe with considerable indelicacy, while Mr Gibbs took up a station by his knee. The two men drank a toast to each other solemnly.

'What is the celebration?' I asked.

Philpott's face broke at once into a rosy smile. 'Why, we took John Taylor up for bigamy this morning at the Bailey.' His face was glowing, apparently with the excitement of the day, and he could not have looked more unlike my own reflection in the window. 'Do you remember? The rascal with a wife in two places, and a propensity to spy for the Ministry. By God, it was the most amusing business I ever saw in my life! Erskine had me act quite the busybody, looking after other men's sins for my own amusement. I proved an excessively talented thespian, which I did not expect, but the judge, God bless him, wasn't taken in for a moment, and was most displeased to have the Ministry's witness tampered with. "I shall expect to see you here every quarter day, Mr Philpott," he said to me, "if you take upon yourself the business of a constable." But we got the fellow locked up for a month, so at any rate he will not testify against Mr Hardy next week.' Philpott smiled so hard his eyes disappeared. 'I begin to hope, Laurence; I begin to believe we shall get him off.'

'Hungry, Laurence?' Erskine had been calling to the landlord for a chop and a jug of sherry.

'No, thank you, sir.' I was still full of Black Drop and I had no appetite as I watched Philpott fold the last piece of slimy honeycomb into his mouth and wipe his chin on his sleeve. Erskine believed in Hardy, and so did Philpott, but scoundrel that I was, I found I almost longed for some new damning evidence that would put his guilt beyond dispute. Real guilt, that had nothing to do with popguns or poisoned darts.

31

THE NOISE WAS DEAFENING as the procession of
condemned men came down Ludgate Hill to the corner
of Fleet Street, where the subterranean river had somehow
burst through its grating and flowed on towards the Thames,
an open sewer once more. The press of bodies was dreadful,
and I knew that somewhere in the middle of the baying mob
was Mr Gibbs. The filthy water writhed like the back of a
snake, and I was seized with a mortal fear that the dog had
been thrown in, like an unwanted pup. A log was drifting
downstream, and there was something tangled in its branches,
some dark object with the texture of hair. I looked about for
a stick to catch on to it, and came face to face with Dora,
wearing a stupid smile. 'Help me,' I said. 'For God's sake, help
me catch this log. It's Mr Gibbs.'

'No, it ain't.' She turned her head to the gallows behind
us, and I saw they had already begun. Corpses, hanging like
the shifts in her kitchen, dangled by the neck limply. More
shackled men had arrived at the scaffold foot, and I turned

to ask Dora what it meant, but she was gone and in her place was Aglantine.

'Is it Hardy?'

As if in answer she spat snuff into the gutter and raised her skirts above her waist. I threw up my hand and turned my head away. There was that log in the water again. Mr Gibbs had it by a branch. 'Good dog, Mr Gibbs.' The log turned over, the matted object bobbed to the surface, and I was looking into Philpott's sightless eyes.

'Jesu.' I sprang out of bed, suddenly wide awake. Mr Gibbs was not fishing heads out of the Fleet but lying by the window snoring, and no doubt Philpott was next door peacefully eating his breakfast. It was still dark, but Hardy's trial was to begin that morning, and Philpott had undertaken to fetch me. I lit a candle, poured a jug of water over my head, and spent a long time at the washstand, looking at myself in the mirror. The pale, long face looked placidly back, as unremarkable as ever. Anne had called me handsome, behind the spectacles and formal wig, but I would never touch her again. I felt a return of the breathlessness that had gripped me at the palace but resisted the temptation of another dose of Black Drop. Its promised balm would only bring more bad dreams.

It was still dark as we came out into the street and turned towards Ludgate Hill and the Old Bailey. I had a couple of hours before work and could hardly have kept away, but there was a long queue of spectators stretching out from the fortress-like entrance of the court, around the corner into Newgate Street. The case had certainly seized the public's attention. Philpott took me by the elbow, propelled me through the queue up to the door itself, amid injured cries of complaint. 'I been here in the pissing rain since five o'clock in the morning! Ain't you got no fucking respect?'

'I respect the press, madam, which I am proud to serve. And so should you.' Then we were inside, past the ushers who seemed somehow to know Philpott well enough not to stop him.

The jury was being sworn as we slipped on to the public benches. Large windows looked out over rooftops and chimneys towards St Paul's. The judges sat under an ornate wooden canopy, and the lawyers were arranged around a semicircular table covered with piles of books and papers. The counsel for the Crown comprised six lawyers and four clerks, while Hardy had only Erskine and my old employer Vinegar Gibbs to defend him. Aust sat in a corner of the public gallery, eyes and ears for Grenville. Next sat George Canning, performing the same role for Pitt, I supposed, and then, with a jolt, I saw Anne beside him, her hands folded in her lap, her soft hair pulled back into a loose knot under her bonnet, the set of her thin shoulders firm under her sober linen jacket. Canning was calmly listening to a clerk whispering in his ear, while Anne's eyes were fixed on a point across the room. It was only when I followed her gaze that I realised Thomas Hardy was already at the bar, facing the jury, so that they could get a good look at him.

What can I say about Hardy, the first time I saw him? The subject of so much speculation, he was in reality a commonplace man of middle years. He looked exactly what he was: a prosperous tradesman, a man who might sell you a bolt of cloth or make you a coat out of it. More than anything he looked like a man who could make you a pair of shoes, if his shop had not been burned to the ground, and himself imprisoned. Dressed in a thoroughly respectable broadcloth suit, he could just as well have been a clerk to some minor government department. Men like Hardy walked down every street in London every day, but if he looked harmless, he also looked very worn. If he looked prosperous, then a prosperous man come to grief.

I could hardly bear to look at him, or at Anne, who was now listening to George Canning, with the ghost of a smile on her pale face. Instead, I turned to Philpott, who was scribbling down his impressions in blotted haste. 'How long will it last, do you think?' The reality of the trial and all it foreboded had finally hit me, and the flavour of a Black Drop dream was upon me again. But Philpott only looked up from his notes and smiled.

'You know as well as I do. I had that scoundrel of a bigamist done and dusted in half an hour. But Erskine has a deal to say, and the Attorney General is never brief. I dare say we shall be here till nightfall.'

And would Grenville burst in before then, with some damning proof of Hardy's involvement with what the papers were now calling the Popgun Plot? It hardly mattered, for suspicion was swilling around Hardy, and no juryman could be ignorant of the rumours and innuendo in the press.

After a clerk read out the lengthy indictment, the Attorney General rose to his feet, and the case for the prosecution began. The public gallery was rapt for about twenty minutes; after that an epidemic of fidgeting and coughing spread gradually through the benches, and even Philpott grew restive, forever going to the door to view the crowd waiting in the rain or consulting his pocket watch. Perhaps in accordance with the Ministry's instructions to spin out proceedings while they elaborated the plot into something that would crush Hardy for good and all, the prosecution started slowly, producing only an endless succession of commonplace letters from one Corresponding Society branch to another. Philpott turned to me after an hour or so. 'Do you see how these letters signify?'

I shook myself from a reverie. I knew none of this mattered. 'That they show their enthusiasm?'

'But for what? Ink, not blood, apparently.'

The Attorney General was doing his best with these meagre materials, drawing out traitorous intent from the most innocuous phrases. 'If this is all they have,' Philpott said, 'we will be drinking the poor man's health by lunchtime.'

I WENT TO WORK AT TEN, leaving the prosecution still mired in literary criticism. But everyone in Downing Street was preoccupied by the events unfolding across town at the Old Bailey. Grenville sent a clerk down to the court every hour for news. By the early afternoon everyone was mystified. 'Nothing yet,' the clerks reported among themselves in the back kitchen.

'Who speaks?'

'Still the Attorney General.'

'But it's six hours gone.'

'He's still making his opening remarks.'

I copied out some treaty clauses, then went back to the Old Bailey at five o'clock, through a crowd pretty evenly split between Guysers and those preoccupied by the trial. Bonfires were beginning to be built on street corners, far bigger than any for a Government illumination. Guy Fawkes Night was the people's festival, and they poured their restless energy into it for days ahead. There were children on every corner with their guys, now often guarded by gangs of rough men with staves, and no one dared deny them a halfpenny.

In the safety of the courtroom, Aust and Canning were still sitting where I'd last seen them, but Anne was gone. Nine hours into the proceedings, everybody looked exhausted, even the spectators in the public gallery. Erskine was very pale, sitting at the desk noting down the heads of the prosecution case, rumpling his hair under his wig abstractedly, while Vinegar Gibbs rifled through law books. The prosecution was still reading out letters seized from Hardy's desk when he was arrested. Parliamentary Reform. Universal Suffrage. Treasonable documents, according to the prosecution. 'No intimation is given,' the Attorney General was saying sonorously as I found Philpott still in his seat, 'that they mean to apply to parliament for this end. On the contrary, they declare they must have recourse to their own power. The jury must make of that what they will.'

As I sat down beside him, Philpott addressed me with the end of a one-sided conversation he was apparently having with himself. 'D'ye think they imagine the jury will hang a poor man regardless, no questions asked?' He grasped my sleeve with a hectic look. 'They are bent on wearying the jury to death. I spoke to Erskine an hour since, and he fears they mean to talk it out, as men do a bill in Parliament. Except here, instead of parliamentary time, they mean to exhaust the jury's patience.'

'What good would that do?'

'At Paine's trial, the jury stopped proceedings – said they'd made up their minds already.'

'Not without hearing Erskine first!'

The ushers hissed their disapprobation as Philpott threw up his hands. 'If they ever get to the evidence, we'll see the truth of it. Good God, they must mean to start calling witnesses soon.'

Hardy was beginning to sway where he stood, and someone behind me whispered that he should be given a chair, but no such leniency looked likely. 'After this written evidence, gentlemen of the jury,' the Attorney General was saying, a valedictory tone creeping into his voice, which made everyone look up, 'we shall produce witnesses to prove that Mr Hardy meant to provide his Society with pikes, guns and other weapons. This will be our case, and we will commence on it directly.'

But even the Attorney General seemed finally to have run out of words, and he sat down exhausted. Philpott consulted his watch. 'Eight hours and fifty minutes! God damn me, you have to admire the stamina of the man.'

The judges were conferring among themselves. 'I thank the Attorney General for his very comprehensive opening statement,' Lord Chief Justice Eyre said. 'I now propose a short adjournment for refreshment. We shall continue the proceedings at five and twenty past six.'

ERSKINE WENT BACK to talk to Hardy, while Philpott dragged me across the road to the Magpie and Stump, an inn of some ill repute where the landlady dispensed ladles of stew into bowls of uncertain cleanliness. There was a dull roar from the restless streets outside, but we sat by a window of such encrusted filth there would be no seeing out even in daylight.

'We should have gone back to the Salutation,' Philpott said regretfully. He looked at his bowl of congealing fat, cautiously conveyed a lump of gristle to his mouth, then picked out the vegetables and dropped them in his ale, where they bobbed for a moment, then sank. I was too preoccupied to find him amusing as he wiped his mouth with the repulsive tablecloth and beckoned the landlady over. 'This ale is tainted, woman. Fetch another, will 'ee?' He shook his head as she went for the jug. 'Drugs and poison. That's what they put in this damned beer.'

I blinked at him owlishly in the gloom. The world seemed to be darkening day by day. I wondered if my sight was failing from the laudanum, or the world blacker than hell.

'Canning came to see me last night,' Philpott said, eyeing me over the rim of his tankard. 'In my own shop, God damn me. Hardly thought he'd demean himself by entering such a place, but it seemed he was too eager to keep away.'

'Eager? Eager for what?'

'Said he'd heard of a letter the radicals from the Corresponding Society had given me. Asked if I still had it.'

'What did you say?'

'That I'd rummage through my papers and see if I could find it.' He winked. 'Don't fear, my boy. I'd not dare let him near you for fear you'd blacken his eye.'

A violent nausea gripped me, and only the need to hear Philpott out stopped me from bolting. 'Did he ask what was in it?'

'He did. I told him it was nothing to do with Hardy, only some nonsense about the menagerie keeper and his lions. Whereupon he gave me a look made the hairs on my neck stand up. I almost thought you was right about him, for a moment.' He grew cheerful again, draining his ale and standing up. 'Time for us to go back to court, I think.' Outside the tavern, he looked at me quizzically. 'Damn, Laurence, how the devil do you contrive to see anything in those eyeglasses, with summer gone and the nights so black?'

A T MIDNIGHT, the Attorney General was still in full flow, but Erskine was rising to his feet having finally lost his patience. 'My Lords, it is absolutely necessary that we come to some determination respecting an adjournment. The court, the jury and the counsel are all but men, and cannot possibly sit up indefinitely.'

The Lord Chief Justice frowned. 'And equally, no jury can possibly be separated till after they have pronounced their verdict.' But even he looked dog-tired, and Hardy could barely stand. My own eyes were stinging from the candles and the guttering fire in the chimney.

The Chief Justice scratched under his wig thoughtfully. 'Yes, yes …' Some of the jury were making it plain they wished to go home. 'I am very sorry for it, gentlemen, very sorry indeed, but the Sheriff calls out he has prepared accommodations for you, and you must submit.'

If Erskine and Philpott were right, this was the moment for the jury to rebel. But perhaps, thank God, they did not know their own rights, and they filed off the bench sullenly but quietly enough and followed in the Sheriff's footsteps.

I spilled out with the rest of the crowd into the emptying street and reeled in the fresh air. After the close press of bodies, I hardly smelled the drains as I walked home. I half thought I heard footsteps behind me, but when I turned to look, the road was empty. I remembered Canning's visit to Philpott and shivered. One slip, one hint of my suspicions to anyone, and I would likely be as dead as the others. But, for now, Fleet Street was asleep as I turned the key in my door.

Dora was not asleep, but standing at the top of the staircase, a candle in her hand and her nightcap rammed down over her eyebrows.

'What's the matter?' My heart thumped. Had Canning been back? Was the time finally come?

'Thank Gawd you're 'ome. There's a spider the size of Beelzebub in the piss pot and I been crossing me legs this last hour.'

32

I MET SIR JAMES IN the lobby of the Foreign Office the next morning. He was on his way to the Secret Committee, to interrogate the Popgun plotters once more, but he took the time to congratulate me on the neatness of my copying, and to ask for another three fair copies of the treaty for interested parties. 'You may sit at my desk if it will be more comfortable for you,' he offered generously.

It was certainly warmer in the Under-Secretary's dark, tapestried room, for the Necessary Woman lit me a fire and even brought me a cup of tea. The trivial and the deadly, side by side in every corner of London. I lowered my face to my copying and tried to block out all thought of anything but the letters forming under my hand. The remains of last night's laudanum lingered in my head and made the letters blacker, hollower – made me feel as though I teetered on the brink of a precipice and might fall headfirst into the paper if I let go my grip on the goose-quill pen.

The clerks came in at intervals. Mr Jay had also gone to

court, they reported. He looked stern, but then he always looked stern. Mr Theodore Jay seemed bored, and no wonder. The prosecution was now testing everyone's patience by reading out reams of Paine's *Rights of Man*, perhaps to remind everybody of what a traitor looked like. News trickled in all day. Erskine had declared the prosecution in love with sedition by quoting from Paine at such exhausting length, and the public had laughed. The prosecution had found a letter written by one Corresponding Society member to another making fun of the King – firm evidence of their design to depose him. Erskine had objected. How could Hardy be responsible for a letter he'd never seen?

But two Society members had been to Paris, praised Robespierre, been kissed on both cheeks, and wildly applauded. Emboldened, they had munificently offered five thousand pairs of boots for the Revolutionary army. Though the public benches laughed again, perhaps this time the prosecution had planted a seed. Hardy was a shoemaker, and where else was this army of boots to come from?

Apprehension warred with dreariness all day, as I churned out more copies of the arid treaty clauses. At four o'clock, I put down my pen and went out into the cold grey drizzle, back to the Old Bailey, where witnesses were finally being called. Anne was there again, still sitting beside George Canning. Sir James and Mr Aust sat at the front, heads together in conference. The jury look dishevelled, unshaven and dirty. The Attorney General had gone home for a rest, but Erskine had no such luxury, and looked nearly as wild as the jury in a grubby gown and unpowdered wig.

'Do you know the prisoner?' Mr Garrow KC was asking, for the prosecution, as I found a seat. A witness had just taken the stand. He looked exceedingly frightened, glanced apprehensively at Hardy's weary face, and then mumbled something indicating reluctant assent, but Hardy didn't meet his eye.

'He once spoke of a person in Sheffield, I believe. A man he said would forge some blades for pikes. Can you recollect the business?'

'Yes, sir.' The man licked his lips apprehensively. A minor sensation was running around the room, but Erskine looked calm from his place at the table.

'What did you hear?'

'That a plan had been formed in Sheffield to forge pikes for the people there. Several of our members wished to have 'em. There was to be a meeting to lay down the money for them, and write off to the fellow. One shilling for each blade. I thought that rather dear, so did not attend the meeting, and only made one at home, for myself.'

Erskine was on his feet. 'You did not attend the meeting, you say?'

'I beg pardon, sir?'

'Mr Garrow asked you if you heard Mr Hardy arranging for the manufacture of pikes in Sheffield. You seemed to say so. But then you went on to say that you did not attend the meeting where the matter was discussed. In fact, did you ever hear of the matter from Hardy's own mouth?'

This seemed rather too hard a question for the witness, and Erskine let the jury watch him wrestle with his recollection a moment, before moving smoothly on. 'You made a pike yourself, you say?'

'Yes, sir.'

'For what purpose did you make it?' Erskine was friendly, leaning on the jury box.

'For fear of any illegal dispersing of our meetings, sir.'

Garrow cupped his ear. 'Do you say *legal* dispersion?'

'No, sir, I said *illegal*, as by a loyalist mob, or summat. They was always hanging about, threatening, like at Mrs Hardy's house.'

'Now, witness, attend.' Erskine seemed serenely oblivious to both Garrow's interruption and the murmur of sympathy that ran round the public bench at Mrs Hardy's name. 'On your oath, had you any intention to use that pike against the King and government of this country, or against the law and constitution?'

The witness spoke very loud, as if making sure he was heard right this time. 'No, sir, not against the King, or the government, or the law.'

'I ask you again, before God and your Country, did you intend to use that pike for the purposes of rebellion?'

'Not for any such thing.'

'Did you believe that any other members of the Society meant to use them so?'

'No, sir.'

'Now, witness, look at the prisoner. Did you ever know him to be disloyal or troublesome, or disaffected?'

All eyes turned on Hardy, but he only gazed at his folded hands on the railing.

'I always looked upon him as a very quiet, good kind of a man,' the witness answered.

'Did you ever hear that Mr Hardy intended to destroy the Constitution or the Government?'

'Oh, no, sir.'

'Or the King?'

'No, sir.'

Erskine turned away with a dismissive wave. 'My Lords, I have done with this witness.'

The man looked relieved, but Garrow came back immediately. 'Witness, do you know a man named Thomas Higgins?'

'He was a member of my division, yes.'

'Did Higgins once tell you of a place in Borough Market you could learn to fire a musket?'

'Yes, sir.'

'And did he not raise a subscription for the aid of Mr Hardy who stands here before us?'

'Yes, sir.'

'And is Mr Higgins not presently in the Tower, on a charge of conspiracy to kill the King with a poisoned dart?'

'Objection, my Lords. Mr Higgins's trial is not yet fixed, nor the indictment even proved.'

I stumbled to my feet and left the courtroom, feeling sick. With all the prosecution's nonsense, Upton's unproven testimony would be a card to play whenever the jury looked inclined to leniency.

I was almost glad to bump into Theodore Jay outside. He looked ominously pleased to see me. 'Laurence,' he piped, apparently oblivious to the crowds all around us, 'does Mr Pitt really go to Moorfields? You said so in Newman Street.'

Roused from the hopeless trance that had held me in its spell these last days, I took him firmly by the collar and marched him into a doorway, close by a pile of horse shit waiting for the dung cart and the broom. 'I was joking. Do you want to be arraigned for slander?'

He sulked. 'I've heard others say so.'

'Only because he shows no interest in women. But he shows no interest in men either, nor boys – nor animals, for all I know. He's only interested in politics.' I looked at the boy's eager face in the shadow, and then across to the lights of the courthouse. 'But what is it? For God's sake, you don't mean to preach to Mr Pitt?'

'Of course not.' He looked at me pityingly. 'He wouldn't let me. But the molly meeting didn't answer, so I thought of Moorfields—'

I began to see where his thoughts were leading. 'Are you out of your mind? You got a black eye in Clements Lane. You'll have your brains bashed out in the molly walks if they take you for a constable. You know the alleys are crawling with informers.'

'But the sin … It's so dreadful, I can't leave them to their fate—'

I was exasperated. 'Yes, yes, hellfire and eternal damnation, I know. Does all this afford you some kind of pleasure? An amusing *frisson* of sulphur?'

Even by lamplight I could see that colour came and went quickly in his pale face. 'By no means! Wickedness gives me no pleasure at all, I assure you.'

'And yet amid all the troubles of this vast city, your charity seems roused only by sensual sins. It is a reckless scheme, and I'll not aid you in ruining yourself.'

He turned as if to go. 'Well then, never mind.'

'What do you mean, "never mind"?'

'I shall find my own way – or find someone else to guide me.' The boy looked up at me, quite cool. My remonstrances had not done the slightest bit of good.

I fervently wished Peter Williams would appear and take the boy off my hands, but there was no sign of his figure among the seething crowd at the courthouse steps. Remembering him, I moderated my own tone. 'I can't let you do that.' There was the usual mutinous set about Theodore's mouth, and I realised with gloomy foresight that if Theodore Jay was discovered in the molly walks, Peter Williams might kiss freedom goodbye for ever. Nor would Philpott forgive me if I let the boy go alone into such danger. And then, with a sigh, I also saw that this was the one case in which I could make a difference to the outcome, and I should save him if I could.

'When do you mean to go?'

Theodore brightened at the capitulating expression on my face. 'Well ... I rather thought tonight.'

33

WE WENT BY WAY OF Fleet Street, where I changed
out of my clerk's suit and picked up Mr Gibbs, for his
teeth might prove useful where we were going. These days
Sodomites' Walk in Moorfields was a respectable row of
houses, and the sinners and sinned against had taken to a new
resort in Saffron Hill, Holborn, a shady alley of grim repute,
bounded by old tenements and home to the poorest of the
poor.

Guy Fawkes fever was growing as we made our way through
the lamplit streets out of the city. I saw a man carrying an
effigy of Pitt, with a notice around his neck listing his crimes,
and another of Fox, the Whig leader, with an equal and oppo-
site list of offences. Some children had already blackened
their faces and would stay that way until the fifth, revelling in
brigandry. Gangs of adult Guysers were roaming the streets
with clubs and some with masks, for what nefarious purpose
did not bear enquiry.

For his own part, Theodore had made no effort to conceal

his true identity, with his shock of curls uncovered. We walked up Fleet Market, over the gratings to the sewer that recalled my bad dream, and into Field Lane, which led directly across the city limits and out into the ramshackle warren of Holborn, where the road narrowed and turned into the alley of Saffron Hill.

Here rickety buildings loomed over the cramped passageway, their upper storeys leaning at crazy angles. The windows glowed only fitfully with guttering rushlights; there were no expensive candles here, no streetlamps. It was full dark except for the odd blaze of a brazier where two alleys met. I heard the smash of a plate, a child's wail. A window opened somewhere ahead, and slops poured down into the passage below.

It was a desperate spot, quite beside its fame as the resort of outlawed sodomites and those that preyed on them, and even Mr Gibbs could sense the danger. He skulked at my heels, growling in the back of his throat, and I put a hand on his fur to quiet him. It felt like the gateway to hell, and any man that ventured here would fight first and ask questions after.

'It won't do, Mr Jay,' I said, pausing at a granite milestone that loomed out of the dark. 'Those poor women you met want only money. But these men have different purposes. Would the men who visit Newman Street listen to you? If you think so, you give yourself more credit than a thousand Sunday sermons.'

'I intend only a friendly discourse.' But even Theodore looked doubtful as he peered into the Stygian shade. I bent to read the milestone with my fingers. Only a mile and a half from Charing Cross, but it already felt like another world. 'The greater the sin, the greater the call.'

'You think so? The most likely victims are the men themselves.' In the pillory at Charing Cross, faces smashed to a pulp. Sometimes even hanged. For the first time in a long time, I thought kindly of the French, for however many others they murdered, they left off punishing such men and driving them into such peril. 'If you are caught, you risk as much.'

But there was a moving shape in the darkness ahead. Someone was coming along the lane towards us, stopping every few paces as if to listen. It might be a man in search of other men, or a constable in search of felons. Before I could stop him, Theodore was gone into the shadows, and with a curse I followed, the dog at my heels. The figure ahead had stopped, and there was the sound of someone pissing against the wall. Theodore was approaching. God damn the boy, he was reckless.

The dark mass of the figure turned and shuffled slowly sideways towards the boy. He was bigger than Theodore, well set and stocky. 'Fine night, sir.' His voice was almost inaudible to me, Theodore's answer entirely so. Theodore followed the fellow into the dark, and I hastened after. Somewhere there was a scream, a burst of wild laughter, and the hiss of a firework that sent up a glow a couple of streets away. Gibbs yapped sharply, and then I heard a step behind me and there was a fugitive scent of orange.

'Aglantine?'

But the apparition melted away into darkness, and I stood still, straining my ears. Suddenly there were footsteps ahead, and then all at once a cry and the sound of a scuffle. Voices raised loudly now. I stumbled into a run as I saw a dim light ahead, and a small knot of figures locked in some struggle.

Aglantine. Theodore Jay. And a fellow holding aloft a lantern in one hand and Theodore's collar in the other. I ran faster, Mr Gibbs surging past me with a yelp, and I charged with all my force into the knot of bodies, knocking the lantern from the man's hand with an outstretched fist. It smashed and went out. My knuckles smarting, I grasped Theodore's sleeve.

'Run!' I thrust my hat into his hand and pushed him in the direction we had come. For a moment he hesitated, then he rammed the hat over his curls and was gone, footsteps drumming down the alley.

The man I had felled struck a new light and held up the flame to my face. Aglantine was at his elbow, looking at me wrathfully. He grasped at me and I struck his hand away, while Mr Gibbs growled and snapped. Windows above us opened, voices called out asking what was the matter, and the child began crying again.

Aglantine put a hand on the watchman's sleeve and lowered the flame, so that all our faces were lit weirdly from below. 'Never mind this one. I know him. He is of no account.'

'Assaulting the watch!' The man was aggrieved, panting slightly from the excitement, and Aglantine's scent of oranges mingled sickeningly with his earthy smell. 'Damned if I'll stand for that.'

Aglantine gave him a push, but he resisted, his hand on my arm again, and this time I couldn't shake it off. There was the murmur of French irritation, the clink of a coin, and then the watchman swore ripely and made off up the alley, hobnailed boots ringing off the cobbles. There was a deserted courtyard ahead, between the tumbledown tenements, lit by a small brazier. I was suddenly cold, my hand hurt and, despite the danger, I needed to rest. I trudged closer and held my hands to the flame.

'You're bleeding.'

I had thought Aglantine close behind me, but she was gone, and it was Peter Williams at my elbow. Good God, was half of London in Saffron Hill tonight? But of course, I should have known he would have been following us all the way from the Old Bailey, and Aglantine would not wish to be seen by him. I looked at my hand, black in the firelight and dripping. I must have cut it on the watchman's lantern as I knocked it from his grasp. I was glad. I deserved to bleed, and it had been worth it, for I had saved the boy from certain humiliation or worse. 'Shouldn't you be seeing Theodore home?'

'I guess so.' He took my hand and held it to the light of the bonfire with gentle fingers.

'I'm all right.' I wiped the blood on my old jacket. 'But perhaps I was a fool. You would have felled the fellow in my stead if I'd held back.'

'I reckon not.'

'You'd have let Theodore be caught? Mr Jay would not be pleased.'

He turned to go, and I followed him, back towards the distant glimmer of the city. We walked slowly in the dark. 'Better a slave than hanged for the sake of that whoreson.' He glanced at me. 'She wouldn't have saved *me* from the constable.'

He knew something of Aglantine, then. After a moment he added, 'She was there in the park when he first preached to them women.'

I remembered being lost in the dark, then as now. 'I saw her, but I thought I imagined it.'

'And she followed you to the bawdy house in Newman Street.'

I remembered a small white face gazing up at the brothel windows as I looked out. No body, so most likely a figure dressed in black. Yes, she was doubtless the woman Theodore had feared. But he had guessed her purpose and left off going.

'Reckon she found that watchman and put him up to catching Theodore.'

Of course she had. The promise of a high-born gentleman lurking in the gloom would have made him eager. He would have been famous in the papers if he'd found any man of repute, never mind the son of the American envoy. Mr Jay would have been mortified, of course. What would she have done? Blackmailed him to destroy the treaty? I realised with some bitter amusement that by this night's work I might have swayed the fate of nations, too.

Peter Williams must have wondered why Aglantine had saved me from the watch, but he didn't ask, and I didn't tell. He took out a flask from his pocket and offered me a drink. It was whisky, burning down my throat as hot as fire. 'No, I ain't risking my neck, even for a year off my term,' he said pensively. '1805 is as good as I'll get, I reckon.'

'1805?' I handed the flask back to him.

'When I'll be free.'

It sounded impossibly distant. A new century, a new world. 'Good God! But that's eleven years. You might be dead by then.'

'Have to make sure I ain't.' He put the flask back in his pocket. 'There's people relying on me, Mr Jago, back in America. My wife, my children.'

I finally saw why he wouldn't leave Jay's service. Fool that I was, I hadn't considered that he had a life of his own across the Atlantic, as a family man, as well as a slave.

I HAD LOST ALL SENSE OF TIME in Saffron Hill, but it was not yet midnight when Mr Gibbs and I reached Fleet Street. St Clement's Church was chiming its several bells for the quarter from beyond Temple Bar, while Gog and Magog clashed their clubs with less sweetness nearer at hand. I jumped as a hand grasped my arm from behind, and I turned to see Aglantine scowling up at me, apparently intending to give me a piece of her mind now I was alone again.

'I have been chasing *cet imbécile* Theodore Jay for half a year and you thwart me, Laurence. I have told you before that the talks must fail.'

I shook off her hand. 'I never said I'd help you with that. And besides, it's too late. The treaty's agreed.'

'All the more reason to prevent it.' Yes, she was angry. 'But you have put back my efforts a good deal.'

'For good, I hope.' I wanted nothing so much as my bed, and to escape her unsettling gaze. 'I'll not be your fool any more, Aglantine, not after this popgun business.'

A procession of carriages was rattling over the cobbles towards us, from the direction of the Old Bailey. The court must have adjourned for the night, late as usual. Even through the subterranean green of my lenses, I recognised the faces behind the glass window of the first carriage. Aust. Anne. And George Canning beside her. Aglantine turned with astonishing speed to stride away, head bent. Canning's eyes swept across me. I did not think he had seen Aglantine, but as the carriage rattled past, I could see him staring back through the small pane in the rear of the carriage, his eyes fixed on Mr Gibbs.

34

EVERYONE WITH THE LIBERTY to follow their own inclinations was in court over the following days, even Grenville. Only the clerks were kept at their desks, and I sat in Sir James's office, head bent over paper and ink, watching the scrupulously agreed words form themselves on the clean page in my very best round hand. The pages grew into an ordered pile, while the rain gusted on the windowpane and the light failed so that I had to light the candles. The other clerks came in and out from court by turn, on the excuse of seeking instruction from the under-secretaries. They had been obliged to fight their way through the growing crowd outside the Old Bailey. The mayor had summoned the militia to control the mob, which seemed to find the conjunction of Hardy's trial and the anniversary of the Gunpowder Plot more than commonly intoxicating.

'We spoke to Mr Philpott,' a clerk said, coming back in at three o'clock on the fourth day, rather tousled, despite the militia's best efforts. 'Mr Erskine has proved half their witnesses paid informers.'

In the absence of any superior to deny me, I gave myself permission to leave my papers and go down to the Old Bailey. The crowd was immense, as large as at any hanging, and my feet left the floor as I fought my way down to the courthouse where, recognising me as a respectable clerk, the guards at the gates let me past. Nothing in the courtroom had changed. Hardy still stood at the bar, paler than ever. The judges still sat in their elevated seats like saints on a rood screen, and the same lawyers sat at the table below. The noise from the street washed in and out every time the doors opened, and the judges looked up irritably at every interruption. Erskine sat at the table exhausted, while Vinegar Gibbs was on his feet, cross-examining another witness. I couldn't see Canning, which made me somehow uneasy as Philpott made a space for me on the bench beside him. He spoke low, under the buzz of conversation on the benches.

'The Crown's evidence is all trash. But saying so ain't enough, for we can all see that already. Erskine can't deny the seriousness of revolt when the French are busy sweeping all before them in Europe.' He shook his head. 'And whenever the jury looks sour, the prosecution can talk some nonsense about Lemaitre and his blowpipe, and bring them back to heel like a pack of hounds.'

I SPOILED HALF A DOZEN sheets of copying, half-written, the next morning. Sleepless, I had doubled my nightly dose of Black Drop, and I now felt sluggish, only half-awake. More than that, I felt old. My bones ached, and yet at the same time I felt light-headed and only the pen in my hand anchored me where I sat in Sir James's comfortable chair.

How had I ever hoped to bring Canning to justice, when Grenville and Pitt were his allies? I was a lowly clerk, and it was all utterly beyond my power to change. My efforts had only made everything worse. Higgins and Lemaitre were still in prison, suffering God only knew what privations, and their names alone would be enough to persuade Hardy's jury to send him to the scaffold.

There were light footsteps crossing the lobby, running up the stairs to the landing, and thence to the door of the room where I sat. Someone for Sir James, no doubt. In fact, it was Canning, advancing into the room towards me, half in shadow from the dull light at the window and the dull red glow of the fire.

'Sir James is at the Bailey.' I took my glasses off and laid them on the desk as if it would render me invisible. Canning was a blur as he approached and sat down on the other side of the desk. 'There's no sense in waiting. He won't be back for hours.'

'I know. I left him there, along with every man in Whitehall. You are aboard a deserted ship, Mr Jago.'

Now I listened, the building *was* quiet – very quiet. No sound of voices, or laughter from the garret, or even the footsteps of the domestic staff downstairs. The activity that thrummed through the building morning till night was silenced.

'It's you I wanted to see, Mr Jago.'

The table between us was some kind of barrier, but his slim frame was poised as if to spring, and my hand closed foolishly around the ink pot as the only weapon to hand. 'I can't imagine why.'

'Can you not? I confess, you have always been an enigma, Jago, and grow more mysterious by the day. You never explained why you sought a duel. Never explained why you blamed me for poor Mr Benson's death. And now at the Secret Committee, George Higgins swears blind you went to their meetings in disguise. That you asked him for a letter which raised some doubt about another man's death. What you do in your own time is your own business, but it is rash to attend radical meetings in the present circumstances. And to deny it is even more curious.'

'Unless I was telling the truth and was not there.'

He only looked at me. The existence of Mr Gibbs hung between us across the table. I was calculating furiously, wondering how much I should confess. How much or how little would provide him with a motive to murder me. I was still listening for movement downstairs. There was none.

'I went to see Philpott,' he said.

'He told me.'

'Among other things, I asked him about your family. Your parentage. Something that might explain your eccentricities. He told me your mother was not well liked in Cornwall. He did not know why, though I surmise he makes his own guesses.'

I wondered how Philpott had imparted this information. Cheerfully, innocently, thoughtlessly? 'Mr Philpott knows nothing at all about it. Quite as little as he knows about your own mother.' I regretted the words as soon as I spoke them. It was more knowledge I should not have.

Canning didn't seem to hear. 'But in fact, Mr Philpott is your great friend, and got you off the hook. At least for some of it. He tells me Erskine asked you to go to the Corresponding Society meetings to help him with Hardy's case, which, though foolhardy, is not, I suppose, a hanging offence.'

'Mr Canning, I don't know what you want with me.'

He stood up. With his back to the fire, his face was hidden, a mere silhouette. 'Nor do I, Mr Jago. You remain a puzzle. But if you'll take a word of advice, I would take great care who you call your friends, and who your enemies. Leave off your snooping, it doesn't become you, and mind your own neck instead of others'.'

I put on my spectacles again to examine him as he turned to leave.

'Oh, and as for Anne Aust,' he said. 'Don't mistake her pity for admiration.'

INSTEAD OF GOING TO court after work I went out to Kensington in the dark, and loitered under the plane tree in the square, leaves falling about my shoulders like dead butterflies. I looked at the lights of the drawing room where I had spent so many hours these last ten years, and wondered what Anne was thinking, and what I would say if I found myself in her presence and had the chance of a private word. Perhaps that George Canning thought so little of her that he had forgotten her name. She had never been Anne Aust, for the Under-Secretary had only ever been her stepfather, and as long ago as '89 she had taken another man's name.

London had been ablaze with candles in the spring of that year, to celebrate the King's return to health and reason, and Aust had held an illumination in Kensington. All the clerks had been invited – I had no special status then, being still stuck in the garret, a papery pallor growing in my face like Pitt's – but, for one last moment, I still had hope as I watched Anne go over to the large window, taper in hand.

'Are we all ready?' Aust had fussed over, rearranging the candles unnecessarily.

'All ready, sir.' She was just nineteen, dressed in white, but there was a crimson shawl around her shoulders I had never seen before.

We all drew near. The garden square had fallen into dusk, and the poor man's bonfire in Hyde Park was well alight, while a footman from a neighbouring mansion seemed to be wrestling with our own. A fellow Aust had introduced as Ned Bellingham of HMS *Cato* pushed forward, the firelight reflecting off his brass buttons, and took it upon himself to offer Anne the candles one by one, the candlelight shining through the fine work of his lace cuffs. I saw his fingers linger on her own, saw her blush – expected her to give him the same frosty stare she turned on me when I betrayed too much of what I was feeling. She did not. And as we turned back into the room to take our tea, and pick at the supper laid out on the table, I saw him rearrange the shawl about her shoulders. Surreptitiously, his fingers slid to her tender throat, and from there to her collarbone.

That shawl was his betrothal gift to her, brought back from the Indies long before they ever met. All hope gone, I wondered in my bitterness what other woman had been the intended recipient, as I lay in the long grass of Roscoff that summer, and tonight, standing in the darkness of the square under the dying leaves, it was tempting to blame her for every-thing. Tempting to pretend it was only anger that opened my lips to Aglantine on my return from France and began the long chain of circumstances that led me here tonight. But I recoiled from this feeling with shame, for every man was an island. In the end, every man had to take responsibility for his own wrongdoing and not waste time in disingenuous excuses.

A carriage had been rattling along the road from London, and now it drew up outside Aust's door. Two figures emerged

– Anne herself, and Canning – probably just returning from the Old Bailey. She was clutching a nosegay of hot-house flowers, an expensive gift on a cold winter night, and I knew then I had no hope of winning her back, and that I did not deserve to do so.

Later, alone in my room, the chimes of London's churches rang in the hour raggedly, and the third of November turned to the fourth. A solitary rocket over the rooftops announced Guy Fawkes Night a day closer, when the traitor would burn in effigy on a thousand bonfires.

Hardy would burn, too. By gifting the Ministry the Popgun Plot I had as good as hanged him myself. I took the largest dose of Black Drop I had ever ventured, and after a moment's hesitation, slipped the bottle into the pocket of my coat. Soon the trial would come to its inevitable end, and when it did, I would need oblivion.

35

'COME TO COURT TODAY, LAURENCE,' Aust said the next morning, waylaying me on my way to Sir James's study. 'Erskine is to give his oration, and the copying can wait another day. Four copies already? Very good, yes, you are excused from further labour until this business at the Bailey is done.'

I felt sick from the drugs of the previous night and still stupid, and the court was so packed I didn't think I'd get a seat. But Philpott caught sight of me, elbowed his neighbour smartly in the ribs, and made a space beside him. I looked around, thinking to see Theodore, for I'd heard nothing since he ran away up the alley in my hat. But he was not there, nor was his father. Indefatigable Anne was back in her place, and so was Canning. Erskine was rising from his seat, Hardy's mild eye fixed upon him with painful hope. Erskine nodded first to the judges, then let his gaze travel over the public benches, over Hardy's lonely figure and then finally, with melancholy brown intensity, over the jury in their box.

'We have heard so much about parliamentary reform in this trial.' Erskine drew a tired hand across his forehead, and spoke with a weary stoicism. He looked as if he had not slept for days. 'The gentlemen of the prosecution have argued that any attempt on the part of the people outside Parliament to persuade those inside to change the franchise, the taxes or the law is an act which must ultimately result in the death of the King. This doctrine, which they have argued in order to damn my client, is so absurd I would have hoped it hardly in need of an answer. But in these perilous circumstances I find I must do so after all.' He turned to the judges, high up on their bench, and suddenly the weariness was gone. 'My Lords, if you will permit me, I have one final witness to call in my client's defence.'

'A witness, Mr Erskine? We had believed you embarked on your closing statement.'

'So I am, my Lords. However, the honourable gentleman in question has been unavoidably detained by the prosecution of the war and can only now make his appearance. It would seem a dreadful pity to send Mr Pitt back to Number 10.'

There was a tremendous sensation in court as Erskine smiled at the jury, triumph apparent under his fatigue, and in the corner, Aust, Sir James and Grenville put their heads together in sudden conference.

'Mr Pitt!' a clerk called over the din of voices. 'Will Mr Pitt be pleased to appear?'

The Prime Minister was certainly not pleased, as he made his way to the witness stand through a roar of conversation and bursts of laughter. In fact, he looked as pale and harried and bad-tempered as ever. The courtroom only quietened down when he was settled in his place and had sworn his oath. Erskine wasted no time on pleasantries but handed Pitt a paper at once and asked him if he knew the hand. Pitt studied it for a moment, then handed it back, looking, if possible, more pained than ever. 'It is my own.'

'And what is the document, Mr Pitt?' The Lord Chief Justice was eyeing the Prime Minister somewhat wildly. Pitt, by contrast, was as stiff as a broom handle.

'A letter on the importance of parliamentary reform, my Lord.'

'And when was the letter written?' Erskine asked, looking between Pitt and the jury with significance.

'Nine years ago. Forgive me, if I do not recollect its contents exactly.'

'To whom was the letter addressed?'

'I believe to a gentleman in Westminster, interested in the same cause. There were several meetings to discuss the matter – one at the Thatched House Tavern, I remember, one at my house. One with the Duke of Richmond.'

'Mr Pitt, is it not true that those meetings and this letter were in support of parliamentary reform, in which you then believed?'

'I have already said so.'

'And is it not also true that your professed scheme then was to garner the sense of the whole people throughout England?'

'I do not recollect the precise details.'

'I think you will find it so. In fact, an opponent in the House objected that you solicited opinion outside Parliament in this way. They declared it might undermine our system of government.'

'I do not recollect such an objection.'

'But you, sir, were of quite a different opinion. You declared that petitions must come from the whole body of the people – from all parts of the kingdom—'

'I have no recollection—'

Erskine bore him down. 'We should never for a moment dream that *you* intended violence or force, sir. But even you said that a degree of awe was necessary, to remind Parliament that they withstood the whole body of the people.'

Pitt's fingers drummed on the witness box, and for a moment it seemed he would not answer. In the end he seemed reluctantly constrained to do so – perhaps by his understanding of perjury, or, to do him greater justice, by the prompting of his own honour. 'I dare say I made some such observation.'

'Well, then, why in God's name were *you* not taken up for treason?'

There was uproar. Pitt flushed red and Lord Chief Justice Eyre hammered on his desk. A boisterous cheer broke out, followed by uproarious laughter. An echo came from the crowd outside, as the news travelled back over the benches and into the street. 'Ha!' Philpott said in my ear. 'The damnedest thing I ever saw! By God, we shall talk of nothing else for weeks!'

'That will do, Mr Erskine. Mr Pitt, you may step down.' Lord Chief Justice Eyre looked harried, and Pitt stalked gratefully out of the courtroom, back to the safety of Number 10. But the noise went on and on, until the ushers began ejecting people from the public benches and the rest fell quiet. In the sudden hush, Erskine's voice was much more cheerful.

'Gentlemen of the jury, you are, of course, all electors, else you would not be here. Your votes send representatives to Parliament, but your choice of candidate is quite constrained. They must be rich enough to work without pay. They must be well connected enough to have their names put forward at all. And you send them to the *House of Commons*. That is a curiosity, is it not?' He pointed a finger at the foreman. 'You, sir. I believe that you are a baker of biscuits, and next to you sits a maker of starch. There are merchants among you – coal merchants, I mean, not fat East India Company men. You, sirs, are the true commons, and within these walls your writ is law. Do not let the prosecution frighten you into injustice. You have no reason to recoil at such a man as Mr Hardy. He is no monster, only a skilled tradesman. Only an arbitrary property requirement stands between him and the vote – between him and yourselves. Times are hard, war is upon us, and our way of life is at risk. But do not entertain so stupid an imagination as that in days like these, a country can be preserved by corrupting one half of the people to defame, bully and persecute the other.'

He turned to address the courtroom at large. 'My wish and my recommendation is not to conjure up a spirit among us to destroy ourselves. By imitating the tyranny of a French tribunal, where an accusation alone is enough to bring its object to the guillotine, we are in danger of abandoning the things we are met here in this place to protect. Gentlemen, patriotism demands that we keep to the old and venerable laws of our forefathers and let a jury of the country weigh the evidence, and the evidence alone. To your care I now commit my client without fear, being confident that you will do him justice.' He sat down heavily in his chair, overcome by emotion.

Lord Chief Justice Eyre leaned over his desk to peer down at the prisoner. 'Mr Hardy! Do you have anything to add to your defence?'

For the first time, the court heard Hardy's voice. For all the talk, and the week of evidence, none of us knew anything of the real man at all. He was merely a symbol for both sides: a cause for one, and for the other an ogre, with which to frighten women and children.

'No, indeed, my Lord,' he said, so quietly the crowd hushed

one another to hear him. 'I have nothing to offer in addition to what has been said for me and am quite satisfied with what my counsel has done.'

THE COURT ADJOURNED, and we shuffled towards the door, behind the departing crowd. Something banged against my hip, and I remembered the Black Drop bottle still in my pocket. I had come to court ready to stun myself with laudanum to stave off despair. I had come with no hope. I had been so caught up with my own affairs that it hadn't occurred to me that Erskine might pull off the customary brilliance that had made him famous. But Philpott, walking ahead of me, only looked tired and morose as people slapped his shoulder in congratulation and shook his hand. 'Words, words, words,' he said. 'And the summing-up still to come.'

I touched his arm. 'You are too gloomy. The jury was spell-bound. Rapt.'

'As rapt as the pit at a playhouse. But 'twill all be forgot tomorrow when the judge tells 'em to kill Hardy anyway. How can twelve men, half of them tradesmen, stand up to the power of the Crown?'

'You think they'll still find him guilty?' It had not occurred to me that such a thing was possible.

Philpott only shook his head and led me down the steps into the tumultuous crowd, where competing groups were singing 'The Roast Beef of Old England' and 'Ça Ira'.

'I don't know.'

He hastened across to the exhausted Erskine, being physically supported to his carriage by Vicary Gibbs, and then Mr Aust was at my elbow. 'Well, well, who would have thought Erskine so damned clever?' He was stirred up, despite himself.

'Come out to Kensington, my boy. I have issued quite a general invitation, so we should have some good conversation. No one wishes to go home after such excitement.'

I hesitated, though only for a moment. 'Thank you, sir. I'll come along presently.' Philpott was too cynical. Everyone else in the lamplit square seemed certain Erskine had triumphed.

But then Sir James and Grenville came up behind me, Sir James full of good cheer, and my sudden hope was punctured. 'There is still the summing-up to come, my Lord, don't fear. Chief Justice Eyre will direct them as to their duty.'

As the cheerful crowds moved off towards the town, my mood darkened again. Philpott, for all his nonsense, was astute. How could so much anguish and despair be dispelled in a moment, by only words, words, words? I lingered in the emptying courtyard in the shadow of the brooding courthouse that had seen so much misery, that had condemned so many men and women to death. The jury could yet betray an innocent fellow man, simply out of fear of the Ministry.

I hardly knew where to go. I took a few steps towards the Magpie and Stump, but I wasn't hungry. Took a few more in the direction of the hackney stand, to take a cab out to Kensington as I was bid. I felt lost and very alone. Even Hardy had his loyal supporters, his counsel, and the vociferous support of Mr Philpott. But if my own wrongdoing was ever exposed, they would all turn away from me, for I had done no one any good. Had only endangered others instead of myself.

A reckless swig of Black Drop was the only possible rejoinder to such thoughts and, being the one dependable player in this drama, it soon did the trick. I felt only numb, though perhaps a little more breathless than usual, as I hailed a Hackney to follow the others out to Kensington. As the carriage rattled through the busy streets, through the fireworks and the flames, tranquillity flooded up into my mind once more like warm candlelight, infusing everything with hope and easy clarity. Erskine had triumphed in court, and better men than me would find the Ministry out in the end and avenge Will Benson and Mr Grant. My guilt would be absolved and I would escape the consequences of my own rashness. Hardy would be acquitted, Anne would eventually see through Canning's lies, and slowly over the coming months I would work my way back into favour. Suicides – murders – the machinations of governments – what were they to me? Only torments I could do nothing to solve. A quiet obedience, like Mr Aust's, would last me into a peaceful old age, and was the best I could hope for. And if it also pleased Anne, it would be quite enough happiness to last me a lifetime.

36

THERE WERE CHEERFUL lights in Aust's broad bay window, and music spilling down the stairs into the street as I came up to the open front door. The breathlessness was back upon me as I climbed the stairs to the drawing room, but I thought I could see Anne at the piano, her face turned away from me. Candles blazed everywhere with their honey perfume. Dazzled, I turned towards sudden loud voices behind me. It was Philpott and Canning coming in together. More arrivals in the street below, and I thought I heard Sir James's laugh in the hallway. 'Where are the Jays?' a voice asked behind me in the crush. 'Ain't seen them for days.'

Do you suppose they've fled back to America without telling anyone?' another answered.

Canning had arrived in the middle of the conversation. 'No such thing. Mr Theodore Jay is merely unwell, and his father stays at home to nurse him.'

'Unwell! Is it serious?'

'I think not. But Mr Jay believes the boy will be confined to his lodgings until they do leave.'

There was a table spread with supper, but the Black Drop had taken away my appetite, and I needed to gather my muddled wits. I went over to the darkening window, only half listening to the conversation behind me, and Anne's modest talents on the piano. Lights were visible from the vast sprawl of London in the east, while the gardens below were sprinkled with lamplight, and the gleam caught in the sleety raindrops that gathered on the windowpane. A fire was roaring in the grate. Behind me, Anne began to sing in her husky voice. She was running through a collection of old folk tunes and modern songs. Her voice suited the old songs best.

Philpott and Canning were close again, standing together beside the fire behind me. Philpott's gloomy mood had turned pugnacious. 'Damn it, Canning, you may quote Mr Burke as it suits 'ee, and call common folks the swinish multitude. But don't he also say they're the wise cattle, quiet beneath the English oak, while fools chirp about their feet like grasshoppers?'

Canning, apparently not counting himself a grasshopper, sounded amused. 'Brute animals in either case, Philpott. I might even misquote another great man, and say it's as curious to see Hardy argue politics as to see a dog stand on its hind legs.'

Philpott was probably quite aware that Canning thought him a dancing dog himself. 'Rid yourselves of the *animals*, as 'ee call them, and what will be left? A wilderness no invader would trouble to disturb. Why, man, the people make everything you eat, drink and wear. They build the carriage you ride in, dig the coal for the fire you sit by, put the roof over your head. They outnumber you twenty to one. What makes their views and desires of no account, when you eat up all that they produce like a succubus?'

'How can a man speak of politics who does not know Plato or Aristotle? Who does not know Pericles or Cicero?'

'How can a man speak on taxation who never did a day's work in his life? Who does not know the price of bread? Hardy is a damned well-educated man in his own field.'

The piano had fallen quiet, and Anne was coming over. She brushed past my sleeve and I opened my mouth to speak to her, but Canning was making a gallant bow, and she did not spare me a glance. Philpott excused himself bad-temperedly, going off to the supper table.

'Do you like to sing?' Canning had already fixed her with his grey gaze. She was dressed in a dusky lavender, and her shoulders glowed under a scant chiffon neckerchief. She coloured as his eyes moved to her bosom. '"Richmond Hill" is a particular favourite of mine,' he added, 'and you sang it beautifully.'

She was gazing up into his eyes with her customary ardour. 'You are very kind, Mr Canning, as always. It's been done to death by so many, I half expect to be pelted like a man in the stocks. But it *is* pretty.'

They were scarcely an arm's length distant from me, but quite oblivious, wrapped up entirely in each other. It seemed imperative now to break the gaze between them, to turn her eyes to me. 'You did sing well, Anne,' I said, and she turned with a reluctant smile. 'The one about the almond tree seemed made for you, with your pale skin and blossom-coloured gown.'

'The one …?'

'Something about an almond tree under the window, with paper-white flowers? I've never heard that one before.'

The look on her face was changing as I spoke. No longer reluctant, she was looking at me as if I had run mad, suddenly quite as stiff and quite as pale as the paper she had just sung about. Why was she angry with me? For competing where I could never win? But Canning was also looking at me narrowly, and Anne's eyes were unreadable dark pools.

'*Un amandier, qui a des fleurs blanches, comme du papier,*' she said, almost in a whisper.

The Black Drop had made me stupid. I felt quite alone, and suddenly afraid.

'How very curious.' Canning was still studying me. 'Did I not say you were an enigma, Mr Jago? Lord Grenville will be mighty interested to learn of your unexpected talents, unless you have some special secret duty I am unaware of?'

I had forgotten to breathe, and the lights were jumping in my eyes. 'No, no, sir. I believe that is your department, not mine.'

He raised his eyebrows. Then, as the words sank in, his eyes widened. His special secret duty. What else could I mean but his relations with Aglantine, perhaps even murder? I spoke French. I owned a dog I had denied existed. I bowed with confusion, turned and fled before he could stop me. I passed Philpott morosely eating a pie by himself in a corner but pushed past his outstretched hand, down the stairs, and out into the quiet square. I spewed up the scanty contents of my belly into the gutter, and then stumbled off into the sleet, towards the city, dressed only in my best clerk's suit and thin leather shoes.

Robespierre tried to escape retribution at the guillotine by putting a pistol in his mouth. But the God whose existence he denied would not let him escape the end he so richly deserved. So it was with me. I had condemned myself unprovoked from my own mouth. So many years of guarding my secrets, all for nothing, blown away as if they had never been.

I passed stragglers from the Old Bailey crowd still singing, still skirmishing with those that opposed them, touting
effigies they would burn come the following night's revelry.
Guy Fawkes, Pitt, Robespierre, and many – far too many – of
Hardy. Perhaps it was my own despair, but there looked to be
as many loyalists as radicals among the crowds.

In Fleet Street a paper blew under my foot, and the name
Watt caught my eye. In the lee of St Dunstan Church I bent
to retrieve it, and held it up to a streetlamp to read. It was wet
from the sleet, only a fragment, but I knew at once what it was.
The traitor's confession, made the night before his execution.

*Remember, reader, that the period is coming when death shall
be as near to you as it is to me. On the brink of eternity, with
the throne of judgement in plain view, dare you approach the
Omnipotent with a lie in your right hand?*

I was shivering violently with the cold, and now without more
warning than a metallic wheeze, Gog and Magog turned their
heads to me, hammers raised, and struck the half-hour.

Send not to know for whom the bell tolls. It tolls for thee. I had
turned Hardy's life to my own use and by doing so had bound
his fortunes to mine. No man was an island, after all, and if
Hardy was condemned, his passing bell would toll for me, too.

All this flashed through my mind in the time it took the
giants to beat out the chimes. When I came to myself, I found
I was leaning against the church door, still looking at the
paper flapping idly in the gutter where I had thrown it.

Will Benson and Grant were beyond saving, but Hardy was
not. And now, my secrets discovered, all hope of escape gone,
what use was there any more in silence? *A lie in your right hand!*
I had lies in right and left, lies on my shoulders weighing me

down to the ground. Lies that had kept me quiet these past weeks, through all the villainy I alone had witnessed. If Hardy was condemned on my idle tale, I was free at last to save him. All that could stop me was Canning himself.

And so, as soon as I reached my room, foot sore and shaking, I drew out pen and paper and, by the light of a candle, wrote feverishly until my fingers seized with cramp. If Canning sends the Runners for me, I will confess everything to them. If he murders me, these pages will speak for Hardy. Who will come for me I do not know. The Ministry to arraign me as a spy. Canning to kill me. Or Mephistopheles and his demons to drag me to hell.

All I know is that this paper will account for my actions and redeem Thomas Hardy if he is still alive to be saved. I will not go into nothingness like Will Benson, a mystery to my parents and the world. Dawn is nearing and I am still at liberty and still alive. As the last candle dwindles, I remember the confession prayer I have heard my mother whisper of a Sunday since I was small. *I have sinned exceedingly, in thought, word and deed. Through my fault, through my fault, through my most grievous fault.*

Amen.

37

WHEN I OPEN MY EYES, I realise I have fallen asleep, my head on the written sheets of my confession. Birds are beginning to chirp hesitantly outside the window, and the dark sky is fading to indigo. The court will be coming into session at any moment, and I cannot be late. I am already dead, and all that can redeem me now is discharging my debt to Hardy.

But, if Canning kills me before I can confess, these pages are his only hope. I put a ribbon around the closely written sheets and carry them down into the street. I find Philpott's shop deserted, for which I am grateful, and lay my confession on his desk. Whatever else happens now, justice will be done. This has been the solution all along, the penance for all my former crimes, but until now I have been too wedded to life to accept this simple truth.

THE COCK, THE MITRE, the Globe, the Cheddar Cheese, all open already, their bonfires lit, and the city one mass of excited humanity. At the corner of Fleet Market and Ludgate Hill a hand grasps my arm, and I turn to see Aglantine.

'My secrets are discovered, and I'm resolved to tell everything about the Popgun Plot.' I set off walking again, pushing through the crowded pavement without looking at her. It gives me courage. 'I have been a fool, but now I'll be my own fool. I'll not see Hardy butchered for something he didn't do.'

'You can't.' She is hurrying to keep up with me and, for the first time in all these years, her composure is slipping. 'They will hang you.'

'They will hang me anyway. I told you, I am betrayed.'

'Then come away with me. I can put you on a coach from the Boar in Holborn that will take you straight to France.'

'And leave Hardy to his fate? Aglantine, it was all our doing, with that damned story.'

'Remember my hands. Remember what I have suffered. If you confess, they will kill me, too, in Paris if not here.'

I pity the panic in her voice, but the scars on her hands are no stigmata. Neither of us is innocent. The only innocent ones are Hardy, Grant and Will Benson. Two are dead, and the other's life is in my hands.

She is still following me up Ludgate Hill. 'But if he is acquitted, what then? You will be quiet? You will come away before they catch you?'

'No.' What use would France be to me? 'I'm resolved to speak out for the other dead, and seek some justice. Will Benson. Poor Grant of the menagerie.'

'Very noble,' she taunts me, with a return to her fierce scorn. But she has finally stopped following, and her voice is fading behind me. She has given up at last, I think wonderingly, and for a moment at least I am free.

I arrive at the Old Bailey only just in time to squeeze in

the courtroom and hear the judge begin his summing-up. The place is more packed than ever, and there is a general hum of conversation that contrives to drown out a good deal of what he has to say, but I hear the names Higgins and Lemaitre through the din, and the jury looks serious. Their moment of decision is at hand, and the burden lies heavy on them.

At least in the crowded courtroom I am safe from murder, and my racing heart settles slowly to a steady beat. There is plenty of time, after all. If the jury condemns Hardy, I will stand up to confess. He will be saved one way or another. But the Lord Chief Justice is not brief, and it is gone noon before he is done. Long enough for my mind to slip back over all the preceding years, and forward to the sorrow I will bring my mother on this day.

'Gentlemen of the jury, you will now withdraw and consider of your verdict,' the Lord Chief Justice says finally, amid a sudden hush. 'As you may have no refreshment after you retire, you may, if you please, have it before.'

'There'll be no need of that,' one of the jurors says, perhaps more loudly than he means, then reddens and falls silent, and the jury men file out, under the combined scrutiny of judges, lawyers and public.

'What do you suppose he meant by that?' someone behind me asks.

'That they'll not be long.'

My heart is so full a pin would burst it as the court adjourns, and Hardy is led back down to the cells, as quiet and unreadable as ever.

The crowd funnels me towards the door, out to the swarming courtyard. Erskine is pale and abstracted, like one just come from a trial of his own, and Philpott is urging him to take some dinner. After some altercation they push through the crowd towards the Magpie and Stump. The crowd is swelling on the pavement beyond the courtyard, more and more people drawn by the news that the jury is out, and despite the presence of the militia, barrow boys and costermongers push through, selling refreshments. There is the eternal smell of Guy Fawkes Night – smoke and gunpowder and baking potatoes – and a rattle of firecrackers echoing down the street. Bow Street Runners are everywhere, watching the crowd anxiously and taking instruction from others who come pushing through the throng at intervals for whispered conclave. I fancy they are looking at me, but no one comes near, and now I realise I have seen no sign of Canning all morning. *Just a few moments more,* I find myself praying. Just until the jury returns, so that I may redeem my soul before death comes one way or another.

The jurors come back to their bench in the mid-afternoon. As the news spreads, every conceivable space in the courtroom is filled. More and more bodies crush in, the court ushers shouting and pushing back, to keep the latecomers from suffocating those at the front of the public benches. It reminds me of the mob in Piccadilly, but six months have changed everything – then they burned Hardy's house, now almost everyone here champions him. If circumstances call on me to speak, I will have an audience for my confession beyond anything I could have imagined. My palms are wet, and I wipe them on my suit. My mouth is dry.

The judge is almost inaudible, as the jury, the lawyers and the prisoner take their places. There is a collective shushing and a burst of excited laughter from the doorway behind us. I am rehearsing phrases in my mind. What will I say? Where will I begin? I imagine shouting 'Objection!' like some lawyer. But the foreman of the jury is on his feet and the clerk to the court is questioning him.

'Do you find the prisoner guilty, or not guilty, of high treason?'

The noise has scarcely abated, and I strain to hear as the foreman leans across his fellows.

'Not guilty, my Lord.'

I am not sure I have heard aright, turn to question my neighbour, begin to stand up anyway to make my statement. But a rising tide of noise has begun at the front of the court and breaks over me like a wave, the news passing back and back until it reaches the street. There is an enormous cheer and another burst of fireworks. God help us all, the crowd has grown larger still. People are talking all around me, but I strain again to hear what is happening at the front of the court. The Lord Chief Justice is thanking the jury for the attention they have paid the business. Then Hardy, pale and weeping, says something beginning with 'Fellow countrymen', but no one can hear him.

PHILPOTT'S WEEKLY CANNON

THE TRIAL OF
MR HARDY CONCLUDES

On this date, one hundred and ninety years ago, Guy Fawkes was thwarted in his plan to destroy Parliament and the King. Today, those that seek discord and rebellion were also thwarted in their designs, not by fire or the gallows, but by the reaffirmation of our British Freedoms.

It was clear that Thomas Hardy was not guilty of Treason, long before the jury of his peers acquitted him. But it was not the brilliance of Mr Erskine that saved his client – though brilliant indeed he was. No, the jury

needed the merest nudge to do their duty and discrimi-
nate guilt from innocence as juries have ever done under
our Ancient Constitution. Happiness filled the courtroom
when the verdict was given, and a cheerful smile spread
across the Defendant's weary countenance as he accepted
the congratulations of his friends.

But to my dying day, I shall remember Lord Chief
Justice Eyre, as he thanked the jury for their verdict and
declared the prisoner free. He gave no sign that he and
his masters had been entirely thwarted by the decision of
the court. This is our glory. This is why we will fight the
French to the death, rather than lose the liberties that we
are so fortunate to enjoy.

The early-winter dusk is falling as we come out into the
courtyard. The lamps have already been lit as the cheerfully
riotous mob drags the horses off the hackney carriage and
men take up the shafts themselves, with much boisterous
noise. Hardy, Erskine and Philpott are lifted by the wave of
bodies and deposited at the carriage step, where Erskine shouts
something to the crowd, and they cheer. He is transfigured. So
is Philpott, who hangs out of the carriage window and waves as
the cavalcade moves off towards Lincoln's Inn, bearing Hardy
in triumph. Philpott sees me in the watching crowd, and shouts
to the carriage men to stop, but they do not hear him. I would
not have gone in any case, for my fate lies elsewhere. The mob
surges forward in pursuit, and it is a good many minutes before
the courtyard is left to the dignified and the defeated.

They all look dismal. The Attorney General comes out to
commiserate with Lord Grenville, but his Lordship is tight-
lipped and makes his excuses. Even the rattle of his wheels
over the cobbles sounds bad-tempered as he drives away. Sir

James and Aust are already discussing what they will do with the dozens of other political prisoners waiting in the Tower to follow Hardy to the bar of the Old Bailey, as they set off back to Downing Street on foot. I will follow in a moment, but I pause to savour the night air and the smell of gunpowder. My own end must still take place, but it is to be a quiet one after all, and for that I am grateful.

What will be happening now in Lincoln's Inn? Erskine may receive a mixed reception from his colleagues, bringing with him a cleared traitor and such a motley mob of supporters. On the other hand, he has achieved such a dazzling personal triumph that men will soon be clamouring at his door for representation. And Philpott will be there at his side, deservedly sharing in the applause. I am glad for them both – heartily glad – but I turn my steps towards Whitehall, for none of this changes my own situation. Canning knows my secrets – Philpott has my confession – and I find that I would rather meet my accusers at a time of my own choosing than wait to be summoned.

The noise is deafening as the revellers come down Ludgate Hill to the corner of Fleet Street, where the sewer flows under the road and on towards the Thames. The press of bodies is dreadful, and I see the Guysers have already begun. Corpses dangle limply from makeshift nooses – Pitt, Grenville, the Whore of Babylon – and now a makeshift sledge has arrived at the scaffold foot, and Guy Fawkes joins them. Outside the debtors' gaol another execution is in progress – God damn me, it is Hardy and Erskine, tied back to back on another sledge, both grinning like clowns, and two such competing groups will be at each other's throats in a moment. I push through, over the junction with Fleet Market and the grating where the filthy water slithers. I stop, arrested, for something bobs up at the grill, and I am seized with the conviction that all this has happened before, but when I cannot say.

I hear a voice behind me. 'That one. In the green spectacles.' There is a shadow at my back, a rush of air, and then blackness.

THE PAIN IN MY pounding skull wakes me. I am being dragged by the heels into an alley, and my head is thumping over cobbles like the wheels of a cart. I don't know where I am. I don't know anything. My glasses are gone, and it is dark. Somewhere, far away, there are shouts and laughter, but here there is only the rasping breath of the man who is dragging me, and perhaps more footsteps behind us. I cry out for help but all that comes is a whisper. I am thirsty, my mouth is parched, and there is something sticky across my lips. Blood, from the taste of it, and my head seems to have a hole in it, for the cold night air is inside my skull.

I raise my hand to beg for water, but it's too dark, and the man dragging me does not see. Once well inside the alley, he stops, drops my feet, and coughs like a consumptive. I had thought it was Canning, but this is not him. A paid assassin, after all.

I am to be killed like poor Will Benson, like poor Grant, and, despite everything I have learned these past months, I find I am astonished. Consciousness comes and goes with the sound of the man's panting. Will was knocked on the head, then hanged, I explain to Philpott, while he nods and smiles over his unlit pipe. Grant was fed to his own lions. And now I am to join them, if I am not much mistaken. What do you think, sir? Is it Canning's footsteps I now hear, coming up quietly behind, to see the thing done?

Philpott has no answers, but his pipe is finally alight. I smell smoke, and when I open my eyes the darkness is gone, and with it, Philpott's imagined presence. A blaze is kindling ahead of me in the darkness. And now hands are under my armpits dragging me towards the brightness as a child might drag a guy. For a moment I am awake, and I see that although the bonfire is stacked up roughly, it is made up of sturdy junk – broken bits of cart, tree branches, a wheel with broken spokes. Sturdy enough to bear a man's weight without scattering uselessly into embers. The flames are catching hold and licking the lichen from the branches like flesh from a bone.

And now Will is with me, laughing as he used to laugh in the park, dancing as he used to do by the bandstand, swirling a woman in his arms. I smell oranges. They turn and it is Aglantine, flying through the air, as a pistol shot shatters the darkness inside my head and I am sinking into unconsciousness again.

Aglantine has come to save me with her own burned hands, as I always hoped she might, but Canning is there too, shouting above the crackle of the fire. Is that a laugh or a cry? My eyes open to see the flames surge, catching hold of black fabric. The hole in my skull no longer freezes but scalds. Good God, it is not Canning or his henchmen at all – what possessed me to think so? It is Mephistopheles, and his demons are with him. I think I see a hand in a lace glove, reaching out to me, but then a boot kicks it into the heart of the flames and I am gone down into oblivion as deep as a Black Drop dream.

38

PAIN WAKES ME. My head, *my hand*. God damn me, my hand is on fire. I jerk away from the flames, but when I open my eyes there is no bonfire, no darkness. The blue light of dawn is stealing through Fleet Street, leaving deep shadows where it cannot yet penetrate the darkness. Under Temple Bar, where I am lying propped against the wall like a drunk, the light picks out only my boots. The roof above me is still as black as Hades.

I move my hand into the light. It is scorched and red – in parts raw, almost as neatly peeled as Will Benson's flesh in the laboratory. The nails are blackened. But apart from my hand, it seems I am otherwise undamaged by the fire. The wind still blows through my head, but I can stir and look about me. There are figures moving in the half-light, Fleet Street awakening for a new day. The clock chimes seven, and a procession of workmen are trudging past, through the city gate, without casting me more than a cursory glance.

'You're alive,' a scornful voice says from the shadows to my left. 'Thank God. Perhaps you'll do me the favour of walking the last steps to your door. I am dog-tired with carrying you.'

There is no mistaking that voice. '*Canning?*' I turn to see him leaning against the archway with one shoulder of his immaculate suit. Not so immaculate, in fact. His face is blackened. Smoke? Gunpowder? His suit is torn.

'You may call yourself the luckiest clerk in Whitehall this morning.' He wipes a hand across his forehead, leaving a black smear, then sits down beside me. 'Here.' He is holding something out to me. 'You would not have wanted *these* left at the scene of the crime.'

My eyeglasses. I take them and put them on. One lens is cracked, and there is a strange jagged line before my eyes, like a fracture in the world. There was a pistol, I am beginning to remember. What does he mean by *the scene of the crime?* Then I remember the fire, the burning dress, the hand kicked into the embers. Will there be anything left of Aglantine to be found?

My head throbs, the pain in my hand is exquisite. I can hardly think and need some relief. My hand goes to my pocket for the Black Drop, and I cry out again. The bottle is shattered, the contents a black stain on my suit, and my unburned hand is bleeding from the shards of broken glass.

'A dangerous remedy for despair,' Canning says, watching. 'Though hardly more than all your other remedies this year. The duel. Conspiring with Aglantine. Fortunately, I am more circumspect.'

I can see him properly now I have my spectacles. He looks tired, but the same haughty Canning. Somehow, for reasons at present inexplicable, he has saved my life.

'You have also treated with Aglantine,' I say sourly. 'I saw you.'

'As have half the clerks in Downing Street, it transpires.'

He watches me pull my sleeve down around my burned hand against the stinging air. The pain is worse for a moment, then a little better. 'She was nothing if not persistent. Thought if she tried everyone, some weak-willed fool would crack eventually.'

The thought is familiar, and then I remember Upton at the Corresponding Society meeting. *P'raps you think summat will stick, if you throw shit hard enough.* Is that all I am? Is that all I've ever been? When I thought she had especially sought me out, that day in Dick's Coffee House, was I wrong?

Canning is still talking. 'She tried Will Benson, too, but of course he was far too loyal to be her spy. Unfortunately, it meant when he saw me with her, just as you did, he jumped to the same conclusions.

'I wish I could say I'd been more prudent than either of you, but I was no less a fool when I told her he was suspicious of me and might warn Pitt I was a traitor. It had not struck me she would value Pitt's secretary higher than a clerk's life, and would not scruple to save such a vital alliance with a murder. When I saw what she meant to do, I tried to warn him – chased him to his lodgings more than once – but she and her devils got to him before I could. They would not risk leaving him lying in a ditch to raise awkward questions in the Department. Flattering, really, that they esteemed me so high they'd go to the lengths of a pretended suicide. But it proved useful, later.'

He is examining the rip in his suit. Looking quite as arrogant as ever. 'Yes, I was a fool with Benson, but not this time. Lucky for you, I have been following you since last night, or you'd be as crisp as Guy Fawkes by now. And even if any trace of Aglantine is found, the Runners won't get to the bottom of it. The ruffian that dragged you in the alley was likely the same man killed Benson, and therefore he won't dare betray us for tonight's work, even if he knew our names.'

I lean back against the wall, closing my eyes, suddenly sick. Perhaps this is a dream, for in what rational world would Canning be sitting beside me on the ground, speaking calmly of murder?

'And lucky for me, too, since I appear to have redeemed my soul in the process.'

I open my eyes again at his suddenly sombre tone. 'Redeemed …?' There is no new man behind his eyes to explain how thoughts so like my own come to be in his mouth.

'I freely confess I was to blame for Benson's death. But I learned my lesson from that catastrophe, and have saved you, Mr Jago. For what you are worth.'

I am not dreaming. Moreover, I am alive. If they arraign me for treason this state of affairs will soon change, but the way my head hurts, death has lost its sting. Still I remember his former words. *Some weak-willed fool.* I try not to look at it square-on; try to pretend the words unsaid until I have leisure to examine them.

'I saw you with Aglantine at the menagerie,' I say instead.

'I guessed as much.'

'She told me she'd offered you money for your mother's upkeep in return for secrets. But later I guessed the Ministry had already told you to court her. Use her.'

'Naturally.' Is there some fractional softening of his expression towards me? Perhaps it is just the excitements of the night that make him forthcoming. 'Sir James came down to Oxford to find me. They knew I'd had some dealings with the radicals at the University. Knew I'd been a French sympathiser but still had the sense to see the Revolution was tending to the guillotine. He asked me to come into politics. Make myself available to be seduced by our mutual friend in black.'

How strange to think the Ministry have known about Aglantine all along, even as I fell in and out of love with her. 'I thought you a French spy at first. I thought you had passed the leaked message to her.'

'Of course I did. We needed to get the army back to Antwerp somehow. But then Paris smelled a rat and leaked the message, and it was damned touch-and-go whether the press would ferret out the whole story and all our pains for nothing.'

'You blamed Will Benson. Planted evidence in his room.'

'He was dead already. I told you it was useful. Would you rather Grenville had had you hanged?'

I remember saying the same words to Philpott all those weeks ago in his shop. *The boy is dead and buried, and well beyond their harm, I suppose.* If chance had kept me away from Mr and Mrs Benson, I would not have discovered the blow to Will's head. It was only luck that I witnessed Canning's meeting with Aglantine in the menagerie that day. It could all have been so different. 'I suppose they have always known about me, too.'

Canning reaches in his pocket and pulls out a box of snuff. Delicately, incongruously, in the shadow of Temple Bar, he takes a pinch.

'In this, if admittedly in nothing else, you have been quite the success. We have not known what to make of you these many months. Thought you merely a piece of her usual cannon-fodder, until you fixed your attention on me so disagreeably and inserted yourself in matters of state.' He offers me the box of snuff, but I shake my head. 'These past weeks I have rather thought *you* a murderer, Mr Jago. Mr Grant knew me pretty well from my meetings with Aglantine at the menagerie – thought me a sympathiser – and told me someone had been asking questions. I told him to keep it to himself, but in the end he must have let something slip to Aglantine, for she sent me a message down to my mother's house in the country to tell me she feared some new betrayal. I sent Grenville a message and he wrote Grant a warning note – tried to get him out of town. But, by God, she was always ruthless. Grant was dead the same night, and you only a street away! One of the first on the scene, and apparently so eager to help Aglantine in all her schemes.'

The vision of another life, in which none of this happened, is still hovering near the hazy edges of my mind, but at this I snap awake again. 'You thought *I* killed Grant?' Was that why they had sent a search party to my rooms? I could almost laugh to think they thought me a danger, when their visit had, in fact, driven me to bed, shivering like a coward under my sheets.

'When you started asking for Grenville's letter at the meetings, I felt sure you had done it, and were covering your tracks. You were Aglantine's puppet, after all. Quite content to put Hardy's neck in the noose with the blowpipe nonsense.'

'*You* did that.' I am suddenly shaking.

'She went to Upton, I'm pretty sure of it – desired nothing more than that Hardy should hang, especially if on such a foolish tale. Those crowds outside the Bailey would have risen to a man. Strung us all up from the lamp-posts. Stormed Number 10.'

He straightens. Gets to his feet. 'But it turns out you are no murderer after all. She strung you along until your foolish bit of French in Aust's drawing room betrayed you. I suppose you told her your secrets were discovered?'

I only nod as he pulls me to my feet.

'Yes, and therefore as dispensable a creature as poor Benson or Grant. Come, let's get you home and for God's sake stay there and stay quiet.'

He puts my arm over his shoulder, and begins to help me across the street. I find I am dizzy, and my voice sounds distant amid a crashing headache.

'You make everything out to your own credit. But you would have killed Hardy, too, if you could. You had the blow-pipe made. I heard Mr Aust say the Ministry wants terror, and you would all have seen Hardy hang on a lie. You're no better than the French and I'll not stay quiet.'

We stop almost under the wheels of a rag-and-bone cart, as Canning turns to face me. 'No one wants your opinions, Mr Jago, and if you persist in hounding the Ministry, it will go very badly for you. No one will riot, still less revolt, over the trial of a disloyal clerk. Keep quiet, and you may slip back into Grenville's favour little by little until the whole business is quite forgot.'

He does not know it is too late for that, for Philpott has my confession and will have read it already. As he deposits me at my door without much ceremony, I reflect that, whatever comes, I am alive against all odds, only a little singed around the edges, and that having been silent for so long, I will at last have my say.

DORA MENDS MY HEAD and wraps it in linen, smears my burned hand with mutton fat, and binds the other with strips from her own petticoat. Reluctantly she brings me a clean shirt, and my second-best suit. 'Eh, must 'ee go? You look dreadful poorly.' But she fetches me a hackney, I tell the driver to take me back to Whitehall, and as we drive away

Mr Gibbs is sitting at Dora's feet. Through my broken glasses everything looks crooked, and I close my eyes, wishing I had laudanum to dull the pain from my wounds and the fear that threatens to overwhelm my resolutions.

There is an urgent meeting between Lord Grenville and several other unnamed gentlemen, the Chamber Keeper informs me, when I arrive in Downing Street, and I must wait to be seen. I wonder if Philpott is already there, laying my confession on Grenville's desk. More likely he is in Fleet Street, totting up the value of my story to his circulation, while here in the Foreign Office they hatch a warrant for my arrest. I always knew I would be alone when the worst came. Clerks pause only to gawp at my wounds. Who else among them did Aglantine approach? They will congratulate themselves on their own superior loyalty when I am dragged off to the Tower in shame.

Grenville's door is opening. His Lordship stands on the threshold, brightness around him like a halo. 'Mr Jago. Would you have the goodness to step into my office?' I can see into the room behind him. No Philpott. But Aust is there, looking grey as ever, Sir James half turned away in profile, and Mr Jay looking at me with chilly disdain, a van Eyck painting once more. Then Canning steps into view and the portrait is complete.

I pause in the doorway, a shaft of wintry sunlight in my eyes that refracts off the cracked lens of my spectacles and makes me squint. The men looking back at me are in no mellow mood, and of all of them, strangely, Jay looks the angriest. I imagine the chains, the Tower, the noose. If they arrest me, I will do my damnedest to take them down with me. If they arraign me for treason, my accusations will only ripple out the wider.

Grenville is frowning as he goes to his desk and sits heavily. 'You are aware, Mr Jago, that you have compromised all that we have worked for these past months?'

'Yes, my Lord.' I remember the confessional in Roscoff, and, after all, the words come freely. I forget my aching head and enflamed hand. This catechism is the welcome preliminary to words that will matter more. Days of testimony in court that, whatever Canning says, will cause a stir that will change government for ever.

'Betrayed our trust most dreadfully.' It is hard to believe the gall of it, from one who has betrayed so many others, but he is serenely righteous. 'Yes, a veritable worm in the apple.'

'A snake in the grass,' Mr Jay adds. 'The tempter, the beguiler of innocence.'

'Quite so.' Grenville turns to the envoy. 'And you, Mr Jay, above all, are the injured party. What would you have me do with him?'

I do not quite see what sudden tangent the conversation has taken, until I notice Theodore Jay behind them, sitting by the fire, his curly head in his hands.

'That is a matter for you, Lord Grenville, of course,' Jay is saying. 'Theodore has only said that he regrets the whole affair most deeply and was quite taken in by Mr Jago's depravity. He begs you will overlook the affair in Saffron Hill, for he remains mercifully ignorant of Mr Jago's exact crimes in those precincts, but otherwise he leaves everything to your discretion.'

Grenville plays with his snuffbox absently. 'Hm. A plodding sort of man, whatever Mr Aust may have hoped, and now it seems with an unfortunate predilection for low company, whoring – and worse.' He flips open the snuffbox lid and takes a pinch. 'We should have overlooked it, I suppose, if you hadn't had the temerity to debauch Mr Theodore Jay amid such delicate negotiations.' He looks up at me as if I am someone already half forgotten. 'Not everyone can rise to the standards of the Foreign Office, of course, but such a want of judgement can't be excused.'

Sir James has a hand under my elbow and is propelling me out of the office before I can speak. I struggle in his grasp, looking back over my shoulder, the words of my accusation dying on my lips as the door behind me closes. There are no farewells, no memorable last words. All I remember afterwards is the ghost of a smile playing about Canning's mouth as he glances from me to Jay and Grenville and then, as the door is closing, his unmistakable wink.

THEY COULD NOT ARREST ME, I see that now, for I know too much to appear at the bar of the Old Bailey. For them it is better, far better, to put me away quietly with a convenient tale than let me speak at all. And it is genius in its way. The charges are unanswerable, and the *entente* between nations will be strengthened by Theodore's escape from disgrace.

But still they do not know that Philpott has my confession. I do not doubt he will publish it, for *he* has no guilty secrets to conceal. Then let the Ministry attempt to silence his unruly pen! And for myself? What will happen next is a blank I cannot begin to fill. But there is one final thing I know. Like Peter Williams, I am adrift in a strange land, and all I want to do now is go home.

39

A BRISK SOUTH-WESTERLY blows us up the channel, the crew of the shabby merchantman ever shortening sail. Gulls follow us up on the tide, and once I imagine I see the splash of a dolphin but lose track of it in the moving water. Empty sea and sky. The subdued chatter of half a dozen men. After the fever of London and Hardy's trial, the peace is passing strange. I take myself and Mr Gibbs to the bow, to vomit in private, and watch the Cornish coast slip by, under a veil of rain. I bought no new Black Drop, and I regret it now as I empty my guts into the turbulent November sea.

A glimpse of whitewashed cottages hugging the hill, the fields on the headland brown and muddy. Fishing boats are out in numbers despite the wind, following fish on the flood around Manacle reef, while close into shore they are lifting their pots, water cascading as the baskets come up on dripping ropes. Such activity on a cold winter day speaks of hunger. The weather has turned wet with a vengeance, as Philpott once predicted, too wet to graze the animals outdoors, and after the dry summer, fodder and bread will be scarce.

Two monstrous warships swing at anchor in Falmouth harbour, their sails furled, their sides gleaming and new painted in readiness for sea. White-trousered sailors lean on the rails and watch us make our ramshackle way between them towards the docks and the Custom House. By the time we reach the quay it is late afternoon, and the windows of the town wink with the first of the lamplight. Until the boat docks and I find myself on dry land it seems like nothing more than a picture, and I can no more imagine walking its peaceful streets than the sunny squares of one of M. de Calonne's Canalettos. Suspended between London and home, I lean on the prow and allow myself to believe neither really exists.

But the town is full by its own standards. Sailors on shore leave from the Navy stand about in groups, mahogany brown and drunk already, well turned out with ribbons in their hats and neatly oiled pigtails. Mr Grant should have stayed among their number. He would have had at least as much chance of surviving the war as he had found in the menagerie. A tender is launching from the shore and takes off in the direction of one of the largest ships at anchor, a midshipman sitting stiffly to attention in the waist, with its orders clutched in his hand. I had thought myself at the hub of affairs in Downing Street, but here I am far closer to the war. It is uncomfortable, walking through this patriotic bustle, to remember my disloyalty, and to imagine Philpott reading my confession. I could buy a bottle of laudanum to blunt the sudden shame, but I tell myself it would be sheer craven weakness. New tendril fingers of fear settle about my heart as I watch the midshipman clamber up the tall side of the ship with his bundle in its oiled canvas wrapping. I can almost see Philpott's eyes gleaming at such a scene of martial purpose. It is only now, as I turn into the doorway of the Old Grapes crouching down by the water, to take a room and a simple supper, that I see how much he may come to hate me.

I TAKE THE MARKET wagon from Falmouth to Helford the next day, through the sunken lanes. Even the ivy is brown and rotting in the hedgerows. At the ferry point the horses wade into the water still harnessed to the wagon and pull us through the heavy drag of the tide. Somewhere in the middle they swim for a moment, before their hooves touch down again, and the wagon begins to climb up the other side of the estuary.

Helford is its usual squalid self, full of waggoners, tinkers and people of no discernible occupation. An officer from the Custom House has a ruffian by the shoulder and is marching him in the direction of the lock-up. Nets are everywhere, in the process of repair by squatting fishermen, who scowl at anyone that trips over them. I sling my portmanteau over my shoulder and hurry through the huddle of thatched cottages, uphill towards home, Mr Gibbs at my heels. It is a steep pull and I pause at the top, out of breath, my head still throbbing for want of Black Drop. I look back down on Helford harbour. It looks no better, even from this distance.

The road up from the creek to the farm is practically impassable with mud, and when I turn in, the yard is in uproar, almost as bad as the building sites on Ludgate Hill. Dogs I don't know run circles around me and snap at Mr Gibbs, while clouds of dust issue from the back garden along with the ringing of hammers. A workman is mixing plaster in the front yard and smashed glass and rubble is strewn everywhere.

But then Peggoty, the old collie, comes running around the

side of the farmhouse, her ears flopping and her tail waving. She looks at me for a moment, before bowling herself into my arms just as my brothers appear from the cow house to see what the racket is. They hasten over to embrace me. 'See now!' John is saying, as he catches me in a bear hug, and then strokes my sleeve, unbelieving. 'It's our Laurence.'

James only smiles. 'Why didn't you write and tell us?'

'Because I came by sea, quicker than the post.'

There is a gawky young man behind them, my brother Anthony grown to manhood.

'Mother's in the kitchen.'

Amid the general racket, she has taken no mind of the noise of my arrival. She has flour in the dark hair that curls out from under her cap, humming a lullaby and baking scones. Peggoty pushes past me, her coat full of wet mud, and shakes vigorously all over the tablecloth. Mother turns, sees me, and the next moment she is in my arms.

THEY ARE BUSY ALL DAY, the men carting straw for the cows' bedding and grinding corn for their fodder, while Grace minds the sheep and poultry and Mother makes what shift she can to feed us. The building works are still in hand, and altogether there is far too little time and money, and a great deal too much mud and mess.

But the days seem peaceful to me, after the turmoil I have come through. I am a little weak and sick from want of laudanum, but I read the newspaper cover to cover, the *First and Last*, repository of all local news and retailer of London affairs to the West Country. Erskine is a hero and Philpott's long-awaited account of his meeting with Mr Hardy in the Tower a sensation. Two more men have been tried and acquitted, and it looks likely the other trials will be dropped. But there is no sign of my confession yet, no news of another traitor fled from Downing Street to the provinces.

My life is in Philpott's hands. In the despair and cold of London I was willing to throw it away for a noble cause. But here, despite my family's troubles, there is still the calm I dreamed of. Mr Gibbs dozes in the inglenook by the fire, like a dog born to country living, and, in the evenings, Grace plays the piano as the soft rain falls persistently on to the saturated ground.

But still there is no justice for Will, though his parents are pacified and the story almost forgotten in Downing Street. Oh, Aglantine killed him and she is dead, but the facts of his murder are mere symptoms, not causes. If Canning had not courted Aglantine, Will would be alive. If war with France had not broken out, Canning would have had no need of Aglantine, and Will would be alive. If the revolution in France had not happened, there would be no war, there would have been no spying, and Will would be alive. Back and back it goes, like mirror reflecting mirror to eternity, and myself in each pane, inflamed by a possibility of change that will likely never come in England and has led only to ruin in France. Yes, I am present in every reflected image, but my actions meant very little. I was a mere straw blown into the breeze by this juggernaut of colossal events. Is it possible that I may one day come to forgive George Canning – and myself?

NOVEMBER TURNS TO DECEMBER, and I am thirty, as I told Aglantine I would be, that summer day at the hanging. I feel older, from the pains of quitting the Black Drop, and yet younger again, being back at home, as if London itself has been only a painful dream. Mother is singing happily in the kitchen, baking the same birthday tea she always made for me as a boy. I am ghostly from lime, mixing plaster for the workmen, when I hear Grace calling from the sheep field. A hat is approaching up the lane, presumably atop the head of a mounted man. I push my new felt cap off my face as the horse comes around the corner and into the yard escorted by the excited pack of farm dogs. They snap and snarl as the rider dismounts, and James appears from nowhere to take the rein politely from his hand. Philpott looks about him with mingled pleasure and disgust until he catches sight of me and halloos loudly, taking off his hat and waving it in the air.

'My dear boy! I find you at last! I have been wandering these damned lanes all the morning and been to half a dozen farms.' His eyes are looking everywhere: at the workmen, the cows and the mud. 'All a good deal neater than this, I must confess. But you are still amid construction, I see.' He sets off around the house into the garden without so much as a by your leave, where I find him standing back, hat in hand, looking at the mellow old house with its gaping wounds, his face as rosy as ever. Two workmen are neatening the holes in the walls in preparation for new windows, while another whistles over a piece of timber.

'Is this what your mother calls improvement? I see a deal of mess and inconvenience, but I'll take her word for it. Will you tell me what they intend, now?' He has surely read my confession, but his eyes are as blank as buttons, and I realise he is not going to tell me his business yet. He is his usual obstinate self, and I will have to make the best of it.

'They have closed up all the old windows that looked out on the muck of the yard and are making new ones with an aspect over the garden.' It is whimsical to talk of flowers when my life hangs in the balance. 'John Barry here is remaking the staircase, and there's a man from Helston in the parlour making good with a new coat of plaster.'

'A parlour, you say?' Philpott frowns and examines some half-finished windows stacked up against the wall. 'I was not used to find such an article in a farmhouse.'

'But it will please my mother. Come, sir. Will you step inside and meet her?'

Philpott stoops as he passes the threshold, and blinks in the sudden dimness, where she stands waiting, wiping her hands on her apron. 'Will you take something to drink, sir?' She is on her best behaviour, her accent almost indiscernible, but it doesn't matter now, I remember, for Philpott has read my story and knows everything.

'Thank you, ma'am. A drop of beer or cider would be most refreshing.'

Philpott takes his mug back out into the drizzle and leads me on an inspection of the barns and even the privy, gathering material, he announces, on the state of the nation. He quizzes my startled brothers on the tithes and the rates. He seems determined not to be asked the reason for his visit, turning every approach to the subject aside with some new exclamation on the state of the farm, and I am none the wiser when we sit down at the table. The birthday provisions are ample, and Philpott stares at the spread with some unaccustomed wonder. If he is come to take me, it will be my last natal day, my last good meal.

My mother is fussing. 'Can I tempt you to some heavy cake, Mr Philpott?'

'Thank you no, ma'am.' He looks wistful. 'I make it a rule to end each meal a little hungry. I am a big man and would be bigger still if I ate all I fancied. I would recommend it as a plan for your strapping sons.'

Everyone looks at John and James, who gaze back placidly, their broad elbows resting on the tablecloth and Mother offers them a plate of scones. 'But they must keep up their strength, Mr Philpott. To farm the land is dreadful heavy work, and heavier since we cannot pay for extra hands at present.'

Anthony takes a large slab of ham and sets it on his plate, apparently pleased that he is still too scrawny to be the subject of Philpott's discouraging advice. 'And are you a colleague of Laurence's at the government, sir?'

'No, indeed. I am William Philpott.'

My family meet this announcement with blank faces, and Philpott looks at them with some surprise. 'William Philpott? Scourge of the American Democrats, the French Jacobins, and of mischief-makers everywhere? Welcomed back to these shores in June by Pitt himself, with a handsome set of china? And just lately involved in the acquittal of the so-called traitor, that fine man, Mr Thomas Hardy? God damn me, I had hoped my name might have preceded me into these parts.'

'Was it in *The First and Last*?' Mother offers him a slice of heavy cake again, which he now absentmindedly takes. 'Well, I confess, even if 'twas, we only read the farming news. You must forgive us.'

'Forgive you! Madam, I look on it as a challenge. Give me five years and every Cornishman, Scotsman and Welshman shall know my name. Hold me to that, madam.'

'I shall be sure to do so, Mr Philpott.'

'And in return I must make a challenge of my own.' He looks around, slowly and somewhat severely, puts the slice of heavy cake on his plate with deliberation, and then presses his palms down upon the table. 'Madam, I fear for my country, when there are wives and mothers like yourself in it, and honest men like these I see before me to suffer the consequences.'

'Indeed, sir! I am sorry to hear it,' she returns calmly, but with some surprise.

'I wish you could make the acquaintance of Mrs Philpott, madam, as my model of a wife and mother. I met her in the jungles of America, nine years ago, a young Englishwoman transplanted to the wilderness by her adventurous father. They had battled snakes and bears, crocodiles and lions, to make as snug a little home as you could hope to find. I took one look at her, Mrs Jago, and whisked her away. I tried my own hand at farming for a spell, and Mrs Philpott was a help-meet such as the Bible praises. She ploughed, she sowed, she baked bread, yea, after grinding the corn with her own poor hands. She kept our little house as clean as a pin, but did she ever turn up her nose at the mud and the muck and the animals? Did she demand windows looking on to flowers? Did she ask for a parlour? No, madam, she did not. She gloried in the mud, as the symbol of our honest toil, as now she glories in piles of papers and ink.'

Mother meets my eye. A ghost of something lurks around her mouth. If I ever had wits enough for Whitehall, I know full well where they come from.

'Mr Philpott, I am quite inspired,' she says. 'Never have I heard the duties of a wife explained so clear. Never before have I pondered the dangerous tendency of my household ambitions. Can you explain more fully the perils of a parlour, so that I may instruct my daughter?'

'I can indeed. I did not stand up for Mr Hardy to bring about the Rights of Man, you know. No, no, I only seek to save the British soul by British ways. As Burke says of the British Constitution, madam, the triumph of this country is in its traditions, and as Mr Erskine argued, we break with the habits of our forefathers at our peril.'

'I should be sorry to meddle with the Constitution, Mr Philpott, but I believe even my grandmother would have fancied a parlour had she seen one.'

'Fancy! Aye, and that is the beginning and end of it. You'll be offering me a cup of tea next, which is, madam, no less an abomination of modern life than parlours, or—' he concludes with some enigmatic bitterness, 'damned potatoes.'

40

THE LIGHT IS FADING as we set out into the lane for a tramp through the mud. A blackbird whistles a winter song, otherwise the world is still, damp and misty, the setting sun gleaming behind a low bank of cloud. After all Philpott's nonsense, I believe he is finally ready to tell me his business, and my own fate, which now lies in his hands.

'Aye, aye. What a year it has been, to be sure.' Philpott sounds easy. He takes off his hat and swings it in his hand, wigless to the elements, and entirely at home in the country lane. I have been waiting all day to hear his purpose in coming here, but now I find myself willing to postpone the reckoning.

'What was happening in London when you left?'

'The treaty is signed, and Grenville triumphant. But there've been two more defeats for the government at Erskine's hands, and all the other suspected men set free.'

'Does the Ministry still fear a rising?'

'No, no, that moment's past. Erskine killed it stone dead with his defence of the Constitution, and ought to get a medal from a grateful government.' He looks at me sidelong. 'But of course, he won't. Not from those devils. Now, what else will interest you …?'

'Mr Philpott, why are you here?' I find I can't bear the anticipation any more. 'Are you come to arrest me and take me back?'

'Arrest you?' He looks at me as if I have run mad. 'No, no, I am merely on my way back to America. I've a berth booked on a ship out of Falmouth in a week's time. 'Twill be vastly convivial, for Theodore Jay and Mr Peter Williams are to go back on the same boat, carrying a copy of the treaty, while Jay goes on to France. He don't trust his boy on the loose in Paris, I assure 'ee, and the paper must reach Congress as soon as may be.'

Somehow, I realise, I have counted on Philpott to make everything right. I would, in fact, gladly surrender to his custody if that was his purpose. But now I see he cares nothing for me or my wrongdoing and will leave me behind without a second thought. While Theodore, Philpott and Peter Williams turn their faces to another continent, the bearers of vital news, my own future stretches out before me, empty and bleak. 'I will miss you.'

Philpott isn't listening. 'Jay means to smooth the feathers of the new government in Paris, but they are mighty displeased about the treaty and will hardly make him very welcome. I suppose he'll kick his heels back in London until April, when he dares brave the sea himself. Mrs Philpott will likely cross with him, for she fears the winter storms as much as he does. In the meantime, I shall be in Philadelphia, and will defend his treaty until he comes. There'll be a dreadful to-do about it.'

He still mystifies me, his opinions slippery and adamantine by turns. 'You still support the treaty? After all this?'

'France ain't the answer to our problems, I assure 'ee, and England is more than those scoundrels in Downing Street, my boy.' He takes out his pipe and chews on the stem as we walk on down towards the water. 'They got rid of you damned neatly, I hear. As the debaucher of innocent youth, you wasn't enough of a gentleman for the Foreign Office.'

'Something like that.'

We come to the head of the creek. The tide is out, and a heron flaps slowly home in the dusk. I open my mouth to ask if he has read my confession, but Philpott goes off at something of a tangent. 'I ain't a gentleman either. Not what they mean by one, at any rate.'

'I never supposed you were.'

'Was in the army when I met Nancy in Canada. Should have done quite well, if I'd learned to keep my mouth shut. But I found the officers were pilfering money meant for the soldiers. Well, you can imagine what I did. I took 'em to court for embezzlement.'

'You ...?'

For once there is no bluster in his tone, no foolishness. 'I hadn't reckoned with their influence. From me court-martialling them, it soon appeared *I* was to be arraigned for disloyalty and such-like offences.'

I stare at him. 'Does Lord Grenville know all this?'

'I doubt it. 'Twas all so long ago. I made myself scarce, and after a discreet period in America returned quite reinvented as the loyal servant of the Crown. How should anyone remember? How could they indeed? The papers are destroyed or filed away somewhere quite forgot.' Philpott is looking at me through the gathering gloom. ''Twill not always be so. I hear they think to examine a man's past before he joins the Government, even in the meanest capacity. At present they know more of what passes in Antwerp than – let us say for an example – in Cornwall.'

'That's true.'

'The day is coming when a man's parentage, his associates, his political opinions will all be under scrutiny. It's only common sense, I suppose, but it shouldn't suit me to have my past raked over. Thank God, I'm an independent man.' He purses his lips and whistles to a song thrush making a racket in the trees above our heads. It falls silent at once, apparently offended at the interruption.

'But I wanted to be discovered. Wanted to have my say in court. Wanted to expose them—'

'Did you?' Philpott's eyes are on me.

'If you published the work I gave you—'

'They would be certain to call you a madman – a fellow with a grievance, having been dismissed in disgrace.' He sees me start to protest and puts up a hand to stop me. 'I read your piece, Laurence, and thought about it for days, I assure 'ee. But whatever else they may be, they are not stupid. They picked your offence very well, for 'tis calculated to make you out either a fool or a knave, and undermine any statement you might make, however true. Men like us can never win, you see. Not me, against the army, nor you against the Ministry. Not until we get Hardy's reformed parliament and all men vote. Perhaps not even then.'

He looks away, out over the mud flats, while I digest his words. What in God's name will become of me? If he is right, I am stranded on this Cornish coast with no future I can see. But Philpott is reaching in his pocket, and he hands me a sealed paper. 'I was charged to give 'ee this.'

'Charged? By whom?' He doesn't answer, and I break the wax seal, holding the paper up to the fast-failing light. I see the Downing Street watermark, Grenville's crabbed hand. There is no direction, no signature.

You need fall no further. If he asks you, accept, and there will be a way back for you. Look for a letter.

What does Grenville mean, *accept?* I turn my eyes from the paper to Philpott's face. I don't understand the message, but then he looks at me and speaks, as if on cue. 'The first time I met you I offered you a job.'

'Did you?'

'Might still have good use for a secretary – provided he laid off the damned Black Drop. Seems to provoke a disagreeable mawkish enthusiasm. I should not like to have him jabbering about devils and angels amid a brisk Atlantic storm.'

I laugh despite everything. The light is almost gone, and a jackdaw lands with a clatter in the trees behind us, before I remember my mother and the farm. 'I can't come with you. Someone needs to pay the mortgage and I am the only candidate. I'd be quite useless to my mother in America.'

'And for that, I have another answer.' He produces a fat bag of coin from his pocket and puts it in my hand. 'Downing Street repents of its harshness, my boy. At least, so I surmise from the contents of this package, which will keep your family housed and fed until you can send them more. Grenville has freed you, you see, and you may begin anew.'

I weigh the bag in my hand. There must be six months' wages in it, and I begin to make out what the Ministry intends. Philpott is quite wrong. I will go to America apparently their enemy, but if I accept this money I will be in their secret employ. It is the antithesis of freedom. 'Did they send you here, Mr Philpott?'

'Send me!' He swells like a toad. 'God damn me, I am no errand boy of theirs, I assure 'ee.'

He takes the pipe out of his mouth and proceeds to stuff it with tobacco. 'Now, what else can I tell 'ee?' He is already moving on. 'George Canning has agreed to succeed Aust as Under-Secretary on the old man's retirement next year.'

'God damn him. I always thought he might.'

'Poor old Aust has aged dreadfully through all this business.' Philpott looks up at me from his pipe, but darkness is falling so fast on this short winter day that I can only see the glint of his eye reflecting the shining mud of the estuary. 'I believe you will also wish to know that his stepdaughter Anne looks likely to be betrothed again before the New Year.'

'Oh, indeed?' I know what is coming.

'Yes. The gossip says she is certain to accept the new Under-Secretary. I have always liked her, even if her ambitions are entirely naked.'

I allow the news to sink in and find, at last, that there is no pain. I have lately wondered how I fixed my suspicions on Canning so easily, instead of on Aglantine where they really belonged. Affronted by his arrogance to all those of us beneath him – Will Benson, Peter Williams and myself – I built a monster out of air. Though he is still a mystery, I remember his solemn wink and find I do not now fear for Anne's safety. She will give him no quarter and expect none.

I wonder what my own future holds. What Grenville will demand of me in America if I accept his offer. I think of Peter Williams, working out his freedom, and see that, if I consent, I will be an indentured servant too.

A pair of tawny owls begin calling back and forth, as Philpott takes out his tinderbox and essays vigorously to produce a spark. 'Yes, they are all so caught up in their own interests they don't see the wood for the trees. Of all of 'em, only Erskine had the sense to know what he wanted from the first, and by God he brought it off.' The sparks afford fleeting glimpses of Philpott's red face and his button eye. 'Grenville, now, well, he's a man in two minds, with his foot in two camps between the right and wrong courses. He has got his treaty, but there are a dozen other things he ain't got, dead men on the scaffold among 'em.'

Philpott gives up on lighting his pipe and puts the tinder-box back in his pocket. 'As for myself, I have contributed my mite to a treaty between great nations, plucked an innocent man from the gallows, learned a great deal about the Indian rhinoceros, and made a prodigious number of delightful new friends. Not bad for a stint of six months, eh? Just think what I might accomplish in the next six.' His voice grows dreamy. 'Jay's Treaty – yes, yes, I will certainly bring that off. And I am inclined to sort out slavery, too, for those damned impractical abolitionists will never do it.' He puts the unlit pipe back in his mouth, takes my arm under his own, and we walk back up the hill towards the light and warmth of the farm.

HISTORICAL
NOTE

In 1794 the war against Revolutionary France was a year old – a struggle that, unknown to the characters in these pages, would endure for another twenty-one years. In 1789 most people – and certainly most youthful intellectuals – had welcomed the Revolution against France's rotten aristocracy and out-of-touch monarchy. Rapidly disillusioned by the Terror, it would take a generation for such enthusiasm to rekindle. Robespierre's attempted 'suicide' was widely believed, but the details are, in fact, moot.

Most of the historical events in these pages really happened, though I have tweaked the timing occasionally, for the exigencies of the story. There were always fears of spies within the Foreign Office. Lord Grenville controlled a wide network of secret agents throughout Europe and Ireland, and George Aust's few surviving papers contain notes of codes, invisible inks and daring missions. John Jay, who ran spy networks in the Independence War, is now hailed as the founder of the CIA.

But there was no leak of military information to the papers, and in 1794 George Aust was, in fact, mourning the loss of his only daughter, and would not marry the childless Sarah Murray until much later, after his retirement. Though George Canning did succeed him as Under-Secretary to the Foreign Office, Canning's relations with Aglantine are pure fiction. Nevertheless, Canning was certainly a controversial Foreign Secretary and later Prime Minister, and was not a likeable character. He was, in reality, an actor in one of history's more famous duels.

John Jay was actually accompanied to London by his eldest son, Peter, who was far better behaved than Theodore, who is a figment of my imagination. Peter Williams is not, and Jay's computational approach to manumission is based in fact.

Mr Philpott is inspired by William Cobbett, inventor of the popular press in England, whom *The Times* called 'a fourth estate in the politics of the country'. I spent a happy if often exasperated decade in his company, which has left me with an abiding love for home-brew and the cottage economy of vegetables and farmyard animals he advocated.

Much of Hardy's trial, the Secret Committee meetings and the conversation of George III are taken from contemporary sources, and Pitt really did reluctantly appear at another of the Treason Trials to admit his youthful radicalism. The ridiculous Popgun Plot is a case of truth being stranger than fiction – I would not have dared make it up – and I'm grateful to John Barrell's *Imagining the King's Death: Figurative Treason, Fantasies of Regicide 1793–1796* (OUP, Oxford, 2000). Finally, though he would not thank me for admitting it, Philpott's delightful account of his mishap at the menagerie is taken almost verbatim from the *Adventures and Recollections* of Colonel George Landmann, published in 1852, which was too perfect to be improved upon.

ACKNOWLEDGEMENTS

Writing a book is a solitary business until it isn't.

I'd like to thank my husband Mark, sons Geoff and Will, my brother Nick Shillito, my friend Alison Little, and friend and former colleague Tim Fulford for reading early drafts of *Black Drop*. Litopia Writers' Colony has also been a wonderful resource, and I'd like to especially thank Peter Cox, Eloise Logan and Emily Rainsford for giving me more insightful criticism than I could reasonably have asked for. Diane Johnstone and Susannah Okret encouraged me to keep writing at a moment when it really mattered.

People are remarkably generous with their time and knowledge. Pamina Husseini corrected my French, Abigail Stanley is a fount of information on all things medical, and the John Jay Papers project pointed me in useful directions for researching Peter Williams. I'd like to make especial mention of Gavin McGuffie at the Postal Museum in London, who answered my obscure questions by email with astonishing promptness.

The internet has, of course, transformed the process of research, and has brought me to all sorts of treasures I would never have found alone. I was directed to Colonel Landmann's memoir by a comment by Dennis Robillard on the website *All Things Georgian*; while the Georgian 'molly' underworld has received marvellously detailed and celebratory attention on a host of sites and blogs.

I would like to thank everyone at Viper for bringing *Black Drop* into the world. Without my agent, Giles Milburn, and editor, Miranda Jewess, this book would not exist.

ABOUT THE AUTHOR

Leonora Nattrass studied eighteenth-century literature and politics, and spent ten years as an English Literature lecturer, including eight at Nottingham Trent University. During this time she published several works on William Cobbett, and was a reviewer for *The Year's Work in English Studies* journal. She then moved to Cornwall, where she lives in a seventeenth-century house with seventeenth-century draughts, and spins the fleeces of her traditional Ryeland sheep into yarn. *Black Drop* is her first novel. Viper will publish the sequel charting Laurence Jago's adventures at sea, *Blue Water*, in 2022.